PERSEPOLIS RISING

BOOK SEVEN OF THE EXPANSE

JAMES S. A. COREY

orbit

www.orbitbooks.net

ORBIT

First published in Great Britain in 2017 by Orbit

1 3 5 7 9 10 8 6 4 2

HB ISBN 978-0-356-51030-9
C format 978-0-356-51031-6

Printed and bound in Great Britain by
Clays Ltd, St Ives plc

Papers used by Orbit are from well-managed forests
and other responsible sources.

MIX
Paper from
responsible sources
FSC® C104740

Orbit
An imprint of
Little, Brown Book Group
Carmelite House
50 Victoria Embankment
London EC4Y 0DZ

An Hachette UK Company
www.hachette.co.uk

www.orbitbooks.net

To Dr. Shank
We never make it easy

Prologue: Cortazár

Almost three decades had passed since Paolo Cortazár and the breakaway fleet had passed through Laconia gate. Time enough to build a little civilization, a city, a culture. Time enough for him to confirm that alien engineers had designed the protomolecule as a bridge builder. They had thrown it into the stars like seeds to hijack whatever organic life it encountered and create ring gates into a pocket universe, a nexus between worlds. Until they died out, the slow zone and its rings had been the hub of an empire that defied human comprehension. And now, it would be again. A little bridge-building mechanism that overcame locality changed everything for all humanity.

Not that Paolo cared about all humanity. For him, the fact of the protomolecule and the technologies it opened was all-encompassing. It not only changed the shape of the universe around him but also altered his personal and professional life. For decades, it had been his only obsession. In the fight that ended their relationship, his most recent boyfriend had accused him of actually *loving* the protomolecule.

Paolo hadn't been able to deny it. It had been so long since Paolo felt anything approaching love for another human that he'd lost the context for what did and didn't qualify. Certainly, studying the protomolecule and all the myriad branches of scientific insight that came from it took most of his time and attention. Understanding the ways in which it interacted with the other alien artifacts and technologies would be the work of lifetimes. He made no apology for his devotion. The tiny, beautiful speck so rich with implicit information was like a rosebud that never stopped blooming. It was beautiful in a way that nothing else could ever be. His lover had been unable to accept this, and the end of their relationship felt inevitable in retrospect. Paolo did miss him, in an abstract sort of way. Like he might miss a lost pair of comfortable shoes.

There were so many other wonderful things to occupy his time.

On the viewscreen in front of him, a latticework of carbon grew and unfolded in intricate, interwoven patterns. Given the correct environmental conditions and the right growth medium, the protomolecule defaulted to building these lattices. The material created was lighter than an equal volume of carbon fiber and had greater tensile strength than graphene. The Technology Directorate of the Laconian Military Council had asked him to explore its possible use in armor for infantry units. The lattice's tendency to permanently bond to human skin made that problematic from an engineering standpoint, but it was still beautiful.

Paolo adjusted the sensitivity of the electron stream and leaned in toward the monitor, watching as the protomolecule picked up the free-floating carbon atoms and neatly wove them into the grid like it was a child focused on its play.

"Doctor Cortazár," a voice said.

Paolo answered with a grunt and a wave of his hand that meant *Go away, I'm busy* in any language.

"Doctor Cortazár," the voice repeated, insistent.

Paolo pulled his gaze away from the screen and turned around. A pale-skinned person of indefinite gender stood in a lab coat, holding a large hand terminal. Paolo thought their name was Caton? Canton? Cantor? Something like that. One of the lab's army of technicians. Competent, as far as Paolo could recall. But now interrupting him, so there would have to be consequences. The nervous look on Caton/Cantor/Canton's face told him they were very aware of this fact.

Before Paolo could speak, the tech said, "The director asked me to remind you that you have an appointment. With"—the tech's voice went low, almost to a whisper—"him. With Him."

The tech did not mean the director. There was only one Him.

Paolo turned off the video display and checked to make sure the monitoring systems were recording everything before he stood up.

"Yes, of course," he said. And then, because he was making an effort these days, "Thank you. Cantor?"

"Caton," the tech replied with visible relief.

"Of course. Please let the director know I'm on my way."

"I'm supposed to accompany you, Doctor," Caton said, tapping on the hand terminal as though this fact was on a list somewhere.

"Of course." Paolo pulled his coat off a rack by the door and headed out.

The bioengineering and nanoinformatics lab of the University of Laconia was the largest research lab on the planet. Possibly in the entirety of human space. The university campus spread across nearly forty hectares of land on the outskirts of the Laconian capital city. His labs accounted for almost a quarter of that space. Like everything on Laconia, it was orders of magnitude larger than it needed to be for the people who inhabited it now. It had been built for the future. For all those who would come after.

Paolo walked briskly along a gravel path, checking the monitor on his forearm as he went. Caton jogged along behind.

"Doctor," the lab tech said, pointing in the opposite direction, "I brought a cart for you. It's in Parking C."

"Bring it around to the Pen. I have something to do there first."

Caton hesitated for a moment, caught between a direct order from him and the responsibility of being his chaperone.

"Yes, Doctor," Caton said, then ran off in the other direction.

As he walked, Paolo scanned through his task list for the day to be sure he wasn't forgetting anything else, then plucked his sleeve down over the monitor and looked up at the sky. It was a lovely day. Laconia had a bright cerulean-blue sky, with a few cottony white clouds scattered about. The massive rigging of the planet's orbital construction platform was very faintly visible, all long arms and empty spaces between, like a massive oligonucleotide floating in space.

The gentle wind carried the faint burned plastic scent of a local fungus analog releasing what passed for spores. The breeze pushed the long fronds of dogwhistles across his path. The grunchers—approximately the same ecological niche as crickets with even a few morphological similarities—that clung to the plants hissed at him when he got too close. He had no idea why the weeds had been named dogwhistles. They looked more like pussy willows to him. And naming an insect analog that looked like a cricket with four limbs a gruncher made even less sense. There didn't seem to be any scientific process to the naming of the local flora and fauna. People just threw names at things until a consensus arose. It annoyed him.

The Pen was different from the other lab buildings. He'd had its walls built from single sheets of high-impact armor plating welded airtight into ninety-degree angles to make a dark metallic cube twenty-five meters on a side. At the building's only entrance, four soldiers wearing light armor and carrying assault rifles stood at alert.

"Doctor Cortazár," one of the four said, holding out a hand in the universal gesture for *Stop walking*.

Paolo pulled his ID badge on its lanyard out from under his shirt and presented it to the guard, who plugged it into a reader. He then touched the reader to the skin on Paolo's wrist.

"Nice day," the guard said pleasantly, smiling as the machine did its work of comparing Paolo's ID to his physical measurements and his identifying proteins.

"Lovely," Paolo agreed.

The machine pinged its acceptance that he was actually Paolo Cortazár, the president of Laconia University and head of its exobiological studies lab. The guards had all known that by sight, but the ritual was important for more reasons than one. The door slid open, and the four guards stepped aside.

"Have a nice day, Doctor."

"You as well," Paolo said as he stepped into the security airlock. One wall hissed as hidden nozzles blasted him with air. Sensors on the opposite wall tested for explosives and infectious materials. And possibly even bad intentions.

After a moment, the hissing stopped, and the inner airlock door slid open. Only then did Paolo hear the moaning.

The Pen, as it was called by everyone in spite of not having an official name in any documentation, was the second highest security building on Laconia for a reason. It was where Paolo kept his milking herd.

That name had come from an early fight with his ex-lover. He'd meant it as an insult, but it was an apt analogy. Inside the Pen, people and animals that had been deliberately infected with the protomolecule lived out the remainder of their lives. Once the alien nanotech had appropriated their cells and begun reproducing, Paolo's staff could drain the bodies of their fluids and filter out the critical particles from the matrix tissue. When the bodies were exhausted, any remaining fluids could be incinerated without losing anything of value. There were bays for twenty-four, but only seventeen were occupied at the moment. Someday, with a wider population base, subjects would be more abundant.

The great works of Laconia depended on communicating with the underlying technology the long-dead alien civilization had left behind. The protomolecule hadn't been designed as a universal control interface, but there was a modularity to the alien technology that let it function that way often enough for the work to proceed. It was Paolo's job to supply the active samples needed. One of his jobs.

As he walked toward his office in the rear of the building, he paused on a catwalk over one of the holding pens. Half a dozen people in early stages of infection wandered around the cramped, metal-walled space. They were still in the pseudo-hemorrhagic fever phase the techs called Pukers. They could manage no more than a shambling walk and occasional violent bouts of vomiting. It was the protomolecule's means of ensuring the infection would spread quickly. Once the bodies had been removed from the space, every centimeter of its metal walls and floor would be torched to destroy any biological debris.

They'd only had one accidental infection in the history of the lab, and Paolo intended to keep it that way.

Dr. Ochida, head of the Pen and Paolo's second in command, spotted him from across the holding area and rushed over.

"Paolo," Ochida said, clapping him on one shoulder in a friendly greeting. "Just in time. We finished pulling the stem cultures an hour ago, and the injections are prepped."

"I recognize that one," Paolo said, pointing at a hairy, muscular man in the Pen.

"Hm? Oh. Yes, he was one of our guards, I think. His intake paperwork said 'dereliction of duty.' Caught sleeping on watch, maybe?"

"You tested them?" Paolo asked. He didn't actually care about the hairy man in the pen, and Ochida's answer had satisfied his curiosity.

It took Ochida a moment to realize they'd changed back to the original subject. "Oh, yes. I tested the samples for purity three times. Personally."

"I'm going directly from here to the State Building," Paolo said, turning to look Ochida in the eye.

His assistant knew what he was asking and replied, "I understand. These injections exactly meet your specifications."

If anything went wrong, they both knew they'd be the next two placed in the Pen. They were valuable, but they weren't beyond consequences. No one was. That was what Laconia meant.

"Excellent," Paolo said, giving Ochida a friendly smile he didn't actually feel. "I'll take them now."

Ochida waved at someone in a corner of the room, and a tech trotted over carrying a silvery metal briefcase. She handed the case to Paolo, then left.

"Is there anything else?" Ochida asked.

"I'm starting to see some growth," Paolo said, pointing at a bone spur protruding from the hairy man's spine.

"Yes," Ochida agreed. "They're nearly ready."

In the time he'd worked with Winston Duarte, Paolo had found much to admire in the man. The high consul was intelligent, given to astounding leaps of comprehension on complex topics but still measured and thoughtful in his decision making. Duarte valued the counsel of others but was decisive and firm once the information was gathered. He could be charismatic and warm without ever seeming false or insincere.

But more than anything else, Paolo respected his total lack of pretension. Many lesser people, holding a position like absolute military dictator of an entire planet, would wrap themselves in pomp and glittering palaces. Duarte had instead built the State Building of Laconia. A massive construction of stone that towered over the rest of the capital city, it still somehow managed to feel comforting rather than intimidating. As though all its solidity and size was merely to house important works and solve serious problems. Not aggrandize those inside it.

Caton drove Paolo's little cart up the wide street that led to the building's front entrance. They were the only traffic. The street ended at a high stone wall, a narrow gate, and a guard post. Paolo climbed out of the cart, taking the metal briefcase with him.

"No need to wait for me," Paolo said to Caton.

The tech hadn't spoken since picking him up outside the Pen,

and seemed relieved to be dismissed. "Yes, Doctor. Call if you—"
But Paolo was already walking away. He heard the car's electric
whine as it left.

The narrow gate opened as he approached, and two soldiers left
the guard post and fell in alongside him without a word. These
were not like the lightly armored guards that stood watch at the
university. These wore strength-augmenting suits of articulated
composite plates, with a variety of weapons mounted on them.
The suits were the same dark blue as the Laconian flag and had the
same pair of stylized wings. A phoenix, he thought, but it might
have been some sort of raptor. The pleasant color made the lethal
war machines under it seem out of place. Their footsteps on the
stone courtyard and the faint thrum of the power suits were the
only noises that followed them to the State Building's entrance.

At the door, his two guards stopped him, then spread out, one
on each side. Paolo fancied he could feel the tickle of X-rays and
millimeter waves bouncing off his body as they scanned him head
to toe. After a long moment one of them said, "The high consul
is waiting for you in the medical wing," and then they turned and
walked away.

"Technically, yes. The dreams have stopped," Duarte said as
Paolo slid a hypodermic port line into a forearm vein and taped
it down. He knew from experience that Duarte was distracting
himself to keep from looking down and seeing the needles go in.
It was endearing that the most powerful human in the universe
was still a bit squeamish about needles.

"Have they?" Paolo asked. It wasn't a casual question. The side
effects of the incredibly experimental treatment Duarte was receiv-
ing were something to be kept close track of. "How long ago?"

Duarte sighed, and closed his eyes. Either relaxing as the first
of the sedative mixture hit his veins, or trying to remember the
exact date, or both. "The last one was eleven days ago."

"You're sure?"

"Yes," Duarte said with a smile and without opening his eyes, "I'm sure. Eleven days ago was the last time I slept."

Paolo nearly dropped the IV line he was connecting to the port. "You haven't slept in *eleven days*?"

Duarte's eyes finally opened. "I don't feel tired at all. Quite the opposite. Every day I feel more energetic and healthy than the last. A side effect of the treatment, I'm sure."

Paolo nodded at this, though it wasn't anything he'd anticipated. His stomach gave a tiny spasm of worry. If there was an unexpected side effect this extreme, then what else was waiting for them? He'd asked Duarte to wait until they had more data, but the man had demanded they move forward, and how could he argue?

"I see that look, old friend," Duarte said, his smile even wider. "You don't need to worry. I've been monitoring it myself. If anything were out of balance, I'd have called you a week ago. But I feel fantastic, I'm not building up fatigue poisons, and the blood work promised I'm not psychotic. And now I get an extra eight hours every day to work. I couldn't be happier."

"Of course," Paolo replied. He finished hooking the IV bag filled with its payload of protomolecule-modified human stem cells into the port. Duarte gave a tiny gasp when the cool fluid started to enter his vein. "But please, do remember to send along these sorts of details, even if they don't seem to be a problem. Animal models are never perfect, and you're the first person to receive this treatment. Tracking the effects is incredibly important to—"

"I will," Duarte replied. "I have full confidence that your lab has everything working exactly as it's supposed to. But I'll make sure my personal doctor sends you all his daily notes."

"Thank you, High Consul," Paolo said. "I'm going to draw some blood as well and have my people do a workup. Just to make sure."

"Whatever you need," Duarte said. "But as long as we're alone, please don't call me 'High Consul.' Winston's fine." Duarte's voice had grown mushy, and Paolo could tell the sedatives were taking effect. "I want us all working together."

"We are working together. But a body needs a brain. Leadership, yes?" Paolo replied. He let the IV bag empty, used the line to draw a small sample of Duarte's blood and put it in the metal briefcase, and quietly went about the process of doing a full body scan. The treatment had begun growing a small number of new organs in Duarte's body that had been designed by the best experimental physiologists on the planet and implemented using lessons taught by the eternal protomolecule bloom. But there were still so many things that might go wrong, and tracking the development of the changes in Duarte was the most important aspect of Paolo's job. Despite Duarte's warmth and the genuine friendship he showed, if anything happened to the Laconian ruler, he would be executed shortly thereafter. Tying Paolo's safety to his own was how Duarte could guarantee the scientist's best efforts on his behalf. They both understood this, and there was no ill will attached. Paolo's death wouldn't be punishment, exactly. Just a clear disincentive to letting his patient die.

As relationships went, it was probably the most honest one Paolo had ever had.

"You know, Winston, that this is going to be a very long process. There may be imbalances small enough that they don't appear for years. Decades."

"Centuries," he said, nodding. "It's imperfect, I know. But we do what we have to do. And, no, old friend. I'm sorry, but I haven't reconsidered."

Paolo wondered if the ability to read minds was yet another unexpected side effect of the treatment. If so...well, that would be interesting. "I wasn't suggesting that—"

"That you should undergo the treatment too?" Duarte said. "Of course you were. And you *should* suggest it. Make the best argument you can. I don't believe you'll change my mind, but I'd like it very much if you did."

Paolo looked at his hands, avoiding Duarte's eyes. Defiance would have been easier for him. The melancholy in the man's voice was disturbing in a way he found hard to understand.

"The ironic thing?" Duarte said. "I've always rejected the great-man idea. The belief that human history was formed by singular individuals instead of broad social forces? Romantic, but…" He waved a hand vaguely, like he was stirring fog. "Demographic trends. Economic cycles. Technological progress. All much more powerful predictors than any one person. And yet here I am. I would take you with me if I could, you know. It's not my choice. It's history's."

"History should reconsider," Paolo said.

Duarte chuckled. "The difference between zero and one is miraculous. But it's as miraculous as it ever will be. Make it two. Three. A hundred. It becomes just another oligarchy. A permanent engine of inequality that will breed the wars we're trying to end."

Paolo made a small sound that could have been mistaken for agreement.

"The best governments in history have been kings and emperors," Duarte said. "The worst ones too. A philosopher-king can manage great things in his lifetime. And his grandchildren can squander it."

Duarte grunted as Paolo pulled the hypodermic port out of his arm. He didn't need to place a bandage over the wound. The hole closed up before a drop of blood could escape. It didn't even scab.

"If you want to create a lasting, stable social order," Duarte said, "only one person can ever be immortal."

Chapter One: Drummer

The habitation ring of the transfer station at Lagrange-5 was three times the diameter of the one Drummer had lived in on Tycho, half a lifetime ago. TSL-5 had a small city's worth of offices with the same fake-marble walls and soft, full-spectrum lighting as the one they'd given her, the same crash-couch beds and water showers as her quarters there. The air had a constant smell of terpene compounds, as if the station were the largest chrysanthemum in the universe. The dome in the center of the station had berths for hundreds of ships and warehouses that seemed so numerous and deep that filling them would leave Earth as empty as a squeezed-out bulb. All those berths and warehouses were at rest now, but starting tomorrow, that would change. TSL-5 was about to be open for business, and even as tired as she was, as annoyed as she felt at having to haul herself halfway across the system for what was ultimately a ribbon-cutting ceremony, there was also an excitement to it. After three decades of struggle, Mother Earth was open for business.

The planet glowed on her wall screen, whorls of high white clouds and glimpses of the still-greenish sea beneath it. The terminator crept across, pulling a blanket of darkness and city lights behind it. The ships of the Earth-Mars Coalition Navy floated around it, dots of darkness swimming on the high sea of air. Drummer had never gone down that well, and now by the terms of the treaty she'd signed on the union's behalf, she never would. Fine with her. Her knees bothered her sometimes as it was. But as an objet d'art, Terra was hard to beat. Humanity had done its level best to kick the shit out of the slowly spinning egg. Overpopulation, exploitation, atmospheric and oceanic imbalance, and then three military-level meteor strikes, any one of which would have fucked up the dinosaurs. And here it still was, like a soldier. Scarred, broken, reimagined, rebuilt, and remade.

Time was supposed to heal all wounds. To Drummer, that was just a nice way of saying that if she waited long enough, none of the things that seemed important to her would turn out to matter. Or at least not the way she'd thought they did.

Time, plus the combined expertise of a Martian terraforming project staggering under the loss of its mandate, the ruthless administration of Earth's political sector, and the huge market of thirteen-hundred-odd worlds all in need of biological substrates to grow food that people could actually eat had hauled Earth, slow and staggering, up to functional again.

Her system chirped, a polite little pop like someone snapping bamboo. Her private secretary's voice followed like a drink of whiskey.

"Madam President?"

"Give me a minute, Vaughn," she said.

"Yes, ma'am. But Secretary-General Li would like to speak with you before the ceremony."

"The Earth-Mars Coalition can wait until after cocktails. I'm not opening this station by jumping every time the EMC clears their throat. Bad precedent."

"Copy that. I'll handle it."

The system made the little woody tock that meant she had her privacy again. She leaned back in her chair, looked over at the images set into the wall behind her desk. All the previous Transport Union presidents before her: Michio Pa, then Tjon, Walker, Sanjrani, and her own thin, stern face looking back at her from the end. She hated that picture. It made her look like she'd just eaten something sour. The first version of it looked like something off a singles forum. At least this one was dignified.

For most of the Transport Union's members, this image was all they'd ever see of her. Thirteen hundred worlds, and within a decade most if not all of them would have their own versions of the TSL-5. Hand-off stations that marked the bubble of void where the planet's sphere of control ended and the union's began. Anything that the colonies needed from humanity's first home or from each other went up the gravity wells. That was the inner's problem. Moving it from one system to another belonged to the Belt. Old terms. Inners. Belters. They stuck because language held on to things that way, even when the reality around them had shifted.

The Earth-Mars Coalition had been the center of humanity once—the innermost of the inners. Now it was an important spoke on the wheel whose hub was Medina Station. Where the weird alien sphere sat in the middle of the not-space that linked all the ring gates. Where her civilian quarters were when she wasn't on the void cities. Where Saba was, when he wasn't on his ship or with her. Medina Station was home.

Except that even for her, the blue-black disk of Earth on her screen was home too. Maybe that wouldn't always be true. There were kids old enough to vote now who'd never known what it meant to have only one sun. She didn't know what Earth or Mars or Sol would be to them. Maybe this atavistic melancholy just behind her breastbone would die with her generation.

Or maybe she was tired and cranky and needed a nap.

The bamboo broke again. "Ma'am?"

"I'm on my way."

"Yes, ma'am. But we have a priority message from traffic control on Medina."

Drummer leaned forward, her hands flat against the cool of the desk. Shit. Shit shit shit. "Did we lose another one?"

"No, ma'am. No lost ships."

She felt the dread loosen its grip a little. Not all the way. "What, then?"

"They're reporting an unscheduled transit. A freighter, but it didn't have a transponder."

"Seriously?" she said. "Did they think we wouldn't notice it?"

"Couldn't speak to that," Vaughn said.

She pulled up the administrative feed from Medina. She could get anything from her realm here—traffic control, environmental data, energy output, sensor arrays in any slice of the electromagnetic spectrum. But light delay made all of it a little more than four hours old. Any order she gave would come through eight, eight and a half hours after the request for it was made. The vast alien intelligence that had engineered the ring gates and the massive ruins in the systems beyond them had found ways to manipulate distance, but the speed of light was the speed of light, and seemed like it always would be.

She scrolled through the logs, found the relevant slot, played it. *Medina here. Conferme.* Traffic Control's usual calm.

The responding voice had a little interference. An artifact of the gates. *This is the freighter* Savage Landing *out of Castila on approach, Medina. Transferring our status now.*

A new window popped up. The ship status of a light freighter. Martian design. Old, but not antiquated. It took a few seconds for Traffic to come back.

Visé bien, Savage Landing. *You are clear to transit. Control code is—fuck! Abort,* Savage Landing! *Do not transit!*

A sudden spike on the safety curve and the alarm status blinked to red. A new drive signature appeared on Medina's control board, the plume sweeping through the starless dark of the slow zone.

It was done. All of it over with hours ago, but Drummer still felt her heartbeat pick up. Traffic was shouting for the new ship to identify itself, the rail-gun emplacements clicked to active. If they'd fired, everyone on the unauthorized ship was dead already.

The safety curve decayed, the disruption created by mass and energy passing through the ring dropping until it passed the threshold. The intruding ship spun, burning hard, and zipped through a different gate, kicking the curve back up again as it escaped.

Traffic cursed in several languages, sending stand-by messages to three other inbound ships. The *Savage Landing* was quiet, but the feed from their system showed a bruisingly hard burn as they peeled away, breaking off the approach to the Castila gate.

She rolled back, the near calamity reversing itself. The reckless asshole had come in from Freehold and passed out into Auberon. Because of course it had. The leaking radiation from the Auberon gate showed that the ship had made it. As close as it had cut the safety curve, it hadn't gone dutchman. But if the *Savage Landing* had gone through as scheduled, one or both ships could have vanished into wherever ships went when their transits failed.

In the short term, it would mean slotting *Savage Landing* in later. There'd be a bunch of pushbacks. Maybe dozens of ships that had to change their burns and coordinate new transits. Not a threat, but a pain in the ass.

And not a good precedent.

"Should I respond," Vaughn asked, "or would you rather deal with this personally, ma'am?"

It was an excellent question. Policy was a ratchet. If she pulled the trigger, gave the order that the next unauthorized ship through was going to be turned into scrap metal and regrets, it wasn't something she could pull back from. Someone much better at this than she was had taught her to be very careful doing something if she wasn't ready to do it every time from then on.

But, Christ, it was tempting.

"Have Medina log the transit, add the full cost to Freehold and Auberon's tabs, and penalties for the delays they caused," she said.

"Yes, ma'am," Vaughn said. "Anything else?"

Yes, she thought, *but I don't know what yet.*

The conference room had been designed for this moment. The vaulted ceiling looked as grand as a cathedral. Secretary-General Li of Earth stood at his podium, shifting his grave but satisfied countenance out at the cameras of dozens of different, carefully selected newsfeeds. Drummer tried to do the same.

"President Drummer!" one of the reporters called, lifting a hand for attention the same way people probably had in the forums of Rome. Her podium told her the man's name was Carlisle Hayyam with Munhwa Ilbo's Ceres office. A dozen others had started clamoring for her attention too.

"Hayyam?" she said, smiling, and the others quieted down. The truth was, she sort of liked this part. It appealed to some long-forgotten ambition to perform on a stage, and it was one of the few places where she felt like she was actually in control. Most of her work felt like she was trying to stuff air back into a leaking balloon.

"How do you respond to Martin Karczek's concerns about the transfer station?"

"I'd have to listen to them," she said. "I've only got so many hours in my day."

The reporters chuckled, and she heard the glee. Yes, they were opening the first hand-off station. Yes, Earth was about to stagger up out of years of environmental crisis to ramp up its active trade with the colonies. All anyone really wanted was a couple politicians being snippy at each other.

And that was fine. As long as they kept looking at the little stuff, she could work on the big things.

Secretary-General Li, a broad-faced man with a lush mustache and a workman's callused hands, cleared his throat. "If you don't mind," he said. "There are always people who are wary of change. And that's a *good* thing. Change should be watched, moderated, and questioned. But that conservative view shouldn't rein in progress or put a damper on hope. Earth is humanity's first and truest home. The soil from which all of us, whatever system we now inhabit, first grew. Earth will always, *always*, be central to the greater project of humanity in the universe."

Whistling past the graveyard. Earth was celebrating a huge milestone in its history, and that was maybe the third most important thing on her agenda. But how do you tell a planet that history has passed it by? Better to nod and smile, enjoy the moment and the champagne. Once this was over, she'd have to get back to work.

They moved through the expected questions: would the renegotiation of the tariff agreements be overseen by Drummer or former president Sanjrani, would the Transport Union remain neutral in the contested elections on Nova Catalunya, would the Ganymede status talks be held on Luna or Medina. There was even one question about the dead systems—Charon, Adro, and Naraka—where ring gates led to things much stranger than goldilocks-zone planetary systems. Secretary-General Li fended that one off, which was just as well. Dead systems gave Drummer the creeps.

After the Q-and-A was done, Drummer did a dozen photo ops with the secretary-general, high-level administrators from the EMC, and celebrities from the planets—a dark-skinned woman in a bright-blue sari, a pale man in a formal suit, a pair of comically identical men in matching gold dinner jackets.

There was a part of her that enjoyed this too. She suspected that the pleasure she took in Earthers clamoring to get mementos of themselves with the head of the Belters spoke poorly of her in some vague spiritual way. She'd grown up in a universe where people like her were disposable, and she'd lived long enough for fortune's wheel to lift her up higher than Earth's sky. Everyone wanted the Belt for a friend, now that the term meant more than a cloud of half-mined-out chunks of debris trapped between Mars and Jupiter. For children born today, the Belt was the thing that tied all humanity together. Semantic drift and political change. If the worst that came out of it was a little schadenfreude on her part, she could live with that.

Vaughn waited in a small antechamber. His face was a network of crags that would have done credit to a mountain range, but he managed to make it work for him. His formal jacket was cut to echo old-style vac suits. The marks of their oppression remade as high fashion. Time healed all wounds, but it didn't erase the scars so much as decorate them.

"You have an hour before the reception, ma'am," he said as Drummer sat on the couch and rubbed her feet.

"Understood."

"Can I get you anything?"

"Encrypted tightbeam and privacy."

"Yes, ma'am," he said without missing a beat.

When the door slid closed behind him, she turned on the system camera and composed herself. The plan that had been forming in the back of her head all through the ceremonies was in place. All the bits and pieces she'd need to make it happen. And sooner was better than later. Punishment worked best when there wasn't a gap between misbehavior and consequences, or at least that was what they told her. But there was also a real advantage in giving the offender time to savor their regret.

Best of all was when she could do both.

She hit Record.

"Captain Holden," she said. "I'm linking you through to the data on an unauthorized transit from Freehold to Auberon that occurred today. I'm also giving you access to the security review of the Freehold system. It's not much. One habitable planet a little smaller than Mars, another one that's exploitable as long as you don't mind too much nitrogen and cyanide in your air. The governor of Freehold is named...."

She checked the records and coughed with contempt and laughter.

"Payne Houston. I'm assuming that's his own choice and not what his mommy called him. Either way, I'm sending you under an executive mandate so that you can get going right now. I'll get Emily Santos-Baca and the security committee to genuflect over this well before you get there, so we'll be fine with that.

"Your official mission is to carry the message that Freehold's repeated violations of Transportation Union guidelines have triggered punitive action, and that I'm banning all traffic in and out of Freehold for three years. When he asks whether it's Earth years, the answer is yes. He's going to make a point of that, because that's the kind of idiot he is.

"Your unofficial mission is not to hurry. I want Freehold and all the systems like it to see a gunship moseying toward them for weeks without knowing what it's going to do when it gets there. I'll have my staff draw up the usual work agreement. If you can't take the job, let me know as soon as possible. Otherwise, I'll have you on the roster to fuel up and make transit in the next fifteen hours."

She reviewed the message, then sent it out with a copy to Ahmed McCahill, the chair of the security committee. Then it was an executive request to push the *Rocinante* to the head of the resupply and transit authorization queues. And then Vaughn was knocking discreetly at her door.

He took her grunt as permission to come in, which it was.

"Secretary-General Li is asking whether you're indisposed, ma'am," he said. "He's getting concerned."

She checked the time. Her hour's respite had ended twenty minutes ago.

"Tell him I'm on my way," she said. "And do I have a change of clothes?"

"In the closet, ma'am," Vaughn said as he slipped out the door again, quiet as a phantom. Drummer changed quickly, shedding the formal jacket and slacks for a bamboo-silk blouse and self-tailoring skirt with a neural net woven into it that was about as intelligent as an insect just to keep the drape right. She considered herself in the mirror with a certain satisfaction. She only wished Saba were here to accompany her. But he'd probably make too many consort-of-the-queen jokes. She shut down the mirror, its screen defaulting back to the image of Earth.

The planet was over half in darkness now, a crescent of white and blue. Belters had tried to kill the Earth, but here it was still spinning. They'd tried to burn the inner planets' ships, and here was the EMC navy, scraped back together and flying.

And on the other hand, Earth had tried to choke the Belters under its boot for generations, and here was Drummer. Time had made them allies in the great expansion of civilization out to the stars.

At least until something *else* changed.

Chapter Two: Bobbie

The transit from the slow zone was behind them and Freehold was still weeks away, but an atmospheric landing in a ship as old as the *Rocinante* wasn't the trivial thing it had once been. Age showed up in unexpected ways. Things that had always worked before failed. It was something you prepared for as much as you could.

Bobbie squinted at a wall panel on the engineering deck and watched as a long list of data scrolled by, ending with the ship's reassurance that it could handle at least one more descent without burning up.

"All greens on the atmospheric braking thrusters," Bobbie said.

"Hmmm?" Alex's sleepy drawl replied from the panel.

"You awake up there? This is your damn landing prep list. I'm down here doing the work. Could at least seem interested."

"Yeah, not sleepin'," the pilot replied, "just got my own list of shit to do." She could hear his smile.

Bobbie closed the diagnostic screen. Verifying the status on the thrusters was the last item on her work order. And short of putting on a suit and climbing outside to physically look into the nozzles, there wasn't much more she could do.

"I'm going to do some housekeeping, then head up," she said.

"Mmhm."

Bobbie put her tools away and used a mild solvent to wipe up some lubricant she'd spilled. It smelled sweet and pungent, like something she'd have cooked with back when she'd been living alone on Mars. Anxiety pushed her toward preparing more for the mission even after she was prepared. In the old days, this was when she'd have cleaned and serviced her power armor again and again and again until it became a kind of meditation. Now, she went through the ship the same way.

She'd lived on the *Rocinante* for more years now than anyplace else. Longer than her childhood home. Longer than her tour in the Marines.

The engineering deck was Amos country, and the mechanic kept a tidy shop. Every tool was in its place, every surface spotless. Other than the oil and solvent, the only other smell in the compartment was the ozone scent that hinted at powerful electricity coursing nearby. The floor vibrated in time with the fusion reactor on the deck below, the ship's beating heart.

On one bulkhead, Amos painted a sign that read:

SHE TAKES CARE OF YOU

YOU TAKE CARE OF HER

Bobbie patted the words as she walked by and climbed onto the ladder lift that ran up the center of the ship. The *Roci* was at a very gentle 0.2 g braking burn, and there had been a time when riding the lift instead of climbing the ladder would have felt like admitting defeat, even if the ship was burning ten times that hard.

But for the last couple years Bobbie's joints had been giving her trouble, and proving to herself that she could make the climb had stopped mattering as much.

It seemed to her that the real sign you were getting old was when you stopped needing to prove you weren't getting old.

The hatches separating each deck slid open at the lift's approach, and then quietly closed after she'd passed. The *Roci* might be a decade or two past her sell-by date, but Clarissa tolerated no sticking or squeaking on her ship. At least once a week, Claire made a complete pass through every environmental system and pressure hatch. When Bobbie had mentioned it to Holden, he'd said, *Because she broke the ship once, and she's still trying to fix it.*

The lift hummed to a stop on the ops deck, and Bobbie stepped off. The hatch up to the cockpit was open. Alex's brown and almost entirely bald head poked up over the back of the pilot's crash couch. The crew spent most of their working time in Operations, and the air felt subtly different. Long hours spent in the crash couches meant the smell of sweat never entirely went away, no matter how hard the air recyclers worked. And, like any room James Holden spent a lot of time in, the comfortable scent of old coffee lingered.

Bobbie ran a finger along the bulkhead, feeling the anti-spalling fabric crackle under the pressure. The dark-gray color had faded, and it was getting harder to tell where the fabric didn't match because it had been damaged and patched and where it was just aging unevenly. It would need to be replaced soon. She could live with the color, but the crunching meant that it was losing its elasticity. Getting too brittle to do its job.

Both of Bobbie's shoulders ached, and it was getting trickier to tell the difference between the one that had been explosively dislocated during hand-to-hand training years before and the one that just hurt from decades of not being gentle with her body. She'd picked up a lot of battle scars during her life, and they were getting harder and harder to differentiate from the normal damage of wearing out. Like the discolored patches on the *Roci*'s bulkheads, everything was just fading to match.

She climbed the short ladder up through the hatch into the cockpit, trying to enjoy the ache in her shoulders the way she'd once enjoyed the burn after an intense workout. As an old drill sergeant had told her, pain is the warrior's friend. Pain reminds you that you aren't dead yet.

"Yo," Alex said as she dropped into the gunner's chair behind him. "How's our girl look?"

"Old, but she can still get around."

"I meant the ship."

Bobbie laughed and called up the tactical display. Off in the distance, the planet Freehold. The mission. "My brother always complained I spent too much time looking for metaphors."

"An aging Martian warrior living inside an aging Martian warrior," Alex said, the smile audible in his voice. "Don't have to look too hard there."

"Not too agéd to kick your ass." Bobbie zoomed in on Freehold on their tactical screen. A mottled marble of brown continents and green oceans, with the occasional white swirl of cloud. "How long?"

"We'll be there in a week."

"Talk to Jizz lately? How's my future baby daddy doing?"

"*Giselle* is fine, and she says Kit is doing great. Picked planetary engineering as his major at Mariner Tech."

"It is the hot job market right now," Bobbie agreed.

She'd been Alex's best man when he'd married Giselle, and she'd waited at the hospital on Ceres when Kit had been born thirteen months later. And now Kit was going into upper university, and Alex had been divorced for over a decade. He was her best friend, but he was terrible husband material. After his second failure at it Bobbie pointed out that if he just wanted something to hurt, she could break his arm for him and save everyone time.

But for all the unnecessary drama, Alex and Giselle's short-lived trainwreck of a marriage had produced Kit, and that made the universe a better place. The boy had all of Alex's laconic charm and all of his mother's regal good looks. Every time he called her Aunt Bobbie, she wanted to hug him until his ribs cracked.

"When you reply, make sure to tell Jizz I said 'fuck off,'" Bobbie said. The failure of the marriage wasn't entirely Giselle's fault, but Bobbie had picked Alex in the divorce, so acting like she blamed his ex for everything was part of the best-friend pact. Alex pushed against it, but she knew he also appreciated her saying all the things that he couldn't.

"I'll send *Giselle* your love," Alex said.

"And tell Kit that Aunt Bobbie says hi, and I want new pictures. Everything I have of him is a year old. I wanna see how my little man is filling out."

"You know it's creepy to flirt with a kid you've known his entire life, right?"

"My love is a pure love," Bobbie replied, then switched tactical to the mission parameters. Freehold had a population of just under three hundred, all Earth-born. They called themselves an Assembly of Sovereign Citizens, whatever that meant. But the colony-ship manifest had included a lot of firearms and ammunition. And with the weeks the *Roci* had spent dropping down toward Freehold's sun, the locals had had plenty of time to work themselves up.

Reading along with her, Alex said, "Captain'll need some backup down there."

"Yeah. Talking to Amos about that is the next thing on my list."

"Taking Betsy?"

"This is probably not a Betsy-level situation, sailor," Bobbie said. Betsy was Alex's nickname for the suit of Martian Marine Recon armor she kept in the ship's cargo bay. She hadn't put the thing on in years, but she kept it operational and charged anyway. It made her feel warm and comfortable knowing it was there. Just in case.

"Copy that," Alex said.

"Where is Amos, anyway?"

It was subtle, the difference between Alex being at ease and Alex trying to sound like he was at ease. "Ship thinks he's in the sick bay," Alex said.

Clarissa, Bobbie thought. *Well, shit.*

The *Rocinante*'s medical bay smelled like antiseptic and vomit.

The antiseptic came from the little floor scrubber that was humming around the room, leaving a trail of shiny decking in its wake. The acid-and-bile smell of vomit came from Clarissa Mao.

"Bobbie," she with a smile. She was on one of the med bay's couches, an autodoc cuff around her upper arm that buzzed and hummed and occasionally clicked. Claire's face would tighten at each click. Injections, maybe, or something worse.

"Hey, Babs," Amos said. The hulking mechanic sat at Claire's bedside reading something on his hand terminal. He didn't look up when Bobbie entered the room, but raised a hand in greeting.

"How're you feeling today?" Bobbie asked, grimacing internally as she said it.

"I'll be out of bed in a few minutes," Claire said. "Did I miss something on the pre-landing check?"

"No, no," Bobbie replied, shaking her head. She feared that Claire would tear the tubes out of her arm and leap out of bed if she said yes. "Nothing like that. I just need to borrow the lunk for a minute."

"Yeah?" Amos said, looking at her for the first time. "That okay with you, Peaches?"

"Whatever you need," she said, gesturing at the med-bay in general. "You will always find me at home."

"All right," Amos stood up, and Bobbie guided him out into the corridor.

Surrounded by the fading gray walls, and with the sick-bay hatch closed behind him, Amos seemed to deflate a little. He leaned his back against the wall and sighed. "That's tough to watch, you know?"

"How is she?"

"Good days and bad days, same as anyone," Amos said. "Those aftermarket glands she had put in keep leaking their rat shit into her blood, and we keep filtering it back out. But taking 'em back out would fuck her up worse, so..."

Amos shrugged again. He looked tired. Bobbie had never really been able to figure out what the relationship between the *Roci*'s mechanic and his tiny counterpart was. They weren't sleeping together, and it didn't seem like they ever had. Most of the time they didn't even talk. But when Claire's health had started its decline, Amos was usually there by her side in the sick bay. It made Bobbie wonder if he'd do that for her if she got sick. If anyone would.

The big mechanic was looking a little thinner himself these days. Where most big men tended toward pudge in their later years, Amos had gone the other direction. What fat he'd had was gone, and now his arms and neck looked ropey with old muscle just under the skin. Tougher than shoe leather.

"So," he said, "what's up?"

"Did you read my briefing on Freehold?"

"Skimmed it."

"Three hundred people who hate centralized authority and love guns. Holden's going to insist on meeting them on their turf, because that's the kind of shit he does. He'll need backup."

"Yeah," Amos agreed. "I'll keep an eye on him."

"I was thinking maybe I should take this one," Bobbie said, nodding her head toward the sick-bay hatch. Not saying, *She doesn't look good.* Amos pursed his lips, considering.

"Yeah, okay," Amos said. "Atmospheric landing will probably shake the damn ship apart. I'll have plenty to do here."

Bobbie started to leave, then something made her stop. Before she knew she was going to say it, she asked, "How much longer?"

"Rest of her life," Amos said, then went back into the sick bay and closed the hatch behind him.

She found Holden and Naomi eating breakfast in the galley.

The smell of scrambled eggs with powdered onions and what passed for peppers competed with brewing coffee. Bobbie's belly growled as soon as she walked into the room, and without a word Holden pushed a plate toward her and began slopping eggs onto it.

"Enjoy, because this is the last of the real eggs until we get back to Medina," Holden said as he dished her up.

Naomi finished chewing a mouthful and said, "What's going on?"

"Did you guys read my threat assessment on Freehold?"

"Skimmed it," Holden replied.

"First-generation colony," Naomi said. "Eight years since founding, and it's still only got one township on it in a semiarid temperate zone. Low-level agriculture, but most of the food supply is salvaged hydroponics. Some goats and chickens, but the livestock is surviving on the hydroponics too, so not the most efficient model. Lithium in the planetary crust and a weirdly lot of uranium trapped in polar glaciers that hopefully means it'll be easily harvested helium if they ever get the infrastructure to mine something. Charter that calls for radical personal autonomy enforced by a citizen militia made up of the whole colonial population."

"Really?" Holden said. "The whole population?"

"So three hundred people who like guns," Naomi said, then pointed at Holden. "This one will insist on getting off the ship and speaking to them in person."

"Right?" Bobbie said, then quickly shoveled a heaping scoop of eggs into her mouth. They were as good as her nose had promised they'd be.

"This *has* to be done face-to-face," Holden said. "If not, we could just have radioed the message to them from Medina and saved ourselves the trip."

"Diplomacy is your thing," Bobbie said. "I'm strictly concerned with tactical issues. And when we talk to the powers that be on Freehold, we'll be telling them there's no reason not to just start shooting and hope for the best."

Holden pushed his half-empty plate away and leaned back with a frown. "Explain that."

"You really should read my assessments."

Naomi grabbed Holden's mug and moved over to the coffee machine. "I think I know where she's going with this. You want any coffee, Bobbie?"

"Yes, thank you," Bobbie said, then pulled up the tactical assessment on her hand terminal. "These are people who left Earth to form a colony based on personal sovereignty. They believe in the absolute right of each citizen to defend themselves and their property, with lethal force if necessary. And they are well armed for this purpose."

"I followed that part," Holden said.

"They are also years from self-sustaining at this point. The reason they're relying on hydroponics is that they're having a difficult time developing soil for their greenhouses. Something about the mineral content. The money they've been able to get from preliminary mining futures is all going to Auberon for agricultural supplies trying to get around that. They don't agree that the Transport Union should be taking tariffs on any basic life-sustaining trade. Which is what got us here."

Naomi handed her a steaming mug of coffee with lots of cream, just the way she liked it. Holden nodded in a way that probably meant trouble. He'd understood what she was saying.

"How long till they have local crops?" Naomi asked, leaning over her shoulder to look at the report.

"I don't know, but that's not the issue here—"

"The issue here," Holden said, "is that we're delivering a death sentence. Isn't that right? We're going to land and tell them they're cut off from trading with other colonies. And they know they're going to run out of usable food in a few months, and won't be able to grow their own for years. The union is putting them in an impossible position. And by *union* right now, I mean us. We are."

"Yes," Bobbie agreed, glad he seemed to understand. "These are people who believe in the inviolate right to use lethal force in defense of their own lives. When we land and tell them they're cut off, we'll leave them with no reason not to try to take the ship."

"I don't understand the penalty," Naomi said. "Seems harsh."

"Drummer's been waiting for this one, I'd guess," Holden said. He didn't look happy. "The first colony to really test how far the union will go to protect its monopoly on gate usage. And she's going to crush this first example so hard that no one else will even try. She's killing one colony now so she doesn't have to kill thirteen hundred colonies later."

The idea hung in the air like smoke over a poker game. Naomi's expression mirrored Bobbie's concern. Holden had the inward focus he got when he was thinking about something too hard for safety. A three-year timeout was rough. A three-year timeout when you'd start starving in less than one was something worse. Motive enough for violence, at least. Maybe something more.

"So," Bobbie said, "this is going to be interesting."

Chapter Three: Santiago Jilie Singh

Singh felt a tingle on his wrist and slid back his sleeve. The monitor wrapped around his forearm saw him look and displayed a notification of his most urgent task: the upcoming audience with the high consul.

He reset the notification timer to one-half hour before the meeting itself. His data pad had been riding on his arm or in his pocket for nearly five years. It knew everything there was to know about him. It was treating his upcoming audience with the high consul as if it were the single most important event of his life.

It wasn't wrong.

He pulled the sleeve back into place, giving it one sharp tug to smooth out any new wrinkles, and inspected himself in his mirror. His blue-and-white dress uniform fit him like a glove, emphasizing the muscular frame he spent an hour every day sculpting in the gym. The newly acquired captain's stars glittered on his collar, polished to a golden gleam. His chin and scalp were freshly shaved, and he imagined it gave him the feral, predatory quality that befit a military man.

"Still preening?" Natalia said from the bathroom. She opened the door and came out in a cloud of steam, her hair dripping wet. "A man so handsome needs to be groped, I think."

"No," Singh said, backing away. "If you get water on me—"

"Too late," his wife laughed, darting forward to grab him. She hugged him tight around the waist, her wet hair on his shoulder.

"Nat," he said, meaning to complain but finding himself unable to. Her towel had come loose when she grabbed him, and in the mirror he could see the gentle curve of her hip. He put a hand on it and squeezed. "I'm all wet now."

"You'll dry," she said, reaching behind him to pinch his butt. The newly promoted captain in the Laconian navy gave an undignified yelp. He felt another buzz in his wrist, and for a moment Singh thought the pad on his arm was disapproving of all this tomfoolery.

He pushed his sleeve back again, and saw that it was just a notification that his car would arrive in twenty minutes.

"Car will be here soon," he said with regret, burying his nose in his wife's wet hair for a moment.

"And it's time to get Elsa up," Natalia agreed. "It's your big day. You pick: wake the monster, or make breakfast?"

"I'll take monster duty this morning."

"Be careful. She'll care even less about not messing up your clean new uniform," Natalia said as she pulled on a robe. "Breakfast in ten, sailor."

But it took nearly fifteen minutes to drag Elsa out of her crib, change her diaper, get her dressed, and carry her into their kitchen. Natalia had already put plates piled high with pancakes and fresh apples on the table, and the smell of chai filled the air.

Singh's wrist buzzed, and he didn't need to look to know it was the five-minute warning for his car. He strapped Elsa into her high chair and put the smallest plate of apple slices in front of her. She chortled and smacked her palm down onto them, spraying droplets of juice everywhere.

"Will you have time to eat?" Natalia asked.

"I'm afraid I won't," Singh said, pulling up his sleeve and scrolling through the day's schedule. "Monster just did not want to put pants on today."

"I think her single biggest disagreement with preschool is their pants requirement," Natalia said with a smile. Then she glanced down at the meeting schedule on his arm and sobered. "What time should we expect you?"

"My meeting is scheduled for fifteen minutes at nine a.m., and I don't have anything else today, so..." Singh said. He did not say, *but I'm meeting with High Consul Winston Duarte, so I control nothing about when the meeting begins or ends.*

"All right," Natalia said, then kissed his cheek. "I'll be at the lab today until at least six, but your father agreed to monster duty if you can't pick her up from school."

"Fine, fine," Singh said. "Until then."

The dark naval staff car pulled up outside. Singh paused at the mirror by the door to give himself one final inspection, and wipe away an errant bit of Monster's breakfast shrapnel. Natalia was at the table now, trying to eat and also get some of Monster's own food in her mouth and off her shirt.

Dread welled up from his belly, swamping his heart. He had to swallow half a dozen times before he could speak. He loved his wife and their child more than he could say, and leaving them was always a little difficult. This was different. Generations of navy men had faced mornings like this. Meetings with superiors that heralded change. Surely, if they'd faced it, he could too.

The imperial view, a history professor at the Naval Academy once said, is the long view. Individuals build empires because they want their names to echo through time. They build massive constructs of stone and steel so that their descendants will remember the people who created the world that they only live in. There were buildings on Earth that were thousands of years old, sometimes the only remaining evidence of empires that thought they would last forever. *Hubris*, the professor had called it. When people build, they are trying to make an aspiration physical. When they die, their intentions are buried with them. All that's left is the building.

While Martian intentions had never been explicitly imperialist, they had a fair bit of this same hubris. They'd built their tunnels and warrens as temporary living space in the stone of Mars, then gotten down to the generations-spanning work of making the surface habitable.

But their first generation died with the work still unaccomplished. And the generation after that, and so on, child following parent, until the children only knew the tunnels and didn't think they were so bad. They lost sight of the larger dream because it had never been their dream. Once the creators and their intentions were gone, only the tunnels were left.

As Singh looked out at the capital city of Laconia whizzing past the car's window, he saw the same masses of material and intention. Giant stone-and-steel buildings designed to house the government of an empire that didn't exist yet. More infrastructure than Laconia on its own would need for centuries. Their columns and spires called back millennia of Terran and Martian culture, and remade them as a vision of a peculiarly human future.

If the dreams of empire failed, they'd just be big buildings that had never been used.

It was an open secret among the high-ranking officers of Laconia's military that the high consul's labs had made incredible breakthroughs in human modification. One of their most important projects was dramatic life extension for the high consul himself. The captain that Singh had served under as a lieutenant had received an official reprimand for getting drunk and referring to the high consul as "our own little god-king."

But Singh understood why that particular project for the high consul was so important. Empires, like buildings, are aspirations made material. When the creator dies, the intention is lost.

And so the creator couldn't be permitted to die.

If the rumors were true, and the high consul's scientists were in fact working to make him deathless, they had a chance to create the sort of empire history had only dreamed of. Stability of leadership, continuity of purpose, and a single lasting vision. Which was all well and good, but didn't explain why he had been summoned to a personal meeting with Duarte.

"We're almost there, sir," his driver said.

"I'm ready," Singh lied.

The State Building of Laconia was the imperial palace in all but name. It was by far the largest structure in the capital city. It was both the seat of their government and the personal dwelling space of the high consul and his daughter. After passing through a rigorous security screening administered by soldiers in state-of-the-art Laconian power armor, Singh was finally ushered inside for the very first time.

It was a little disappointing.

He wasn't sure what he'd expected. A ceiling fifty feet high, maybe, held up by rows of massive stone pillars. A red velvet carpet leading to a towering golden throne. Ministers and servants lining up for a word with the high consul and plotting intrigues in whispers. Instead, there was a foyer and waiting area lined with comfortable chairs, easy access to restrooms, and a wall monitor displaying the security rules inside the State Building. It all seemed very mundane. Very governmental.

A short, smiling man with a red jacket and black pants entered through the room's largest door and gave an almost imperceptible bow.

"Captain Santiago Singh," he said, not making it a question.

Singh stood up, only barely stopping himself from snapping out a salute. The man didn't wear a military uniform or any rank insignia, but they were inside the home of their ruler. It carried a weight beyond protocol.

"Yes, sir. I am Captain Singh."

"The high consul hopes you will join him in the residence for breakfast," the little man said.

"It would be my honor, of course."

"Follow me," said the little man as he exited through the same large door. Singh followed.

If the foyer of the State Building was underwhelming, the rest of the interior was positively utilitarian. Corridors lined with office space radiated off in every direction. The halls bustled with activity, people in suits and military uniforms and the same red jackets and black pants as his guide moving about. Singh made sure to salute any time he saw a rank that required it and tried to ignore everyone else. The whole human population of Laconia were the original colonists, Duarte's fleet, and the children born there in the last few decades. He hadn't imagined there were this many people on the planet he hadn't met. His little guide moved through as though he didn't see any of them and kept his same vague smile the entire time.

After a ten-minute walk through a maze of corridors and chambers, they arrived at a set of glass double doors that looked out on a large patio. His guide opened one door and ushered him through, then disappeared back into the building.

"Captain Singh!" High Consul Winston Duarte, absolute military ruler of Laconia, called out. "Please join me. Kelly, make sure the captain has a plate."

Another man in a red jacket and black pants, this one apparently named Kelly, set a place for him, then pulled out his chair. Singh sat, dizzy and grateful he wouldn't have to try to keep from swaying on his feet.

"High Consul, I—" Singh started, but Duarte waved him off.

"Thank you for joining me this morning. And I think we can use our military titles here. Admiral Duarte, or just Admiral is fine."

"Of course, Admiral."

Kelly had placed a single egg in an egg cup in front of him, and was now using tongs to put a sweet roll next to it on his plate. Singh had eaten an egg before, so while it was a luxury, it wasn't a total mystery. The table was small—it would have been crowded with four diners—and overlooked a large patch of what looked like lovingly tended terrestrial grass. A girl of maybe twelve years sat in the middle of the grass playing with a puppy. Real chickens and Terran dogs. Unlike Noah's ark in the old story, the ships of the first fleet had carried only a few species of animal to Laconia. Seeing evidence of two in the same sitting was a little overwhelming. Singh tapped on the shell of his egg with his spoon to crack it, and tried to keep his bearings.

Admiral Duarte gestured at Singh's coffee cup, and Kelly poured for him. "I apologize," Duarte said, "for pulling you away from your family so early this morning."

"I serve at the pleasure of the high consul," Singh said automatically.

"Yes, yes," the admiral replied. "Natalia, right? And one daughter?"

"Yes, Admiral. Elsa. She is nearly two now."

Admiral Duarte smiled out at the girl in the grass and nodded. "It's a good age. Not the toilet-training part, but she's sleeping through the night?"

"Most nights, sir."

"It's fascinating to watch their minds start to grow around then. Learning language. Learning to identify themselves as a separate entity. The word *no* becomes magical."

"Yes, sir," Singh said.

"Don't pass up trying that pastry," the admiral said. "Our baker's a genius."

Singh nodded and took a bite. The pastry was too sweet for him, but the bitter black coffee paired with it perfectly.

Admiral Duarte smiled at him, then said, "Tell me about Captain Iwasa."

The bite of sweet roll he'd just swallowed turned into a slug of lead in his belly. Captain Iwasa had been stripped of rank and dishonorably discharged based on a report Singh had given to the admiralty. If his former commanding officer had been a personal friend of the high consul, Singh could be witnessing the end of his career. Or worse.

"I'm sorry, I—" Singh started.

"It's not an interrogation," Duarte said, his voice as soft as warm flannel. "I know all the *facts* about Captain Iwasa. I want to hear your version. You filed the original dereliction-of-duty report. What moved you to do that?"

One of his professors at the military academy had once said, *When there's no cover, the only sensible thing to do is move through the field of fire as quickly as possible.* Singh sat up straight in his chair, doing his best version of standing at attention from the sitting position.

"Sir, yes sir. Captain Iwasa failed to enforce the newly delivered naval code of military conduct, and then when asked a direct question about those guidelines, he lied to Admiral Goyer, his commanding officer, in my presence. I sent a memo to Admiral Goyer that disputed Captain Iwasa's statements."

Duarte eyed him speculatively, no hint of anger on his face. That didn't mean anything. From all accounts, the high consul was not a demonstrative man.

"The revised code that made dereliction of duty an offense punishable by being sent to the Pen?" Admiral Duarte said.

"Yes, sir. Captain Iwasa felt this punishment to be excessive, and spoke openly about it. When two Marines were found sleeping on duty, he gave them administrative punishments instead."

"So you went over his head to Admiral Goyer."

"Sir, no sir," Singh said. He lowered his eyes to look directly into the high consul's. "I witnessed an officer lying to his superior in response to a direct question about his chain of command. I notified that officer, as was my duty."

Singh stopped, but Duarte said nothing. Just kept looking at him like he was a particularly interesting bug pinned to a corkboard. Then, as if it were a casual question, "Did you dislike Iwasa?"

"If I may speak frankly, sir," Singh asked. When Duarte nodded, he continued. "Operating within the code of military conduct is the sworn duty of every officer and enlisted man. It is the instrument by which we are a military and not just a lot of people with spaceships and guns. When an officer shows a disregard for it, they are no longer an officer. When Iwasa demonstrated a repeated and deliberate failure to uphold that code, he was no longer my commanding officer. I merely informed the next person up the chain of command of this fact."

"Do you feel now, knowing what the consequences to Iwasa were, that you did the right thing?" the admiral asked. His face and voice betrayed no opinion on the topic. He might as well have been asking if Singh wanted sugar.

"Yes, Admiral," Singh said. "Duty isn't a buffet where you pick what you want and ignore the rest. Provisional loyalty isn't loyalty. Captain Iwasa's duty was to enforce the code of conduct on those in his command. When he lied about failing to do so, it was my duty to notify his commanding officer."

The high consul nodded. It could have meant anything. "Do you miss him?"

"I do. He was my first commanding officer when I left the academy. He taught me everything I needed to know. I miss him every day," Singh replied, and realized he wasn't exaggerating. Iwasa's fatal flaw had turned out to be his affection for those in his command. It made him an easy man to love.

"Captain," Duarte said. "I have a new assignment for you."

Singh stood up, nearly knocking his chair over, and saluted. "Captain Santiago Singh, reporting for duty, High Consul." He knew it was ridiculous, but something about the entire conversation was surreal and ridiculous, and in the moment it just felt like the right thing to do. Duarte had the grace to treat it with respect.

"The first phase of our project is coming to an end. We are now moving on to phase two. I am giving you command of the *Gathering Storm*. The details of your orders are in the captain's safe on that vessel."

"Thank you, Admiral," Singh said, his heart pounding in his chest. "It will be my honor to carry those orders out to the letter."

Duarte turned to look out at the girl playing with her dog. "We've been hidden away from the rest of humanity long enough. Time we showed them what we've been doing."

Chapter Four: Holden

Holden had been in his twenties when the Earth Navy kicked him out. He looked back at that version of himself with the kind of fondness and indulgence that people usually extended to puppies that were overly proud of themselves for scaring off a squirrel. He'd signed up to work ice-hauling runs with a sense of turning his back on the whole corrupt, authoritarian, cynical history of his species. Even the name of the company he'd signed on with—Pur 'n' Kleen—had seemed rich with meaning. A promise of integrity and purity. If it was also a little cartoonish, it hadn't felt like that at the time.

Back then, the Belt had been the rugged frontier. The UN and the Martian Congressional Republic, the political gods of a solar system more isolated than an ancient island in the middle of the ocean. Belters had been a structural underclass fighting to have people on the inner planets even notice when they were dying.

Now humanity was scattered to more than thirteen hundred new solar systems, and Earth might not even be the most hospitable planet for human life. Anytime a few like-minded people could put together the resources for a colony and the fees for passage through the ring gates, the seeds of a new society could be sown out there among the stars. Even the most populous of the new systems only had eight or ten cities on a whole planet. It was a massive parallel experiment in the possible forms of human collective, a chance to remake the structure of culture itself. But somehow, it all wound up seeming very familiar.

"What makes you people believe you have the right to dictate trade between sovereign states?" Governor Payne Houston of Freehold demanded. "We are a free people. And despite what your masters on Medina may think, we do not answer to *you*."

When Houston had come into the meeting, he'd already been pretty worked up, and Holden hadn't had much opportunity to talk him back down to a meaningful, productive level of raising hell just yet. Instead, he watched and listened and tried to decide whether the governor's anger was based more in fear, frustration, or narcissism. Fear, Holden could understand. Frustration would have made sense too. All the planets connected by the ring gate had their own biomes, their own biologies, their own unexpected obstacles for someone trying to carve out an environmental niche for humans. Being able to trade for what they needed was quite often the difference between life and death. Anyone who thought they and the people they cared about were being arbitrarily blocked from the things they needed would be scared down to their bones.

The more the governor went on, though, the more it seemed like the guy was just an asshole.

"Freehold is an independent sovereign state," Houston said, slapping his table with an open palm. "We will engage in trade with willing partners, and we will not pay tribute to parasites like you, sir. We will *not*."

The council chamber was built like a courtroom, with Holden and Bobbie sitting at a low table and the governor and his eleven cabinet members above them looking down like a panel of judges. Their table was a dark-stained wood analog. Windows behind Houston and his cohort silhouetted them. Interior design as a political tool. The sidearms that all the Freeholders wore underscored it.

He glanced over at Bobbie. Her expression was calm, but her gaze shifted between the people looking down at them, then to the guards at the door. Calculating who she'd take out first, how she'd disarm them, where to take cover, how to escape. It was something Bobbie did the way other people knitted.

"So here's the thing," Holden said as Houston took a breath. "You think I'm here to negotiate with you. I'm not."

Houston scowled. "There is a right given by God to all free men, and we will have no tyrants or kings—"

"I understand why you're confused," Holden said, his voice louder, but still friendly. "You see a gunship coming out. Takes weeks to get here. You think this must be something where we're expecting a lot of give and take. Light delay would make back and forth awkward, so it makes sense to have someone right here breathing your air, right? You say something, we say something. No lag. But the thing is, the Transport Union has already decided what's going to happen. We aren't mediators. We're not looking for an amicable solution."

The woman to Houston's left put a hand on his arm. Houston leaned back. That was interesting. Holden shifted a little, speaking to the space between the two of them to include her in the conversation.

"We're all adults here," Holden said. "We don't need to pretend with each other. The union sent us here in person because they don't want to have to do this kind of thing over and over with a bunch of other colonies. They wanted to make sure that everyone else was watching this situation. Especially your friends and trading partners on Auberon."

"Political theater," Houston said with contempt in his voice. Which was kind of funny coming from a guy sitting a meter and a half higher than he needed to.

"Sure," Holden said. "Anyway, here's the thing. You sent a ship through the gates without authorization. You endangered the other ships using the gates—"

Houston huffed and waved a dismissive hand.

"—and there are consequences for that kind of thing," Holden went on. "We're just here to tell you what they are."

Bobbie shifted her chair, turning it out so her legs were free. It might have been a casual gesture, except that it wasn't. Holden ran his hands over the top of the table. Whatever it was made from wasn't wood, but it had the same hardness and subtle texture. Houston and his cabinet were quiet. He had their attention now.

Holden needed to decide what to do with it. Follow instructions or fudge it a little.

"There are two ways this can go," he said, fudging a little. "The first one is the union cuts off gate access to Freehold for three years."

"We aren't self-sustaining yet," one of the other cabinet members said. "You're talking about a death sentence for three hundred people."

"That's a decision you folks made when you sent your unauthorized ship through the gates," Holden said. "Or maybe you can find some way to up the timetable. Get a way to feed people sooner. That's up to you. But for three years, any ship going in or out of the Freehold gate gets killed without warning. No exceptions. Communications in and out of the gate are jammed. You're on your own. Or, option two is Governor Houston comes with us for trial and probably just a whole lot of jail time."

Houston snorted. His expression looked like he'd taken a bite of something rotten. The other people on the bench were less demonstrative. Freehold was a colony of pretty good poker faces.

"You forget the third option," Houston said. "Being the ambassador of tyranny is a job with risks, Captain Holden. Very. Real. Risks."

"Okay, so let's do the math on that," Holden said. "We're here, and there are a dozen of you up there and four guards at the doors—"

"Six," Bobbie said.

"Six guards at the doors," Holden said, not missing a beat. "If you just look at the hundred or so meters around this building, we're totally outnumbered and outgunned. *But* if you expand that to half a klick out, I have a gunship. My gunship has PDCs. It has a rail gun. It has twenty torpedoes. Hell, it's got an Epstein drive that can put out a plume that would glass this whole settlement if we pointed it at the right angle."

"So force," Houston said, shaking his head. "Taxation always comes at the end of a gun."

"I thought of it more as an argument against shooting ambassadors," Holden said. "We're leaving now and going back to our ship. Twelve hours after we get there, we're taking off. If we have Governor Houston here on board, you can start scheduling ships with the union again. If not, we'll send someone back in three years to check in."

Holden stood up, Bobbie following his lead so closely that she was on her feet before him. Houston leaned forward, his left hand on the table and his right at his side like it was resting on the butt of a gun. Before the governor could say anything, Holden started for the door. The guards watched him step forward, their eyes cutting from him to Bobbie, then up to Houston. In Holden's peripheral vision, Bobbie settled a little deeper into her legs, her center of gravity solidifying. She was humming softly, but he couldn't quite pick out the melody.

As they reached the door, the guards stood aside, and Holden started breathing again. A short corridor to the anteroom, then out to the dirty street. He eased his hand terminal out of his pocket as they walked. Alex picked up the connection as soon as he put in the request.

"How's it going out there?" Alex asked.

"We're on our way back now," Holden said. "Make sure the airlock's open when we get there."

"You coming in hot?" Alex asked.

"Maybe," Holden said.

"Copy that. I'll have the welcome mat out and the PDCs warmed up."

"Thank you for that," Holden said and dropped the connection.

"You really think they'll be dumb enough to make a play?" Bobbie asked.

"I don't want to bet my life on other people being smart," Holden said.

"Voice of experience?"

"I've been hurt before."

Freehold was the name of the town and the planet and the solar system. Holden couldn't say which had come first. The town nestled in a valley between two ridge mountains. A soft breeze smelled faintly of acetate and mint, by-products of whatever chemistry the local biosphere had figured out for its life cycles.

The sunlight was subtly redder than Holden expected, making the shadows seem blue and giving the sense of permanent twilight. Or maybe dawn. A flock of local bird-analogs flew overhead in a V, their wide, transparent wings buzzing in an eerie harmony. It was a beautiful planet in its way. The gravity was a little less than half a g—more than Mars, less than Earth—and the planetary tilt and spin made the daylight just eight hours and change, the night a little over nine. Two minor moons were tide-locked to a big one almost a third the mass of the planet. The large moon even had a thin atmosphere, but nothing lived there. Not yet, anyway. If Freehold made it another few generations, someone would probably put another little town up there too, if only to get away from the locals. That seemed to be the human pattern—reach out to the unknown and then make it into the sort of thing you left in the first place. In Holden's experience, humanity's drive out into the universe was maybe one part hunger for adventure and exploration to two parts just wanting to get the hell away from each other.

It was always strange seeing the *Rocinante* on her belly. The ship had been designed to rest that way when it came down the gravity well. It didn't do any damage. It just seemed wrong. The PDCs that studded her side shifted as they got closer, restless and active.

The crew airlock stood open, a length of ladder leading down to the ground. Amos sat with his legs dangling over the lip of the open airlock door, a rifle resting across his thighs. Holden was a little surprised that Clarissa wasn't there with him. Bobbie waved as they drew close, and Amos lifted his hand in response without taking his eyes off the trail behind them.

Holden went up first, then turned, standing between the ladder and Amos while Bobbie clambered up to them. Back toward the town, four people stood in a clump, not coming close, but clearly watching. At this distance, Holden wasn't sure if they'd been at the meeting or if they were new. Bobbie hit the panel, and the ladder retracted into the ship.

"How'd it go?" Amos asked, levering himself to his feet and stepping back from the outer door.

Bobbie cycled the door closed, raising her voice over the sound of the servos. "Back with no shots fired. I count that as a win."

The inner door opened, and Amos stowed the rifle in a locker that their weird orientation made look like a drawer. Holden walked along the wall, heading toward the ops deck. Which should have been up, but was, for the moment, to the left.

"I'm going to be glad when we're out of here," he said.

Amos smiled, the expression amiable and empty as ever, and followed after. Naomi and Alex were sitting in their crash couches, playing a complex combat-simulation game that they'd picked up in the last couple of years. Holden was reassured to see an exterior feed of the path to the town on both of their screens. Whatever else they were doing to pass the time, everyone was keeping their eyes on the town. Just in case.

"Hey, there, Captain," Alex said, his drawl a little thicker than usual. "We ready to pull up stakes and mosey on out of here?"

"We're waiting twelve hours," Holden said, sitting in his couch. The gimbals didn't shift. The fixed gravity of the planet meant all the couches were locked in place, their workstations rotated to the correct orientation. Naomi twisted to look at him.

"Twelve hours? For what?"

"I may have renegotiated the deal a little," he said. "I said if they turned over the governor to us for trial, there wouldn't be a quarantine."

Naomi lifted an eyebrow. "Does the union know about this?"

"I figured I'd send them a message when I got back here."

"You think Drummer'll be okay with it?"

"Cap changing the rules?" Amos said with a shrug. "That's just a day that ends in y far as I can tell. If she didn't leave some wiggle room for it, that's her mistake."

"I'm not going to hold the whole colony responsible for what a few administrators did," Holden said. "It's collective punishment, and it's not the kind of thing that the good guys should do."

"At least not without twelve hours' warning?" Naomi said.

Holden shrugged. "This is the window they have to make a choice. If they have the chance to do something different and they still double down, I feel a little better about closing them off. At least we'll have tried."

" 'A little better' meaning 'not totally guilt-ridden.' "

"Not totally," Holden said, lying back. The gel was cool against the back of his head and shoulders. "Still don't love the whole cutting-people-off-from-supplies-they-need thing."

"Should have agreed to run the union when you had the chance," Alex said. "Then it could all be the way you wanted."

"It'd be pretty to think so anyway," Holden said.

Twelve hours. A night and part of a day, for Freehold. And not quite enough time for a message to go from the *Roci* to Medina to the office of the president of the Transport Union and come back again. If Drummer threw a fit, they'd still be burning for Medina before her message came through. He'd have given the Freeholders more time to think things through if he could have. But lightspeed was lightspeed.

It was the irony of making threats while having mass. The messages and voices, culture and conversation, could move so much

more quickly than even the fastest ship. In the best case, it would
have made persuasion and argument much more important. Moving ideas across the gap between planets was easy. Moving objects
was hard. But it meant that whoever was on the other side had to
be listening and willing to let their minds be changed. For all the
other times, it was gunships and threats, same as ever.

Holden was asleep when the answer finally came.

"Wake up," Naomi said. "We've got visitors."

He wiped his eyes, swung his feet to the wall that was now
temporarily the floor, ran his hands through his hair, and looked
blearily at the screen. A crowd of people were outside the ship. He
recognized a couple of the faces from the council meeting. And in
the middle of them, Governor Houston was hog-tied in a wide,
gray ceramic wheelbarrow. The relief that poured through Hold-
en's body was only tempered a little bit by the prospect of months
on the burn with the disgraced governor on board.

He opened a connection. "This is Captain Holden of the *Rocinante*. Hang tight. We'll be right out."

"Be careful," Naomi said. "Just because this looks like one
thing, that doesn't mean it can't be something different."

"Right," he said, opening a connection to ops. "Alex? You
there?"

"He's sleeping," Clarissa answered. "I have the PDCs warmed
up, and Amos and Bobbie are on their way to the airlock. If it's an
ambush, it will be a very unsuccessful one."

"Thank you for that," Holden said, walking along the side of
the lift shaft toward the airlock. The mixed voices of Bobbie and
Amos already echoed down toward him.

"Give the sign if you need me to do more than watch," Clarissa
said, and cut the connection.

When the airlock opened and they lowered the ladder, Holden
went first. A woman with sharp features and thick gray-black hair
pulled back in a bun stepped out toward him.

"Captain Holden," she said. "I'm Interim Governor Semple
Marks. We're here to accede to your government's demands."

"Thank you for that," Holden said as Bobbie slid down the ladder behind him. Amos followed, his shotgun clanking as he came.

"We're lodging a formal complaint with the union about this infringement on our sovereignty," Marks said. "This should have been handled internally in Freehold."

"I'll let you take that up with the union," Holden said. "Thank you for being willing to bend on this one. I didn't want to quarantine your system."

Marks' eyes said, *I think you did,* but she stayed silent. Bobbie helped the prisoner to his feet. Houston's face was gray where it wasn't red. He seemed unsteady.

"Hey," Amos said. A moment later, Houston seemed to find him. Amos nodded encouragement. "I'm Amos. This is Bobbie. We've done this kind of duty before, so there's some rules about how this goes you're going to want to listen to very carefully..."

Chapter Five: Drummer

Drummer didn't want to be awake, but she was. The couch was built for the two of them, Saba and her. Acceleration gel over a frame designed to give them freedom to spoon while People's Home, first and largest of the void cities, was spun up or under gentler thrust or to divide them if they went into an unexpected hard burn while they were asleep. Balancing to keep from shifting the couch and troubling Saba, she checked the system console in the wall nearest her bedside. It was still two hours before she needed to get up. Not long enough for a full sleep cycle. Not short enough to ignore. She was, by some measures, the most influential woman in thirteen hundred worlds, but it didn't fix insomnia.

Saba shifted in his sleep and muttered something she couldn't make out. Drummer put a hand on his back, petting down his spine, not sure if she hoped to quiet him back to sleep or wake him up. He picked the former, snuggling himself down into the gel the way animals in their nests had been doing since before humanity had been more than an upstart hamster trying to avoid the dinosaurs.

She smiled in the darkness and tried not to be disappointed. She needed to pee, but if she got up now, it would wake Saba for certain, and then she'd feel bad. She could suffer a little instead. People's Home muttered around her like it was glad to have her back.

There were ways that she didn't have a home anymore. Hadn't since she'd accepted the presidency. Their quarters on Medina near the administration levels. The captain's cabin of Saba's ship, the *Malaclypse*. Back before she'd become the leader of the Transport Union, they'd been enough. Now she had more space devoted to her than she would ever see. Like a palace minced and scattered across light-years. Medina Station, Ganymede, Ceres, Pallas, Iapetus, Europa. The *Vanderpoele*, which was at her disposal as long as she held office. TSL-5 had quarters set aside for her, as would all the transfer stations when they were built. And the three void cities that made up the spine of the Belters' dominion: Independence and Guard of Passage and People's Home.

At rest, the central core of People's Home stayed on the float, seventy decks of permanent facilities and infrastructure that wore the drum section like a cloak. The dock at one end, the drive at the other. Magnetic fields more powerful than a maglev track held the core separate from the drum levels and corrected when the drum spun up, holding the core stationary while the body shifted from thrust gravity to spin. The rooms and hallways in the drum were fashioned to shift, their floors orthogonal to the direction of thrust when the drive was on, their feet pointing down to the stars at a constant tenth of a g when they were at rest. Enough to make a consistent up and down, but light enough for even the most float-adapted. Not a ship, but a city that had never suffered a gravity well.

Saba yawned and stretched, his eyes still shut. Drummer ran a hand over his wire-brush hair, a little more insistently this time. His eyes opened and his wicked little half smile flickered on and then off again.

"Are you up?" she asked, trying to keep her voice soft, but really wanting the answer to be yes.

"Yes."

"Thank God," she said, and hauled herself up off the couch and went to the head. By the time she was back, Saba was standing naked at the little tea dispenser that had been provided for the exclusive use of the president. Saba had been with her for almost a decade now, and if his age showed a little in the softness of his belly and the roundness of his face, he was still a very pretty man. Sometimes, seeing him like this, she wondered whether she was aging as gracefully. She hoped so, or if not, that he didn't notice.

"Another beautiful morning in the corridors of power, ah?" he said.

"Budget hearings in the morning, trade approval in the afternoon. And Carrie Fisk and her fucking Association of Worlds."

"And fish on Friday," he said, turning to hand her a bulb of hot tea. As little time as People's Home spent on the float, she might as well have had Earther cups. But she never would. "What's an Association of Worlds?"

"That's the question, isn't it?" Drummer said. "Right now it's a couple dozen colonies that feel like I'd listen to them better if they spoke with one voice."

"Are they right?"

He took another bulb for himself and leaned against the wall. He had a weirdly intense way of listening. More than his eyes, it was what made him pretty. Drummer sat on the couch, scowled at nothing in particular and everything in general. "Yes," she said at last.

"And so you don't like them?"

"I don't dislike them," Drummer said and took a sip of her

tea. It was green and flavored with honey and still just a little too hot. "They've been around since Sanjrani, in one form or another. It's all been sternly worded press releases and political grandstanding."

"And now?"

"Sternly worded press releases, grandstanding, with occasional meetings," she said. "But that actually means something. I didn't use to have to make room on the agenda for them. Now it seems like I do."

"What of Freehold?"

"Auberon is more the issue," she said. "There's talk that they're making progress toward a universal polypeptide cross-generator."

"And what is that, when it's at home?"

It was a mechanism for pouring whatever toxic, half-assed soup the biospheres of the scattered planets had come up with into one end of a machine and getting something that humanity could eat out the other. Which meant sometime in the next ten or fifteen years, the effective end of Sol system's monopoly on soil and farming substrates. And it meant Auberon was about to become the new superpower in the wide-flung paths of the human diaspora, provided that Earth and Mars didn't decide to fly a navy out through the gates and start the first interstellar war.

All assuming, of course, that the breakthrough wasn't vapor and tricks, which she wasn't ready to discount. Every great nation, they said, was founded on a knife and a lie.

"I'm not supposed to talk about that," she said. "I'm sorry. I shouldn't have mentioned it."

Saba's face went hard for a moment, but he pushed it back into a smile again. He hated it when she closed him out of things, but however much she trusted him—however much the union's security division had cleared him—he wasn't in the chain of authority. Drummer had spent too much of her life enforcing security protocols to ignore them now.

"The upshot is," she said, trying to bring him in enough to salve his feelings and still not say anything compromising, "that Free-hold is, among other things, a warning to Auberon not to get too cocky, and Carrie Fisk and the Association of Worlds is sniffing around to see if there's any opportunities in it for them. Including how far they can push me."

Saba nodded and, to her mild disappointment, started to get dressed. "So more palace intrigue, savvy sa?" he said.

"Comes down to that," Drummer said, apologizing and also being angry for apologizing, even if it was only by implication.

Saba saw the storm in her almost before she knew it was there. He stepped over to her, knelt at her feet, and put his head in her lap. She coughed out a laugh and patted his hair again. It was an obeisance that he didn't mean, and she knew it. He knew it too. But even if it didn't mean he was actually abasing himself before her, it still meant something.

"You should stay another night," she said.

"I shouldn't. I have crew and cargo and a reputation as a free man to maintain." The laughter in his voice pulled the sting a little bit.

"You should come back soon, then," she said. "And stop hooking up with all the girls on Medina."

"I would never be unfaithful to you."

"Damned right you wouldn't," Drummer said, but there was laughter in her voice too now. Drummer knew that she wasn't an easy woman to love. Or even to work with. There weren't many people in the vast span of the universe that could navigate her moods, but Saba was one of them. Was the best at it of anyone.

The system made its broken bamboo tock. Vaughn, making the first approach of the day. Soon, there would be briefings and meetings and conversations off the record with people she liked or trusted or needed, but never all three at once. She felt Saba's sigh more than she heard it.

"Stay," she said.

"Come with me."

"I love you."

"Te amo, Camina," he said, and rose to his feet. "And I will flitter off to Medina and back so quickly you'll hardly know I was gone."

They kissed once, and then he left, and the cabin seemed empty. Hollow as a bell. The system made another little tock.

"I'll be there in five," she said.

"Yes, ma'am," Vaughn replied.

She dressed, did her hair, and was in the office in slightly less than fifteen minutes, but Vaughn didn't chide her for it.

"What's up first today?" she asked as he handed her a little cup of white kibble and sauce.

His hesitation was almost too small to notice. But only almost. "Message came in from Captain Holden of the *Rocinante*."

"Sum it up?"

The hesitation was more pronounced this time. "Perhaps you should watch it, ma'am."

The meeting room was on the outermost deck of the People's Home drum. Coriolis in the void city was trivial to anyone who'd spent time on a ring station, but outsiders who'd only known mass and acceleration gravity before still found it bothersome. The walls were a pearlescent gray, the table a veneer of blond bamboo over titanium that was bolted straight to the deck. Drummer sat at its head, seething. Most of the others around her—Emily Santos-Baca, Ahmed McCahill, Taryn Hong, and all the other representatives of the board and budget office—knew her well enough to gauge her mood and tread lightly. The poor man making the presentation had never met her before.

"It's been a question of priorities," the man said. His name was Fayez Okoye-Sarkis, and he'd come to speak on behalf of some kind of nongovernmental, nonacademic group that pushed for science research. Chernev Institute, based out of Ganymede and Luna. "Over the last decades—really since the bombardment of

Earth—the vast, *vast* majority of research has been in increasing food yield and infrastructure. And mostly, it's been reverse engineering the technology that made things like the protomolecule and the ring station. Every planet we've been to has had artifacts and old technologies."

"Yes," Drummer said. Meaning *Get on with it*. Okoye-Sarkis smiled like he was used to people finding him charming.

"When my wife was an undergraduate, back in the day," he said, "her fieldwork involved tracking rodent species that had adapted to live in high-radiation zones. Old reactors and fission test sites. They had evolved to fit into environments that were specifically created. By humans. Well, we're those rodents now. We're adapting ourselves into spaces and environments that were left behind by the vanished species or groups of species that created all this. The changes in technology we've seen are immense, and they promise to be just the beginning."

"Okay," Drummer said. Okoye-Sarkis took a drink of water from a bulb. The furrows in his forehead said he knew he was losing her. Hopefully it would make him tighten the presentation up, skip the boring parts, and get to what he wanted so she could say no and get back to her job.

"There has been a lot of speculation about what sort of beings built all the things we've found. Whether they were conscious individuals like us or some kind of hive mind. Whether they were one species in a community or a variety of interconnected species acting in concert. Whether—and I know this sounds weird—whether they had the same relationship to matter that we do. There's been a lot of great thought. Great theory. What there hasn't been is testing. The Chernev Institute wants to be the spearhead for a new generation of scientific research into the deepest questions that the ring gates embody. Who or what built them? What happened to those species between the time they launched Phoebe and the creation of the Sol gate? Did they leave records that we can translate and understand? Our belief is that somewhere in the systems on the far side of the gates or within the gates themselves, we will find something that acts like a kind of Rosetta stone. Something that places all the other discoveries in context. Our goal is to crack the present work in materials science, high- and low-energy physics, biology, botany, geology, even the philosophy of science wide open."

Drummer leaned back in her chair, tilted her head. "So...you think the problem is that things aren't changing fast enough?"

"Well, I think that progress is always better and more efficient when—"

"Because it seems to me," Drummer interrupted, "like we're on the ragged edge of being able to deal with what's already on our plate. I don't see how more growing pains are going to help us."

"This is meant to help us with growing pains," the man said. He delivered the line with a certainty and authority that Drummer respected as a performance. He was a charismatic little shit. She saw why they'd sent him. To her left, Emily Santos-Baca cleared her throat in a way that might have meant nothing, but if it meant anything, it meant a lot. Drummer was being an asshole. With a conscious effort, she pulled her irritation back.

"Fair enough," she said. "And how does the union fit in with this?"

"There are several things that the Transport Union can do to help with the effort. The first being, of course, a contract to grant passage to Institute ships. We've got fieldwork proposals for sites on half a dozen planets whose preliminary surveys look most promising. But we have to get there first." His grin was an invitation for her to smile back.

"That makes sense," Drummer said. His grin lost its edge.

"The other thing that we'd like to open a conversation about... the Transport Union is in a singular position. The fruits of our work stand to benefit the union as much or more than anyone else in any system."

"And so you'd like us to underwrite your work," Drummer said. "Is that it?"

"I had some more preliminaries that help lay the groundwork for why," Okoye-Sarkis said, "but yes."

"You understand we aren't a government," Drummer said. "We're a shipping union. We take things from one place to another and protect the infrastructure that lets us do that. Research contracts aren't really in our line."

Okoye-Sarkis looked around the table, searching for sympathetic eyes. Maybe he even found a few. Drummer knew that her reaction might have been different if the proposal had been made a day earlier. But Holden's message from Freehold...

"The Institute respects that, ma'am," Okoye-Sarkis said. "This is a very new project, but one I think has the potential to yield real benefits for everyone. I have a breakdown of our mission proposals I can leave with you and whoever in your staff wants to look at them."

"All right," Drummer said.

"And the passage agreement. I don't mean to press, but we're still getting our backers together, and the fees—"

"Give us your proposals," Drummer said. "The board can go over them. Whatever conclusion they make about reducing or waiving the contract fees will be fine with me."

"Thank you, Madam President. That's wonderful. Thank you very much."

The scientist practically bowed himself out of the room. Drummer ticked off the last entry in her morning agenda. The afternoon's list looked just as long and at least equally irritating. Santos-Baca caught her eye and lifted an eyebrow.

"It's an interesting proposal. It should make for a lively debate," she said, meaning *I see you just gave the board another issue to deal with.*

"It's important that the board be involved in any serious decisions," Drummer said, meaning *Suck it up.* Emily Santos-Baca chuckled, and half against her will, Drummer smiled. But only for a few seconds.

She suffered through the small talk and pleasantries that came before and after all meetings like social plaque, then went back to her private office as soon as she could. Vaughn or one of his staff had left a bowl of soy pasta with mushrooms and a glass of wine for her. She started with the wine.

She pulled up the display of the full Sol system. Planets, void cities, stations. The asteroids swirling in the complex orbital dances where gravity and system geography made pools of stability. It looked like images of a snowstorm on Earth. She'd never seen snow to know how accurate that was.

She cut out most of the data, simplifying it enough for a human eye to make sense of. There was People's Home, in Mars' orbit, but not near the planet. And there, nearer the ring gate, was Independence. She placed a query, and the *Malaclypse* appeared—a single bright-yellow dot that seemed like it was almost on top of People's Home. Like the ship had never left.

It was a failure of scale. That superposition of light in the display was a hundred thousand kilometers by now. More than the circumference of Earth twice over and getting larger every second. It was just that the unbridgeable distance between her and Saba was nothing compared to the vastness around them. Here in the system, and then out in all the other systems beyond the gates.

Even for a woman born to the void, it was overwhelming. And everyone seemed to want her to control it for them. To take responsibility for it all so that they could feel like someone, somewhere was in charge.

She'd never have said it aloud, but there was part of her that missed the way it had been in her youth. The Belt had been the OPA. Earth and Mars had been the enemy. That had seemed overwhelming at the time. It was only everything that had happened since then that made it seem small and manageable by comparison. A nostalgia for the age that had forged her into who she was. That had given her all the skills she'd needed and then changed into a place where half the time she felt like an impostor in her own clothes.

The *Rocinante* was light-hours away through the gates. Light-centuries by more traditional paths. She pictured Holden as if he were across the table. She took a deep breath, let it out slowly, and then started the recording.

"Captain Holden. I've gotten your status report about the situation on Freehold. Politely put, your proposed solution isn't going to work…"

Chapter Six: Holden

"Politely put," Drummer said on the screen, "your proposed solution isn't going to work. What you're doing would fundamentally change the union. Jailing someone isn't a thing we do. We're a transport union, not a police force. We don't have prisons. We don't have prisoners. We don't have judges. We have *contracts*. When someone breaks the terms of the contract, we object. Then we levy fines and penalties. And then, if they still won't do what they said, we stop playing with them. What we don't do is *arrest* them."

"She sounds pissed," Alex said.

Holden paused the message playback. The ops deck was dim, the way Alex liked it. The air recycler clicked and the drive hummed through the bones of the ship, as familiar as silence.

"Yeah," Holden said. "That doesn't sound like her happy voice, does it?"

Alex scratched at his beard and gave Holden a sympathetic shrug. "You want to finish that someplace private?"

"I don't think that'll make it better." Holden took the pause back off, and Drummer sprang back into motion.

"The other thing we don't do is let everyone who captains a ship on our registry make their own policies for the union as a whole. What you did on Freehold doesn't get to set precedent for what I have to do on every other system that decides to break the rules. I sent you out there with a mission to deliver a message. Not negotiate. Not broker deals. You were there because it was important for everyone else who's watching—and *everyone's* watching—to see what happens when you break the terms of your contract with the Transport Union."

"So it was theater first, and *then* an execution," Holden said to the screen. Not that she could hear him. Still, she paused, looked down, and gathered herself as if she had.

"My problem now," she said, "is how to fix what you've broken with the least amount of damage. I will be consulting with the board and our legal counsel, and when we decide what needs to happen, I'll tell you. And you'll do it. I really hope this is clear enough that it doesn't confuse you."

"I'm getting the feeling she may not actually like me," Holden said.

"She's working herself up a little," Alex said. "I wouldn't take it personally."

"For now," Drummer said, "I am instructing you to proceed on to Medina with Governor Houston. I will have someone ready to meet your ship when you dock. At that time, I will expect you to read a statement that I will put together for you. It may be an apology. It may be a clarification of the Transport Union rules. Whatever it is, I'll deliver it to you before you get there. And you'll recite it word for word.

"You don't get to make the universe be what you want just by saying it, Holden. There are other people who live here too. Next time, show some respect."

The message ended. Alex blew out a long, slow breath. "Well, maybe take it a little personally," he said as Holden closed the message out. The screen returned to its series of rolling system reports. Drive output, environmental stability, waste-heat management. The *Rocinante* doing what she did best. What she always did. The knot in his stomach sat there, quietly. He couldn't tell if it was anger or disappointment or something altogether else.

Alex cracked his knuckles. "You've got that look," he said.

"No, I don't," Holden said. "I don't look like anything."

"She's got a point. There's a lot of colonies out there. If we're going to start hauling in bad guys from all of them... well, there's a lot of mission creep in that. Telling them they can't come play if they won't play nice? It's rough, but it doesn't change what the Transport Union *is*, you know?"

"It's more convenient," Holden said more sharply than he'd intended. "It is. No, I see that. I understand that it's easier to run the union if everything's in terms of who's violated the terms of the contract and withholding service and... and give it a few more decades so the colonies are all able to support themselves, maybe cutting off trade will be a slap on the wrist. But the fact of the matter right now? It's a death sentence."

"Maybe," Alex said. "What I heard about Bara Gaon Complex and Auberon, they're already—"

"This isn't Bara Gaon Complex or Auberon. This is Freehold. If we cut them off for three years, the colony would collapse, and they'd all starve. So right now, yeah, she's saying we should kill them. Only she's phrasing it so it sounds like it's just the natural consequence of *their* choices and not also *ours*."

"Well, yeah," Alex said, but Holden wasn't done. The words kept pushing their way out of him.

"They didn't vote for Drummer," he said, tapping hard on the screen. "They can't appeal her decisions, and she has the power of life and death over them. She needs to be held to a higher standard than 'whatever's most convenient.' And in every military service in history, when the commander gave an immoral command, it was the *duty* of the soldiers to disobey it."

"Every military service in history?"

"All the good ones."

"All right," Alex said. Then a moment later, "They didn't elect us either."

"Exactly! That's my *point*."

"Right," Alex said.

"So we're agreeing with each other."

"Yes. But it still kind of sounds like we're fighting."

"It does," Holden said, and leaned back. His crash couch shifted under him, hissing. The tightness in his gut hadn't lessened at all. He'd really hoped it would. "Shit."

"You think she's going to shut them out again? Put the quarantine back in place?"

"I don't know," Holden said. "Except if she was going to do that, she'd probably make us take Houston back to die with his friends. And it doesn't do great things for your political dog-and-pony show when the captain of one of your pet gunships starts refusing your orders. She'll have to give us this one."

"That sounds right," Alex agreed. "Next one's going to be interesting, though."

"Yeah."

They were quiet for a moment. He knew Alex was going to speak even before the words came. Decades of living and working in the same place meant you never had to ask for someone to pass the salt at galley time. This was just the same.

"If you want, we could yell at each other some more."

"Thanks," Holden said. Alex nodded. It was an open invitation, and only half a joke. He consulted his gut again, then pulled himself up and headed for the lift. Alex didn't ask where he was going. He probably knew.

The galley still had the ghost of the ginger tea Clarissa drank to soothe her stomach, but neither she nor Amos was there now. The food dispenser showed their supply levels, and he saw them without really seeing them. He'd lived on the *Rocinante* longer than anyplace else in his life. He knew the ship better than he knew himself.

As he walked down the corridor to their room, he tried to shrug off the bitterness and the anger. The sense of guilt that was rising in his throat. Even so, he knew she'd see it.

Naomi was in the crash couch, her arm thrown over her eyes, but her breath didn't have the deepness of sleep. Her nap was already over or else it hadn't yet begun. She smiled, and the deep lines at the sides of her mouth were beautiful.

"How bad is it?" she asked even before she took her arm away.

Holden took a deep breath and let it hiss out through his teeth. His gut didn't loosen, but it did shift. The anger turned toward something deeper. Grief, maybe. He crossed his arms. She shifted to look at him. The gray at her temples had started appearing a few years ago, and was slowly spreading. There were lines at the corners of her eyes that the antiaging meds they all took now weren't going to rub away. They were beautiful, too.

"I think it may be time for us to do something else," he said. "For me to do something else, anyway."

She shifted, the crash couch moving to adjust to her. If there had been a joke waiting, an impulse to lighten the moment, it died when she looked at him. Seeing her reacting to him told him how serious he really was. How bad he looked.

"Walk me through it," she said.

He gave her the basics—what Drummer had said, what he and Alex had talked about, what sense he'd made of it—and with every word, every phrase, he felt a confusion he hadn't known he was suffering start to clear. Just saying it to her, knowing that even if he got the words or thoughts wrong, she would hear the meaning underneath them, let him find his own clarity. The tightness in his gut didn't go away.

"When we were hunting down pirates, I could accept their surrender," he said. "Even the Free Navy could have set down arms and we'd have arrested them. But now I'm working for a bureaucratic system that's willing to kill people as a matter of policy. I don't feel like I'm enforcing rules, I feel like an executioner, and...I don't think I can do it."

Naomi shifted, making room for him on the crash couch. He lay down beside her. The couch adjusted to their combined mass. She made a low sound, part hum and part sigh. "Tough to do our jobs, then."

"These colonies? They're all dependent on the Transport Union, and maybe they won't always be. But until they're self-sustaining, they should have a voice in how the union makes the rules. How it enforces them. They didn't elect Drummer."

"They didn't elect any of them. Walker, Sanjrani, Pa."

"The others weren't cutting off trade. Drummer is. And yes, I know. Looking at it, this was probably inevitable. Maybe it's a miracle it took this long to happen. But now it *has* happened, and..."

"And when one thing changes, other things change too."

A voice came from the galley. Bobbie, talking to someone— Alex or Amos or Clarissa. He didn't hear the response, but Bobbie laughed a little at it. The knot in his gut grew heavier.

"I can put out a press release," he said, and the words seemed to sink him deeper into the gel. "Get the message out to all the colonies about what Drummer wants to do, why I think it's wrong. Try to lead some kind of...I don't know, reform coalition. Maybe talk to the Association of Worlds, see if they want to take it on."

"Big fight to pick," Naomi said, neither approving nor disapproving. Just saying it because it was true.

"It'll mean grounding the *Roci* or keeping to one system for a while. There's a lot of trade between Earth and Mars, still. Ganymede. Ceres. Maybe there are some colony worlds with enough infrastructure in place that we could find a niche there. Or make one. Or I could tell a few people what's going on—"

"They already know," Naomi said. "Drummer sent us out here to make a statement. Everyone's already watching. Nothing you've said isn't already on news and discussion feeds all around the colonies."

"So maybe I could let someone else take point on this battle," he said, closing his eyes. "Just get some in-system contracts and see what happens. It's important. But...I don't know. But I'm tired. Too tired to fight this one."

"Or."

He opened his eyes, turned to his side. Her head was tilted the way it was when she hid behind her hair, only without the hiding. Her mouth tensed. Her eyes met his.

"You remember when we first got the *Roci*?" she said. "We were on the run from, oh, I think everyone? Flying this stolen ship. You asked if we wanted to sell her, split the money, and all of us take an early retirement."

He chuckled. "She was worth more back then."

" 'Retirement' meant more years back then too," she said. She wasn't laughing. "What if this isn't a decision you need to make for everyone?"

"Meaning?"

"We both know Alex's going to die in that pilot's chair. Bobbie's at home here. Clarissa's health isn't great. And I don't know, but if she decides to try a skilled-nursing facility on Ceres or something, I get the feeling Amos may go with her."

Holden let that idea sink in. He didn't understand the bond between Amos and Clarissa except that it was fierce and platonic and had lasted through years. If it was love, it didn't look like any version he'd ever experienced, but it didn't look like anything else either. He ran his mind over the idea of Amos still on the *Rocinante* without Clarissa. He'd never considered it before. It was a melancholy prospect.

"Yeah, maybe," Holden said. Then, a moment later, "Yeah."

"We're getting up to the same age Fred was when he stroked out on a burn. And you've been on daily anticancer meds for more than half of your life now. It doesn't matter how good they are, that's going to take a toll on your system. Leave you a little more fragile. So the other thing we can do? Sell our shares. Head down to Titan, pick a resort, and enjoy our retirement."

No, Holden thought. *No, I will never leave this place and these people. This is my home, and no matter what the dangers and threats and fights are, I will stand this ground. This is where I belong. Where we all belong.*

Only what came spilling out of his mouth was "*God*, that sounds wonderful. Let's do that."

Naomi leaned forward, her brows furrowed. "Really? Because I've got a half dozen other arguments I've been working on for why it's not a terrible idea."

"Oh yeah, hold on to those," Holden said. "I'm going to flip my opinion back and forth for weeks. But right now, living in a dome on Titan with you sounds like the single best idea anyone has ever had."

"You wouldn't feel like it made you less of a man?"

"Nope."

"That you were letting the universe down by not taking on every fight there was? Because I worked on that one for a while. I've got some good lines practiced up."

"Keep 'em," Holden said. "You'll need them later. But right now, I'm sold."

Her face relaxed. He could still see the woman she'd been when they were on the *Canterbury*. Time and age, sorrow and laughter had taken some of the curve out of her cheek, left her skin a little looser at her neck. They weren't young anymore. Maybe you could only really see that someone was beautiful when they'd grown into themselves. He moved to kiss her—

—and drifted off the crash couch.

With the thrust suddenly cut, leaning up had pushed him into the cabin, twisting as he floated. He reached back with his foot automatically, trying to hook it into one of the holds, but the ship was flipping, so it took a couple tries. Naomi had already braced herself on the frame of the crash couch.

"Well," Holden said. "I guess Drummer changed her mind about letting Houston come to Medina. That's disappointing."

"Weird that Alex wouldn't sound the alert first, though," Naomi said, and then tapped her system console. "Alex? Everything all right?"

"I was about to ask you," the pilot said through the speaker. "We have a change of plan?"

Holden pulled his hand terminal out of his pocket. "Amos? Did you just do a flip-and-burn?"

"Hey, Cap," Amos' real voice said behind him as the big man floated into the doorframe. "Wasn't me. We got something going on?"

A chill ran down Holden's back that had nothing to do with temperature. Naomi was already on it, querying the *Roci*'s logs and control systems, but Clarissa's voice came from the speaker before she could find anything.

"I received an alert from the air recyclers," she said, her reedy voice stronger than usual. "It got a manual command from engineering to drop oxygen output to zero and flood nitrogen."

"That's not good," Holden said. "We shouldn't do that."

"I had an aftermarket override in place. No one changes my environmental settings without my say-so," Clarissa said, as calmly as if she didn't mean, *My paranoia just saved our lives.* "I'd like to know what's going on, though."

"Engineering, the machine shop, and the reactor are all locked down," Naomi said, scrolling through system screens faster than Holden could follow. "I think I've got the drive shut down, but I can't—"

But Holden was already pulling himself out of the room. Amos hauled himself flat against the wall of the corridor as he flew past, then followed along behind him. Through the galley, to the lift, then down one level. His heart was tripping over, the pulse tapping at his eardrums, but it was just adrenaline. Just fear. There wasn't anything wrong with the air.

He hoped that was true.

The brig wasn't really a brig so much as one of the crew cabins that had been set aside, the door controls isolated from the system and disabled on the inside. Over the years, nearly a dozen prisoners had spent days or weeks or months in it. Now the door stood halfway open, the control panel flickering and throwing error codes. Holden pulled himself toward it cautiously—doors and corners were where they got you—but when he reached it, he was already sure what he'd find.

The cabin stood empty apart from bits of floating debris. Anti-spalling cloth floated in ribbons. Bits of fluff from the mattress, like February snowflakes that never fell. Bright lines showed where the storage drawer had been pried off its runners and a length of the guide pulled free. A wall screen floated beside the bunk, and the exposed electronics showed where the door locks had been shorted out.

The governor of Freehold was nowhere to be seen.

"Well," Amos said. "That's new."

Chapter Seven: Bobbie

There was a certain luxury to the thrust gravity of steady acceleration. Hooking your nethers to a vacuum toilet was one of the indignities space travel occasionally forced you into. On the float, with nothing to pull your waste away, it was that or have pee globes sharing your living space. Being able to just sit on a toilet in the crew head and relax for a moment while you did your business was something to appreciate. The fact that it felt like a luxury was also probably not very dignified, if you looked at it too closely.

Bobbie was just reaching behind her for the cleaning-pad dispenser mounted on the bulkhead when the gravity went off with no warning. The momentum of her twisting torso sent her floating off the toilet seat and into the air, pants still around her knees. Thankfully, the *Roci* immediately fired up the vacuum system on the toilet and spared her having to dodge floating waste.

While she tumbled through the air tugging at her waistband, she yelled, "*Roci*, get me the bridge!"

"Yo," Alex replied almost immediately. "Where are you—"

"Not even a fucking warning light? I'm down in the head, taking a leak, and suddenly I'm trying to pull my pants up on the float!"

"Wasn't my plan," Alex said. "Looks like…Ah. Hold on."

The system link picked up Naomi's voice coming through a different channel. *Alex? Everything all right?*

"I was about to ask you," Alex said. "We have a change of plan? Naomi? Um, Bobbie? I think we may have a situation."

All it took was the tone of Alex's voice. Bobbie planted one foot against a bulkhead, hooked a handhold with the other, and yanked up her pants.

"Copy that," she said, the flat, emotionless tones of the old Marine taking over. "On the move."

She found Holden and Amos floating just inside the door of their makeshift brig when she arrived. They were examining a wall screen that someone had pried out of the wall. The prisoner wasn't there.

"How long has he been out?" Bobbie asked as she came to a stop with one hand on the doorframe.

"*Roci* started throwing errors from this door almost an hour ago," Amos said with a grimace. "This is on me, Cap. Shoulda been paying attention, but I was—"

"Forget it," Holden said. "Let's just keep him from doing any more damage."

"He's down in engineering, if he was able to kill the drive and spin the ship," Bobbie said.

"That's where he is," Holden said. "Naomi's working to keep him from making too big a mess, but she's working remotely, and this guy has demonstrated surprising technical skills."

"Options?" Bobbie asked. The tactical situation wasn't optimal. If the prisoner was locked in engineering and had also managed to seal off the machine shop above it, then they'd need to cut or breach two doors just to get to him. Even with Naomi hacking the control systems, physical proximity to the reactor gave Houston options she just didn't have. And Bobbie didn't like him having.

Holden drummed his fingers on his leg for a moment, the movement imparting an almost imperceptible spin to him as he floated.

"If he feels like he has no way out, he might blow the reactor out of spite," Holden said, mirroring Bobbie's own thoughts. "So a standard breach has to be last choice. Amos, you're in charge of that. Have Clarissa help you hotwire the door sensor to the machine shop so you can cut it without Houston knowing. Then put a mining charge on the door to engineering and wait for my signal."

"Got it," Amos said and pushed off down the corridor. He already had his terminal out, and was saying, "Peaches? Meet me at the machine shop hatch…"

"If I'm not breaching, then—" Bobbie started, but Holden cut her off with a shake of his head.

"I want you using the aft maintenance hatch. You can come in from behind. Keep us from doing a very risky breach."

"Okay," Bobbie said, stretching the word out. "But, that access is unusable with the drive on."

"Naomi will make sure it stays off."

"And if she doesn't."

"You'll get cooked," Holden said with a nod. "But we're playing against the clock here. We don't know how long we've got until Houston decides dying in a fireball is more romantic than jail."

"Betsy won't fit into that tight maintenance crawl."

"No, she won't," Holden agreed. "Pretty sure you can still kick this guy's ass, though."

"Not in doubt."

"Then gear up, Marine. You're going outside."

Bobbie wasn't really much of a ship mechanic, but she knew how to turn a wrench or draw a straight bead with a welding torch.

Over her last couple decades of making the *Rocinante* her home she'd spent a fair amount of time outside the ship. Sometimes with Amos, who called her Babs for a reason only he understood, and who often assumed she knew what she was doing even when she didn't. Sometimes with Clarissa, who occasionally slipped and called her Roberta, and who explained every procedure in the exhaustive detail you'd use with someone who knew nothing.

And, almost without her knowing it, they'd become her family. She still had brothers and nieces and nephews back on Mars related to her by blood, but she rarely spoke to them. Even then it was always in a recorded message fired across space on the end of a laser. Instead, she had Amos, the gruff big brother who'd let her fuck up on a repair job and just laugh at her, but then fix it later and never mention it again. And she had Clarissa, the annoying know-it-all little sister who wrapped herself in rules and procedure lists and formality like a shell around her fragile center.

And then Holden and Naomi, who couldn't help but become the parents of the ship. Alex, the best friend she'd ever had, and the person she'd realized recently she had every intention of growing old with, in spite of never having seen him naked. It was an odd group of people to fall in love with, to adopt as your own kin and tribe, but there it was, and she wasn't ever going back.

And now Payne Houston was threatening them.

"You fucked up, man," she said to herself as she drifted to a stop over the reactor-bay emergency-access panel. "You just fucked all the way up."

"Repeat?" Alex said quietly in her ear. Bobbie realized she'd left the channel open and the volume low as she'd made the climb down from the crew airlock to the rear of the ship.

"Nothing," she said, turning the volume back up. "I'm in position."

"Patching you back into the master channel," Alex replied, and then suddenly there were half a dozen voices breathing in her ear.

"Sound off," Holden said.

"We got through the machine shop door okay, and Peaches

says no alerts were triggered. Breaching charge is ready. Just call it." Amos' voice, calm and faintly amused. He could have been reporting football scores.

"I've got the *Roci* in diagnostic mode, so she's asking me to verify any orders coming from the engineering console," Naomi's voice said. "But that can't last. Pretty soon he can just start breaking things the old-fashioned way."

"Draper here. I'm outside the emergency-access hatch."

"How long once that door opens?"

Bobbie ran through the layout in her head. It was an old habit, beaten into her by years of training in the toughest military outfit humanity had ever created. Plan it through before you go in, because once the bullets start flying, the time for thinking is over. All you can do is move and react.

"Fifteen seconds to cycle the hatch closed. A few seconds to squeeze past the reactor housing; it's a tight fit. But a good thirty seconds to equalize the pressure, so that's our speed bump. Once the atmo in the crawlspace is equalized, I can be through that inner hatch in less than five."

"Naomi? Can you keep our guest out of the controls for the next minute so we don't cook our only good Martian?"

"Hey, Cap, that's low," Alex said with a laugh. Bobbie found it reassuring and terrifying that they could joke at a time like this.

"Bobbie," Naomi's voice said, gentle but firm. "No way he gets that reactor on while I'm alive."

"Copy that. Draper is a go on your mark."

Holden simply said, "Okay."

The hatch in front of her vibrated under the palm of her vacuum suit's glove as Naomi cycled it open. A faint puff of vapor escaped as the hatch popped open. Bobbie pulled herself inside, squeezing into the curved space between the inner hull of the ship and the outer shielding of the *Roci*'s reactor core. The hatch began to cycle closed behind her.

"Governor Houston," Holden said over the radio. "I'm sending this over the 1MC so I know you can hear me. It won't compromise your position at all to at least open a dialogue."

Bobbie pulled herself around the curve of the reactor to the inner hatch. The panel glowed red with the lock symbol, and the status read, NEG ATMOSPHERE. The timer in her HUD showed only ten seconds had elapsed, so the outer door wasn't even finished cycling. Almost forty seconds, then, before she could pop the inner hatch and go kick this Houston's ass up one side of the ship and down the other. She pulled the heavy recoilless pistol from the harness on her chest and double-checked the ammo counter. Ten self-propelled high-explosive antipersonnel rounds. If Houston forced her to shoot him, they'd be cleaning up red stains for a month.

Bobbie had served on ships most of her life. She wasn't scared of a little mopping.

"Come on, man," Holden said. "At this point, we can keep you from doing just about anything. Sooner or later, you'll need a snack."

To her surprise, Houston's voice answered. "Naw. Found your mechanic's beer fridge down here. Had a big bag of sesame sticks in it. Jalapeño-flavored. Bit spicy for me, but still tasty."

"Better not be drinking my fucking beer," Amos said in that same nonchalant voice.

"Anyway," Holden cut in, "we still have a situation. You're not going to be able to take the ship, and I'd really like to start using it again. How do we come to some sort of agreement?"

Bobbie heard the first hiss of the atmosphere system outside her suit. The pressurization was almost done. She held the pistol in her right hand and gripped the door with her left. The second it showed green, she'd be in the room with that asshole.

The asshole said, "I don't know that we do. You're right. I can't get past that diagnostic lockdown. That was smart work, by the way. But I figure I can probably get the reactor back online from in here, and then I figure I can collapse the bottle if I just find the right wires to pull. You figure the same way?"

"Well," Holden started, but the light on the inner hatch clicked green and Bobbie yanked it open.

The main console for the reactor would be to her left as she entered the compartment. It was likely that Houston was using that workstation, so that was her first target. If she pushed off hard, she'd come out of the small hatch like a missile, do a quick flip to land feetfirst on the opposite bulkhead. From there she'd have open sight lines to the entire engineering deck. Nowhere for Houston to hide.

Bobbie gripped the edge of the hatch and pulled with all her strength to launch herself into the room. She had to—

Something crashed into the side of her helmet and sent her into a flat spin through the air. She tried to get her hands up to keep from crashing facefirst into the bulkhead, and only half succeeded. Her left arm crumpled under her, and she felt something tear with a wet heat in her shoulder. She bounced off the wall and saw Houston standing on the bulkhead above the access hatch, mag-booted in place, and holding a heavy fire extinguisher with a dent in the bottom.

Miraculously, the gun was still in her hand. Blackness creeping in at the edge of her vision, Bobbie tried to line up a shot. Houston launched himself off the wall with one strong kick and brought the extinguisher down on her hand in a baseball-bat-style swing. She felt two of her fingers break, and the gun and extinguisher flew off in opposite directions across the room.

The deck seemed to swim up to meet her. She caught a glimpse of Houston spinning off toward the ceiling. She managed to turn on the mags in her glove and pull herself down long enough to get her boots locked onto the deck plating. If this was going hand-to-hand, she'd want leverage, and that meant planting her feet. She turned the boots' mags almost up to full, and watched Houston catch himself on the ceiling.

She spread her arms wide, though from the tearing sensation in her left shoulder, she didn't think that one was going to be much use. And the broken fingers in her right hand made grappling or throwing a punch problematic.

"You're lucky you're wearing that suit," Houston said, gulping to catch his breath. "I put a dent in that helmet woulda knocked your brains out without it."

"And you," Bobbie said, "are very lucky it's *this* suit. I've got another one."

"Well. We gonna talk or are we gonna dance?"

"They're playing my—" Bobbie started, then Houston launched himself off the ceiling straight at her. She was expecting it. Getting someone else to talk while you threw a punch was an old trick. The moment he left the bulkhead above her, she was already shifting her body to the left and rotating through her hips. As Houston sailed past, she brought her right elbow into his chin.

Houston's teeth slammed shut with a crunch that meant he'd cracked a few, then his whole body cartwheeled past her and into the wall with a thud. She kicked her mags off and pushed over to him, wrapping her right arm around his neck for a choke hold. It was unnecessary. His eyes were rolled up in his head, and he was breathing blood bubbles out of his ruined mouth. One and done. Just like the old days.

"I put our guest to bed," Bobbie said over the radio, then hauled Houston over to the wall panel and removed the locks on the hatch. "Amos, take that bomb off the door before I open it, 'K?"

Bobbie sat in the galley, her left arm in a sling, and her right hand in a cast that the ship had spun for her out of carbon fiber. Holden sat across from her, a steaming cup of coffee on the table held down by the gentle 0.3 g Alex was flying them at.

"So," Holden said, then paused to blow across the top of his coffee. "Turns out that guy had a few more skills than I clocked him for. Thanks for saving my ship."

"I kind of feel like it's mine, too," she said with a smile. Holden was Holden. He'd need to take the weight for every bad thing that happened, and to overstate his appreciation for the good ones. It's what made him *him*. He projected selfless heroism on everyone because that's what he wanted to see in people. It was the same thing that caused most of the problems in his life—most people weren't who he wanted them to be—but this was a nice moment. Ship safe. No one dead. Not even Houston, though if someone didn't keep an eye on Amos, that might change.

"So it's funny you should say that," Holden said. He'd paused over his coffee long enough that she'd sort of forgotten what she said. "Would you like to buy the ship from me?"

"I—" Bobbie started, then, "Wait, what?"

"Naomi and I are thinking of pulling the ripcord. We've been doing this shit for a lot of years. It's time to find a quiet spot somewhere. See how we like that for a while."

It was more of a hit than anything Houston had managed. The ache started just below her ribs and spread up. She didn't know what it meant yet.

"Is everyone else on the crew…?" Bobbie said, then wasn't sure how to finish the sentence.

"No. As Naomi recently pointed out to me, Alex will die in that pilot's chair. Whoever buys the ship will have to be okay with that. I can't speak for what Amos plans to do, you know, after."

After. He meant after Clarissa died.

"I've been saving my money, mostly, but I'm not sure I can afford a gunship," Bobbie said, keeping her tone light, trying to make a joke of it.

"We'll finance it. Split the joint account six ways, then set up a payment plan for the rest. Based on our past income, it should be an easy nut to cover. You pay any new crew out of your end. The *Roci* is your ship."

"Why me? Why not Alex?"

"Because there isn't anyone on this ship *I'd* rather take orders from, and I'm the world's worst person at taking orders. You'll make a fantastic captain, and you'll protect the reputation of this ship. It's weird, but that's something I find myself caring about."

Bobbie swallowed something that had become stuck in her throat, and she straightened up her back. It was all she could do to not stand up at attention. Military tradition died hard, and a captain handing over command of their vessel bordered on sacred trust.

"I would, you know," she said. "I'd see us become a cloud of gas before I'd violate the honor and good name of this ship."

"I know. So is that a yes?"

"I do wonder..." Bobbie said.

Holden nodded and drank his coffee, waiting for her to finish.

"I wonder what the universe looks like without James Holden trying to ride to the rescue."

"I imagine everyone will find things running a lot more smoothly," Holden said with a grin.

"I wonder," Bobbie repeated.

Chapter Eight: Singh

Singh was dreaming of wandering, lost in the halls of a vast spaceship, when the comm on his desk buzzed him awake.

"Yes?" he croaked even before he'd opened his eyes. There was nothing wrong with his taking a nap in his quarters. He wasn't shirking any of his duties. And the shakedown of his ship, the *Gathering Storm*, had meant working for sixteen and sometimes eighteen hours a day for weeks now. He couldn't continue as an effective leader and officer if he didn't take every opportunity to grab a little shut-eye.

And yet, something inside him didn't want his crew to know. As if having the same biological requirements as other humans was admitting weakness.

"Sir, we are nearing rendezvous with the *Heart of the Tempest*," came the reply. Lieutenant Trina Pilau, his navigation officer. "You asked me to—"

"Yes, yes, quite right. I'm on my way," Santiago said as he rolled out of his couch and waved on the lights.

His quarters were also his office, and the red folder containing his orders from the admiralty was still sitting on his desk. He'd been reviewing them for the fiftieth time or so when he'd fallen asleep. Leaving them out was a breach of operational security, and one he'd have reprimanded a junior officer for. As he returned them to his safe, he told the ship to make a note of the lapse in his private log. At least it would be part of the permanent record, and his superiors could decide later if it required further inquiry. He hoped they wouldn't.

He took a moment to wash his face in his private lavatory. The cold, biting water was one of the perks of his station. He put on a fresh uniform. A captain set the standard for his officers. Appearing on duty clean and pressed was the minimum level of professionalism he expected from them, and so he was responsible for it in himself. When he was presentable, he opened the door that separated his private space from the bridge of the ship.

"Captain on the bridge!" the chief of the watch snapped. The officers who were not actively manning stations stood and saluted. Even the consoles, polished to a spotless shine, seemed to radiate respect, if not for him as a man then at least for his authority. The blue of the wall matched the flag, and the sigil of his command— three interlocking triangles—had been built into the surface. It made him feel a deep, almost atavistic pride seeing it. His ship. His command. His duty.

"Is Colonel Tanaka here?" Singh asked.

"The colonel is in her briefing room with her senior officers, sir."

A twitch of annoyance troubled him, as much with himself as with his chief of security. He'd meant to have a quiet conversation with her before meeting with Admiral Trejo. He'd heard unofficially that Tanaka and Trejo had known each other before, and he'd intended to get her assessment of the man. But it was too late for that now.

"The con is yours," said Davenport, his executive officer.

"I have the con," Captain Singh said, and sat in his chair.

"The *Tempest* has cut thrust and is awaiting our arrival," his flight control officer said, pulling up the range map on the main screen. "At current deceleration we'll make final docking approach in twenty-three minutes."

"Understood," Singh replied. "Comm, please send Admiral Trejo my compliments and request permission to dock with *Heart of the Tempest*."

"Aye, sir."

"I'd love to get a good look at her," said Davenport.

"All right, let's take a peek," Singh agreed with a nod.

The truth was, he was just as curious. Of course they'd all been briefed on the configuration of the *Magnetar*-class battle cruisers, of which *Tempest* was the first. The old *Proteus* class had been retired, and this new generation was only now being deployed. He'd seen dozens of concept sketches and photographs of the ships under construction, heard rumors of the new technologies that they would support. This would be his first chance to see one of Laconia's most powerful battleships flying free and in her element. "Sensors, let's take a close-up look, shall we?"

"Aye, sir," said the officer at sensor control, and the main screen shifted from the docking map to a telescopic view of the approaching ship.

Someone let out a quiet gasp. Even Davenport, an officer with nearly a decade in the fleet, took an unconscious half step back.

"Good God, she's a big one," he said.

The *Heart of the Tempest* was one of only three *Magnetar*-class ships to come out of Laconia's orbital construction platform. The *Eye of the Typhoon* was assigned to the home fleet and the protection of Laconia itself. The *Voice of the Whirlwind* was still being grown between the spars and limbs of the alien orbital arrays. And while the fleet now consisted of over a hundred ships, the *Magnetar*s were the largest and most powerful by far. The *Gathering Storm*, his own ship, was one of the *Pulsar*-class fast destroyers, and he was fairly certain the *Tempest* could fit a dozen of them inside its hull.

The *Pulsar*-class destroyers were tall and sleek in design. To Singh's eye they were almost reminiscent of old Earth naval ships. But the *Heart of the Tempest* was massive and squat. Shaped like a lone vertebra from some long-dead giant the size of a planet. It was as pale as bone too, even where the curves fell into shadow.

Like all ships built by Laconia's orbiting construction platforms, it had the sense of something not quite human. The sensor arrays and point-defense cannons and rail guns and missile tubes were all there, but hidden under a self-healing plate system that made the surface of the ship seem more like skin than not. Grown, but not biological. There was something fractal about its geometry. Like crystals showing the constraints of their molecular architecture in the unfolding of shapes at higher levels.

Singh wasn't an expert in the protomolecule or the technologies that it spawned, but there was something eerie in the idea that they'd built things partly designed by a species that had been gone for millennia. Collaboration with the dead left questions that could never be answered. Why did the construction array make the choices it made? Why place the drive here instead of there, why make the internal systems symmetric and the exterior of the ship slightly off? Was it a more efficient design? More aesthetically pleasing to its long-vanished masters? He had no way of being certain, and probably never would.

"*Tempest* acknowledges," the comm officer said.

"Remote piloting for dock now," his helm added, and the main screen shifted from telescopic shots of the battleship to a wire frame course ending at the *Tempest*.

"Very well," Singh said with a smile. The admiralty had entrusted him with one of Laconia's state-of-the-art ships, and they'd filled it with serious and focused officers and crew. As a first command, he couldn't have asked for better.

That he and his ship were the tip of the imperial spear was just icing on the cake.

"Admiral Trejo sends his compliments," the comm officer said. "He asks that you join him for dinner in his private mess."

Singh turned to his XO. "Stay on the *Storm* and keep the crew alert. We have no idea what reception we're getting on the other side of the gate, and may need to deploy at a moment's notice."

"Aye, Captain."

"Rig for docking. I'll be in the bow-crew airlock. Mister Davenport, you have the con."

The *Tempest*'s operations officer, Admiral Trejo's third in command, was waiting for him on the other side of the airlock. Technically they were the same naval rank, but as a ship's captain, tradition dictated that Singh be treated as the superior officer. She saluted and granted him permission to board.

"The admiral would have greeted you personally," she said as she led him out of the airlock and they floated down a short corridor to a lift. The walls in the *Tempest* looked like sheets of frosted glass, and glowed with a gentle blue light. Very different from the bulkheads of the *Gathering Storm*. "But this close to the gate he doesn't like to leave the bridge."

"Fisher, right? I think you were a year behind me at the academy."

"I was," she replied with a nod. "Engineering track. Everyone said logistics was the faster path to command, but I just love working with exotic tech."

She stopped and tapped on the wall panel to call a lift. While they waited, the bulkheads began to pulse from blue to yellow.

"Grab a handhold," Fisher said, pointing to one close by. "Drive is about to come online."

A moment later they both drifted to the deck, and Singh felt his weight grow until it was about half a g.

"Not in a hurry," Singh said, and the elevator made a gentle beep and the doors opened.

"The admiral's a cautious man."

"Speaks well of him," he said as they began to rise.

Admiral Trejo was a short, stocky man, with bright-green eyes and thinning black hair. He came from the Mariner Valley region of Mars, but the traces of his accent were almost imperceptible. He was also the most decorated officer in Laconia's military, with a career that stretched back to pirate hunting for the Martian Navy even before the gates opened. They studied his tactics in the academy, and Singh thought the term *military genius* was justifiably applied to his career.

He'd expected the private mess of an admiral and fleet commander to be larger, more luxurious than the one he claimed on the *Gathering Storm*. It turned out to be a table that pulled down from one bulkhead in Admiral Trejo's slightly larger office/living quarters. The aesthetics were different only because the ship itself was.

"Sonny!" Trejo said, waiting to return his salute and then grabbing his hand and shaking it vigorously. "Finally all the pieces are in place. It's an exciting time. Would you like to sit, or do you want the tour?"

"Admiral," Singh replied. "If there's a tour to be had, I'd be honored to see a little more of the ship."

"She's a sight, isn't she? Call me Anton, please. No need for formality in private, and we'll be working very closely together in the coming months. I want you to feel like you have complete freedom to speak your mind. An officer who won't share his opinion and insight is of no use to me."

It was an echo of the high consul allowing him to use his military title, the permission of a little familiarity in private to build a sense of approachability and rapport. Now that he'd seen it twice, he understood it would be expected of him as well.

"Thank you, sir. Anton. I appreciate that."

"Come on along, then. It's too large to take in all at once, but we can hit the highlights." Admiral Trejo led the way down a short corridor to a lift that stood wider than the one on the *Gathering Storm*, with rounder edges that left Singh thinking of the mouth of some deep-sea fish. "I've been re-familiarizing myself with your career to date."

"I'm afraid that, like most of the officers trained after the transition to Laconia, I have very little in the way of operational experience."

The admiral waved this away. The lift door opened, and they stepped in. The anti-spalling padding on the walls was gently scalloped, like the presentiment of scales.

"Top of your class in logistics. That's exactly what this posting will need. Me? I'm an old combat commander. Spreadsheets give me hives."

The lift descended with a hushing sound like a million tiny bearings spinning at once, or the hiss of a sunbird. The small hairs on the back of Singh's neck rose a little. There was something uncanny about the *Tempest*. Like he'd entered into a vast animal and was waiting to see its teeth.

"Yes, sir," he said. "My orders were quite specific on—"

The admiral waved him off again. "Forget your orders for a moment. Plenty of time to get to that later. For now, I want to get to know you a little better. You have a family?"

Another point. Duarte had touched on his home life as well. Another piece of the secret teachings of Laconian command. He'd read that a command structure took its tone from those at the top. He'd never seen it so clearly in practice before. He wondered whether he'd been meant to. If this was a conscious lesson passed from Duarte to Trejo to him. He had the sense that it was.

"Yes, sir. My spouse is a nanotech scientist with the lab in Laconia City. She specializes in genetics. We have one child. Elsa."

"Elsa. Unusual name. Very pretty."

"My grandmother's. Nat— Natalia, my spouse, insisted."

The lift stopped. The doors opened on a wide and flowing deck. There were no stairs, but a gentle undulation in the deck raised some workstations above others. It seemed almost random until he saw the captain's station that could command direct line of sight to all the flight-deck crew at once. The design was elegant and utterly unfamiliar at the same time.

The XO caught sight of them and stood at attention, surrendering command, but Trejo waved him back. The admiral was present, but not to take command.

"Connection to the past is important," Trejo said as they walked across the gently sloping deck. "Continuity. We honor those who came before, and hope that those we bring into the world do the same for us."

"Yes, sir."

"Anton, please."

"Anton," Singh agreed, but knew calling the admiral by his first name would never feel natural or correct. "We almost never call her Elsa."

"So what, if not Elsa?" the admiral asked.

"Monster. We call her Monster."

The admiral chuckled. "Named for another grandparent?"

"No," Singh said, then stopped. He worried that he might be oversharing, but the admiral was staring at him, waiting for the rest of the answer. "We were not really ready when Nat got pregnant. She was just finishing her postdoc, and I was doing two- and three-month patrol tours as the XO on the *Cleo*."

"No one is ever ready," the admiral said. "But you don't know that until after it's happened."

"Yes. So when Elsa was born, I'd just rotated back to an administrative position, and Nat had moved to a more permanent research job, and we were both learning the ropes while a very insistent one-month-old made her demands."

Trejo led the way down a curving ramp at the side of the room. Hatches irised open as they approached them and closed again once they'd passed. The light came from thumb-sized recesses in the wall, perfectly regular in their spacing, but rounded and soft. Organic life subjected to military engineering.

"So," Singh continued as they walked, "we were exhausted.

And one morning, at about three when Elsa started crying, Nat rolled over to me and said, 'That monster is going to kill me.' And that was it. She was Monster from then on."

"But you say it with a smile now, yes?"

"Yes," Singh agreed, thinking of his daughter's face. "Yes, we do. And that's why I'm here."

"Why you're here, hm? You don't seem like the type of man who'd choose to go without his family."

"It will hurt to leave them behind for this deployment. It will be months, at least, before they can join me on Medina Station. Possibly years. But if I can give my daughter the version of humanity that the high consul has planned, it will all be worth it. A galactic society of peace and prosperity and cooperation is the best legacy I can imagine for her."

"A true believer," the admiral said, and Singh felt a flush of shame that perhaps he appeared naïve to the man. But when Trejo continued, there was nothing mocking in his tone. "This will only work because of the true believers."

"Yes, sir," he said. And then, "Anton."

The admiral led the way into a broad corridor, larger than anything he'd ever seen designed in a ship. The *Tempest* didn't have the closeness of other ships, the design constrained by the need to cut back every kilogram, to waste no space at all. It was a ship that claimed power by the shape of its walls. Singh felt a little awe at it. As he supposed he was meant to.

Two midshipmen sat at a table, laughing and flirting until they saw Trejo. The old man scowled, and the pair saluted and scurried off to their duties. Singh realized that no one had spoken to them in the time since they'd left the admiral's cabin. The tour might seem casual, but it was intended to be private as well.

In the same tone of voice one might use to ask what the time was, the admiral said, "Explain to me the tactical and logistical problems with controlling Medina."

Singh stood a little straighter. Comfortable discussions of family were over. Now it was time to work. He pushed his sleeve back a bit to pull the monitor off his wrist, and flattened it onto the abandoned table. He pulled up the briefing. He'd been preparing it for weeks, and the sudden, irrational fear that he'd overlooked something obvious, something that would show the admiral that he wasn't a serious person after all, still lurked in him. It was an old, familiar kind of fear, and he knew how to push it aside. A wire frame rendering of Medina floated in the air above the surface.

"Medina Station," Singh said. "Assuming our intelligence is correct, it houses the hundreds of members of the planetary coalition and their personal staffs, including security. Add in the permanent staff and crew of the station, as well as trade union members passing through, and you get a conservative estimate of between three and five thousand people on the station at all times. I would guess the number is actually double that."

"Assuming our intelligence is correct?"

"Passive monitoring, even over the course of years, will always have a greater opportunity for error than active examination. And the surface interference of the gates adds an additional level of error," Singh said. The admiral grunted and waved him to continue. He spun the rendering of the station, and hard points on the surface became highlighted in red.

"The station itself is equipped with some defenses. A PDC network that provides missile defense brackets the station, and one torpedo launcher remains intact and usable from its *Behemoth* days. Eight rails, automated reloading system, we estimate a total capacity of forty missiles."

"Nuclear?" the admiral asked.

"Almost certainly not. The lack of maneuvering capability and the confined nature of the ring hub makes high-yield weapons dangerous to the station itself."

Singh adjusted the image and focused in on the hub station, a perfect sphere several kilometers across that sat at the center of the gate network. The purest and most active alien artifact in all the worlds they knew of. Dotted on the surface of the sphere were six massive rail-gun turrets.

"The station's primary defense is an aging rail-gun network, first installed by Marco Inaros' people, and disabled during the final conflict with his faction. These guns are placed so that at least three guns and as many as five can fire at any of the rings. They're our design, from back when we were still supplying the Free Navy with weapons. Older, out of date now, but capable of sustained fire at thirty rounds per minute. Assuming, of course, that they haven't made modifications to them."

"The rail guns. In the ancient days back on Earth, they'd have cannons that could fire down into the harbors when enemy ships appeared. The defense of the sea from the land. We got rid of the land and the sea, but the logic of it stays the same. The more things change, eh?"

"Yes, sir."

"What do you think of them?" Trejo asked.

"The design is elegant. Placing the defense battery on the alien station is brilliant," Singh said. He felt anxiety growing in his throat. Was this the answer Trejo was looking for? "Anyplace else, and the rail guns would have to compensate with thrusters. The station doesn't move. Or maybe it moves and drags its entire local context with it. Either way, it avoids having to worry about Newton's third law. And as long as it has ammunition, it can hold off attacks from any of the rings, or even several at once. Honestly, I'm going to be sorry to see it go."

Trejo sighed. "Rebuiding them won't be quick, that's true. But we have to look at the long term. Even if a replacement battery takes months to install and test, it will last centuries. I wish we could take control of them ourselves. But that's the *Tempest*'s first target, while you disable the station's defenses. Then board and secure the station," the admiral said.

"Yes, sir. Logistically, once the station's defenses are secured and the rail-gun network is taken offline, the *Gathering Storm*'s Marines, which we've designated Task Force Rhino, can take operational control of the station within minutes. When we control their comm array and access to the hub space, we effectively control all communications and trade for the thirteen hundred worlds."

"You'll have operational control of the landing and securing Medina Station. Is the task force prepared?"

"Yes, Admiral. They've been drilling for this assignment for months, and my security chief is Colonel Tanaka. She is well respected."

"Tanaka's good. And good personnel are critical," Trejo said. "What obstacles do you anticipate?"

"The ship traffic coming into and out from the hub space is unpredictable. It's very likely that there will be one or more additional ships with some defensive capability beyond the use of drive plumes as weapons. How many and what their armaments are can't be stated with certainty until we pass through the gate. Also, Medina Station has been in operation for decades, and with a mission significantly different from her original design. The information we have about the initial configuration will be badly out of date. When we take control, there is the possibility of some local resistance, though that should be minimal. After that, it's a question of co-opting and improving the existing infrastructure, and coordinating the supply chains between the newer planets and the better established ones. Sol system included."

"And then you fly a desk for a while," the admiral said. "I'd have to think that's the toughest part of your assignment. Getting thirteen hundred squabbling children to cooperate."

"High Consul Duarte wrote the book on governmental trade-control theories, back when he was with the Martian Navy. It's still the book we study at the academy. I'm prepared to enforce the new orders absolutely to the letter."

"I'm sure you are. Duarte has an eye for talent, and he selected you personally," the admiral said, then pointed at the briefing diagrams floating in the air between them. "And you certainly seem to have done your homework."

"Yes, sir," Singh said, then cleared his throat. "If I may speak freely, sir?"

"I think I already made my feelings on that clear."

"Yes, sir," Singh said, but the anxiety still tugged at him. "I'm absolutely certain of this portion of our plan. My worry is the Sol system. Intelligence says that the Earth-Mars Coalition has been steadily refitting and rebuilding their fleet. And that it is at least at the prewar levels of preparedness. When external resistance to our plan comes, it will come from them. And while we have newer ships, they have the benefit of an officer corps that fought in two serious wars in the last few decades. They will have vastly more battlefield experience to draw on."

The admiral paused, considering him. The bright-green eyes seemed to dig under his skin. Singh couldn't tell if the man was pleased or disappointed. When he smiled, it seemed genuine.

"Experience and home territory are real advantages for them, you're right. But I think you shouldn't worry about it overmuch," the admiral said. "The *Tempest* was built for one purpose, and one purpose only. To render every other power in the known galaxy irrelevant."

Chapter Nine: Bobbie

They sat in the galley, the same way they always did. Amos and Clarissa beside each other, Alex at the end of a table across from her. Holden a little apart, and Naomi closer to him than to the others. Bobbie felt the anxiety humming in her throat and legs like she was about to get in a fight. Worse, because there was a moment of calm that came with violence, and there wasn't going to be one of those here.

The dinner was—had been—mushroom noodles in black sauce. But everyone had stopped eating when Holden cleared his throat and said he had an announcement. When he'd broken the news, he'd seemed rueful more than anything else, and he covered it up by talking about numbers and business. Going over their last few years, and the projections for the next few. His decision to step down, and Naomi's too. His nomination of Bobbie to take his place and all his arguments for it. The others listened in silence while he turned to the details of the sale. The noodles had all gone cold and sticky in their bowls.

"Naomi and I are cashing out a quarter of our shares in the ship," he said, "with a payment plan that pays out the remainder over the next ten years. That still leaves a pretty fair balance in the operating account. The payment plan has a sliding structure, so if things get a little tight at some point, we're not going to sink you, and if things go really well, you can also pay us out early. So there's flexibility built in."

He thought he was being kind. That by making things formal, it would hurt the others less. Maybe he was right. Bobbie kept glancing around the room, trying to get a sense of how they were taking it. Was Alex leaning forward on his elbows because he was feeling aggressive, or did his back just ache a little? Did Amos' affable smile mean anything? Did it ever? Would they agree to the idea? If they didn't, what happened then? The anxiety in her gut stung like a scrape.

"So," Holden said. "That's the proposal at least. I know we've always voted on these kinds of decisions, and if there's anything in this that anyone wants to look at or a counterproposal that anyone wants to make..."

The silence rang out louder than a bell. Bobbie clenched her fists and released them. Clenched and released. Maybe this whole thing had been a really bad idea from the start. Maybe she should have—

Alex sighed. "Well. Can't say I didn't see it coming, but I'm still a little sad now it's here."

Naomi's smile was a ghost, barely there and unmistakable. Bobbie felt something like the beginning of relief loosening the knot in her stomach.

"As far as putting Bobbie in the captain's chair," Alex went on, "that's barely going to be a change. She already bosses me around plenty. So sure. I'm good with that."

Holden tilted his head the way he did when he was surprised

and a little embarrassed, and Naomi put her hand on his shoulder. The unconscious physical grammar of long, intimate years together.

"You saw it coming?" Holden said.

Alex shrugged. "It's not like you're all that subtle. You've been getting more and more stressed for a while now."

"Have I been an asshole and just didn't know?" Holden asked, making it about half a joke.

"We'd have told you," Amos said. "But there's this thing for the last couple years, I guess, where you kept looking like you had an itch you didn't want anybody seeing you scratch."

"This has been a long damned tour," Alex said. "If I'd re-upped for another twenty back in the day, I'd be out again by now."

"Except your navy didn't last that long," Amos said.

"I'm just saying a good run's a good run. I love you two, and I'm going to miss the hell out of you, but if it's time for something new, then it is."

Naomi's smile grew less ambiguous. Holden rocked back a few centimeters on the bench. In her imagination, Bobbie's best scenarios had involved weeping and hugs. The worst, anger and recriminations. This felt like relief only slightly colored by sorrow. It felt...right.

She cleared her throat. "When we get back to Medina, I'm looking to put out a call for some new hands. So, no rush, but I'm going to need to know if I'm filling more than two couches."

Alex chuckled. "Not mine. The one thing I think my life experience has been unambiguous about is whether I'm good outside a pilot's station. I'm here as long as you'll have me."

Bobbie relaxed another notch. "Good." She shifted toward Amos. He shrugged. "All my stuff's here."

"All right. Clarissa?" Claire was looking down. Her face empty and paler than usual. She put her hands on the table, palms down like she was pressing it back into place. Like there was something that could be put back. Her smile was forced, but she nodded. She would stay.

"Well," Holden said. "Um. All right, then. That's...I mean, I guess that's it. Unless someone else has something they wanted to bring up?"

"Kind of a hard act to follow," Naomi said.

"Well, yes," Holden said, "but I mean—"

"How about this," Alex said, standing up. "I'm going back to my cabin and getting the Scotch I've been saving for a special occasion. Let's all have a toast to Holden and Nagata. Best damn command staff a ship could hope for."

Holden's expression shifted and his eyes took on a shine of tears, but he was grinning. "I won't say no," he said, then stood.

Alex went in for the hug, and then Naomi put her long arms around them both. Bobbie looked over at Amos and pointed a thumb at the knot of three. *Is this a thing we should do?* Amos rose and trundled over to them, and Bobbie followed. For a long time, the crew of the *Rocinante* stood locked together in a long, last embrace. After a few seconds, Bobbie even felt Clarissa against her side, pressing in as soft and fleeting as a moth.

Officially, nothing changed after that. The long float before the deceleration burn toward the gate and Medina Station beyond it went the way they'd planned it. Houston, in his cell, was sullen and uncomfortable but secured. Their duties and schedules, habits and customs, all had the same shape. The only thing that had altered at all was what they meant. This had become their last run together. Bobbie felt like something in her body had shifted.

James Holden had been a strange person from the start. Before she'd ever known him, he'd been the man who'd slandered Mars. Then the one who saved it. To judge from what the greater chunk of humanity thought of him, he was an opportunistic narcissist or a hero of free speech, a tool of the OPA or the UN or a loose cannon answerable to no one. She'd seen him that way too, more than she'd known, when she took her place on the *Rocinante*. Since then, day by day, sometimes even hour by hour, the man and his reputation had peeled away from each other. Captain James

Holden of the *Rocinante* was a name to conjure with. The Holden she knew was a guy who drank too much coffee, got enthusiastic about weird things, and always seemed quietly worried that he would compromise his own idiosyncratic and unpredictable morality. The two versions of him were related the way a body and its shadow were. Connected, yes. Each inextricably related to the other, yes. But not the same thing.

And now he was moving on. And Naomi with him. Losing her was a strange thought too, but different. Naomi had fought against being a persona in the greater world, always letting her lover take the stage so that she wouldn't have to. When she stepped away, it wouldn't change the story that other people told about the *Rocinante* the same way, but Bobbie was going to feel her loss more. As much as Holden was the public face of the ship, Naomi was the person Bobbie had come to trust in their practical, day-to-day lives. Whatever Naomi said was true. And if that wasn't strictly accurate, it was close enough that Bobbie and the others relied on it with confidence.

When they were gone, nothing would be the same. Bobbie felt the sorrow in that. But, to her surprise, the joy too. She found herself going through her rounds, moving through the ship to check everything that had already been checked, marking anything that looked off—a gas pressure level that was dropping a fraction too quickly, a doorway that showed wear, a power link that was past its replacement date—and the ship itself had changed too. It was hers now. When she put her palm on the bulkhead and felt the thrum of the recyclers, it was her ship. When she woke strapped into her crash couch, even the darkness felt different.

She'd been a Marine—she would always be a Marine, even after that role didn't fit her anymore. Becoming the captain of the *Rocinante* felt right for her in a way she hadn't expected. The prospect of taking the captain's chair had the same sense of threat and anticipation that pulling on her power armor had back in the day.

It was as if her old suit had changed with time—changed as much as she had—and become a ship. A worn one, yes. Out of date, but dangerous. Scarred, but solid. Not just a metaphor of who Bobbie was but also who she wanted to become.

She believed the others—Alex, Amos, Clarissa—were as comfortable with the shift as they claimed. And before, she'd have left it at that. Before it was her ship.

Now that she was going to be captain, it was her job to check.

Amos was in the machine shop, as he usually was, paging through feeds on the strategies for keeping an old gunship like theirs flying and safe. A stubble of white along the back of his skull caught the light where he hadn't shaved it in a couple of days. They were on the float, conserving reaction mass, but he was braced against the deck like he was anticipating a sudden change. Maybe he was, even if only out of habit. His thick, scarred hands tapped at the monitor, moving from subject to subject in the feed's tree—lace-plating structural repair, overgrowth in microflora-based air recyclers, auto-adapting power grids. All the thousand improvements that study of the alien technologies had spun off. He understood them all. It was easy to forget sometimes the depth of focus and intelligence behind Amos' cheerful violence.

"Hey, big man," Bobbie said, pulling herself to a stop with one of the handholds.

"Hey, Cap'n Babs," he said.

"How's it going?"

He looked over at her. "Well, I'm a little nervous about the plating we put down by the drive at that depot back on Stoddard. Lot of folks are seeing flaking with that batch under radiation bombardment. Figure when we hit Medina, I should hop outside and take a peek. Hate to have that turn into baklava on us when we were counting on it."

"That would suck," Bobbie agreed.

"Lace plating's great when it's great," Amos said, turning back to his screen.

"How's the rest of it?" Bobbie asked.

Amos shrugged, flicked through the feed. "Is what it is, I figure."

The silence settled between them. Bobbie scratched her neck, the soft sound of nails against skin louder than anything else in the room. She didn't know how to ask if he was going to be okay with Holden and Naomi leaving him behind.

"Are you going to be okay with Holden and Naomi leaving?"

"Yup," Amos said. "Why? You worried about it?"

"A little," Bobbie said, surprised to discover that it was true. "I mean, I know you saw it coming before Holden did. I think all of us did. But you've shipped with them for a lot of years."

"Yeah, but my favorite thing about Holden was knowing he'd take a bullet for any one of the crew. Pretty sure you actually *have* taken a few for us, so that ain't changing," Amos said, then paused for a moment. "You might should check in with Peaches, though."

"You think?"

"Yup," Amos said. And that was that. Bobbie pulled herself back out.

Clarissa was in the medical bay, strapped into one of the autodocs. Tubes ran from the gently purring machinery into the port on the woman's side, blood flowing out of the thin body and then being pumped back in. Her skin was the color of a wax candle and stretched tight against her cheekbones. She still smiled and raised a hand in greeting when Bobbie floated in. As a technician, Clarissa Mao had always been one of the best Bobbie had worked with. She had the sense that the thin woman's drive came out of a kind of anger and desperation. Working to keep some greater darkness at bay. It was an impulse Bobbie understood.

"Rough patch?" Bobbie asked, nodding toward the blood-filled tubes.

"Not a great one," Clarissa said. "I'll be back on my feet tomorrow, though. Promise."

"No rush," Bobbie said. "We're doing fine."

"I know. It's just..."

Bobbie cracked her knuckles. The autodoc chimed to itself and took another long draw of Clarissa's blood.

"You wanted something?" she said, looking into Bobbie's eyes. "It's okay. You can say it."

"I'm not your captain yet," Bobbie said. "But I'm going to be." It was the first time she'd said the words out loud. They felt good enough that she said them again. "I'm going to be. And that's going to put me in a position where I'm responsible for you. For your well-being."

She hadn't thought about her team in years. Her old team. Hillman. Gourab. Travis. Sa'id. Her last command before this. For a moment, they were in the room, invisible and voiceless, but as present as Clarissa. Bobbie swallowed and bit back a smile. This was it. This was what she'd been trying to find her way back to all these years. This was why it mattered that she do it right this time.

"And if I'm responsible for your well-being," she said, "we need to talk."

"All right."

"This thing with your old implants. That's going to get worse instead of better," Bobbie said.

"I know," Clarissa said. "I'd take the implants out if it wouldn't kill me faster." She smiled, inviting Bobbie to smile with her. Making the truth into something like a joke.

"When we get to Medina, I'm going to hire on fresh crew," Bobbie said. "Not co-owners in the ship the way we are. Just paid hands. Part of that is Holden and Naomi leaving."

"But you can also hire someone for my place," Clarissa said. Tears welled up, sheeting across her eyes as she nodded. The autodoc chimed again, pushing her purified blood back down into her.

"If you want to stay on Medina, you can," Bobbie said. "If you want to stay with the ship, you're welcome here."

On the float, Clarissa's tears didn't fall. Surface tension held them to her until she shook her head, and then they'd form a dozen scattered balls of saline that in time would get sucked into the recycler and leave the air smelling a little more of sorrow and the sea.

"I…" Clarissa began, then shook her head and shrugged helplessly. "I thought *I'd* be the first one to leave."

She sobbed once, and Bobbie pushed over to her. Took her hand. Clarissa's fingers were thin, but her grip was stronger than Bobbie expected. They stayed there together until Clarissa's breath grew less ragged. Clarissa brought her other hand over and rested it on Bobbie's arm. There was some color in her cheeks again, but Bobbie didn't know if it was the flush of emotion or the medical systems doing their job. Maybe both.

"I understand," Bobbie said. "It's hard losing someone."

"Yeah," Clarissa said. "And…I don't know. Something about it seems less dignified when it's Holden. You know what I mean? Of all the people to get choked up over."

"No," Bobbie said. "You don't need to make light of it."

Clarissa opened her mouth, closed it again. Nodded. "I'll miss him, is all."

"I know. I will too. And…look, if you don't want to talk about it now, I can just check your file for your medical plan and end-of-life choices. Whatever you and Holden worked out, I'm going to honor it."

Clarissa's pale, thin brows knotted. "Holden? I didn't work out anything with Holden."

Bobbie felt a little tug of surprise. "No?"

"We don't talk about things like that," Clarissa said. "I talked to Amos. He knows I want to stay here. With him. If things ever get too bad, he promised he'd…make it easier for me. When the time comes."

"Okay," Bobbie said. "That's good to know." *And important,* she thought to herself, *to fully document so that if it happens in someone else's jurisdiction no one gets arrested for murder. How the hell could Holden not have done that?* "You're sure Holden never talked about this with you?"

Clarissa shook her head. The autodoc finished its run. The

tubes detached from the port in Clarissa's skin and slid back into the body of the ship like overly polite snakes.

"Okay, then," Bobbie said. "I know now. I'll make sure you're taken care of. And Amos too."

"Thank you. And I'm sorry."

"About what?"

"I've been a little self-pitying about Naomi and Holden," Clarissa said. "I didn't mean to make it anyone else's problem. I'll get back to duty."

"Everyone gets to mourn how they need to," Bobbie said. "And *then* everyone needs to get their asses back to work."

"Yes, sir," Clarissa said with a sharp if ironic salute. "I'm glad we had this talk."

"I am too," Bobbie said as she pulled herself to the door. *And I'm amazed that Holden never did.* For the first time, Bobbie had the sense that there were some ways—not all, but some—in which she was going to be a much better captain than he'd been.

Chapter Ten: Drummer

O kay," Drummer said, it felt like for the thousandth time, "but are these things naturally occurring or not?"

Cameron Tur, the union's science advisor, was an impressively tall, gangly man with an Adam's apple the size of a thumb and faded tattoos on each of his knuckles. He'd come into the service when Tjon was president of the union, and kept the job through Walker and Sanjrani. As old as he was and as much as he'd seen, she had expected him to have an air of condescension, but he'd only ever come across as a little ill at ease. His chuckle now was apologetic.

"That's a good question, semantically speaking," he said. "The difference between something made by nature and something made by beings that evolved up *within* nature, sa sa?"

"Difficult," Emily Santos-Baca agreed. She was the representative of the policy council for the union's board. Officially, she didn't have a higher rank than any of the other councilors, but she got along with Drummer better than any of the others. It made her a sort of first-among-equals. She was younger than Drummer by exactly two years. They even had the same birthday. It made Drummer like the woman just a little bit, even when she was being a pain in the ass.

Drummer looked at the images again. The whatever-it-was was little longer than two hand-widths together, curved like a claw or a seedpod, and shining green and gray in the sunlight outside Gallish Complex on Fusang. She started the image playback, and the young man sprang into life, slotting one—claw, pod, whatever the hell it was—into another with an audible click to create an empty space roughly the shape of an almond. Light flickered into the space, shifting shapes that danced on the edge of meaning. The young man grinned into the camera and said the same things he had every time she'd watched him. *Watching the light is associated with feelings of great peace and connection with all forms of life in the galaxy, and appears to stimulate* blah blah fucking blah. She stopped it again.

"Millions of them?" she asked.

"So far," Tur agreed. "Once the mine goes deeper, they may find more."

"Fuck."

The colony worlds had begun simply enough. A few house-holds, a few townships, a desperate scrabble against the local bio-sphere to make clean water and edible food. Sometimes colonies would falter and die before help could arrive. Sometimes they'd give up and evacuate. But more than a few took root on the rocks and unfamiliar soil of the distant planets. And as they found their niches, as they became stable, the first wave of deep exploration had begun. The massive underwater transport arches on Corazón Sagrado, the light-bending moths on Persephone, the program-mable antibiotics from Ilus.

Evolution alone had created all the wonders and complexities of

Earth. That same thing thirteen hundred times over would have been challenge enough, but added to that were the artifacts of the dead species of whatever the hell they'd been that had designed the protomolecule gates, the slow zone, the massive and eternal cities that seemed to exist somewhere on every world they'd discovered. Artifacts of alien toolmakers that had been able and willing to hijack all life on Earth just to make one more road between the stars.

Any of it could be the key to unimagined miracles. Or catastrophe. Or placebo-euphoric snake-oil light-show bullshit. The images from the seedpods could be the encrypted records of the fallen civilization that had built miracles they were still only beginning to understand. Or they could be the spores of whatever had killed them. Or they could be lava lamps. Who fucking knew?

"The science stations on Kinley are very anxious to get a shipment for study," Santos-Baca said. "But without knowing whether these are technological artifacts or natural resources—"

"Which," Tur apologized, "is difficult to determine with only the resources on Fusang—"

"I get it," Drummer said and shifted to look at Santos-Baca. "Isn't this kind of decision pretty much within *your* wheelhouse?"

"I have the votes to allow the contract," Santos-Baca said, "but I don't have enough to override a veto."

Drummer nodded. The question wasn't whether moving psychoactive alien seedpods between worlds was a good idea so much as whether someone was going to lose face in front of a committee meeting. Thus were the great decisions of history made.

"If we don't think they pose any immediate danger, ship them as alien artifacts with a third-level isolation protocol, and I'll let it pass."

"Thank you," Santos-Baca said, rising from her seat. A moment later, Tur did the same.

"Stay with me for a minute, Emily," Drummer said, shutting

down the demonstration video from Fusang. "There's something else I wanted to talk to you about."

Tur left, closing the door behind him, and Santos-Baca sank back into her seat. Her empty half scowl was a mask. Drummer tried a smile. It worked as well as anything else.

"One of the things I learned working for Fred Johnson back in the day?" Drummer said. "Don't let things sit for too long. It's always tempting to just ignore the things that aren't actually on fire just at the moment, but then you're also committing to spend your time putting out fires."

"You're talking about the tariff structure Earth and Mars are proposing for Ganymede?"

Drummer's heart sank a little. She'd managed to forget about that nascent issue, and being reminded felt oppressive. "No, I mean the *Rocinante* problem. And how it relates to—" She jerked a thumb toward the empty monitor where the seedpod video had been. "We've just taken control of the governor of a colony planet. The Association of Worlds hasn't formally asked about his status with us yet, but it's just a matter of time. I can feel Carrie Fisk rubbing her stubby little fingers together. It would make me very happy to get out in front of this."

"So," Santos-Baca said. "Well, I have had some informal conversations about it. The idea of asking the UN for a charter is... it's a hard sell. We didn't come all this way to go back down dirtside to ask permission for things, now did we?"

Drummer nodded. The enmity between the inners and the Belt was still the biggest obstacle Drummer faced. And even she didn't have *much* use for the Earth-Mars Coalition.

"I understand that," Drummer said. "I don't like it either. But it gives us a level of deniability for things like James Holden's new policing schemes. What I don't want is thirteen hundred planets deciding that the union is the problem. If the UN is behind a crackdown—even just nominally—it spreads out the responsibility. This Houston and his band of merry men can rot in a UN jail, and then we're still just the ships that take things from one place to another. Prisoners, among other things."

"Or," Santos-Baca said, "we admit what we've been playing footsie with since we crawled up out of the starving years. We start treating the union like the government of the thirteen hundred worlds."

"I don't want to be president of thirteen hundred worlds," Drummer said. "I want to run a transport union that regulates trade through the gates. And then I want all those planets and moons and satellites to work out their own issues without it gumming up our works. We're already stretched too thin."

"If we had more personnel—"

"Emily," Drummer said, "do you know the one thing I am absolutely sure won't fix any of our problems? Another committee."

Santos-Baca laughed, and a soft chime came from Drummer's desk. An alert from Vaughn. High priority. She let it ride for a little bit. If it wasn't People's Home about to break apart, another minute wasn't going to hurt. If it was, it wouldn't help.

"You've seen all the same logistical reports that I have," Drummer said. "Expecting the union to police the whole—"

The chime came again, louder this time. Drummer growled and tapped the screen to accept. Vaughn appeared, and before she could snap at the man, he spoke.

"Laconia put out a message, ma'am."

Drummer looked at him. "What?"

"The warning message from Laconia gate was taken down," Vaughn said. "It's been replaced by a new message. The report from Medina came in"—he looked away and then back to her—"four minutes ago."

"Is it broadcast?"

"Yes, ma'am," Vaughn said. "Audio only. Not encrypted either. This is a press release."

"Let me hear it," she said.

The voice, when it came, was low and warm. It reminded her of a scratchy blanket she'd had once, comforting and rough in equal measure. She didn't trust it.

"Citizens of the human coalition, this is Admiral Trejo of the Laconian Naval Command. We are opening our gate. In one hundred and twenty hours, we will pass into the slow zone in transit to Medina Station with a staff and support to address Laconia's role in the greater human community going forward. We hope and expect this meeting will be amicable. Message repeats."

"Well," Santos-Baca said, and then stopped. "Didn't see that coming."

"All right," Drummer said, and looked into Santos-Baca's wide eyes. "Emily, get me everyone."

The void city People's Home was still in Mars orbit, down close to Earth and the sun, and hell and gone from the moons of Jupiter and Saturn. It took ten hours to hear back from all the experts in the union hierarchy, and five more for the system to review everything and build a unified report. Every question, every clarification, every new nuance or caveat would take about as long. Drummer was going to be spending most of the hundred and twenty hours before Laconia reopened waiting to hear from people. Their messages were flying between planets and moons, void cities and stations at the speed of light in vacuum, and it was still too damned slow.

The voice on the message matched Anton Trejo, a lieutenant in the MCRN who had gone to Laconia with the breakaway fleet after the bombardment of Earth. Yes, it was possible that the voice was faked, but the technical service tended to accept it as genuine. Medina Station reported light and radiation spikes coming through Laconia gate consistent with ships approaching on a braking burn. How many ships and of what kind, there wasn't enough information to guess at.

Mars had lost almost a third of its ships when the Free Navy made its brief, doomed grab at power. Those had been divided between the Free Navy's forces in Sol system and the breakaway fleet going to Laconia. In the decades since, Earth and Mars had slowly rebuilt their navies. Technological breakthroughs based on reverse engineering alien artifacts—lace plating, feedback bottles, inertial-compensating PDC cannons—were standard now. Even if the ships on the other side of Laconia gate had been able to glean some details of how the manufacturing processes worked, they would have to build shipyards and manufacturing bases before they could start using them. Thirty years without a refit was a long time.

The most likely scenario was that something in Duarte's private banana republic had finally gone wrong enough that he was being forced back into contact to threaten or beg or barter whatever he—or whoever was in power by this time—needed to prop things up.

The flag in the intelligence report speculating about the fate of the active protomolecule sample that the Free Navy had stolen from Tycho during the war tripped Drummer up a little when she read it. She remembered that day. Fighting in her own corridors, her own station. Even now, she remembered the cold rage that came from discovering betrayal in her ranks. And Fred Johnson's leadership in the face of it.

She still missed Fred. And, sitting in her crash couch with the intelligence reports waiting patiently on her monitor, she wondered what he would have made of all this. Not just Duarte and Laconia, but all of it.

Her monitor chimed and the orange temporary-priority flag appeared. A new report from Medina with the updated analysis of the drive signatures from the far side of Laconia gate. She blew out a breath and opened it. Certainty factors were still thin, but the drives were either unregistered or altered so much they no longer matched the database. She ran her finger over the accompanying text to keep her tired eyes from sliding off them. There had been at least one *Donnager*-class battleship in Duarte's stolen fleet. Given the size of the incoming plume, it was possible this was that ship. Older, yes. Worn down. But still a powerhouse.

She stood, stretched. Her back ached from between her shoulder blades up to the base of her skull. She'd been spending too much time reading reports that she should have given to Vaughn. Digesting information down to the critical pieces was part of his job, after all. Used to be, it had been hers too. She trusted herself more than she did him.

She located Emily Santos-Baca on the ship. It was late, but the younger woman hadn't left for her quarters either. The system put her in the administrative commissary. The idea of food woke her stomach, and a hunger she hadn't noticed rose up like a flame. Drummer sent a quick message asking her to wait there for a few minutes. She shut down her monitor, put it in security lock, and made her way out.

The hallways of People's Home still had a sense of newness about them. The foot- and hand-holds on the walls didn't have the wear of a lived-in ship or station. The lights all had a brightness, subtle but unmistakable, that spoke of recent installation. Not enough time for anything to age or break. Their great floating city would develop all of that in time, but for now, it and the others like it were the bright, perfect Singapores of their age. The well-regulated city. Now, if she could just push that out as far as the stars, everything would be just ducky.

She found Santos-Baca sitting with an older man in a gray jumpsuit. He nodded to Drummer as she approached. When she sat down, he left. Santos-Baca smiled.

"You look like you could use some food."

"It's been a while since lunch. I'll get to that in a minute. You saw the reports?"

"I'm not quite caught up. But yes."

"Where's the board on this?"

The younger woman settled into herself, thoughtful and closed as a poker player. When she spoke, her voice was careful. "It's hard to get too worried about a fleet of out-of-date Martian warships commanded by the remnants of a decades-old coup. Frankly, I'm a little surprised to find out there's anyone alive there."

"Agreed."

"The message isn't coming up with any particular flag of high stress in the vocal patterns. Or any demands, at least not as yet."

"I know, Emily. I read the reports. I'm asking what you think of them."

Santos-Baca opened her hands, an old-school gesture that said, *It's right here in front of you.* "I think we're about to see a bunch of self-centered assholes who've realized that their glorious independence isn't going to work out in isolation. If we can keep them from losing face, we can probably find a negotiated path to reintegration. But Mars is going to be a problem. They're going to want all of them trotted back to Olympus Mons and hung as traitors."

"That's what I was thinking too. Any idea how to approach them about this?"

"I've been trading some messages with Admiral Hu. She's Earth, but she has friends in Martian high command," Santos-Baca said. "Nothing formal. And McCahill in security."

"Of course."

"The other possibility is that they're going to try force."

"With ships that haven't resupplied or seen a shipyard in decades," Drummer said. "And with our rail-gun emplacements all warmed up and ready to poke holes in anyone that gets too rowdy. Are we thinking that's a realistic possibility?"

"It's not the odds-on bet. Even when their fleet was new, taking out the rail-gun emplacements would have been a mighty tall order."

Drummer considered. "We can get a couple ships as backup, just in case. If it turns out Laconia needs its ass kicked, I'm not sending our ships through their gate. But it may make that charter an easier sell. Let Mars smell blood and vengeance and see if the EMC gets more interested in enforcement and policing than it was before?"

"It would be a very different case," Santos-Baca agreed. It was good that they were on the same page with this. Drummer had half-feared that the board was going to come up with their own strategy. Her job was herding kittens. Only thankfully not this time. She was trying to avoid being a police force. She sure as hell didn't want to command a full military. If there was going to be a war on the far side of Laconia gate, let Mars fight it.

"All right then," Drummer said. "Nothing we can't handle."

Chapter Eleven: Bobbie

When the *Roci* pulled into port at Medina, the security detail was there to take Houston into custody. Bobbie watched Holden as the prisoner marched away. She thought there'd been a melancholy look in Holden's eyes. The last thing he'd done as captain was hand over a man to live in a cell. Or she might have been reading more into the situation than was there. Drummer's threatened press release didn't appear.

After that, they'd all gone out to a club. Naomi rented a private room for all of them, and they'd eaten a dinner of vat-grown beef and fresh vegetables seasoned with mineral-rich salt and hot pepper. Bobbie tried not to get drunk or maudlin, but she was the only one. Except Amos. He'd watched all the hugging and weeping and protestations of love like a mom at a five-year-old's birthday party, indulgent and supportive, but not really engaged with it.

After they'd eaten, they went out to the floor of the club and danced and sang karaoke and drank a little more. And then Holden and Naomi left together, their arms around each other's hips, strolling out into Medina Station's corridors as if they were going to come back. Only they weren't.

The four of them made their way back to the port talking and laughing. Alex was reciting lines and acting out scenes from one of the neo-noir films he collected. She and Clarissa egged him on. Amos grinned and ambled along behind them, but she saw him watching the halls in case four old half-drunk space jockeys attracted any trouble. Not that there was a reason to expect it. It was just something he did. She noticed it in part because she did it too.

Back at the ship, the others scattered, floating to their rooms. Bobbie waited in the galley sipping a bulb of fresh coffee until they were gone. There was still one more thing she wanted to do before she called it a day, and it was something she wanted to do alone.

Around her, the *Rocinante* ticked as the residual heat of their journey slowly radiated out into the absolute vacuum of the slow zone. The air recyclers hummed. A sense of peace descended over everything like she was a child again and this was the night after Christmas. She let her breath deepen and slow, feeling the ship around her like it was her skin. When she finished the last drop of coffee, she put the empty bulb into the recycler and drew herself down the corridor to Holden's cabin. The captain's cabin.

Hers.

Holden and Naomi had taken everything out already. The drawers were unlocked. The captain's safe was open and scrubbed, waiting for a new access code. The double-sized crash couch—the one Holden and Naomi had shared for so long—gleamed, clean and polished. The slightly acrid smell of fresh gel told her that Naomi had replaced it all before she went. Clean sheets for the new tenant. Bobbie let herself drift into the space, stretching out her arms and legs. Eyes closed, she listened to the peculiar quietness of this cabin, how it was like the one she'd been using these last years. How it was different. When she reached out to take a handhold, the wall was still a half a meter away. A double-sized crew cabin, created so Naomi and Holden could share the space, had become the privilege of being the *Rocinante*'s captain. She smiled at the thought.

The safe waited for her passcode. She fed it the prints from her thumb and two index fingers, then typed in the password she'd chosen and spoke it out loud for the system to learn. Sixteen digits long, committed to her memory, and not associated with anything outside itself. The safe closed with a solid clack, magnetic locks falling into place where it would take a welding torch and a lot of time to force. She pulled up her partition on the wall screen, checking to see that everything was in place. The drive was quiet, the reactor shut down, the environmental systems well within the green. Everything just the way it should be on her ship. It was going to take a while, she figured, before that thought didn't seem like she was playacting. Better that she got used to it, though. *Her ship.*

Four messages waited for her in the queue. The first two were automated messages, one confirming the docking agreement and fee structure for their present stay on Medina, the other showing the withdrawal from the group account of Holden and Naomi's lump cash-out. The *Rocinante* already sending her the things it used to route to Holden. The third was from Medina traffic control, but the fourth was from the man himself. James Holden. She opened that one first.

His face appeared on the screen, floating in the same room she was in now, back when it had been his. He was smiling, and she felt herself smiling back.

"Hey, Bobbie," he said, and his voice seemed loud in the quiet. "I just wanted to leave this here for you as a note. I've spent a lot of time on the *Roci*. My best moments are part of this boat. And a bunch of the worst ones. And most of the people I love. I can't think of anyone else in thirteen hundred worlds I'd trust with it the way I trust you. Thank you for taking this cup from me. And if there's ever anything I can do to help out down the line, just say so. I may not be part of the crew anymore, but we're still family."

The message ended, and she flagged it to be saved. She opened the one from traffic control. A young man with deeply black skin and close-cropped hair nodded into his camera at her.

"Captain Holden, I am Michael Simeon with Medina Station security. I am sending this to inform you that, in accordance with union policy, the *Rocinante* is being called to a mandatory security contract. Your presence is required at a briefing on the incoming ambassadorial contact from Laconia at the location and time embedded in this message. Please confirm that you or your representative will be attending."

Bobbie tapped the reply, considered herself in the screen for a moment before she pulled her hair back into a bun, and scowled her reply.

"This is Captain Draper of the *Rocinante*," she said. "I'll be there."

Ten minutes into the briefing, Bobbie thought, *Oh. This is why he didn't want the job anymore.*

The room was in the drum section of the station, up near the non-rotating command decks. The desks were lined up in rows like the worst kind of classroom, with hard seats and built-in drink holders that didn't quite fit the cheap ceramic mugs they'd given out. There were around forty people in the uncomfortable seats with her—representatives of all the ships presently in the slow zone—but she and the executive officer of the *Tori Byron* had places of honor. Front row, center. Where the smart kids sat. The *Rocinante* and the *Tori Byron* were, after all, the only gunships around Medina at the moment. All the rest were tugs and cargo haulers.

The man at the front of the room wasn't the one who'd summoned her, but his boss. Onni Langstiver was the head of the security forces and so, for the length of her mandatory temporary contract, technically her boss. He wore a Medina Station uniform like it was a mech driver's undersuit. Dandruff dotted his shoulders.

"The biggest thing is we don't want to seem aggressive," Langstiver said, "but we don't want to look passive either."

In her peripheral vision, the others nodded. Bobbie tried to crack her knuckles, but she'd already done it twice since she sat down and her joints were silent. Langstiver went on.

"We've got the rail-gun emplacements on the hub station, same like always, sa sa? So that anyone tries anything, we spark those up and—" The director of station security for the Transport Union cocked his fingers into little gun shapes and made pew-pew noises. "Probáb they come through like any ambassador. Dock, talk, and los politicos do their dance. But if they come through with ideas, we're ready. Not starting, but not a clean shot too, yeah?"

A general murmur of assent.

"You have to protect the guns," Bobbie said. "The rail-gun emplacements on the hub station? If they get a force onto the surface—"

"Savvy, savvy," Langstiver said, patting the air. "This is the *Tori Byron*, yeah?"

"What we need is intelligence about what's coming through that gate before it comes through," Bobbie said, knowing as the words passed her lips that she wasn't going to be thanked for them. Still, now that she'd started… "A dozen probes going through the gate now could relay back whether we're looking at a *Donnager*-class battleship or a few gunships or just a shuttle. How we get ready for any of those should be different—"

"Yeah, thought of that," Langstiver said. "Don't want to be provocative, though, yeah? And anyway, we're not going to act much different no matter what. Working with what we're working with."

"So send a ship through with a fruit basket," Bobbie said. "Greet them on their territory and get a report back."

Langstiver stopped and stared at her. She stared back. The room was quiet for a long breath. Then another. He looked away first.

"Can't send a manned ship through. Union rules. Is in the work agreement, yeah? So we put *Tori Byron* up like an honor guard. The *Rocinanate* in Medina's shadow, make sure no one lands that isn't welcome. Everyone else in dock or cleared out enough to put a clear path between Laconia gate and Medina. Everyone that gets delayed, the union picks up the fees. *Tori Byron* gets full security contract schedule. *Rocinante* gets three-quarters for support role. Standard."

Bobbie wondered what Holden would have done in this moment. Made an impassioned speech about how the union rules were restricting them past the point of tactical competence? Smiled his I-don't-actually-like-you-very-much smile, then gone back to the ship and done whatever the hell he wanted to do anyway? Or sucked it up as a battle that wasn't worth fighting?

Only it was her battle now, and while she was very clear that she was in the right, it was also evident that her position wasn't going to help her change Langstiver's plan. She couldn't beat sense into a stone. Not even when it seemed fun to try.

"Understood," Bobbie said.

All the way back to the dock, her jaw was clenched. It was just people. They were the same everywhere. She'd dealt with bureaucracy when she was in the service and when she'd done her veteran's outreach work. She'd run up against it when Fred Johnson had the idiotic plan to make her kind of an ersatz Martian ambassador during the constitutional crisis. And when she'd taken her place on the *Rocinante*, she'd been happy to let Holden or sometimes Naomi take point on the bullshit diplomatic dance-and-kiss charade.

It wasn't even that she was worried about the outcome of this particular encounter. It was that there was a better approach, she'd told them what it was, and they weren't going to do it. And her ship—her people—were going to shoulder some part of the unnecessary risk. There was no scenario ever that was going to make that okay with her.

As a generation ship, the *Nauvoo* hadn't expected to berth a lot of ships. As a battleship, the *Behemoth*'s needs had been mini-mal. What hadn't been there, time and necessity had added. The major docks on Medina Station were outside the drum, down near the engineering decks and the long-quiescent drive that had been designed to launch the ship on a centuries-long voyage to the stars. A smaller dock had been built on the far end of the drum, near the command decks, but it was used more for private shuttles and diplomatic meetings. The *Rocinante* was berthed in the main docks, not far from the *Tori Byron*, and Bobbie cycled into the airlock with her sense of rage starting to fade. A little. She could hate it and still do the job. That was all she could do, really.

"Welcome back," Alex said over the ship comms as the inner doors of the airlock cycled closed. "There a plan?"

"Plan is to hang back and see if the new Laconian ambassador needs to show everyone how big his dick is," Bobbie said. "The *Tori Byron* and the rail-gun emplacements are taking point. We'll hang back and splash any boarding teams that get close."

She pulled herself past the lockers, out to the lift, and up toward ops. Alex's voice shifted from the comms to his actual voice as she got close.

"Well, good that we won't be the first ones getting shot at. I mean, assuming anyone gets shot at all. Got to admit I'm a little bit hoping they try something."

"You mean because Duarte and his people are a bunch of trai-tors to the republic who all deserve to hang for treason?"

"And theft. Don't forget theft. And not warning anyone when the Free Navy was looking to kill a few billion people. I mean, I'm all for forgiveness and bygones being bygones, but it's easier to stomach that after the assholes are all dead."

Bobbie strapped herself into a crash couch. "This may not even be Duarte's people. For all we know, he got stabbed in his bathtub fifteen years ago."

"A man can hope," Alex agreed. The dimness of the ops deck meant most of the light on his face was splashing up from the moni-tor. "I shifted the *Roci* back to a four-person-crew configuration."

"It's not enough," Bobbie said. "We need more crew."

"We did it this way for years before you and Claire joined up. It works better than you expect. Hey...Look, since there's a chance that someone might be trying to poke holes through Medina Station, would you mind if I kept Holden and Naomi on the ship's channel? Just in case?"

Bobbie hesitated. Part of her bridled at the prospect of having personnel who weren't on the operation still be in the communications chain. But it was Holden and Naomi, and cutting them out also felt strange. Alex was waiting for an answer. She made a gesture as if she'd been thinking of something else.

"Of course not," Bobbie said. "They're family." Alex's faint smile meant he'd known she'd say it, and was glad she'd said it that way. She opened a connection to Amos and Clarissa. "Okay, everyone. Preflight checks. Let's get ourselves into position."

The slow zone—gates, Medina Station, and the alien hub station with the rail guns—was only tiny if compared to the vastness of normal space. The whole volume was smaller than the sun, and with the guesses she'd seen about how much energy it took to hold the gates open and stable, probably equally energetic, but controlled by forces they were still struggling to make sense of. And between the gates, a darkness that matter and energy slipped into, but from which nothing ever came back. The not-emptiness past the gates left her feeling a little claustrophobic, with only a sphere a million klicks across to move in.

Even that constrained, Medina Station would have been too small to see on her monitor if it had all been rendered to scale. Instead, she had a window with the full system—gates, stations, the *Roci*, the *Tori Byron*, the rail-gun emplacements—on one side of her monitor and three smaller displays showing tactical displays of the *Roci* in the needle-thin radar shadow of Medina, the *Tori Byron*, and Laconia gate respectively. A countdown timer marked the minutes and seconds until this Admiral Trejo said he'd be coming through. Her shoulders were tight. She felt like they were in the moment between throwing dice and seeing what numbers had come up. The gambler's high. She didn't like how much she liked it.

"Medina's sensors are getting something," Clarissa said from the engineering deck.

"Throw me the update, please," Bobbie said, and the screen with Laconia gate on her monitor shifted to a live feed of the gate itself, enhanced in false color to make the darkness legible. The weird circle of the gate. The wavering stars beyond it, and a looming shadow coming through. Even just watching the stars go out behind it, Bobbie could tell it was a big ship. Maybe it was their *Donnager*-class battleship. And that in itself would be the Laconians making a statement.

Unless it was something else.

The ship that came through first looked *wrong*. It was something more than the weirdly organic shape of it. The way the false color struggled to make sense of its surface was like a graphical glitch or something out of a dream. She found herself looking for seams where its plating came together, and there was nothing. Her mind kept trying to see it as a ship, but defaulting to some kind of ancient sea creature from the deep trenches of Earth.

"That ain't one of ours," Alex said. "Shit. Where did they *get* that?"

"I don't like this," Clarissa said.

Me neither, little sister, Bobbie thought.

On the traffic-control channel, the captain of the *Tori Byron* was hailing the Laconian whatever it was, ordering it to come to a full stop. Bobbie nodded at the screen, willing Trejo to respond. To make this a more normal interaction. Instead the strange ship continued on its course, placid and implacable. Another drive plume still showed on the other side of the gate. Much smaller, but a second ship all the same. After a moment, the *Tori Byron* lit its main drive, moving itself in on an intercept. It was like watching a house cat preparing to face down a lion.

This is your final warning, the *Tori Byron* announced. Bobbie's monitor updated. The *Tori Byron* had hit the big ship with a target lock—

And then it was gone. Where the *Tori* had been, only a sparkling cloud of matter so strange the *Roci*'s sensors didn't know what to make of it.

"What the fuck!" Alex breathed. "Did they shoot something? I didn't see them shoot anything!"

Bobbie's stomach felt so heavy, it seemed like it ought to be dragging her down, even on the float. She opened a channel to the rail-gun emplacements before she was consciously aware she'd done it, the certainty growing in her even as she got the lock that it wouldn't be enough. That nothing would be. But there was a way you did these things. An order to battle, even when the battle was doomed.

"Fire, fire, fire!" she shouted.

On her screen the rail guns spat.

Chapter Twelve: Holden

The Transport Union comptroller's offices were buried three levels deep in the thick walls of Medina Station's rotating drum. It made the Coriolis slightly less noticeable than inside the drum, but also meant that they were inside gray metal cubes with desks in them and no screens to even give the illusion of a window. Holden couldn't say for sure why it felt more depressing than sitting in the metal cubes of a spaceship compartment, but it was. Naomi sat beside him, watching the newsfeeds on her hand terminal, unaffected by the grim locale. The *Rocinante* was doing a mandatory security contract. The first gig since they'd left. Maybe that was what he was reacting to.

"Form 4011-D transfers your retainer and future contracts to Roberta W. Draper, and states that she is now the legal captain of the *Rocinante*, and president of Rocicorp, a Ceres-registered corporate entity."

The Transport Union representative who was processing their paperwork handed Holden an oversized terminal covered in legalese. She had a pinched face, deep frown lines on her forehead and around her mouth, and wore her hair in short spikes dyed flaming red. Holden thought she looked like a disgruntled puffer fish, but recognized his unflattering opinion was at least partly a reaction to the mountain of forms she'd made him fill out.

"You do know," the puffer fish said, "that this is a temporary change of status, pending the legal change-of-ownership registration?"

"Our next stop is the bank, where we'll be finalizing the loan to sell the ship."

"Mmhmm," Puffer said, making it a sound of deep skepticism.

As Holden filled out the next of the endless forms, he listened to the small voices coming from Naomi's terminal. He only caught about every third word, but the hot topic of conversation was definitely the approaching Laconian ships.

"Luna," Naomi said.

"Something happening on Luna?"

"No, I mean, let's try Luna first. It'll be easy to find consulting gigs, what with all the work going on down on Earth."

"I'm not sure I—" Holden started.

"Not you. Me. I could get consulting gigs. I like the gravity there. And you could pop down the well whenever you wanted to visit your parents."

"True." His parents were all pushing the centenarian mark, and while he'd been lucky and they were all in pretty good shape, he didn't want them doing orbital launches to visit him if they could avoid it.

"And it's all very far from this," she said, pointing at her screen.

"Not a bad thing," he agreed, and handed his filled-out screen back to the puffer. "But I did like the idea of living in exuberant decadence on Titan."

"When we have enough money to do that for another three decades. Two hours," Naomi said, and Holden didn't need to ask what she was referring to. Two hours until the first representatives from Laconia to come through their gate in decades would arrive.

"We done here?"

The puffer agreed that they were.

"I could use a drink," Holden said. "Let's go get a drink and watch the big arrival on the screens in a bar or something."

They did.

It didn't go well.

Holden ran across the open fields of the rotating drum, heading toward the lift up to Medina's command enter. The adrenaline pumping through his veins only seemed to make his heart beat faster without speeding him up. It occurred to him, with a sort of surreal detachment, that this was exactly like many nightmares he'd had. He reached the lift station, pressed the call button, and willed the doors to open.

Bobbie was yelling *Fire, fire, fire* on the *Roci*'s group channel, her voice coming out of his terminal loud, but not panicky. Commanding. On the screen, Alex was sending him the *Roci*'s tactical display. Three of the rail guns on the hub station fired at the massive Laconian ship. The shots all hit, tearing holes in the hull, but the breaches closed almost as fast as they were created. It didn't look like damage-control systems. It looked like it was healing.

Holden had seen that sort of nearly instantaneous repair before. But not on human technologies. It took a really bad situation and made it a nightmare.

"Bobbie," he yelled back at the terminal. "Keep the ship—"

He didn't get to finish, because the screen flashed white and died. Medina actually shuddered. The entire station shook and rang like a bell.

"Jim," Naomi said, and then couldn't finish because she was still gasping for breath from their run. She made the Belter hand signal for emergency. *Should we be looking for a shelter?* It was a valid question. If the Laconians started poking holes in Medina, they'd want to be in a sealed emergency compartment with its own air supply.

"Go find one," he said. "But I need to get up to command."

"Why?"

Another valid question. *Because I've fought in three major wars*, he thought. *Because the Belters running the station are the ones that didn't join Marco's Free Navy, so they've never been in this kind of fight. They'll need my experience.* All perfectly true and probably valid reasons. But he didn't say them out loud, because he knew Naomi would see through them instantly to the truth. *Because something terrible is happening, and I don't know how not to be in the middle of it.*

The doors finally opened, and the car recognized him as a captain with union clearances and gave him access to the overrides. As they went up, the feeling of gravity slowly turned into a lurching sideways motion and then disappeared. The lift opened onto corridors that Holden remembered fighting through under heavy fire, back when humans first found their way into the ring system. That astonishing moment in human history, passing through a stable wormhole into an alien-created network of interstellar gates, had just led to a whole bunch of people deciding to shoot each other. And now, a group of people who'd been isolated from humanity for decades were rejoining society just as things seemed to be going pretty well. And what did they do? Start shooting.

Holden's terminal gave a gentle ping and then reconnected to the network. A moment later, Alex's face appeared.

"You still there, Cap?"

"Yeah, just outside Medina ops. Did that thing hit the station? Not seeing any atmo-loss alerts here."

"It shot the—" Alex started, then said, "It's easier to show you. Take a look at this shit."

"Just a minute."

Holden slapped the wall panel, and the door slid open. He pulled himself inside the ops center.

The duty officer put up a hand. "You can't come in here, sir. I mean, Captain Holden. Sir."

"Who's in charge right now?"

"Me?"

Holden had met her once before at a Transport Union function. Daphne Kohl. A competent technician. Somebody who'd done an engineering tour on Tycho. Perfect for noncombat ops duty on a station like Medina. Absolutely out of her depth now.

"Holden?" Alex said. "You still there?"

Holden turned his hand terminal so that the duty officer could see it too.

"Go ahead, Alex."

On his hand-terminal screen, the massive Laconian ship was floating past the ring gate. It had a thick lozenge shape, not quite circular in cross-section, and with a variety of asymmetrical projections jutting out from the sides. More organic than constructed.

It came to a gentle stop just inside the ring gate. The *Tori Byron*, the Transport Union's cruiser tasked with defending Medina Station, moved toward it. Holden couldn't see or hear them, but he imagined the stream of hails and demands the *Byron* was throwing at the Laconian ship. Then, happening so fast it was like a glitch in the graphic, the *Byron* turned into a rapidly expanding cloud of superheated gas and metal fragments. In the playback, Bobbie was yelling, *Fire, fire, fire,* and the rail guns on the hub station opened up.

The image jittered, and the rail guns were ripped away from the hub and sent spinning off, fracturing into a cloud of ceramic shrapnel as they went.

"That's what you felt," Alex said. "The second time they fired that weapon, every ship in the zone shook, and half the electronics blew out."

"What," Holden said, "the fuck was that?"

Alex didn't answer. His expression was as eloquent as a shrug.

"Okay, I assume Bobbie's got you guys hiding in the station's radar shadow still, since I'm talking to you and you're not dead."

"Yeah," Alex said. "She seems pretty strongly in favor of not doing anything to make it mad."

"Let me see what we can find out here, and I'll call back."

"Copy that," Alex said. "*Roci* out."

"It's...magnetic?" Naomi said, her tone managing to be authoritative and astounded at the same time. *This is what it is, but I don't believe what I'm seeing.* She'd floated across the ops center to one of the consoles and was working with the tech there. "It's reading as an incredibly strong magnetic field focused down to a narrow beam."

"Is that possible?" the duty officer said, her voice small and tight.

"Only if you define 'possible' as things that have already happened," Naomi said, not turning to look at her.

"So anything made of metal is vulnerable," another tech said.

"It isn't just metal," Holden replied, then pushed off to drift over to Naomi's station and look at the data she was pulling up.

"Everything has a magnetic field," Naomi added. "Usually it's too weak to matter. But at the levels that beam is hitting, it could spaghettify hydrogen atoms. Anything it touches will be ripped apart."

"There's no way to defend against something like that," Holden said, then went limp. In microgravity, it was not as satisfying as collapsing into a chair would have been.

"That's what shook Medina," Naomi added. "Just the beam passing near us. The maneuvering thrusters had to fire to hold us still."

"Holden, this is Draper," his terminal said.

"Holden here."

"Looks like that big bastard is ignoring us as long as we stay really still and keep the weapons unpowered."

"That's a good sign," Holden said. "It might mean they're not looking to kill everyone. Just making a point of destroying anything that's a threat."

"Point loudly and clearly made," Bobbie agreed. "But be aware, there is a second ship. Smaller. And it's heading for Medina."

"Tactical assessment?"

"Based on how thoroughly they took out our defenses," Bobbie said, "I'd bet they do a hard breach, storm ops and the reactor room, and grab full control of the station. If their ground troops have tech like that ship does, it shouldn't take long."

"Copy that. I'm going to try to minimize casualties down here. Wait for me to make contact. Holden out."

"Hard breach?" Naomi asked, though her tone said she already knew the answer.

"They'll drop fire teams all over the station to take over access points, control centers, power, and environmental support," Holden replied, more to the room at large than to Naomi. He turned to Daphne Kohl. "I think you should have everyone here start making calls. Get every union and planetary rep in secure locations, but tell their security details to stand down. No visible weapons. Tell them we're *not* attempting to repel boarders. That'll just get people killed, and maybe piss off that monster of a ship."

"Yes, sir," she said. "Are you taking command?"

"No, I'm not. But this is the right thing to do, and we need to do it now. So we should do it. Please."

Her expression fell a degree. She'd hoped someone in authority had arrived. Someone who knew what to do. He recognized the hope and the disappointment both.

"We're not going to fight back at all?" Kohl asked.

He gestured toward the screens. The dust that was *Tori Byron* and the rail-gun emplacements. Kohl looked away. Still, he couldn't bring himself to say no.

"Not yet," Holden said. Naomi was already collecting sidearms from the other techs in the ops center and putting them in a duffel bag. *Not yet.*

The second ship looked to be about destroyer sized, to Holden's eye. It did a slow flyover of Medina Station, taking out the torpedo racks and PDC emplacements with pinpoint-accurate rail-gun shots, then dropping a dozen Marine landing craft.

As it came, Kohl did as he suggested, passing the word throughout the ship not to resist. Live to fight another day. After the last call, she seemed to sway for a moment, then turned, spat on the deck, and pulled up something that looked like a security interface.

"What are you doing?"

"Purging the security system," she said. "No census. No biometric records. No deck plans. No records. We can't stop the fuckers, but we don't need to make it easy for them."

"Fou bien," Naomi said, approving. Holden wondered whether the forces coming in would be able to track the decision back to her. He hoped they wouldn't.

Each landing craft held a fire team of eight Marines, all wearing power armor of an unusual design—like Bobbie's but with different articulation at the joints, and all in a vibrant blue that made them seem like something that had hauled itself up from the sea. The Marines were methodical and professional. Where the doors opened for them, they entered without causing damage. Where they found locked doors, they breached with ruthless efficiency, blowing the door seals and hauling the plates back in a single, well-trained motion. When they passed unarmed civilians, they moved on by with nothing more than a warning not to resist. The few times they ran into someone with a hero complex who tried to fight back, they killed whoever presented a threat, but no one else. That it wasn't a straight-out massacre was the only comfort.

Watching it all happen from his position in the ops center, Holden found that he had to admire the level of training and discipline the Laconians displayed. They left no doubt that they were absolutely in charge, and they responded to any aggression with immediate lethal force. But they didn't abuse the civilians. They didn't push anyone around. They showed nothing that looked like bravado or bullying. Even the violence didn't have any anger behind it. They were like animal handlers. Holden, Naomi, and the rest of the ops-center techs did what they could to keep the station populace from panicking or foolishly resisting, but it was almost irrelevant. Nothing kept the people calmer than the calm their invaders demonstrated.

When the door to the ops center opened and one of the fire teams entered, Holden told everyone in the room to raise their hands in surrender. A tall, dark-skinned woman in armor with insignia that looked like a modified Martian colonel rank walked toward him on magnetic boots.

"I am Colonel Tanaka," she said, her voice booming with electronically augmented volume. "Medina Station is under our control. Please indicate that you understand and are complying."

Holden nodded and gave her his best fake smile. "I understand and as long as you continue to not abuse the people here, we will not violently resist."

It was a deliberate provocation. If Tanaka were there to flex her muscles and show how important and in charge she was, she'd point out that her people could abuse the populace to their heart's content and there wasn't a damn thing he could do about it.

Instead she said, "Understood. Prepare a hard dock at the reactor level of the station for our ship."

When the dockmaster indicated that it was ready, Tanaka touched a control on her wrist and said, "Captain Singh, a berth is being prepped for docking. The station is ours."

"I am Captain Santiago Singh of the Laconian destroyer *Gathering Storm*," the young man said. "I'm here to accept your surrender."

His uniform was trim and spotless. The design looked Martian, except for the blue-gray color scheme where Holden was used to red and black. Kohl floated before him, confusion in her eyes.

"This is an act of war," she said, her voice trembling. Holden felt an urge to step in, refocus the man onto him just to make her safer. It was a stupid impulse. "The union. The Earth-Mars Coalition. The Association of Worlds. They won't stand for this."

"I know," the young man said. "This is going to be all right. But I have to accept your surrender now, please."

She braced to attention, and it was over.

It had taken less than four hours from the first transit. Marines in Laconian power armor patrolled the corridors and command points of the station. Naval personnel in sharply designed uniforms hurried about hooking equipment into various communication and environmental systems with a well-practiced efficiency. The people of Medina mostly watched in a sort of dazed shock.

It had all happened so quickly. It was impossible to process.

He and Naomi were swept up along with the hundreds of representatives from the colonized worlds, several dozen reps from the Transport Union, the senior staff of Medina Station. He didn't have any actual authority. He wasn't even technically the captain of a ship or a member of the Transport Union anymore, but no one argued. They all gathered in the coalition-council room, an amphitheater with two thousand seats and a stage with a podium on it that consciously aped the layout of the General Assembly of the UN back on Earth.

Admiral Trejo was a stocky older man, with the relaxed air of a person who'd spent so long holding a military posture that he looks comfortable in it. He took his place at the podium flanked by a pair of Marines. Captain Singh and Colonel Tanaka stood respectfully behind him and off to one side.

"Greetings," the admiral said, smiling out at them. "I am High Admiral Anton Trejo of the Laconian Empire, and personal representative of High Consul Winston Duarte, our leader. And now your leader as well."

He paused as though waiting for applause. After a moment, he continued.

"As you know, we have accepted control of Medina Station. And yes, we intend to take control of all the thirteen hundred worlds it leads to. This isn't an act of aggression, but necessity. We bear no ill will or animosity toward any of you. As you've seen, this will be as bloodless a transition as *you* allow it to be. I'm bringing you here to implore you to please, *please*, contact your home worlds. We will make communications available for anyone who will tell them to peacefully relinquish control to us. If they do this, there will be no need for violence of any kind."

"I admit I kind of like these guys," Holden whispered to Naomi. "I mean as conquistadors go."

"There'll be a 'but,'" she said. "There's always a 'but.'"

"Cooperation is the coin of the empire," Trejo continued. "The beginnings were already in motion here. Your Association of Worlds. The Transport Union. All of these things will continue. High Consul Duarte *wants* input and representation from all the systems humanity has colonized and will colonize. The Transport Union is a vital apparatus in supporting those efforts. Both organizations can and must continue their important work.

"The only thing that has changed is that High Consul Duarte will be expediting the process. The Laconian fleet will be the defenders of a new galactic civilization of which you will all be welcome citizens. The only price is cooperation with the new order, and a tax to be paid to the empire that will not be onerous, and will be entirely invested back into the creation of new infrastructure and aid to fledgling or struggling planetary economies. The golden age of man will begin under the high consul's leadership."

Trejo paused again, his smile slipping. He looked pained and saddened by what he was about to say.

"Here it comes," Naomi whispered.

"But to those who intend to defy this new government and try to deny humanity its bright future, I say this: You will be eradicated without hesitation or mercy. The military might of Laconia has only one function, and that is the defense and protection of the empire and its citizens. Loyal citizens of the empire will know only peace and prosperity, and the absolute certainty of their own safety under our watchful eye. Disloyalty has one outcome: death."

"Ah," Naomi said, though it was more a long exhalation than a word. "The nicest totalitarian government ever, I'm sure."

"By the time we figure out all the ways it isn't," Holden said, "it will be too late to do anything about it."

"Will be?" Naomi asked. "Or *is*?"

Chapter Thirteen: Drummer

McCahill, head of the security council, spread his hands before him like he was trying to talk a gunman into putting down his weapon. "We were all taken by surprise. And I think we can all agree this was a failure of intelligence."

"Well, if we all agree, then I guess it's not a problem," Drummer said. McCahill flinched a little. "What the hell *happened* out there?"

The meeting room was small—McCahill, Santos-Baca, and the present liaison of the Earth-Mars Coalition, Benedito Lafflin. And Vaughn haunting the back of the room like a funeral director at a wake. There were others in her feed. Messages from every division of the union and dozens of organizations outside it too. A kicked anthill the size of the solar system, and all of them wanting answers and leadership from her. It would take days to view all of them, weeks to reply, and she didn't have the time or the energy. She needed answers.

Answers and a way to turn time backward long enough to undo what had already happened.

Lafflin was a thick-faced man with a tight haircut that made him look like a particularly self-satisfied toad. He cleared his throat. "Data on Laconia has always been thin," he said. He had a reedy voice and the manner of a doctor explaining why he'd left a sponge in someone's belly by mistake. "The defecting forces from Mars have been playing their keep-away message since before the Transport Union was chartered. They've flooded the gate from the realspace side with chatter along the whole electromagnetic spectrum—radio, visible light, X-ray, everything. We've had no passive intelligence to speak of. The few times that probes were sent through, they were disabled or destroyed.

"The official doctrine put in during the first years of the union was blockade. The navies of Earth and Mars were both badly damaged in the fight against the Free Navy, the focus of governance was disaster recovery on Earth and minimizing the collapse of infrastructure. Laconia never presented an active threat, and…"

"You're telling me the missing navy was just never a priority?" Drummer said, but she already knew the answer: Yes, that's what he was saying.

Sleeping dogs had been left to lie until they were good and rested. And the sting of it was worse because some of that at least had been during her watch. She was as guilty as anyone of taking her eye off the ball.

The images that had come through from Medina were surreal. The ship that had sailed through from Laconia didn't resemble anything that had gone out through the gate decades ago. The blast that had scattered the *Tori Byron* was more like high-energy stellar phenomena than a weapon humanity had conceived. And the destruction of the rail-gun emplacements had been accompanied by a blast of gamma radiation from the gates themselves that Cameron Tur had described as the energetic equivalent of a solar flare. It had destroyed the *Sharon Chavez*, a freighter that had been waiting for clearance from Medina's traffic control. Her crew died in the blink of an eye, and not even from a direct attack. It wasn't something Drummer could get her mind to accept. It was too big. Too strange. Too sudden.

"The attacker has disabled the relay network," Vaughn said, answering something Santos-Baca had asked. "There are no new signals coming in or out of the ring space. Medina is effectively cut off."

Drummer squeezed her fists until they ached. She couldn't let her mind wander like that. It didn't matter that she felt traumatized. The union was under attack, and it was all on her. She had to keep focus. "We do have some record from the freighter that was parked outside the gate. The interference is too severe to get anything with high definition, but enough that we can say with some confidence that Medina Station was boarded. We have to assume it's been taken."

"Can we get data through the gates?" Drummer asked. "Radio loud enough to carry through the interference on both sides? Or tightbeams? Something to get messages to the other systems?"

"It's possible," Lafflin said in a tone of voice that meant he didn't actually think it was possible. "But it would certainly be monitored. And our encryption schema aren't breakable by any known tech, but we're not looking at known tech." His hand terminal chimed. He glanced at the message and lifted his eyebrow. "Excuse me for a moment. Someone's made a mistake."

Drummer waved her permission, and the inner left them to themselves. When the doors had closed behind him, she turned to Santos-Baca and McCahill. "Well, seeing as it's just us, what are the options?"

"If we can find a way to communicate with the other systems, we can coordinate a counterattack," Santos-Baca said. "I've been putting together a spreadsheet of the resources we have in each system."

"Let me see," Drummer said. Santos-Baca flipped the data to Drummer's display. More than thirteen hundred gates, each opening onto a new solar system. Almost all of them with colonies that varied from barely functioning villages to scientific complexes that were on the ragged edge of self-sustainability. The union's void cities were the largest ships, but she could only pour attacking forces through so quickly without losing them to the gate's glitches. She'd be sending them through one at a time to be mowed down. She pressed her fingers to her lips, pinching the flesh against her teeth until it ached a little. There was a way. There had to be a *way*.

She had to put first things first. And that meant reestablishing communications with all the union forces in all the systems. Some kind of stealth relay system had to be put in place. Maybe some kind of feint that would draw the enemy's attention long enough to let her sneak new repeaters on either side of if not all the gates, then a strategic few—

"Ma'am," Lafflin said from behind her, "please, you can't—"

An unfamiliar voice answered. "Give it a fucking rest, Benedito. I can do whatever the fuck I want. Who's going to tell me not to? You?"

The old woman moved slowly, using a cane even in the light gravity of People's Home. Her hair was blindingly white, thinning, and pulled back in a bun at the base of her skull. Her skin was slack and papery, but there was an intelligence in her eyes that the years hadn't dimmed. She looked up at Drummer, and smiled with the warmth of a grandmother. "Camina. It's good to see you. I got the first shuttle I could. How's your brother doing?"

Drummer pushed through a flurry of reactions—surprise that the woman was here, a flicker of starstruck awe, disorientation at being called by her first name in public, distrust that Chrisjen Avasarala—the retired grand dame of inner-planet politics— knew about her brother at all, and finally the solid certainty that every feeling she'd just experienced had been anticipated. More than anticipated. Designed. It was all a manipulation, but done so well and with such grace that knowing that didn't make it ineffective.

"He's fine," Drummer said. "The regrowth went well."

"Good, good," Avasarala said, lowering herself into a chair. "Astounding what they can do with neural replacement these days. When I was growing up, they cocked it up more than they got it right. I had most of my peripheral nervous system redone a couple years ago. Works better than the old stuff, except my leg gets restless at night."

Santos-Baca and McCahill both smiled, but with anxiety in their eyes.

"Ma'am," Lafflin said, "please. We're in the middle of a meeting."

"You can finish it later," Avasarala said. "President Drummer and I need to talk."

"I didn't see you on my schedule," Drummer said mildly. Avasarala turned back to her. The warmth was gone, but the intellect was there, sharp and feral.

"I've been where you are right now," the old woman said. "I'm the only one in the whole human race who has. The way your stomach feels when you try to eat? The part of you that's screaming all the time, even when you're acting calm? The guilt? Anyone who's had a child in the hospital has suffered through that shit. But the part where all human history rides on what you do, and you only get one shot? That's only you and me. I came because you need me here."

"I appreciate—"

"You're about to fuck up," Avasarala said, and her voice was harder than stone. "I can keep that from happening. And we can have that conversation here in front of these poor fucking shit-heads, or you can roll your eyes and humor the crazy old bitch with a cup of tea and we can have a little privacy. You can blame me for it. I won't mind. I'm too old and tired for shame."

Drummer laced her fingers together. Her jaw ached, and she had to focus to unclench it. She wanted to scream. She wanted to have Avasarala thrown out of the city in a plastic emergency bubble with a note tacked to her cane that said *Make an appointment first*. She wanted to see McCahill and Santos-Baca look at her with awe and fear at the violence of her reaction. And none of those things had anything to do with Chrisjen Avasarala. They were all of them about what had happened to Medina.

"Vaughn," Drummer said. "Could you get Madam Avasarala a pot of tea? We'll take a recess of an hour or so."

"Of course, Madam President," Vaughn said. The others rose from their chairs. Santos-Baca took a moment to shake Avasarala's hand before she left. Drummer scratched her chin even though it didn't itch and kept her temper until the room was empty except for the two of them. When she spoke, it was with a careful, measured tone.

"If you ever undermine me like that again, I will find a way to make everyone in the EMC stop taking your calls. I will isolate you like no one this side of a prison door has ever been isolated. You'll spend the last days of your life trying to talk interns into getting you coffee."

"It was a dick move," Avasarala said, pouring a cup of tea for herself and then another one for Drummer. "It's my fault. I overreact when I'm scared."

She hobbled across the room and set the mug down in front of Drummer. An act of submission as calculated as everything she'd done. Whether it was sincere or insincere didn't matter. She'd kept the form. Drummer picked up the tea, blew across it, and sipped. Because keeping the form was all that was keeping her together now too. Avasarala nodded her approval and went back to her seat.

"I'm scared too," Drummer said.

"I know. That was some frightening shit that came back from Medina. That ship? I've never seen anything like it. I've never seen *speculation* about anything like it." Avasarala picked up her own mug, sipped, and nodded toward the tea. "This is good."

"We grow it here. Real leaves."

"All the food chemists in the system will never do better than evolution at making a decent tea leaf."

"How am I about to fuck up?"

"By trying to get back your losses," Avasarala said. "It's not just you either. You're going to have advisors on all sides who want the same damn thing. Mass a force to reclaim Medina, find a way to coordinate, take the fight back to Laconia. Through a massive effort and at tremendous cost, push our way back to the status quo ante."

"Sunk-cost fallacy?"

"Yes."

"So you don't think—" Drummer had to stop. The words were physically gagging her. She swallowed more tea, the heat of it loosening her throat. "You don't think we can get the slow zone back?"

"How the fuck would I know? But I do know you can't get it back as your first step. And I know how much you want to. It feels like if you're just smart enough, fast enough, strong enough *now*, it won't have happened the way it already did. But that's not how it's going to work. And I know how consuming that grief can be. Grief makes people crazy. It did me."

It was like the air mix in the room was wrong. Nothing Avasarala was saying was news to her, but the sympathy in the old woman's voice was worse than shouting. A vast fear, wide and cruel, welled up in Drummer's gut. She put her mug back down with a click, and Avasarala nodded.

"I was briefed about Duarte, back in the day," the old woman said. "Mars didn't want to share anything back then. I thought at the time it was because they'd just been surprise ass-fucked by one of their own, and it was shame. That was true as far as it went, but after I retired, I made him a hobby of mine."

"A hobby?"

"I'm shitty at quilting. I had to do something," she said, waving a hand. Then a moment later, "I found his thesis."

The little book she held out was printed on thin paper with a pale-green cover. It was rough against her fingertips. The title was in a simple font with no adornment: *Logistics-Based Strategy in Interplanetary Conflict*, by Winston Duarte.

"He wrote it at university," Avasarala said. "He tried to have it published, but it never went anywhere. It was enough to get him a position in the Martian Navy, put him on a career path."

"All right," Drummer said, thumbing through the pages.

"After the Free Navy, the best intelligence services in two worlds went over that man's life in so much detail you could get the Christian names of every flea that bit him. I've read...fuck, fifty analyses? Maybe more than that. It all comes back to those hundred and thirty pages there."

"Why?"

"Because that's a plan for Mars to take control of the solar system away from Earth and the Belt without firing a shot. And it would have worked."

Drummer frowned, opened the book to a random page. *The control of resources can be achieved through three strategies: occupation, influence, and economic necessity. Of these, occupation is the least stable.* A chart on the facing page listed minerals and their locations in the Belt. Avasarala was watching her, dark eyes fixed and penetrating. When she spoke, her voice was soft.

"At twenty years old, Winston Duarte saw the path that none of his superiors did. That no one on Earth did. He laid it all out, point by point, and the only reason history ran the way it did is that no one took much notice. Then he was a good, solid career officer for decades, until he saw something—an opportunity, maybe— in the data from the first wave of probes that went through the gates. Without changing the time of day when he got his hair cut, he shifted into engineering the biggest theft in the history of warfare. He took the only active protomolecule sample, enough ships to defend a gate, and engineered the chaos that knocked Earth and Mars on their asses."

"I know all that," Drummer said.

"You do," Avasarala said. "And you know what that means. But you're scared and you're traumatized and you don't want to look it in the face because your husband is on Medina Station."

Drummer picked up her tea and sipped without tasting it. Her stomach felt tight. Her throat was thick. Avasarala waited, letting the silence stretch between them. Saba was on Medina Station. It was a thought she'd been avoiding, and it was like touching a wound.

"Duarte's good," Drummer said at last. "He's very good at what he does. And he came back in his own time and on his own terms."

"Yes," Avasarala agreed.

"You're telling me he won't overreach."

"I'm telling you he came back because he thinks he can win," Avasarala said. "And if he thinks that, you should prepare yourself for the idea that it's true."

"There's no point, then," Drummer said. "We should just roll over? Put our necks under his boot and hope he doesn't step on us too hard?"

"Of course not. But don't talk yourself into underestimating him because you want him to be the next Marco Inaros. Duarte won't hand you a win by being a dumbfuck. He won't spread himself too thin. He won't overreach. He won't make up half a dozen plans and then spin a bottle to pick one. He's a chess player. And if you act on instinct, do the thing your feelings demand, he'll beat us all."

"Give up Medina. And the slow zone. And all the colony worlds."

"Recognize that they're occupied territory," Avasarala said. "Protect what you *can* protect. Sol system. Reach out where you can, if you can. There are still people loyal to the union on Medina. And Duarte's intelligence on the last few decades is going to be thin, at least at first. Find angles he doesn't know. But don't take him on straight."

Drummer felt a little click in her heart, the physical sensation of comprehension. Avasarala was making the case for defending Earth. That was why she'd come to her. Drummer and the union, the void cities and the gunships, were critical to keeping Earth and Mars safe. The strategy she was arguing for was all about playing defense, and the thing Drummer would be defending was, in the final analysis, the inner planets. That's what she and her people would be asked to die for: Earth and Mars and all the people who'd made their civilizations on the back of the Belters back in the days before the union. It wasn't just strategy. It was naked self-interest.

Also, it was right.

Medina was behind enemy lines now. And Drummer wasn't going to be able to take it back. That didn't mean she was powerless.

"So," she said, "what do we have to work with?"

"The coalition fleet," Avasarala said. "The union fleet. And whatever agents we can coordinate with on Medina."

"We can't reach anyone on Medina," Drummer said. "The communications channels are all under Duarte's control."

Avasarala sighed and looked at her hands. "Yours are," she said. It took a moment for Drummer to understand.

Avasarala shrugged. "Everyone spies on everyone, Camina. Let's not pretend to be outraged at water for being wet."

"You have a way to get messages to Medina?"

"I didn't say that," Avasarala said. "But I know a *lot* of people."

Chapter Fourteen: Singh

There have been significant changes to the internal structure of the station," Colonel Tanaka said. "Not that surprising. This was all supposed to be a generation ship that spun at a full g for a few centuries. Now it's a waystation at a third. A lot of the infrastructure would want rethinking, and there's never been a Belter ship that didn't get modified to suit the moment. If they hadn't purged their security and maintenance databases, we'd know a great deal more. But there's nothing lost there we can't build back, given time."

"I see," Singh said, considering the possible methods of recapturing the lost data.

"In addition, we've recovered one thousand two hundred and sixty-four firearms in our sweeps, the vast majority of which were handguns," she said, scrolling through a list on her monitor.

"Areas with complex compounds that can easily be used in bomb making are under strict security watches, but we'll need to make some extensive redistribution and security changes before everything can be effectively locked down."

"Anything else?" Singh asked.

"They still have kitchen knives and power tools. And anything we missed."

Tanaka was out of her power armor, and her long, lean form was insolently stretched out across a chair in Singh's office. She was older than him by almost two decades, and he could see her reaction to his relative youth in the way she held her shoulders and the shape of her smile. She playacted respect for him.

The office—his office—was small enough to be functional. A desk, chairs, a small decorative counter with its own bar. The workspace of an important administrator. He'd taken over a complex that had once been accounting space, based on the names and titles they hadn't scraped off the doors yet. The ops and command decks, like engineering and the docks, were in the part of the station that was permanently on the float, and he found the idea of working in null g uncomfortable. And more than that, he'd seen from Duarte and from Trejo what a real commander's space looked like, and it looked humble.

He went back to the issue that bothered him most.

"Twelve hundred guns? There were less than a hundred security personnel on the whole station."

"Belters have a long tradition of not trusting governmental authorities to protect them," Tanaka replied with a shrug. "Nearly all of these weapons were in civilian hands."

"But the Belters *are* the government here."

"They're Belters," she said, as if her experiences before Laconia explained everything that was happening now. "They resist centralized authority. It's what they do." She gave the report one last glance, then slapped the monitor against her arm, where it curled up into a thick bracelet.

"I have meetings today with their 'centralized authority,' so that should be illuminating," Singh said, surprised at the contempt in his voice. Tanaka gave him a little half smile.

"How old were you during the Io campaign?" she asked.

It felt like a bit of a dig. He remembered the Io campaign the way most children in his generation did. The newsfeeds announcing the launches toward Mars. The gut-clenching fear that one of the missiles bearing the alien hybrids would make it as far as the Martian surface. Even after the crisis had passed, the weeks of nightmares. He'd been a child then, and the memory had the near-mythical feel of a story retold until it barely resembled its truth. Those terrible days that had convinced his parents that something more would have to be done to protect humanity from itself and its new discoveries. It had planted the seeds that bloomed under the skies of Laconia.

But bringing up his age now felt like a power play. A way to point out how little experience he had. He tried not to show that it got under his skin.

"Not old enough to think of it as the Io Campaign, though of course I'm thoroughly versed on the history."

"I was a JG when that shitstorm went down," Tanaka said. "We were actively fighting with Belter factions back then. You probably think these people are a half step up from spear-carrying savages—"

"I don't—"

"And you'd be right," she continued. "They can be the most stupidly stubborn people you'll ever meet. But they're tough as nails, and resourceful."

"I think you misunderstood me," Singh said, fighting to keep a flush out of his cheeks.

"I'm sure," Tanaka said, then stood up. "I have an interview with the technical-assessment crew. I'll report in when I'm done with them. In the meantime, don't leave this office without your monitor on. Security directive."

"Of course," Singh said, the flush of shame he'd felt shifting over into anger. Personnel security fell under Tanaka's operational command while they were occupying the station. It was one of the few areas where Singh could not countermand her orders. So, after dressing him down and questioning his understanding of their situation, she was now delivering a direct order. The humiliation stung.

"Appreciated," she said, and headed for the door.

"Colonel," Singh said at her back. He waited until she'd turned to look back at him. "I am the provisional governor of this station, by direct order from High Consul Duarte himself. When you're in this office, you will stand at attention until I offer you a seat, and you will salute me as your superior. Is that understood?"

Tanaka cocked her head to the side and gave him another of her enigmatic little half smiles. It occurred to Singh that Aliana Tanaka had risen to the rank of colonel in the most punishingly trained combat unit humanity had ever known, and that he was alone in his office with her. He wanted to look down at her legs, see if she was rolling up onto the balls of her feet or shifting her stance. Instead, he stared her in the eye and clamped his stomach down into a knot. If he was supposed to be kind and humble, to ask about her family and trade familiarities with her, he was doing a poor job of it.

"Sir," Tanaka said, coming to attention with a sharp salute. "Yes, sir."

"Dismissed," Singh said, then sat down and looked at his monitor as though she'd already disappeared. A moment later, his door opened and then closed.

Only then did he collapse back into his chair and wipe the sweat off his face.

"Give me one reason we don't tell you to go fuck yourselves," the head of Medina Station's Air, Water, and Power Authority said. "The AWP—"

"The AWP works for us now," Singh replied, keeping his voice level.

"Like hell we do."

It's shock, Singh told himself. *It's surprise and confusion and sorrow that the universe doesn't behave the way they thought it did.* And everyone on Medina Station—maybe everyone on the colonies and in Sol system too—was going to be struggling with it. All he could do for them was keep telling the truth, as clearly and as simply as he could, and hope it sank in.

"You do," Singh continued. "And if you do not order your workers to resume their duties, I will have technicians from the *Gathering Storm* take over for them, and then I will have every single member of your organization arrested."

"You can't do that," the AWP chief said with bravado, but he rubbed his bald head, and his expression wasn't as certain.

"I can," Singh said. "Everyone on your staff is back at work by next shift rotation or I start issuing arrest orders."

"You won't—"

"Dismissed," Singh said, then gestured at one of his Marine guards, who ushered the AWP chief out of the room. Putting Medina Station in order was messy. He had imagined, coming out, that as governor of the station, he would be kept apart from the normal rank-and-file citizens and laborers. That he would have a status that kept those around him a little more in awe, with underlings to deal directly with the hands-on administration. In practice, Admiral Trejo had the role of power, and he was the underling. He accepted it with good grace. It would all be more pleasant in a few months, when the new defense emplacements were complete and the *Tempest* could progress to the next phase of their mission.

The briefings he'd had on the way out—all information gleaned from passively monitoring the backsplash radio that leaked through Laconia's ring gate—were accurate, but wildly incomplete. It left him feeling a half step behind himself all the time. It wasn't even the basic structures—those were constrained by the biological and energetic needs of the ships and station and so were, in a sense, predictable. It was the cultural forms and expectations. The absurdities and accidents of human character that affected the flow of goods and information in ways that were as unpredictable as they were exhausting. Like having to throw an entire branch of Medina's infrastructure staff in the brig.

"Who's next," Singh asked his aide, a junior lieutenant named Kasik he'd grabbed from the admin pool on the *Storm*. Kasik scrolled through a list on his monitor.

"You have Carrie Fisk next," Kasik said.

"The president of the Association of Worlds," Singh said with a laugh. "Bring her in."

Carrie Fisk entered his office, her frown lines and fidgety hands telling Singh she'd be trying to hide her fear with anger. She was a short, thin woman, with a severe face and beautiful black hair piled up on her head. Her clothes were expensive. Someone from one of the richer colonies, then. He knew her from the newsfeeds they'd captured. She looked thinner and less pleasant in person.

Singh gestured at the chair across from his desk and said, "Please sit, Madam President."

She sat, the anger dissipating at his politeness.

"Thank you."

"Madam President, I have news," Singh said, flicking a document from his monitor at her. The hand terminal in her pocket chimed. "And it will be good news or bad news, depending on how seriously you take your job, and how much you like doing actual work. You may read that later, to get all the details."

She'd started to take the terminal out of her pocket, but slid it back in at his words. "I take my job very seriously."

"Excellent, because it seems you used to have a title that held no actual power, except that you presided over the Association of Worlds in their meetings here. Which is a body that negotiates interplanetary laws it has absolutely no ability to enforce. Earth and Mars haven't formally joined your coalition, and the Transport Union has been in a position to dictate terms in all your agreements. Or so I am led to understand. My access to the newsfeeds has been limited." He tried for a self-deprecating smile, and thought he probably got about three-quarters of the way there.

"It's a start," Fisk said, the frown returning to her face. "At least we have people here talking out their problems, rather than immediately reaching for a gun."

"I agree," Singh said. "And more importantly, so does High Consul Duarte. The document I just sent you empowers the Association of Worlds to make laws that will have binding authority on the member systems, which now includes every human colony. You, as president of that body, will be granted a variety of legislative powers to aid in that cause."

"And who is granting us this new power?" Fisk asked. Her face had twisted up like he'd asked her to eat something distasteful. She knew the answer to his question, but she wanted him to say it so that she could begin her counterargument. A counterargument Singh had no interest in entertaining.

"High Consul Winston Duarte, who is now the supreme executive authority of the Association of Worlds and all subsidiary governments. All edicts passed by this body that are not vetoed by executive power will have the force of law, backed by the military power of Laconia."

"I don't know if—"

"Madam President," Singh said, leaning forward and waiting until her attention was fully on him before he continued. "I advise you to take this very seriously. The high consul wants a fully functioning legislature and bureaucracy, and believes that the existing one, with some modification of course, fits the bill. I strongly advise that you not give him a reason to think it's better to tear this down and build something new in its place. Do we understand each other?"

Fisk nodded. Her hands were fidgeting in her lap again.

"Excellent," Singh said. He stood up and extended his hand. Fisk stood and took it. "I look forward to working with you as High Consul Duarte's representative. We have much to do, but I believe it will be exciting and rewarding work."

Singh released her hand and gave a small bow.

"What comes next?" Fisk asked.

"I would recommend you begin by familiarizing yourself with the document I sent you. It contains all the provisional rules for the Association Legislature, until such time as more permanent protocols can be voted into place."

"Okay," Fisk said.

"I know you will be quite busy," Singh told her, gently guiding her past his Marine guards and over to the door. "But I look forward to our next meeting."

Once she'd left, he let out a long sigh and leaned against the wall.

"One more, Lieutenant, then we can break for lunch," he said.

"Yes, sir," Kasik said. "Next is Onni Langstiver, head of station security for Medina."

Singh smiled a little, thinking how Tanaka would have reacted to hearing that title. "*Former* head of security," he said as he returned to his desk. "Give me a moment. Let him wait."

"Yes, sir," Kasik said. "Can I get you anything in the meantime? Water? Coffee?"

"The water here tastes like old piss, and the coffee tastes like old piss run through a gym sock," Singh said. "The recycling systems on this station are decades out of date and badly maintained."

"Yes, sir," Kasik replied. "I can have water brought from the *Storm* for you."

"Or," Singh said, turning to his aide, "we can go about actually fixing the problems here."

"Yes, sir," Kasik said, bobbing his head. If Singh hadn't been tired already and irritable, he would have let it sit there. But the constant pushing back from his own people and the natives of Medina had scratched him enough to raise welts, and he couldn't quite rein himself in.

"If the posting here becomes permanent," he said, "and there is no reason to think it won't, I will be bringing my family to this station. I won't have my daughter drinking badly recycled water, breathing badly filtered air, and attending badly run schools."

Kasik had found a bottle of water from somewhere, and was pouring it into the coffee machine.

"Yes, sir," he said, like it had become an autonomic reaction.

"Lieutenant, look at me."

"Sir?" Kasik said, turning around.

"What we're doing here is important. Not just for Laconia but for all of humanity. These people? They need us. They even need us to show them *that* they need us. When you have children, you'll understand why that matters. Until then, you will behave at all times as an example of Laconian character and discipline. If you don't understand why that's critical, you will *act* as though you understand, or I will place you in charge of personally scrubbing the water-recycling system until it produces laboratory-grade potables. Are we clear?"

If there was a flicker of resentment in the man's eyes, it was a natural reaction to discipline.

"Crystal, Governor Singh."

"Excellent. Then send their former head of security in."

Onni Langstiver was a lanky Belter type in a sloppy Medina Security uniform, with greasy hair and a permanent sneer curling his lip. He looked over Singh's Marine guards just inside the door, then gave Singh himself a look of such low cunning that he almost had the man turned back out again.

"I'm here," Onni said. "You want, bossmang?"

"We're going to discuss your change in status on this station," Singh said.

"Discuss? Bist bien. Let's discuss." Onni shrugged, then walked toward the guest chair.

"Do not sit," Singh said. Something in his tone brought Onni up short, and the man frowned at him as if really seeing him for the first time. "You won't be here long."

Onni shrugged again, a short lift of both hands that did not involve the shoulders. The psy-ops briefing on Belter culture had talked about this. That most of their physical gestures had evolved to use the hands only, because they spent so much time in vacuum suits that body language was invisible. It also talked about their cultural conviction that they were the put-upon victims in all interactions with non-Belters. Well, if this Onni had come into the room expecting to be victimized, Singh would oblige him.

"You are no longer the head of security on Medina Station," Singh said.

"Who's the new boss?" Onni replied. He wasn't angry, which was interesting.

"It doesn't matter to you," Singh said with a smile. "Because you no longer work for station security. In fact, you no longer hold any official duties of any kind on this station. The last official task you will perform is to hand over all personal files related to this station that are not in the official database. Failure to do this will result in arrest and prosecution by a military tribunal of the Laconian Navy."

"Sure, sure, jefelito. Only you know most that's gone. Purged," Onni said.

"What you have, you will surrender."

"You're the man now."

"You may leave."

A smile passed over Onni's face, soft and ingratiating. Singh had seen this before, from the playground to the academy. He'd seen it as a boy in the eyes of the science team that had been on Laconia when Duarte's ships arrived and on the football team when the woman who'd been their coach was reassigned and a new man stepped in. Respect for power, yes, but also the scent of opportunity. The opportunism of making good with the new powers.

"One thing, bossmang," Onni said, as Singh had known he would.

"No, not one more—"

"No, no, no. Wait. You've got to hear this one."

"Fine," Singh said. "Out with it."

"So that weapon your big ship used? The magnetic one?"

"The *Tempest*. Yes, what about it?"

"Yeah, so," Onni said, then paused to scratch his greasy hair and smirk. "When you hit the hub station with it? Where the rail guns were?"

"Yes," Singh said. "We have extensive experience with similar artifacts, and judged the risk to be minimal."

"Okay. So when that beam thing hit the hub station that pinché ball glowed bright yellow for que, fifteen seconds. Anytime anything hits the ball that dumps any energy into it, you get these little flashes of yellow. This is the first time the whole damn thing lit up, and fifteen seconds is a long time."

"I'm having trouble understanding your point," Singh said.

"So during that fifteen seconds, all thirteen hundred rings dumped a massive gamma-ray burst into their systems. Hard enough that four ships on approach to the rings had their crews cooked. Emergency systems kicked in, autopilot stopped the ships, so we don't have four unmanned projectiles flying through the rings at us, but…"

Onni lifted his hands as if he was presenting a gift. Singh blinked and sat back. Something shifted in his belly. An emotion he hadn't felt since he'd arrived at Medina. Surprise. Maybe even hope. The ring space was, by the best understanding of the science teams, one of the most energetically active things in the perceivable universe. The power required to keep the space itself from collapsing was astounding even to people who routinely built things like *Magnetar*-class battleships. The effect Langstiver described wouldn't even be a rounding error in the overall system, but the application of it could mean a significant windfall.

"How do you know this?"

The Belter spread his hands. "I live here. I know things not everybody knows."

"Is this correct?" Singh said, not to Onni but to Kasik.

"I'll have a report prepared immediately," Kasik replied, and left the room already talking at his wrist.

"So, yeah," Onni continued, laughing a little now. Acting as if he'd already ingratiated himself. If he wasn't corrected, it would become true. "Transport Union's gonna be pissed you just cooked four of their freighter crews."

Singh considered the man. He would need local contacts.

Natives of Medina Station who were loyal to the new power structure and supporters of Laconian rule. The prospect of having this
bootlicker as one of the first among them was beneath his dignity.

"Dismissed," Singh said to the man. He needed to call Trejo on
the *Tempest* and report this.

Onni's face fell. The smile faded first into surprise and then
indignation and resentment. Rejection bloomed into hatred while
Singh watched. He'd rarely made a decision proven right so definitively or so quickly. People of this low character would never be
part of his administration, and it was telling that Onni had managed to gain power on Medina.

"Bossmang, you gotta listen to me," Onni said.

"I said you're dismissed," Singh barked at him, then looked to
one of his Marine guards. She immediately grabbed Onni by the
arm, halfway lifting him off the ground with her armor's augmented strength.

"Ouch! Fuck!" Onni yelled as she dragged him out of the room.

"Have a cart brought around," Singh said to the remaining
Marine. "I want to go to the ops center and look over the data
about this gamma-ray burst."

"Aye, sir," the Marine said, then stepped out of the room.

Singh needed to corroborate Onni's story first, then get a full
report to Admiral Trejo. If the man was correct, then they had
the ability to release a lethal gamma-ray burst through the gates
whenever they wished. Could there be a more powerful means
of controlling travel through the network? It had the potential to
shave *months* off their timetable in establishing control over the
various colony worlds.

For the first time that day, Singh felt himself relax. He might
have just won the empire for Laconia, all without firing a shot in
anger.

Chapter Fifteen: Bobbie

As an operator in the Orbital Drop Task Force, Bobbie had trained with Spec Ops personnel from every command in the Martian military for a single purpose: the invasion of Earth. And while the old axiom "If you wish for peace, prepare for war" was not without its skeptics, that skepticism wasn't shared by the Martian military. The doctrine that drove Mars in the century and a half following its declaration of independence relied on it. Mars would never have as large a population or as big an industrial base as Earth. The only thing that prevented Earth from reconquering her wayward colony was a constant demonstration of Mars' willingness and ability to hit back hard. As long as they could land on Earth streets, Earth would hesitate to fight in their tunnels.

Bobbie and her fellow Marines in Force Recon regularly and visibly trained for that day. They took drugs and worked out in full gravity until Earth would be merely uncomfortable, not

bone-crushing. They practiced dropping from orbit in troop car-
riers and one-person pods. They trained in urban pacification and
insurgent elimination. They learned to make up for what they
lacked in troop numbers by using aggression and intimidation to
keep the conquered people in line. She had literally spent years
preparing to move through the streets of Earth commanding obe-
dience through the threat of death.

The invasion and conquest of Medina Station was civilized by
comparison. She wondered whether that would last.

Four Laconian Marines in their power armor stood watch in the
dock offices, mag boots locked to the deck, and kept a close eye on
the line of people waiting to talk to the dockmaster. But while they
appeared vigilant, they were not aggressive. They acted like their
presence was sufficiently intimidating to keep the populace in line.
With some sort of slug thrower built into the armor in each forearm,
and a pair of what looked like grenade launchers on each shoulder,
Bobbie decided they were right. There were probably thirty people
on the float waiting for the dockmaster. The four Laconians looked
like they could have handled ten times that number.

She'd been like them, once.

"I like your suit," she said to the Laconian closest to her.

"Excuse me?" he said, not looking at her, continuing to scan the
room.

"I like your suit. I wore an old Goliath back in the day."

That got his attention. The Laconian looked her over once, feet
on up. He was so much like the teams she'd trained with when
she'd joined up, it felt like looking back through time. She wondered if he was as ignorant as she'd been back then. Probably.
Hell, maybe more so.

"MMC Force Recon?" he said. There was something like respect
in his voice.

"Once was," she agreed. "You guys have made some improvements."

"Studied the Recon operators at the academy," the Laconian
said. "You guys were the real deal. Heart breakers and life takers."

"Less and less of both, as time goes on," Bobbie said, and tried out a smile. The Laconian smiled back. He was half her age, at most, but it was nice to know she could still pull 'em when she wanted to. She could have imagined the kid on the tube station back at home. Shit, he probably had family back on Mars.

"I bet you do okay," he replied, still smiling. "You see any action?"

She smiled back, and the kid realized what he'd said. A little blush touched his cheek.

"Some," Bobbie said. "I was on Ganymede in the lead-up to the Io Campaign. And I was on Io."

"No shit?"

"I don't suppose there's any way an old Marine could try one of those suits out, is there?" Bobbie said, ratcheting the smile up a notch. *I don't use sex as a weapon*, she thought to herself. *But I'd love to get my hands on your outfit.*

The Laconian started to reply, then got a distant look on his face that Bobbie recognized. Someone on the group comm was talking in his ear.

"Move along, citizen," he said to her, the smile gone.

"Thanks for the time," she said, then pulled herself to the back of her line.

The wait was long and uncomfortably warm. The others there with her had flight-suit patches from a dozen other ships, and the same hangdog expression. It was like they were being treated this way because they'd done something to deserve it. Bobbie tried not to look like that.

The dockmaster's office was small and harshly lit. She identified herself and her ship, and before she could give any context, the new dockmaster cut her off.

"As a military vessel, the Ceres-registered ship called *Rocinante* is now impounded by the Laconian Naval Command." He was a small, dark man in a Laconian naval uniform, and the look on his face was the mix of boredom and irritation shared by all natural-born bureaucrats. A screen on the wall listed all the ships in the slow zone and their statuses: LOCKDOWN in red, over and over again like it was a mantra. The counter in front of him glowed with the name CHIEF PETTY OFFICER NARWA.

"Okay," Bobbie said. She'd waited in line for nearly two hours to get up to the window, and she certainly hadn't done it to be told things she already knew. Behind her, the press of bodies was enough to give the office a little extra warmth, the air a little too much closeness. "I understand that. But I have questions."

"I feel like I've told you everything you need to know," Narwa said.

"Look, Chief," Bobbie said, "I just need to get a few clarifying details and I'm out of your hair."

Narwa gave her a delicate shrug of his shoulders. If there had been any spin gravity, he'd have leaned on the counter. He looked like a guy who ran a noodle shop in Innis Shallows. She wondered if they were related.

"I own that ship," Bobbie continued. "Is this a permanent impound? Are you commandeering it? Will I be paid any compensation for the loss of the ship? Will I or my crew be allowed on board to get our personal effects if the ship is being confiscated?"

"A few points?" Narwa said.

"Just those," Bobbie agreed. "For now."

Narwa pulled something up on the counter and flicked it over to her. She felt her hand terminal buzz in her pocket.

"This is the form you can fill out to file for return of property or compensation for the loss of the ship. We are not thieves. The navy will provide one or the other."

"What about our stuff," Bobbie asked. "While the naval wheels of justice slowly turn?"

"This form," Narwa said, and her terminal buzzed again, "is to get an escorted pass onto the ship to get your personal items off it. They're usually processed within forty-eight hours, so you shouldn't have to wait long."

"Well, thank—" Bobbie started, but Narwa was already looking at the person behind her in line and yelling, "Next."

"Any word from Holden and Naomi yet?" Alex asked.

"Not yet," Amos said, tapping his hand terminal with a thumb. "System's pretty loaded up right now, though. May be getting stuck in queue."

"They have it in lockdown," she said. "There's not going to be free comms on Medina that aren't getting scanned by their systems."

"Sounds like that could add some time to delivery," Amos said.

"Standard occupation protocols care a lot more about security than convenience," Bobbie said. "Message tracking, air-gapped encryption, pattern-based censorship, human-review censorship, throttled traffic. You name it."

It fit with everything else that was suddenly changed and beyond her control. She couldn't have her ship. She couldn't get her people back together. She had to ask permission and an escort to let her retrieve her own clothes. So of course their messages were getting stuck in Medina's system. They'd found a bar on the inner face of the drum. The long ramp from the transfer point at the center of spin had been thick with carts and people on foot, some heading up toward the docks, and many—like them— coming back down. The grim expressions had been the same both ways.

"I was captain for about a week," Bobbie said, the beer in her cup sloshing dangerously as she jabbed at the air with it. "I mean, depending on if you count from when Holden offered it to me. Or when we did the paperwork. The paperwork came later, so *officially*, I guess. Houston clocked as much time in control of the *Rocinante* as I did."

"You're drunk," Alex said, gently pushing her beer hand back down to the table. He was sitting next to her at a long, faux-wood table. Amos and Clarissa sat across the table from them. Amos had a beer in his hand and half a dozen empties on the table and didn't appear impaired in the slightest. Clarissa had a plate of cold, soggy french fries in front of her and was using them to push ketchup into spiral art.

"I'm a little drunk," Bobbie agreed. "I was just starting to like the idea of being captain of my own ship and these Laconian assholes took it away."

She punctuated the word *Laconian* by jabbing her glass toward one of their Marines walking past the bar. Beer splashed across the table and into Clarissa's fries. She didn't seem to notice or care. Bobbie plucked up her napkin and dabbed the worst of it away anyhow, with only a little pang of guilt.

"And that's why you need to ease down on the brews, sailor," Alex said, just taking the glass away from her now. "We need to skip past this grief stage and get on to the kickin'-ass and gettin'-our-ship-back stage."

"You got a plan?" Amos asked. His tone said he found this dubious.

"Not yet, but that's what we need to be doing," Alex shot back.

"Cuz, a couple hundred Marines, one destroyer in the docks, and one whatever the fuck that flying violation of the laws of physics is," Amos said, pausing to sip his beer and smack his lips. "That's gonna be one hell of a plan. I gotta get in on that action."

"Hey, asshole," Alex said, half standing up from his chair. "At least I want to do something more than feel sorry for myself."

"This here?" Amos said. He pointed at the Marine outside, the security drones that now hovered over every part of Medina's drum, the people in Laconian Navy uniforms everywhere. "I've seen this before. This is us getting paved over. All we can do now is try to find some cracks to grow through."

"Cracks?" Alex said, then sat back down with a thump. "How long I known you? Half the time I still got no idea what the fuck you're talking about."

"No one is doing anything," Bobbie said. "Not till I give the order. We get this pass to get our stuff off the *Roci*, maybe we can start making a strategy from there. I may not have a ship, but I can sure as hell still have my crew."

"Be nice to sneak a gun or two off the ship," Amos agreed.

"Be nicer to find a way to get Betsy off," Alex said to her. "If that's possible."

"So until then, we wait," Bobbie said, then started pressing on the table trying to order another beer. "I just wish I understood what this Duarte asshole wants."

"They haven't started killing people," Amos said. "I mean, it's still early days. Lots of room for shit to go pear-shaped."

"But why now?" Bobbie waved her arms around at the bar, at Medina, at all of human space beyond them. "We were *just* starting to figure this shit out. Earth and Mars working together, the colonies talking out their problems. Even the Transport Union turned out to be a pretty good idea. Why come kick the table over? Couldn't he have just pulled up a chair with the rest of us?"

"Because some men need to own everything."

The voice was so quiet, it took Bobbie a moment to realize Clarissa had spoken. She was still making ketchup art with her french fries and not looking at any of them.

"What's that, Peaches?" Amos said.

"Some men," Clarissa replied, louder and looking up at them now, "need to own everything."

"Hell, I *met* this Duarte guy," Alex said. "I don't remember him being—"

"This sounds like personal experience," Bobbie said, cutting him off. "What are you thinking, Claire?"

"When I was a little girl, I remember my father deciding to buy up a majority share in the largest rice producer on Ganymede. Rice is a necessity crop, not a cash crop. You'll always sell everything you can grow, but the prices aren't high, because it's easier to grow than a lot of other things. And at that time, his companies had an annual revenue in excess of one trillion dollars. I remember an advisor telling my father that the profits from owning rice domes on Ganymede would add a one-with-five-zeroes-in-front-of-it percent to that."

"Not sure I—" Alex started, but Clarissa ignored him, so he trailed off.

"But the largest food producers were the rice growers. They had the biggest domes and farms. The most real estate. By owning a controlling share in their company, my father was in a position to dictate policy to the Ganymede Agriculture Union. It meant, in terms of Ganymede food production, he couldn't be ignored by the local government."

"What did he use that for?" Bobbie asked.

"Nothing," Clarissa said with a delicate wave of one hand. "But he had it. He owned an important piece of Ganymede, a thing he hadn't controlled before. And some men just need to own everything. Anything they lay their eyes on that they don't possess, it's like a sliver in their finger."

Clarissa pushed her soggy fries away and smiled at them all.

"My father could be the kindest, most generous and loving man. Right up until he wanted something and you wouldn't give it to him. I don't know why I think this, but Duarte feels the same. And these are men who will mercilessly punish anyone who won't comply, but with tears in their eyes and begging you to tell them why you made them do it."

"I knew a few guys like that," Amos said.

"So, he won't stop until he has it all," Bobbie said. "And it looks like he has the tech to make it work. The armor, that destroyer, and that planet killer floating outside. All of this? They all look like they came out of the same factory to anyone else?"

"Yeah, it's protomolecule shit," Amos agreed. "Some of it looks like the stuff growing on Eros."

"I'm seeing a timeline here," Bobbie said.

"We were looking into those missing ships when I talked to this Duarte guy," Alex said. "It was about the time Medina was throwing a lot of probes through the gates to get a gander at the usable planets."

Bobbie finally got the ordering screen to come up on the table, but on impulse bought a glass of club soda instead of another beer. It felt like something important was on the tip of her mind, and she didn't want to drown it in booze.

"So," she said, letting the words come out of the back of her head, hoping her subconscious had an insight it hadn't shared yet. "A probe finds something in the Laconia system, something that makes ships and armor and who knows what else."

"What, like a big volumetric printer that says, 'Insert proto-molecule here' on the side?" Amos scoffed.

"Hey," Alex replied, "we found a planet-sized power generator with moons that could turn off fusion."

Amos considered that for a moment. "Yeah. Fair enough."

"Marco's people are running a fifth column on Medina by that point," Bobbie continued. "Duarte must have been working with them already. Said he'd slip them a fat payday for early info on the ring probes. They call him up and say, 'Hey, we found this awesome thing.'"

"He hands them a bunch of Martian ships," Alex said.

"And Marco starts fucking up the solar system while Duarte takes the rest of his fleet and a bunch of like-minded Martians and takes over in Laconia," Bobbie finished.

"Where he spends a few decades making ships and fancy armor and whatnot, then rolls through the gate ready to name himself king," Alex said as her club soda arrived.

"Which means Marco was just a tool," Bobbie said.

"Kind of knew that," Amos chimed in.

"Free Navy kept everyone distracted while Duarte got set up on Laconia. And we've been sitting here patting ourselves on the back and trying to keep all the food supplies where they need to be for thirty-odd years while he's been getting ready to kick the shit out of us," Bobbie said. "Alex, maybe you should write up your thoughts on meeting him. What kind of guy he was."

"I sat in his office for a few minutes. There are probably some people on Medina who served around the same time he did," Alex said. "If we can find where the Martian vets hang out, we could see if anyone knew him."

"Yeah, that's a good—" Bobbie started, then stopped when she noticed Amos stiffen in his chair. The big mechanic's hand drifted toward his right hip and the gun that was no longer there since the Laconian weapon sweeps.

"Amos?" she said.

"Trouble on the move," he replied with a gentle tilt of his head.

The people he'd nodded toward were a group of Belters, old-school OPA by the tats. They were walking through the drum section nearby. They wore coats too large and heavy for the constant perfect weather of Medina's drum section, and several carried large bags. They kept their heads down and moved fast, like people with a purpose. She recognized one of them. Onni Lang-stiver, the asshole head of security.

"What's over there?" Bobbie asked.

"Some offices? The banking section, and some administrative stuff," Alex replied.

"The Laconians took it over," Clarissa added.

"Here we go," Amos said, and stood up. In the distance, the Belters were pulling things out of their coats and bags. Bobbie felt the surge of adrenaline in her blood the same moment as the calm descended on her: danger followed immediately by the well-cultivated response to danger. It felt like being home.

Bobbie looked around the little bar for likely cover. Nothing within ten steps looked like it would stop a bullet, so she grabbed Alex with one arm and Clarissa with the other and pulled them both to the ground with her. Amos was still standing up, watching the drama play out.

"Get down, you idi—" Clarissa started, but whatever else she was about to say was drowned out by the gunfire.

Chapter Sixteen: Singh

As he stepped out of the office complex, Singh made the mistake of looking up. The thin line of blazing full-spectrum light that ran down the center of Medina's habitat drum blinded him, just a little. It cut a glowing streak across his vision, and filled his eyes with tears. Like looking into a sun, if instead of an orb several light minutes away, it was a line drawn in the sky and very close.

"Hold on a moment," he said to his Marine escort, as he tried to get his vision back.

"Copy that," the Marine replied, then said, "we're oscar mike, triphammer two minutes from the cart. Rolling teams for cover to station ops."

It took Singh a moment to realize that most of that was comm chatter to his security detail. He had nothing but respect for the Marines under his command and for the security they provided, but they did love their jargon and code names. A moment later he'd shaken most of the water out of his eyes, and the yellow-green afterimage line across his vision was fading.

"Okay, I'm ready."

"Copy that," the Marine replied, and pointed to a parking area about fifty meters away with three electric carts lined up and waiting. Lieutenant Kasik was hurrying toward him from the carts, waving a monitor that had been extended to its full size. He met them a few seconds later, puffing with exertion.

"I have the initial defense reports," Kasik said, handing the monitor to Singh.

"Excellent." Singh scrolled past a spreadsheet of incomprehensible numbers. "I hope there's a summary?"

"Yes, sir, and the tech group is waiting for you in station ops to answer any questions. But the initial findings are very exciting."

"Tell me."

"What we can see," Kasik said, "is the ring system converted all of the energy from the *Tempest*'s field projector into gamma rays released through the rings."

"We knew that," Singh replied with a frown.

"But…the energy released was orders of magnitude more than the energy the central sphere absorbed. The ring system amplified it. Exponentially. If the factor is consistent, we can create predictive models for input versus output very quickly."

It was exactly what he'd hoped. The alien rings could be made into their own defenses, and the reconstruction of the defense battery skipped entirely. The *Tempest* would be free to move into Sol system months ahead of the original plan. Any attack would fail, even if it were coordinated through every ring at once. One *Magnetar*-class battle cruiser could guard thirteen hundred gates at once and never miss its shot. The battle to seize control of every human-controlled world in the galaxy was already over.

After that, it was just administration of the new empire. Singh tried to imagine the high consul's pleasure, the possible rewards, and his imagination failed him. But one thing still bothered him.

"Why was it, Kasik, that we heard about this from a local? If this had gone overlooked—"

"I'm sure we'd have found it, sir. But we weren't looking at the logs. We have additional data in Operations," Kasik said. "And I've requested technicians for more analysis."

Singh realized his daydreaming of the high consul's patronage had stretched into an awkward pause. Before he could reply, something shifted at the edge of his vision. Someone walking toward him with the purposeful stride of a messenger making a delivery. Except that the person striding toward him was Langstiver. The man who'd brought him the news of the new and glorious discovery. A small group of Belters were following him. He assumed Langstiver was coming to demand a reward for his information.

"I don't want—" Singh began, but his Marine guard had put one hand on his chest and shoved him back. Kasik nodded at him sharply one time, then spit berry-colored saliva all over his face.

The Marine yanked Singh to the ground, hard, then knelt over him, shielding him with her body. Her knees pressed into his spine until it hurt. Singh heard her shouting orders, muffled by her helmet, to the rest of her detail. And then he heard nothing but the deafening ripping-paper sound of multiple rapid-fire weapons opening up. His guard was sitting on top of him and blocking his view, but the space between her thigh and calf as she crouched created a small triangular window on the carnage.

Langstiver and half a dozen other people were dancing backward as four Laconian Marines cut them to pieces with streams of high-velocity plastic safety rounds. It felt like the firing went on forever, like the bullets were keeping the assassins from falling. In reality it could only have lasted a few seconds. He experienced a little discontinuity in his consciousness, like he'd fallen briefly asleep, though that was impossible, and his Marine had yanked him to his feet and was shoving him back toward the administrative offices. The other members of her fire team slowly backed toward them, weapons at the ready.

Lieutenant Kasik still stood near the carts, not having moved during the entire firefight. He looked like he'd spit raspberry pie filling onto his lips, and he was twitching like an epileptic experiencing a grand mal. Singh understood something that had been eluding him.

"Kasik's been shot," he said. The pie filling on his face was the ruins of his lips from where the bullet had exited. The spray of red on Singh's face and uniform wasn't spit, it was his aide's blood.

"Medical has already been alerted," his Marine said, thinking he was talking to her.

"But no," Singh said. She didn't understand. "He's been *shot*."

She shoved him through the admin-building door and slammed it shut behind her. Just before it closed, the shocked silence that had followed the gunfire ended, and from a hundred voices outside the screaming started.

Kasik died on an operating table three hours after the attack. According to the report, he'd been shot in the back of the head, the bullet fracturing the occipital lobe of his skull and nicking his medulla oblongata. It then passed through the back of his throat and nearly severed his tongue, before shattering five teeth and exiting through his lips. Singh read the surgeon's section of the incident report half a dozen times. Each time felt like the first.

None of the Marine security detail had been harmed in the exchange of fire, though several civilians had received minor injuries from bullet fragments, and one boy of nine had broken his arm while attempting to flee down a short flight of steps. All seven of the Belter radicals who'd attempted the assassination were dead. The intelligence people were digging into their past associations to see if the rebellion had roots that spread farther.

Rebellion.

The word felt wrong to Singh. The most Langstiver and his accomplices could have hoped for was his death. It would have done nothing to hand control of the station back to the Belters who'd once run it. Trejo would simply have assigned another officer to fill his place until a new governor could be dispatched from

Laconia. It was all so short-sighted. So *wasteful*. Seven people had decided to toss their lives away on a symbol.

These are people who have a history of resisting centralized authority, Colonel Tanaka had said. He hadn't understood. He did now. They weren't rational. They weren't disciplined. They valued their own lives less than the prospect of his death.

What struck him most—what offended him as much as the still-implausible idea that he'd watched Kasik be murdered—was the monstrous ingratitude of it. The hubris of believing that Duarte's path for humanity's future was worth killing innocent people to resist. And after Trejo had been so generous with them.

He tapped the monitor lying on his desk, and the comm officer in security replied with a crisp, "Yes, sir."

"Please have Colonel Tanaka report to me in my office immediately."

"Sir, yes sir."

Singh killed the connection almost before the officer finished speaking. He looked around his office, not to take in anything new so much as to judge his own mind. He wasn't feeling the shuddering in his hands anymore. His eyes were able to move from the door to his desk to the little ferns in their planters beside the wall without jittering back and forth of their own accord. He'd been in shock. Only a little. And only for a short time. It was normal. Natural. Expected. The physiological effects were only the consequence of being an animal in a stressful situation. There was no reason for him to feel ashamed.

And yet, when Tanaka entered the room with that little half smirk on her lips, he had to rein his anger in. *Is this funny to you?* He didn't say it.

"Sir," she said, bracing. "You wanted to see me?"

"I was almost murdered today," Singh said. "I found your silence on the matter disturbing."

Tanaka's expression shifted. A little chagrin, maybe? It was hard to tell with her. Her voice didn't have the crispness he'd expect of someone being dressed down. "I apologize. After your safety was established, my focus was on the response and investigation. I should have reported in sooner."

"Yes, well," Singh said. "Are you ready to make your report now?"

Tanaka gathered her thoughts visibly, then nodded to the chair across the desk from his, silently asking his permission to sit. He waved a hand. She sat, leaning forward, her elbows resting on her knees.

"The basic facts appear straightforward. The attempt was instigated and organized by Langstiver. He was the head of security before we came, and his co-conspirators were drawn from the ranks of the local security force."

"Why weren't we monitoring them?" Singh asked.

"We were. But it appears that Langstiver wasn't using the station network. My team is still digging into it, but it looks like he did his coordination and planning on an encrypted network set up in the power conduits. Physically separate from the main system the way the *Storm* is from Medina. Air-gapped. From what we can tell, it was put in by criminal elements in Medina Station. Langstiver also had relationships there."

Singh leaned back a centimeter in his chair. "Criminal elements? You mean he was *corrupt*?"

"It's not unusual on this side of the gate," Tanaka said. "And it makes the investigation more complicated than I'd like. Add to that, he appears to have purged several caches of data he still had access to and inserted false entries into what we have got. And Langstiver and his little friends aren't going to be questioned by anyone but God at this point."

"But you've found the network they were using."

"One of them," Tanaka said. "There may be others. Part of the problem is that Medina wasn't run as a military installation. There were—and probably still will be—competing levels of culture and infrastructure. Controlling the official channels is trivial, but even the officials were using additional undocumented frameworks. It's not like the locals have to create ways to get around our surveillance. All those ways were built in before we showed up."

She lifted her hands in a shrug. Singh had a stark flashbulb memory of Kasik, and with it a powerful, all-pervading dread. In his imagination, Nat and the monster were looking at a picture of him with blood spilling down his chin. It wasn't the prospect of his own death that brought the flush of rage. It was how cavalier Tanaka was being with *them*.

"Well, we'll have to address that directly, then," Singh said. "Mandatory curfews and roaming checkpoints will be a start. And restrict the station security forces to quarters until they can be interrogated and evaluated for service. And I'll want a list of anyone who might pose a threat moving forward for precautionary monitoring. And…hm. Yes, and coordinate that through the *Gathering Storm*. If we can't be sure the local system's clean, we should use our own. The most important thing is that the systems on the *Gathering Storm* not be compromised."

"I've already set up an encryption strong room," Tanaka said, nodding without seeming to agree. Her sigh was like grit on his skin. "But you want to be careful about a crackdown, sir. Especially this early on. It could send the wrong message."

"The wrong message," Singh repeated, stretching out each syllable into a question and a confrontation.

"Belter culture and identity is built around pushing back against authority. This is what that looks like in practice. We knew something like this was possible, and—"

"We did?" Singh said, his voice sharp. "We *knew* that, did we?"

Tanaka's eyes flattened and her lips thinned. "Yes, sir. We did. It's why I had a fire team with you at all times. And, respectfully, it's why you're alive."

"Pity there wasn't one for Kasik."

"Yes, sir," Tanaka said. The languor in her tone was gone. She had the tightness in her voice that said that at last she was taking him seriously. "I'm sorry to have lost him. But that doesn't change my assessment. Bringing Laconian focus and discipline to Medina Station and the other systems isn't a matter of imposing our customs and rules on them."

"I'm surprised to hear you say that."

"Our discipline is *ours*, sir. The same actions can have different meanings in different contexts. What would be routine back home would seem draconian here. Anything harsher than routine will read as a wild overreaction. I believe the high consul would agree that underreacting to this would be a more persuasive show of authority."

Singh stood up. He hadn't meant to, but the need to move, to occupy the space inside his office, was suddenly overpowering. Tanaka stayed still. Her expression was like someone tracking a target on a firing range—focused, but emotionless. He walked to his sideboard and poured himself a drink since his aide wasn't there to do it for him.

"It's an interesting perspective, and I can respect it," Singh said. "But I don't share it. You have my instructions." The alcohol was sharp and strangely acrid in his mouth. His gut rebelled a little at it. He swallowed anyway, trying to enjoy the bloom of warmth in his throat. Kasik had had a better hand at this than he did.

"Governor," Tanaka said, not standing. It was the first time he could remember her using the title. "I strongly urge you to reconsider this. At least sleep on it before we implement it."

He turned to look at her. He imagined himself as she saw him. A young man, off Laconia for the first time as an adult. Having been the target of enemy action for the first time. Seeing an unplanned death by violence for the first time. He must seem shaken and weak to her. Because as much as he hated the fact, he did feel shaken and weak. And naked before her implacable and judging gaze. She thought he was being irrational. Letting his fear make his decisions.

And if he changed his course now, it would prove her right.

"Respectfully," Tanaka said, "as your head of security and a woman with a lot of years of experience in her bag? This isn't a set of orders I can support."

Singh took in a long breath between bared teeth. His gums went cold with it. Whether he was right or wrong didn't matter now. He was committed.

"Your second is Major Overstreet?"

"Yes, sir."

"Please send him in on your way out. You're relieved of your command."

There it was in the flash of her eyes and the lift of her chin. The contempt he'd known would be there. Giving in to her would only have helped cultivate it. Tanaka had never respected him. She thought herself better suited to make the policies of governance than he was. It didn't matter whether she was right or not.

She stood wordlessly, braced, and stalked out of the room. He more than half expected her to slam the door as she left, but she closed it gently. He finished his unpleasant drink in a gulp and went back to his desk.

The alcohol did what it was supposed to do, taking his too-sharp mind back just half a degree. Letting him relax, just a little bit. He wouldn't have another one.

He pressed his palms flat against the surface of his desk, feeling the little bite of cool fading quickly. He took a deep breath, let it out slowly. Then again. When his calm was more or less reestablished, he opened his personal log and reported his decision and the reasoning behind it. *Visible weakness to my chief of security undermines confidence in the chain of command. Tanaka's expertise is admirable, but her placement on Medina proved unsuitable. Recommend her without prejudice for more appropriate duty.*

Hopefully his superiors would approve of his actions. If not, he'd know soon enough. It was done. Time that he got back to work. He felt better now. More centered. More nearly in control. It had been a bad day. Maybe the worst he'd ever suffered through, but he was alive and his command was intact. And it was just a bad day.

He opened a fresh message, flagged it for immediate delivery. For a moment, he felt the impulse was to send his first message home to Nat. To be with her even if it was only a little bit. This attenuated, one-way presence would be better than nothing. But it would wait until he'd done his duty. Duty always came first. He routed the message for the *Tempest* instead of home.

"Admiral Trejo," he said into the system's camera. "I am including preliminary data provided by former Medina Security Chief Langstiver and confirmed by my own staff—"

His own staff meaning the dead man. Meaning his first sacrifice to the empire.

"Ah. Yes. Confirmed by my own staff concerning an unexpected side effect of our actions while securing Medina Station. If command agrees with my assessment that this windfall provides a significant defense and is willing to position a ship equipped with a USM field projector permanently to the ring space, it is my belief that the timetable for further occupation can be moved up considerably. If the *Tempest* adopts a more aggressive schedule, the local forces in Sol system will have a considerably reduced period to prepare defenses. We can have absolute control of Earth and Mars in weeks."

Chapter Seventeen: Holden

Stay still," the Laconian said. "Look at the red dot."

Holden blinked and did as he was told. The sack of rations tapped against his leg like it was trying to get his attention, but he didn't shift his weight. The dot on the hand terminal seemed to look back at him, and something flashed filling one eye with yellow. The guard's hand terminal chimed, and he shifted to Naomi. His other hand was on the butt of his gun. "Stay still. Look at the red dot. You can move along, sir."

"I'm with her."

"You can move over there, sir," the guard said, gesturing down the corridor with his chin. His voice didn't make it a request. Holden walked a few steps, then paused while he was still close enough to go back if something happened. Not that he knew what he'd do.

The hand terminal chimed again and the guard nodded Naomi

forward, waiting until she was back with Holden and the two of them were moving down the gently curving hall of the crew decks before he turned back to the line and the next identity to check and record. An older man with a close-cropped beard who was smiling at the guard like a dog hoping it wouldn't get kicked. "Stay still," the guard said. "Look at the red dot." And then Holden and Naomi turned the corner and left the checkpoint behind.

He felt his gut release a little, the tension backed off a notch just by not being in a direct line of fire.

"Well, this sucks," he said.

The security announcement had changed Medina like dye dropped into water. The rolling curfew meant no one in public spaces off-shift, and three one-hour periods each cycle when no one could be out of their quarters. A congregation ban—no more than three people in a group. Anyone with a weapon would be arrested. Anyone making unauthorized use of the comm system would be arrested. Anyone that the security forces deemed a threat would be arrested. With every new edict, the nature of the station itself shifted, and the fragile thought that maybe everything would work itself out, that maybe it would be all right, receded.

He knew the station architecture hadn't really changed. The walls were still at the same angles as before, the hallways curved around the drum the same as they ever had. The air smelled the way air smelled anywhere. It was only the faces of the people that made everything seem smaller, closer, more like a prison. The faces and the checkpoints.

They reached their rented quarters, and Naomi tapped in the manual override code, since their hand terminals were still locked out. The door slid open. When it slid closed behind them, Naomi sagged against it like she was on the edge of collapse. Holden sat at the little built-in table and unpacked the bag in silence. Pad thai and red curry, both with tofu and both spiced enough to make his eyes water a little bit just at the smell of them. On another day, it would have felt like a luxury.

Naomi went to the bath, washed her face in the little sink, and came back out with droplets of water still clinging to her hair and eyelashes. She dropped down across from him and scooped up a fork.

"Any thoughts?" she asked.

"About?"

She waved the fork in a small circle, indicating the room, the station, the universe. Then she speared a cube of tofu and popped it in her mouth.

"Not yet," he said. "I've got to say, I wish that those assholes hadn't tried to kill this Singh fella."

"Or that they'd done a better job," Naomi said, and Holden felt a twitch of anxiety in his gut. Was station security monitoring their cabin? Was that kind of offhanded joke going to get them sent to the brig? Naomi saw it in his face.

"Sorry," she said, half for him and half for the microphone that might or might not have been there. "Bad joke."

"I'm thinking this takes the Luna consulting gigs off the table, though."

"Seems like it. And Titan."

"That's a shame. I would have liked Titan."

"If only we'd gotten out a week earlier," Naomi said. "Things were different then."

"Yeah," Holden said. The pad thai was rich and hot, and it tasted almost like they'd used real limes and peanuts to make it. Almost, but not quite. He put his fork down. "I don't know what to do."

"Eat," Naomi said. "And when you're done with that, come take a shower with me."

"Seriously?" he said. She hoisted an eyebrow and smiled.

They ate in silence after that. He thought about putting on some background music, and even reached for his hand terminal before he remembered that it was dead. After, Naomi put the plates and forks into the recycler and led him into the bathroom by the wrist. She pulled off her clothes slowly, and he felt himself responding to her body despite the stress and fear. Or maybe because of it. Lust and anxiety mixed into something that was more than one kind of desperation. She got the water to a decent temperature while he stripped, and then they were there together, arms around each other as the warm cascade filled the curves where their bodies made cups and reservoirs. She leaned her head against his, her lips beside his ear.

"We can talk now," she murmured. "We've got about fifteen minutes before the rationing kicks in."

"Oh," he said. "And here I thought this was just my masculine charm."

She grabbed him gently someplace sensitive. "That too," she said, and the laughter in her voice was better than anything that had happened in days. "We need to make a real plan. I don't know what's going to happen with our money. We only had this room to the end of the week, and I'm not sure whether we'll keep it past that or if they'll throw us out early. Or anything else, really. Not at this point."

"We've got to get back to the *Roci*," he said.

"Maybe," Naomi said. "Unless that calls more attention to the kids. It might not be a kindness to have James Holden of the *Rocinante* ride again. Unless that's a fight you want to be part of."

"You think there's going to be a fight?"

She shifted against him, their skin slipping distractingly under the flow of water. "What would Avasarala say?" Naomi asked.

Holden moved his arms around the small of her back, pulled her gently against him. Kissed her gently. "That Governor Singh fucked up," he said softly. "That cracking down on the enemy this hard shows that you're afraid of them."

"Yup," Naomi said. "The people who went after him? They were assholes and amateurs. There's a real underground going to start now, and it's going have the professionals. If you and I keep our noses very, very clean, we might be able to stay out of that. If we start reaching out to the crew, security may think we're putting the band back together."

"So leave them out of it. Commit fully to our new lives as war refugees?"

"Or suck it up, get the band back together, and die as dissidents."

"I'm really wishing Titan were still on that list of options."

"That's waiting for yesterday, sweetheart."

He rested his head against her shoulder. The water ration warning cleared its throat. Just the first one, though. They still had time.

"Why do I get the feeling I'm more freaked-out about this than you are?" he asked, and felt her smile against his cheek.

"You're new here," she said. "I'm a Belter. Security coming down on you just because they can? Checkpoints and identity tracking? Knowing that you could wind up in the recycler for any reason or no reason? I grew up like this. Amos did too, in his way. I never wanted to come back here, but I know how this all goes. Childhood memories, sa sa que?"

"Well, shit."

She ran her hand down his spine and pushed him back. The wall was cold against him. Her kiss was rough and strong, and he found himself pushing into it in a way he hadn't in years. When they came up for air, Naomi's eyes were hard. Almost angry.

"If we do this," she said, "it's going to be ugly. We're outgunned and outplanned, and I don't see how we win."

"I don't either," he said. "And I don't see how we stay out of it."

"Getting the band back together?"

"Yeah. And we were so close to out."

"We were," she said.

The water ration chimed again, a little more urgently. Holden felt some vast emotion move in his chest, but he didn't know what it was. Grief or anger or something else. He turned off the water. The rush of white noise stopped. The gentle chill of evaporation brought goose bumps up his arms and legs. Naomi's eyes were soft, dark, unflinching.

"Come to bed," he said.

"Yes," she answered.

In the darkness, the control pad on the door glowed amber. Green would have meant unlocked. Red, locked. Amber meant override. It meant that they weren't in control of it. That, in a fundamental way, it wasn't their door anymore. It belonged to station security. Naomi was still asleep, her breath deep and regular, so Holden sat in the darkness, not moving to keep from waking her, and watched the amber light.

It was the dead hour of curfew between each shift. Right now, all the hallways in Medina were empty. The curved fields and parks of the drum. The lifts in lockdown. Only the Laconian security forces could travel freely while everyone else huddled in place. Including him. Measured in work-hours, it was a massive tax. If it had just been the *Roci*, it was the same as losing someone for eighteen hours a day. Medina put a coefficient on that with at least three zeros at the end. Someone in the Laconian chain of command thought it was worth the sacrifice. That alone told him something.

Naomi murmured, shifted her pillow, and fell back into it without ever quite breaching up to consciousness. She would be awake soon, though. They'd been sleeping in the same couch long enough that he knew the signs her body gave out without even being certain what he was reacting to. He felt it when she was heading back up. He hoped she could stay down until it was their door again. Maybe she wouldn't feel the same kind of trapped that he did.

Over the years, the *Roci* had done its fair share of prisoner transport duty. Houston had been the most recent, but they'd taken on half a dozen like him one time and another since the *Tachi* had become the *Rocinante*. Now that he thought about it, the first had been Clarissa Mao. All of his prisoners had spent months in a cabin smaller than this, staring at a door they couldn't control. He'd always known in a distant, intellectual way that had probably been uncomfortable for them, but it wouldn't have been that different from being in a brig, and he'd been in brigs.

It wasn't the same, though. A brig had rules. It had expectations. You were in a brig until your lawyer or union rep came to talk to you. There would be hearings. If it went badly, there was prison. One thing followed another, and everyone called it justice, even when they all knew it was an approximation at best. But this was a cabin. A living space. Turning it into a prison cell felt like a rupture in a way that an actual prison cell wouldn't. A brig had an inside and an outside. You were in it, and then you passed through a door or a security lock, and you were out of it. All of Medina was a prison now, and would be for another twelve minutes. It left him feeling claustrophobic and oppressed in a way he was still trying to wrap his head around. He felt like the station had just become small as a coffin.

Naomi shifted again, pulling the pillow over her head. She sighed. Her eyes stayed closed, but she was with him again. Awake, but not ready to admit it.

"Hey," he said, softly enough that she could pretend not to have heard him.

"Hey," she said.

Another minute passed, and Naomi pulled the pillow back under her head, yawned, and stretched like a cat. Her hand landed on his, and he laced his fingers between hers.

"Been brooding the whole time?" she asked.

"Some of it, yeah."

"Did it help?"

"Nope."

"Right. Spring into action, then?"

He nodded at the amber door alarm. "Not yet."

She glanced down. The override light flickered in her eyes like a candle flame. "Huh. All right. Brush teeth, pee, and spring into action?"

"That'll work," he agreed, and hauled himself up out of the bed. The way it worked out, he was brushing his teeth when the door clicked over to red—locked, but under his control. The relief and resentment at the relief came packaged together.

The hallways in the residential deck were no busier than usual. The checkpoint they'd passed through earlier was gone, relocated to some other intersection of hallways. Keeping the surveillance unpredictable and visible, he assumed. If the security systems were in Laconian control, the guards and checkpoints were all theater anyway. A show of force to keep the locals scared and in line. The transport was down—no lifts, no carts. If anyone wanted to go anywhere, the only option was to walk.

In the drum, the false sunlight was as warm as ever. The fields and parkland, streets and structures, curved up and around the same way they always had. Holden could almost forget that it was an occupied station until they interacted with anyone.

The man they paused to get bowls of noodles and sauce from gave them extra packets of peanuts and a twist of cinnamon sugar candy, on the house. An older woman they walked past as they headed aft toward engineering and the docks smiled at them, then stopped and stroked Naomi's shoulder until little tears appeared in the older woman's eyes. A group of young men heading the other way made room for them to pass long before they needed to and nodded their respect. It wasn't, Holden decided, that people recognized him and deferred to his celebrity. All the citizens of Medina were treating each other like everyone was made from spun sugar. Likely to shatter if you breathed on them too hard. He recognized it from being on Luna after the rocks had fallen on Earth. The deep human instinct to come together in crisis. To take care of each other. In its best light, it was what made humanity human. But he also had the dark suspicion that it was a kind of bargaining. *Look, universe, see how kind and gentle and nice I am? Don't let the hammer fall on me.*

Even if it was only grief and fear, he'd take it. Anything that helped them all treat each other well.

Beside a little café that served tea and rice-flour cakes, a dozen people in Laconian uniforms were building something—a wall made from cubes two and a half meters to a side, eight wide, and three high, with steel walls and backs and wide mesh doors facing the pathway. Like kennels. Half a dozen locals stood watching, and Naomi went to stand beside them. A young woman with mud-brown hair and a scattering of freckles across her cheeks made a little space for them. Another small kindness, like a coin in a wishing well.

"Are they expecting prisoners, then?" Naomi asked the woman as if they were friends. As if everyone who wasn't Laconian was part of the same group now.

"That's the thought," Freckles said, then nodded a greeting to Holden. "Making a show of it. Supposed to keep us all in line, isn't it?"

"That's how it works," Holden said, trying to keep the bitterness out of his voice. "Show everyone what the punishment is. Enough fear, and we'll all be obedient. They'll train us like dogs."

"That's not how you train dogs," Freckles said. She made a little, deferential bow when he looked at her, but she didn't back down. "You train dogs by rewarding them. Punishment doesn't actually work." Tears glistened in her eyes, and Holden felt a lump in his own throat. *They'd been invaded. They'd been taken over. They could kill everyone on the station, and no one would be able to stop it. This couldn't be happening, and it was happening.*

"I didn't know that," he said. Banal words, the closest he could offer to comfort.

"Punishment never works," Naomi said, her voice hard. Her face was unreadable. She shifted her weight like she was looking at sculpture in a museum. The spectacle of power considered as art. "Not ever."

"Are you from here?" Freckles asked. She hadn't recognized them.

"No," Holden said. "Our ship's in the dock. Or our old ship anyway. The one we came in on. And the crew we flew with."

"Mine's in lockdown too," Freckles said. "The *Old Buncome* out of New Roma. We were slated to go home next week. I don't know where we're going to stay now."

"Not on your ship?"

She shook her head. "The docks are off-limits. No one's allowed on their ships without escort. I'm hoping we can find rooms, but I've heard we may have to camp out here in the drum."

Naomi turned, and he saw everything that he was thinking mirrored in her face. If the docks were off-limits and the crews turned out, the others wouldn't be on the *Roci*. And with the network down, they couldn't put through a connection request. They didn't have any way of contacting Bobbie or Alex or Amos. Or Clarissa. Counting each deck and the inner surface of the drum, it was something over fifty square kilometers of hallways, cabins, access tubes, and warehouses. Recycling plants. Hydroponic farms. Air storage. Medical bays. A maze the size of a small city, and somewhere in it, four people he needed to find.

Holden coughed out a small, harsh laugh. Naomi tilted her head.

"Nothing," he said. "It's just not very long ago I was thinking how *small* Medina felt."

Chapter Eighteen: Bobbie

A rope defined the line to the ships. Two and a half, maybe three hundred people, each with their fist on it, went the length of the dock and switched back twice. Men and women in the jumpsuits of dozens of different companies jostled in place in the dock's microgravity, inching forward along the line as if registering their silent impatience would make the whole operation move faster. Laconian guards floated along the perimeter, rifles drawn and ready for violence. If it came to that, Bobbie thought, it wouldn't be surgical. Not in a mob like this. If anyone started anything, the air recyclers would be spitting out blood clots for months. She hoped everyone else knew that too. She hoped they cared.

Every now and then, a team of Laconian military escorts came, took the people from the moored end of the line, checked their authorization, screened them for weapons, and led them off to their ship. Everyone on the rope would pull a little forward, grabbing on another half meter closer to their turn, feeling the weave of the strands, the grease from all the palms before their own. The unmoored end floated free, waiting for the next hapless crew to join the waiting horde.

They were lucky, Bobbie told herself. Most of the ships had full crews of twenty or thirty people. The *Roci* just had the four of them. They could all go aboard at once. Small blessings indeed. Almost too small to see.

The guards led away another group. They moved down the rope again, that much closer.

"How you holding together, Claire?" Bobbie asked.

Clarissa took a long, shuddering breath and nodded. When she spoke, the words came just a little too fast, and all the consonants had sharp edges. Like she was trying to rein them in and couldn't. "It would be very nice to get to the med bay. But right now, it's just euphoria and nausea. Nothing I can't handle."

"That changes," Amos said, "you let me know."

"Will," she said. Bobbie wasn't sure she liked the sound of that. There weren't many actions Amos could take that would make the situation better. If putting their heads down and enduring wasn't enough to get Clarissa to her medications, the options got bad fast.

"Anyone else think it's cold in here?" Alex said.

"It is," Clarissa said. "I think the pressure's a little low too. The environmental systems are all off."

"That doesn't sound like a good thing," Alex said.

"Belters," Bobbie said. "We trained for this."

"You trained for low air pressure?" Amos asked. He sounded amused. That was better than sounding frustrated.

"We trained for occupying Belter stations. One of the base tactics that Belters used was throwing environmental stasis off just enough that we'd have to keep bumping it up our priority queue.

Someone somewhere on the station is trying to make it harder for these folks."

"Huh," Amos said. "That's pretty ballsy."

"It only works if the occupying force isn't willing to just kill everyone and start over. So yeah. There's an element of playing chicken."

The group in front them on the rope wore gray-black jumpsuits with CHARLES BOYLE GAS TRANSPORT logos in green on the back. The one floating nearest them looked back over his shoulder, catching Bobbie's eye almost shyly. She nodded, and the man nodded back, hesitated, tilted his head a centimeter forward.

"Perdó," he said, nodding toward Clarissa. "La hija la? She's sick?"

Bobbie felt herself tense. It wasn't a threat. It wasn't an insult. It was just someone who wasn't part of her crew putting themselves into her business. But maybe she was feeling as tense as Amos. She took a little breath and nodded.

The man tapped his compatriot ahead of him on the rope. They spoke for a moment in Belter cant so thick and fast, Bobbie couldn't follow it, then they all released the rope and gestured Bobbie forward. Giving up their place in line so that Clarissa could get to the *Roci* a few minutes sooner. It was a tiny thing. A gesture. It shouldn't have hit her as hard as it did.

"Thank you," Bobbie said, and ushered the others forward. "Thank you very much."

"Is is," the man said, waving her thanks away. It wasn't an idiom she'd heard before, but his expression explained it. *We do what we can for each other.*

The Laconians were efficient. The line moved quickly. Even with as many people as were waiting, the *Roci* crew reached the head of the line in only a couple of hours. An escort of four Marines checked her authorizations, scanned them all for weapons. Apart from a momentary hit of panic when they were looking at Clarissa's scan—would her modifications keep them from letting her on?—everything went smoothly. And after all, her mods had been designed to get past security unnoticed. Good to know they were still doing their jobs, even while they killed her.

The *Rocinante* was waiting for them in the dock, loyal as a dog. When they cycled the airlock and pulled themselves in, Bobbie felt her shoulders relax. The air smelled familiar. It wasn't even a particular scent so much as a sense of rightness. Of being home. Bobbie let herself imagine they were getting on board to leave, that they'd be burning for one of the gates. Diving down toward one sun or another.

Someday, maybe. Not now.

"You have one hour," the escort lead said.

Bobbie shook her head. "My mechanic needs to be in the med bay for longer than that. She has to have a blood flush."

"She'll have to do the best she can in an hour. She can visit medical facilities on the station."

Bobbie looked at the guard. The man had a wide face and skin just a shade darker than Bobbie's own. A lifetime of habit mapped out how Bobbie would try disarming him, controlling his weapon, getting into cover. Chances weren't great. The Laconians moved like they'd been well trained, and the oldest of them still looked to be hauling around a decade less than she was.

"It's fine, Captain," Clarissa said. "I can set the system to do a fast push and get blockers. I've done it before."

"If you need another waiver," the guard said, "you can apply for it once you've left."

"Fine," Bobbie said. "Let's get on with this."

They moved through the ship like they were visiting someone in prison. The guards went with them everywhere, examined everything they took from their cabins, watched every command they gave the ship, copied every report the ship returned. The resentment in Bobbie's gut ached, but there wasn't anything to be done about it. Their pass allowed them to retrieve personal items and any tools they needed for their work, provided they didn't present a security risk. Which was a shame. There was a part of her that would have liked to explain that she worked as a mercenary so that she could walk out of here with Betsy around her like a shell.

As she packed her things from the captain's cabin, her guard watching wordlessly from the doorway, she opened a connection to Alex.

"What's the good word?" she said.

"*Roci*'s a little bored, but she's in good condition," Alex said from the flight deck. "A little impurity in the water supply we should look at, but it's likely just a seal that's wearing out. A little stray leaching."

"Okay," Bobbie said. She wanted to stay. She wanted to spend her hours polishing her ship and fixing every flaw they could put hands to. She had thirty-five minutes left. "Flag it. We'll dig in next time."

"Next time, Cap'n," Alex agreed. Because there would be a next time. Even if there wasn't, they were going to pretend there would be. She locked down her cabinets, checked the message queue from the ship's system to make sure everything was getting to her hand terminal—or at least that the Laconian censors were locking everything down equally—and pulled herself back down the corridor and toward the lift.

"This a Martian ship?" her guard asked.

"It is," Bobbie said as they reached the lift and headed down for the machine shop.

"I've seen some like her back home. First fleet had a lot like this."

First fleet meaning all the ships that Duarte had stolen when he'd escaped to Laconia. But also, Bobbie realized, meaning there was a second fleet. One with ships like the monstrosity that had killed the *Tori Byron*.

"Must look pretty quaint, eh?" she said, trying to make light of it, inviting the guard to give something away. But if there had been an opportunity there, she'd missed it.

In the machine shop, Amos had almost finished collecting a set of safety-approved tools into a small ceramic toolbox. He nodded to her as she floated in, stopping herself on a handhold. She saw his sign again: YOU TAKE CARE OF HER. SHE TAKES CARE OF YOU. The words had more weight now. She'd barely had a chance to take care of the *Rocinante*, at least not as her captain. She hoped another chance would come.

"You ready to roll out?" she asked.

"Yep," Amos said.

Clarissa and Alex were already in the airlock with their guard when Bobbie and Amos got there. Clarissa looked more relaxed, and there was more color in her skin. Alex would have seemed relaxed to anyone who didn't know him, but Bobbie saw how he looked at the ship, how his hand lingered on the bulkhead. He knew as well as she did that there was no guarantee they'd ever be back.

The guards escorted them along the nearly empty docks, back toward the transfer point to the drum and spin gravity, then went back for the next crew to the next ship. When they were alone, Bobbie cleared her throat.

"All right. How did that go?" she asked.

"They've locked her down pretty tight," Alex said. "But they didn't get everything. Give me twenty minutes, I can probably get her working."

"I've got a decent kit," Amos said, holding up the toolbox. "Could get some low-level work with just this. Not cutting through any decking, though."

"Claire?"

Clarissa smiled and shrugged. "I feel a little better, and I've got enough blockers."

Bobbie put a hand on her thin shoulder. "We'll take care of you," she said.

"I know you will," Clarissa said.

"All right, then," Bobbie said. "The way I see it, the next step is find someone who can get messages back to the union. Or Earth-Mars. See if there's anyone out there with a plan, or if we're going to have to make one up on our own."

"We can do that," Amos said. "Shouldn't be hard."

"You sure?" Alex said. "This is Medina Station under occupation by a bunch of splinter Martian military expats. It's not Baltimore."

Amos' smile was as placid as always. "Everywhere's Baltimore."

Bobbie had known and worked with Amos Burton for years, and he kept being able to surprise her. For the next two days, Amos took the lead, moving through Medina Station apparently without any particular aim or purpose. They went to sit in a bar by the water recycling plant, went to interview with a pop-up service that was matching people who'd been locked off their ships with accommodations, played a little dirt football with a crew of technicians whose old split-circle OPA tattoos had been softened and smudged by the years.

Every now and then, Bobbie caught something—a phrase or a gesture—that didn't quite feel right, like there was a second conversation going on at some frequency her ears couldn't pick up. She took up her position at Amos' back and watched for threats, either from the Laconians or the locals.

Everywhere they went, the station seemed to be on the edge of something. It was in the air and the voices of everyone they spoke to. Guards in power armor. Checkpoints. The Laconians had erected an open-air jail, and filled it with men and women living behind bars like animals at a particularly shitty zoo. With hand terminals locked down and the internal communications network restricted to the point of uselessness, every conversation seemed fraught and dangerous. *Anything worth encrypting is worth not putting on a network in the first place*, Amos would sometimes say. Bobbie had never really thought about how much communication changed when every time you spoke, you had to be close enough that the other person could stab you if they wanted to. Never before, anyway.

And then, after three days, the old Belter who'd been the opposing goalie at their football game came to them at the little public table where they were eating mushrooms and noodles, nodded to Amos, and walked away. The big man got up, stretched his neck until it popped, and turned to Bobbie.

"We've got a thing," he said.

"A good one or a bad one?" she said.

"One or the other."

Bobbie took a last mouthful of her breakfast, chewed, and swallowed. "Understood," she said. "Let's go."

Clarissa and Alex stood when she did. Part of her wanted to order them to stay back. If things went south, they'd be safe. As if anywhere was safe. She didn't say anything.

The old Belter led them to an access corridor with a ramp that sank down, out toward the skin of the drum and the emptiness beyond it, the void always just underfoot. They passed two different concealed guard posts that she saw, and while she didn't think there were any others that had escaped her notice, she couldn't be sure. The old Belter didn't say anything, and Amos didn't try to strike up a conversation.

The warehouse they ended up in was half filled with storage boxes fixed to the deck with maglocks. The lighting was harsh, restricted-wavelength worklights with a flicker that made her feel like her vision was strobing if she moved her hand too quickly. Three men leaned on the crates, their arms loose at their sides so they wouldn't have to spend the quarter second uncrossing them if things came to violence. Bobbie felt a warmth in her gut, a presentiment of trouble that was almost welcome. Invading ships with unimaginable weapons, protomolecule technology that could rip atoms apart, sudden empires imposed without warning or precedent. She'd grit her teeth and move forward because there wasn't another option. But thugs in warehouses was territory she understood.

The man in the middle of the three was a Belter, tall and muscular. His skin was the same brown as his hair and eyes. Even if he hadn't been pretty, he'd have been striking. And he was pretty.

"Heard you wanted to talk," he said.

Amos looked back at her, and pointed to the pretty man with his chin. He'd gotten them this far, but she was the boss. This was hers now.

"Who'd you hear we wanted to talk *to*?" Bobbie asked, stepping forward. Clarissa shifted out to her side. As weak and compromised as she looked, they'd underestimate her. Bobbie didn't know what using the implants would do to Clarissa, but by the time it took its toll, all three of the men would be incapacitated or dead. And that was without her and Amos weighing in.

The pretty man tilted his head.

"Names are dangerous, coyo," he said.

Bobbie pointed a thumb to herself. "Captain Bobbie Draper." She turned to the others. "Alex Kamal. Clarissa Mao. Amos Burton. Now, who the fuck are you?"

The pretty man scowled, tilting his head like he was trying to recall a song that was just at the edge of memory. It was a look she'd seen before, and she didn't feel like helping him place her. Not yet, anyway.

"Saba," the man said at last, "and that's enough for you right now."

"You're playing this all pretty close to the chest, Saba," Bobbie said.

"Not interested in being under the authority of the authorities," he said. "I've got reasons for that."

"Well, I'm not working for Laconia, so we can stop the bullshit, right?"

"Not sure we can," Saba said. His hand terminal chimed—a sound Bobbie didn't remember hearing since the crackdown—but he ignored it. Interesting that he had a working hand terminal, though. The chances that he was the real deal went up in her estimation.

"Heard you were looking to get in touch with the underground," Saba said. "Leaves a man wondering why. You looking to trade with the new boss?"

"Nope," Bobbie said.

"Then you thinking you're going to come tell us what to do?"

Bobbie smiled. She could feel her teeth against her lips. Either they were going to back each other down, or this was going to end in blood. She hoped it was the former, but it wasn't her call. "We were there when that fucking idiot tried to kill the governor. If that's the level you people are working at, then yes, I'd be happy to help organize. Someone ought to."

Saba's face was cool. "Belters been standing under the oppressors' boot for generations. You think you've got something to teach *us*?"

"Apparently so," Bobbie said. "Seems like some of you assholes have gotten pretty rusty."

A little darkness came to Saba's olive cheeks. He stood up, stepped forward. Bobbie took her own step in to meet him. If she showed weakness now, they'd never take her seriously again. The chirp of his hand terminal seemed to come from another universe.

"What?" Bobbie said, not giving him the tempo. "You planning to do this without any allies? Without any support? You against the Laconian Empire? I've seen how that went up to now, and—"

"Saba!"

The new voice came from behind her. She didn't want to turn her back on the three Belters, but she didn't want someone unknown at her back either.

"Saba!" the voice said again. It sounded young. Excited. Bobbie threw a glance over her shoulder. A young woman in a green jumpsuit, grinning like someone had just given her a present.

"Que, Nanda?" Saba asked.

"Found someone," the girl said. "Look."

And from behind the girl, Holden and Naomi came into the room, squinting at the ugly light.

"Hey!" Holden said, and then "Bobbie. This is great. I wasn't sure how we were going to find you."

Saba whistled low. "James fucking Holden. You'll no believe how much I've heard about you."

"All good, I hope?" Holden said, walking forward, oblivious

to the tension in the room. Or maybe choosing to ignore it. It was always hard to tell with him. "You've met my old crew already?"

"You crew?" Saba said, then looked at Bobbie as if seeing her for the first time. He laughed. "Savvy I did. Well, then. Welcome to the underground."

She smiled, but something ugly plucked at her guts. *James fucking Holden*, Bobbie thought. Three magic words, and just like that, someone else was in charge.

Chapter Nineteen: Drummer

The image was grainy, the sound almost as much noise as signal. Half a dozen encryption layers poured on and then stripped back out left their artifacts in the flattened audio and near-false colors. Drummer's heart softened all the same, because there in the middle of it—unmistakably—was Saba. His eyes had the little puff at the lower lid that he got when he was tired, but his smile was luminous.

"No savvy you how good it was to get your message, Cami," he said. "Heart outside my body, you are. And no one better than us two to be where we're sitting."

"I love you too," she told the screen, but only because no one else was in her office.

Avasarala's covert contacts had come through faster than Drummer had hoped. That they'd come through at all was something of a shock. She had been willing to believe the old woman was overstating her powers, claiming a level of influence that retirement and age had long since taken from her. But here was evidence that, whatever else she was, Chrisjen Avasarala wasn't completely full of shit. Saba had burrowed deep into Medina Station like a tick, making connections with as many union operatives as he safely could. And by union, more often than not, he meant OPA.

She listened and took notes by hand as he went through his full report. Writing it out helped her to remember. Sixty-eight people on Medina Station broken into independent cells that went from three to eight. The amateur, botched assassination and the crackdown that followed. Saba didn't have to say that he was using it to recruit more for his effort. That was obvious. The focus moving forward was intelligence gathering and infrastructure. Avasarala's network was all well and good, but having multiple backups, blind zones in the station where the Laconian security couldn't reach, and opening backdoors into the communications of the enemy were how to prepare for the next wave. And find out what the next wave was going to be.

Drummer found herself nodding with his words, thinking through their implications. The Laconians were routing their comms through a destroyer-sized ship docked on Medina with heavy encryption and an off-ship decrypt local to the station to physically isolate the two. No good way to gather intelligence there, and no chance of breaking into the enemy's system. She'd need to find the firmware code for the antennas and repeaters. Maybe Avasarala's henchmen in the Earth-Mars Coalition had some exploits they'd been sitting on that she could pass on to Saba. The Laconian checkpoints were tying up a third of their ground force. That kept the soldiers busy in the known and public corridors, and gave Saba's people more time to create bolt holes and blind zones. If the crackdown slacked off, they'd want to do something provocative to keep the enemy busy with identity checks and traffic control. Trivial security theater, while the underground dug more tunnels into the body of the station. It was possible that all the updated plans for Medina were in Laconian hands. Any known holes, they had to assume were known to all the players, but making new ones wouldn't be hard for Saba. He understood smuggling as well as she ever had, and maybe better.

The message ended with Saba's impish grin.

"You watch you, m'dil," he said, and blew a kiss to the camera. "Live like you're dead."

Drummer touched the screen as if it were his cheek, but it was cold and hard. *Live like you're dead.* There was a phrase she hadn't heard in a long time. Once, it had been the motto of the Voltaire Collective. A call to courage with a fatalistic bravado that angry adolescents found romantic. She'd found it romantic once too.

She checked the time. Saba's message had run almost twenty minutes. Part of her found it hard to believe it had been that long. She could have drunk in the sound of his voice for another hour and still been thirsty. From her screen after screen after screen of written notes, it was astounding that he'd fit so much information into so short a time.

She went through all she'd written again, committing it to memory, then wiped her notes. Information couldn't be compromised if it didn't exist. She put in a comm request for Vaughn. He answered immediately.

"Where do we stand with the military attaché?" she asked.

"Waiting on word from you, ma'am," Vaughn said.

"Have them in the conference room in ten minutes."

"Yes, ma'am," Vaughn said. There was a surreptitious pleasure in his voice. The diplomats and coordinators from the Earth-Mars Coalition had been flooding into People's Home since the fall of Medina, and Vaughn enjoyed telling them what to do. It was probably a vice, but she didn't mind indulging it.

Drummer rose from her desk and stretched. Her spine popped once between her shoulders, loudly. She yawned, but not from fatigue. It was the kind of yawn that a runner made before a race. The deep inhalation of someone anticipating great effort. If she'd been keeping a normal schedule, her watch would almost be over.

That wasn't how she lived anymore. Now she was awake when she needed to be awake, and asleep when she could. *Sin ritma* they'd called that lifestyle back when she'd been younger. It was harder on her body now, and it took an extra bulb of coffee to sharpen her mind sometimes, but it also left her smiling in a way she didn't wholly understand.

Benedito Lafflin, the EMC liaison, was waiting for her twenty minutes later. His fist was closed around a bulb of soda water that was already half collapsed. His wide, toadlike face looked less smug than usual. "Madam President," he said, standing.

Drummer waved him back down. As she sat, Vaughn brought her a bulb of tea. She took a sip. Hot, but not scalding. Vaughn drifted back to the wall like he was part of the ship's machinery.

"What are we looking at?" Drummer said.

Lafflin cleared his throat. "Candidly? I think you're going to be quite happy with the plan."

"Are you giving me direct control over your fleets?"

He blinked. "Ah...Well, that's..."

Drummer smiled. "I'll probably still be okay with it. What do you have?"

He took out a hand terminal and threw the data onto the conference room wall. The solar system unfolded before them. Nothing quite to scale, of course. Space was too huge and too empty for that. The fleets of Earth and Mars and the Transport Union were all outlined—location and vector for everything in transit, planetary body and orbital period for everything else. All of it tracked through time. Nothing was ever at rest.

And on the edge of the system, hell and gone from anything, the gate where the enemy would arrive.

"Given what we know about the enemy battleship," Lafflin began, "we have worked up several scenarios that we think will give our combined forces the best tactical advantage. The first, of course, being to interrupt it in transit."

"Walk me through it," Drummer said.

For the next two hours, Drummer reviewed scenario after

scenario after scenario. Lafflin made his case for each of them. Another person like him was with every member of the union board making all the same arguments. Soon the debates would start. With the void cities, the union had a fleet at least as powerful as the EMC. If Saba could make contact with ships in the colonies, it might be possible to coordinate attacks on the slow zone, no matter what Avasarala thought. If not, there was local action to be done on Medina that might be just as good or better.

Time after time, his plans came back to the same thing—protecting Earth, protecting Mars. Keeping the inners from being disrupted, no matter what the cost. Her guess was that the board would see the same things she did. And then...

She hadn't wanted to be a police force for the thirteen hundred worlds. She certainly hadn't wanted to lead a military. But with every new twist, every tactical suggestion, she heard the imagined voices of the board, of Secretary-General Li, of Avasarala. It wouldn't work. Someone was going to have to take charge, and she didn't see many scenarios where that wasn't her.

"Thank you," she said when the last of the imagined battles had played out on her monitor. "I appreciate your time. Let me confer, and we'll talk again in the morning?"

"Thank you, Madam President," he said as Vaughn escorted him out of the room.

As soon as he was gone, she pulled up the scenarios, paging through them all again without him. They'd considered mining their side of the gate with a wall of high-yield nukes, but abandoned it because no one was really sure if the ring could be damaged or not. A safer plan was a series of ships looping up above the ecliptic, doing a high burn and dumping gravel that could make a stone veil over the mouth of the gate. She would be able to control when there were gaps that allowed passage and when any ship making the transit would step into a shotgun blast. And it would last until they ran out of reaction mass and gravel. It was a Belter tactic. Another gift from the old days. She thought about putting the idea in her response to the EMC, but the truth was she didn't need their permission, and the void city Independence was close enough to the gate that if they went on the burn now, they could have something in place before the board even finished debating...

Drummer let her head sink into her hands. Her neck ached and a deep, vague craving bothered her—something like thirst, but without a clear sense of what could slake it. If anything could.

She heard the door open behind her, but she didn't bother looking up. Whoever it was, she didn't care. And anyway, it would only be Vaughn.

"Madam President," Vaughn said.

"Yeah."

"Something's come through you should probably see."

"Something wonderful that's going to fill my life with joy?"

"No."

She sat up, waving one hand in a circle. *Get on with it.*

"There's been a new transmission from Medina," Vaughn said. "On the official feeds."

"More threats and posturing from Laconia? Or have they made the war official?"

"Neither one," Vaughn said, and took the monitor focus. A simple video feed of a podium in front of a few tiers of chairs. Drummer was a little surprised by the simple blue curtains at the back. She'd expected more imperial pomp. A Signa Romanum with a double-headed eagle. The chairs were filled with people meant to look like journalists, whether they were or not.

Carrie Fisk walked into the frame and took her place at the podium. Drummer felt her mouth go hard.

"Thank you all for coming today," Fisk said, nodding to her audience. She gathered herself. Looked out, then down again. "Since its creation, the Association of Worlds has been a staunch advocate of independence and planetary sovereignty. As such, we have tracked issues of self-rule in the newly colonized systems and fought for the rights of people living on them. The hegemonic power of Sol system and the Transport Union have proven time and again that those in power have valued the systems unequally. Sol and the union have claimed a de facto sovereignty over what they have, through their actions, made clear they consider second-class planets and governments."

"Oh, fuck you," Drummer murmured. "Fuck you and your quisling bullshit."

"I have had the opportunity to meet several times with the representatives of the Laconian system about the future of the ring gates and the nature of commerce and governance between the worlds. And I am very happy to be able to say that the Association of Worlds has voted unanimously to accept Laconia's offers of protection and the coordination of trade. In exchange, High Consul Duarte has accepted the association's requirements for self-rule and political autonomy. With this—"

Drummer killed the feed. Duarte had planned this too. Not only the military campaign but the story that made it something other than a blatant conquest. *He came back because he thinks he can win, and if he thinks that, you should prepare yourself for the idea that it's true.* Carrie Fisk would be on the newsfeeds of thirteen hundred worlds—worlds that Drummer was cut off from— and the story she told would find rich enough soil to take root.

"Self-rule and political autonomy?" she said. "At the end of a gun? How does that work?"

"Tribute," Vaughn said. "A pledge of financial and resource support if called on, but with very little suggestion that there will be occasion for it."

"Plus the promise that he won't kill the shit out of them, I'm guessing?"

Vaughn's smile was flinty. "Fisk didn't make that explicit, but I think the implication's there, yes."

Drummer pressed her hand to her chin, stood up. Part of her wanted to send Vaughn to the med bay to come back with something to keep her awake. Amphetamines, cocaine, anything stronger than another bulb of tea.

"It's been a long day," she said. "When the EMC's messages

start coming through, tell them to calm their shit down, and that we're going to address this."

"And for the board members?" Vaughn asked.

"Tell 'em the same," Drummer said as she walked out. "Tell 'em it's all under control."

Back in her quarters, she stripped, leaving her clothes in a pathway from the door to the shower. She stood under the near-scalding water, letting it run down her back and over her face. It felt wonderful. Heat conduction as raw, physical comfort. Eventually, she killed the water, took a towel to sluice off most of the moisture, and then dropped to her crash couch, one arm flung over her eyes. Exhaustion pulled down into the gel more powerfully than the spin of the drum. She waited for the despair to come.

It didn't. The union was facing an existential threat. The fragile fabric of human civilization in the colonies was ripping before her eyes, and she was relieved. From her first memories to the death of the Free Navy, she'd been a Belter and a member of one faction or another of the OPA. Her brain and soul and identity had all matured with the inners' boot at her throat. At the throat of everyone she loved.

The respectability of Tycho Station and then of the union and now of the presidency had been her dream from the start. The prospect of a Belter reaching power equal to the inners had guided her on, if not for her, then at least a Belter like her. And like all dreams, the closer she'd come to it, the better she understood what it really was. For years, she'd worn power and authority like it was someone else's jumpsuit. Now, with Duarte and Laconia, everything she'd built was falling away. And part of her was happy about it. She'd been raised to fight against great powers. To wage wars she couldn't win, but also couldn't lose. Returning to that now was a staggering loss, but it also felt like coming home.

Her mind began to slip away, her consciousness falling into dream. History was a cycle. Everything that had happened before, all the way back through the generations, would happen again. Sometimes the wheel turned quickly, sometimes it was slow. She could see it like a feed gear, all teeth and bearings with her on the rim along with everybody else. Her last thought before forgetfulness took her and she fell deeply into slumber was that even with the gates, nothing really ever changed so much as repeated itself, over and over, with all new people, forever.

Which, in light of the next morning's first meeting, was more than a little ironic.

"We've never seen anything like this before." She'd known Cameron Tur professionally since she'd first taken a job with the union, and he'd never registered as more than vaguely interested in anything.

Now he sat across the table from her, gesturing with a tortilla like he was conducting an orchestra with it. His eyes were wide and bright, his voice higher and faster than usual, and she couldn't make out what the hell he was saying.

"Hot places in space," she repeated, looking at the schematic. "So, like stealth ships? Are you saying there are stealth ships waiting outside the ring gate?"

"No, no, no," Tur said. "Not that kind of hot. Not *temperature* hot."

Drummer gave a short, frustrated laugh and put the hand terminal down. "Okay, maybe we should try this again like you were talking to a civilian. There are these areas we've seen that are... what exactly?"

"Well," Tur said, nodding more to himself than to her. "Of course you know that a vacuum isn't really empty. There are always electromagnetic waves and particles that pop in and out of existence. Quantum fluctuation."

"My background is in security and politics," she said.

"Oh. Right," Tur said. He seemed to notice his tortilla, took a bite from it. "Well, vacuum state isn't at all just emptiness. There are always spontaneous quantum creations and annihilations. Hawking-Zel'dovich radiation that allows for—"

"Security, Tur. Politics and security."

"Sorry. Really small things just show up and then they just go away," Tur said. "Much smaller than atoms. It happens all the time. It's perfectly normal."

"All right," Drummer said, and took a sip of her morning coffee. Either it was a little more bitter than usual or she was overly sensitive today.

"So when we turned all the sensor arrays on the gate? To try to get more information about the war and all that? There was interference we couldn't make sense of. It was like the kind we see when signals pass through the gates, but it wasn't localized there. It was out in normal space." He pulled the schematic back up. "Here and here and here. That we know of. There may be others, but we haven't done a full sweep looking for them. But we never saw anything like this, and the logs make it seem like they may have appeared about the same time that the Laconian ship went through the gate. Or when it fired at the ring station. We don't have great data on timing."

"All right," Drummer said again. She was growing impatient.

"It's the rate, you see. The rates of quantum creation and annihilation are...they're through the roof. The uptick is *massive*."

She was still struggling to get her mind around the idea that emptiness wasn't empty, but something about the awe in Tur's voice sent a chill down her back all the same.

"So you're telling me...what exactly?"

"That the space near the ring started *boiling*," Tur said. "And we don't know why."

Chapter Twenty: Singh

Santiago Singh spent a very unpleasant few days dealing with the fallout from his newly announced security protocols for Medina Station. One by one, every bureaucrat and functionary called him to express their concerns over how the crackdown might negatively impact morale and efficiency on the station. However the conversations were phrased, what he heard in them was always the same. *The new rules will make people unhappy. They won't work as hard. Sabotage will increase. Are you sure we want to do this?*

His responses, however he put them, were also of a piece: *I don't care if people are unhappy about the new rules, if they fail to do their jobs, they will be fired, sabotage is punishable by imprisonment or death, yes, I'm sure.*

In High Consul Duarte's seminal book on logistics, he'd pointed out that of all the methods by which one can exert political and economic control over another state, occupation by military force was the least effective and the most unstable. The justification for occupation of Medina Station was that, as the checkpoint of all thirteen hundred colony worlds, it minimized the need for any further military action and let the imperial government move on quickly to economic trade and cultural pressure, which were much more stable long-term strategies for exerting control. And in fact, demonstrating to the people of Medina that the Laconian takeover would lead to better lives for all of them was the test case. If Singh could convince a station full of people bred for anarchy that imperial rule was desirable, the still-nascent colonies beyond the gates should be a piece of cake.

He understood all of this well enough. But it didn't change the fact that he'd had to spend his afternoon explaining to stupid, angry people why attempting to assassinate the governor of the station carried consequences.

When he cut the connection on what he hoped was the last of those complaints, he yelled out for someone to bring him coffee or tea or whatever else passed for a potable on that festering armpit of a station. No one replied. Because Kasik was dead and he hadn't yet brought himself to assign anyone new to his duties. As if by keeping the dead man on the roster, some part of him still remained that history hadn't erased.

For a moment, the buzz of activity and conversation, irritation and confrontation that he'd cultivated since the incident slipped away, and he saw Kasik spitting raspberry jam that was really his brain and his blood and part of his tongue—

Singh lost a few seconds. When he became aware again, he was on his knees next to his desk, vomiting into his trash can. From the state of the bin, he'd been at it for a while. The smell and look of the mess set off a new round of vomiting that only ended when his stomach clenched up painfully on nothing and a thin trickle of bile bit at the back of his throat. Delayed shock. Trauma reaction. It was normal, he told himself. Anyone would go through it.

"I'm so sorry, Kasik," he said, face suddenly covered in tears for a man whose first name he couldn't even remember.

The comm unit on his desk politely beeped. "Leave me the fuck alone," Singh yelled at it.

"Admiral Trejo is here for you, sir," a carefully neutral voice replied.

"Here?"

"In the security lobby, sir."

Singh cursed under his breath, soft but vicious. He grabbed the liner out of his trash can and stuffed it into the recycler. The air probably still smelled of sick. He turned the air recyclers as high as they would run to cut it.

"Put him through in one minute, please," Singh answered, then used the sixty seconds to wash his face and rinse out his mouth. Trejo had returned to Medina. It could have meant a number of things, but all of them meant he wanted to have a face-to-face conversation instead of trading messages through the comparatively glacial security apparatus that surrounded official communications. And that meant talking about sensitive issues.

"Sonny," Admiral Trejo said as he walked into the room. "You look a fright."

"Yes, sir," Singh agreed. "I'm afraid that recent events have shaken me a bit more than I expected. But I'm getting it secured. Shipshape and ready to sail, sir."

"Have you slept at all?" Trejo asked. He sounded genuinely concerned.

"Yes, sir," he said. And then, because it felt like lying, "Some, sir."

"It's hard losing someone. Especially someone you worked with closely."

"I'll be fine, sir," Singh said. "Please, take my desk."

Trejo's smile was sympathetic as he sat. He took the offered desk. "I have good news for you, at least. I passed along your findings on the gamma-ray bursts through the rings, along with your recommendation about using a ship with an ultrahigh magnetic field projector stationed in the slow zone to control access and passage. Naval high command was very intrigued. They took it all the way to the top."

The top meant only one person on Laconia. "I'm very flattered it got so much attention, Admiral."

"He agrees with you," Trejo said. His voice had a flatness that Singh didn't entirely understand. His green eyes flicked up to meet Singh's gaze and they stayed there. "They're sending out the *Eye of the Typhoon*. It'll take a bit for her to outfit. She wasn't scheduled to come through for another four months, but you'll have her with all deliberate speed. She'll have Medina Station defense as her official mission, but holding the ring system using your new data will be part of her parameters."

"Rear Admiral Song has that command, as I recall."

"Yeah, that's Song's boat," Trejo agreed. "But you're still governor of Medina. You'll have operational command over the defense of the station, and that includes determining when and if our new ring strategy is appropriate."

"Yes, sir," Singh replied.

"It'll be heady stuff, knowing an admiral has to dance to your tune, Sonny. Just remember that this posting won't last forever. Don't make any enemies you can't unmake." There was a weight to Trejo's words, like they carried more than just what they said. They landed on Singh's chest like a gentle rebuke.

"Understood and appreciated, Admiral," Singh said. "Will the *Tempest* remain here until the *Typhoon* arrives to take over?"

"No. We are moving up the timetable, per your analysis. The *Tempest* is leaving through the Sol gate in four hours. Unless you've reconsidered your position?"

Singh felt an offer in the question. This was the chance for him to say that he was out of his depth. That he needed backup and help. The temptation to claim perfect fitness was strong, but he couldn't dismiss the fact that he was, in fact, compromised. The question was whether his own frailty was enough to risk giving Sol system more time to prepare. The most dangerous part of the *Tempest*'s mission in Sol system was the transit through the gate and the hours immediately after it. The longer the enemy had to exploit that period of vulnerability, the less the time he'd won with his discovery of the gamma burst would gain them. He didn't want to undercut the advantage he'd just provided.

And still…

He started to reply, but stopped when the bitter-lemon taste of bile crept up the back of his throat again. *Not now.* He swallowed furiously, hoping this would be enough to hold off yet another round of vomiting into his trash bin. Trejo's eyes widened with what looked like genuine concern.

"Sonny," Trejo said, "have you seen a doctor?"

"Immediately following the attack. I sustained no injuries beyond a bruise on my knee and a bit of pride."

"That's not what I mean," Trejo said.

"I'll be fine," Singh lied, but Trejo didn't call him on it. "I know that the ring emissions were never part of the defensive strategy before, but I find myself worried about leaving such a powerful tool behind."

"Understood. I'll be honest, I'm not totally happy moving the timetable up. Slow and steady, that's the strategy I like best. But there's nothing so far to indicate the locals have made any breakthroughs we don't know about. The high consul thinks we can afford to pull the *Tempest* out past the gate early. It does feel a bit like I'm leaving you here with your ass hanging out. But there is exactly one fleet in known space that poses a threat to our plans here. And it's bottled up in the Sol system. You won't need to worry about defending Medina from it at all, because I'm going to force them to fight me on their home ground. I don't expect the colonies are going to cause you any trouble a destroyer can't handle."

"I agree, sir," Singh said. "We'll hold and wait for the *Typhoon*'s arrival, or word of your success in Sol, whichever comes first."

Singh expected this to end the conversation, and waited for Admiral Trejo to stand. Instead, the old man stared at him with thoughtful eyes until the silence had become uncomfortable. Etiquette dictated that he not close the interview until his superior dismissed him, so he stared back and tried for a vague smile.

When Trejo spoke again, his voice was lower. "Tanaka filed her report. She'll be boarding a shuttle shortly to take up a post on the *Tempest.*"

"Oh," Singh replied, hoping it came off as casual.

"Don't misunderstand me. She's a fine operator, and her experience is more than welcome there. But if there are problems with her, I would like to know what they are."

"I'm sure her talents will—" Singh started, but Trejo cut him off without raising his voice.

"If she's going to take a command role on my ship, I'm going to need to understand why you removed her from yours," the admiral said, his voice as gentle as though he'd asked for the time. "That's what I'm asking you for."

"Yes, sir," Singh replied. *If I understood it myself,* he thought. The fury at everyone and everything that had followed the attack had faded, leaving behind only a vaguely unsettled feeling, like the adolescent fear of forgotten homework. Like there was something that needed to be done, something that would cause trouble if it wasn't, but he had no idea what the thing was or even how to find out.

"Anytime, Sonny," Trejo said.

Singh took a deep breath that stuttered a little. He hated that it did. "It was my feeling, at the time, that failing to respond to the attack on my person, and by extension on the authority of the high consul and the empire itself, would only serve to embolden any dissident elements here on the station. I felt that a strong response was needed to enforce the message that this was now our station, that we weren't going anywhere, and that any attempt to hinder our work would fail. End the idea of a rebellion before it could begin."

"And you believe Colonel Tanaka didn't understand or support this position?" Trejo asked.

"She counseled a more conciliatory approach. I believe her

experience in the Martian military guided her here, but that it was not experience that translated well to this new situation. She disagreed, and stated that she would not support the new security measures, deeming them too harsh. I relieved her at that point."

"Why did her considerable experience not translate, do you think?" Trejo asked. The words could have been taken as mocking or rhetorical, but something in the old man's voice made it seem like genuine curiosity.

If there's no cover, the only thing to do is charge. How did he keep finding himself in these situations?

Singh cleared his throat. "Colonel Tanaka learned about rebel pacification by dealing with a belligerent but unaligned population. The Belters were *not* citizens of Mars, though they fell under Martian influence and regulation. To some degree, 'winning hearts' was always part of the mandate. She still thinks that way. She wants to approach this insurgency in that way. Crack down on only those involved in the attack, and attempt to win the cooperation of the rest of the populace through kindness."

"You disagree with this assessment," Trejo said.

"I do. By mandate from the high consul himself, all humans are citizens of the Laconian Empire. The people on Medina are not a neutral third party placed between us and an insurgent faction. They are *Laconians*, and the insurgents are not a foreign government resisting conquest, they are criminals. Any other reaction defies the imperial mandate and legitimizes them. I don't need to win their hearts. I need them to understand that all the previous political bodies and relationships are irrelevant. We are not conquering new territory, we are enforcing the law in our empire."

Trejo smiled. "That could have come straight out of a political theory class at the academy. I wasn't asking for a book report, Captain. Do you believe all of that is true?"

It was a strange question. "I wouldn't be here if I didn't, Admiral."

"It is certainly the official position of the empire, and accurately stated," Trejo agreed.

"Sir, if that's all, I—"

"Why," Trejo asked, as if Singh hadn't spoken at all, "did the high consul place you here, do you think?"

"Sir?"

"Your educational credentials are impeccable. I've read your paper analyzing Duarte's theories on empire through logistical control. And I'd bet even he was impressed. You attributed some truly unique ideas to his text that I'm pretty sure aren't actually in there."

"Thank you, sir," Singh replied, trying to keep it from sounding like a question and failing.

"But you did exactly one tour on a naval vessel prior to this posting. And there are probably a hundred more like me and Tanaka on Laconia who have actual combat-command experience. Why you and not any of them?"

Singh had wondered that himself. "I honestly can't answer that, sir."

"And that's the only right answer, Sonny. No, you don't know. But I'm going to give you a hint. Do you know how to polish a rock?"

"No, sir."

"You put it in a tumbler with a lot of other rocks and some sand and you roll them around for a couple of weeks until all the edges are worn off and they're nice and shiny. We're taking control of thirteen hundred different worlds, and we've only got a hundred old farts like me and Tanaka, and a couple thousand university-educated greenhorns like yourself."

Singh had no idea what a greenhorn was. It sounded like a Mariner Valley idiom. But the context was clear. And so was the point.

"Colonel Tanaka was placed here to—" Singh started.

"To rub some of the stupid off you. Tanaka's been fighting insurgents since before you were born. She's killed more people than you've met. But we've already got a Colonel Tanaka. Putting her in charge doesn't create anything new. Hopefully this little dust-up has knocked some of your edges off, or this will be a waste of everyone's time. Tanaka's scheduled to fly out in an hour. I think you owe her a conversation."

"Yes, sir," Singh replied. It tasted like more bile in his mouth, but the admiral was right.

Trejo rose. The meeting was ended.

"Dismissed, Captain. Make sure Medina's still here when I get back."

"Understood, Admiral."

The bravest thing would have been to go to the *Tempest*. The easiest thing, to record a message and send it through the Medina system where the security measures would forgive not having the conversation in real time. He split the difference.

The Belter whiskey that someone had left in his old cabin on the *Storm* tasted like acid and mushrooms, but Singh drank it anyway. The alcohol seemed to finally cut through the last of the bile in his mouth and throat. He kicked his boots off, propped his heels on his desk, and waited for the knot in his chest to loosen, even if only a little bit.

It should have been obvious from the start. Looking back on it, the only thing Singh had to recommend him for the governorship was his absolute commitment to High Consul Duarte's vision. But that's all they'd asked from him. They needed to take the inexperienced true believers like himself and drop them into the deep center of the lake, then hope they learned enough to swim back to shore. And everything about Tanaka: her arrogance, her contempt for his inexperience, her refusal to just accept his orders at face value. All of those were *exactly* the reason she'd been placed under his command. Throwing her out in a fit of pique was the sort of adolescent behavior they were trying to burn out of his system.

He had fucked it up.

The fact that Admiral Trejo understood that he'd done it in the blind panic that followed his first time under fire was both a relief and a humiliation. It was also probably the only reason he hadn't been relieved of command. Trejo saw what had gone wrong and still felt like Singh had something to offer. That he wasn't fit for the rubbish bin just yet. Comforting and humiliating, again.

He took another drink of the whiskey. It left his throat warm. That was about the best he could say for it. That was enough.

There was another trap ahead. Singh found that he could sense it. He could feel Trejo's attention, waiting to see how he'd navigate his way out now that his mistake had been made clear. The admiral had practically ordered Singh to speak with Tanaka before she left, so that's where the trap lay. He had a dozen different impulses about what that conversation would be, and he second-guessed every one of them as quickly as he recognized them. This was his command. So it was his to lose.

Maybe the right thing was to be willing to fail honorably. Even if he did get sent home to Nat and the monster, the disgrace would be less if he knew he'd done the fully adult thing.

He pulled the screen off his wrist and flattened it out on his desk. "Colonel Tanaka, video and voice," he said to it.

"Tanaka here," she said a moment later. On the small screen, her face was compressed down to only the most prominent features. Dark, heavy eyebrows. Wide jaw. Flattened, slightly off-center nose. It made her look dangerous and angry. She was probably both right now.

"Colonel," Singh said, trying to keep his tone even and informational. He thought he mostly succeeded. A call to finalize some trivial bureaucratic details.

"Governor," she said, actually achieving the emotionless affect he was only trying for.

"I spoke to Admiral Trejo about your transfer. He said he was happy to move you into a command position on the *Tempest*, and I did nothing to dissuade him from this."

"Thank you for not attempting to torpedo my career," she said, not sounding grateful at all. The fact that she didn't say, *Fuck you, little man, you couldn't have hurt me even if you wanted to* was as polite as this was likely to get.

"I want you to know that I recognize that in my heightened emotional state following the attack, I made some poor decisions, not least of which was removing you from your command."

There was a pause. A fraction of a fraction of a second, but it was there.

"Really," she said. The large eyebrows moved up a millimeter.

"Yes. And if I could take that back without compounding my error, I would. But the most important thing now, to both my staff and to the citizens of Medina, is the appearance of calm authority at the top. To make so drastic a move as relieving you only to rescind it would make us...make *me* appear weak and indecisive. So your transfer will be recorded as a move to put additional combat experience on Admiral Trejo's staff, now that we've secured the station and he's moving into the attack on Sol. It will not put a blemish on your outstanding record. Unfortunately, my apologies and regrets will have to remain unofficial for now."

Tanaka frowned, though it looked more like surprise than anger. "I appreciate that, Governor."

"Good luck and godspeed in Sol, Colonel. We will all be waiting for word of your mission's success. Singh out."

He closed the connection and drank off the last of the terrible Belter whiskey. He wasn't sure if it was the alcohol, but he felt like a weight he'd been carrying ever since landing on Medina was lifting. This was *his* station now. His command, to fail or succeed at entirely on his own merits. And now he felt that the worst mistake he was likely to make was behind him, and it hadn't actually been all that bad.

Things could only get better from here.

Chapter Twenty-One: Holden

Rather than leave them sneaking into and out of the refugee camps in the drum or Laconian-assigned quarters, Saba gave Holden and the crew access to a smuggler's cabin: a six-rack berth his people had carved out of a service tunnel where the station records were out of date and missing. It was a tight fit, and Alex snored a little, but it was better than the alternatives.

The room where they spent most of their time had been meant for midlevel storage. Not the deep pockets of the generation ship traveling through the vast abyss between the stars. Not the immediate, day-to-day pantry of the men and women whose lives would begin and end in the journey without seeing either end. Built-in yellow guides marked where crates of tools and imperishable rations would have been stacked along the deck and walls. History hadn't taken the room that way.

Cushions of gel and fabric covered the floor around a half-dismantled holographic display that acted as a low table. The air recyclers were set to minimum to keep the usage footprint of the space as low as it could be, and a battery-driven fan moved the thick air. Lengths of printed textile—Holden couldn't tell if it was cloth or plastic or carbon mesh—draped the walls and rustled in the little breeze. He didn't know if those were functional somehow, or if the impulse to decorate interiors just outlived all political circumstances. Mostly, it reminded Holden of a Moroccan restaurant he used to go to on Iapetus, back when he'd been hauling ice for Pur 'n' Kleen.

Saba and four people Holden assumed were his lieutenants sat across from him and the crew and refilled their cups with a smoky tea whenever they got low. In addition to being captain of a supply ship called the *Malaclypse* that was stuck in dock just like the *Roci*, Saba was married to Drummer. At first, Holden had been worried that what he'd done with Freehold was going to haunt him, but when he brought it up, Saba had waved it away. *It happened in a dream*, Saba said, which was a little confusing until Naomi told him it was an old-timey Belter idiom for *Don't worry about it*.

Even after a long life spent outside Earth's gravity well, Holden was impressed by all the things he didn't know.

"Perdón," a Belter woman said, squeezing her way past the guard at the door. "Saba? Are you ready for food yet?"

Saba mostly managed to keep his smile polite. "No, Karo. Bist bien."

The woman bobbed her hands, nodding like a Belter. She swept her gaze over the rest of them, but paused a little bit at the *Rocinante*'s crew—Holden, Naomi, Bobbie, Alex, Amos, and Clarissa. "Any of you? We've got mushroom bacon."

Bobbie cracked her knuckles meditatively. Holden was pretty sure that was a sign of annoyance.

"That's fine," he said. "We're good. Thank you."

The woman bobbed her hands again and squeezed back out. It was the third interruption of the morning. That was a little strange, but Holden put it down to a level of general anxiety for everyone. With the occupying force settled in, the freedom Saba's underground had to operate was thin as a razor blade, but everyone still wanted to be doing something.

"I'm sorry," Holden said, shifting which leg was folded under him. If he was always going to have one leg asleep, better to alternate them, he figured. "You were saying?"

Saba leaned forward. It didn't seem like sitting on the cushions made his legs go to sleep, but he was younger than Holden by a decade or two. "We need to find the balance, sa sa? The more of our own that we build, the more there is for us to use. But the more there is for them to find."

One of Saba's lieutenants, who'd spent the morning arguing for building a fully separate comm system by threading hair-thin cables through the water system, cleared her throat.

"The way I see it, we serve three masters: making space for ourselves, making tools for ourselves, and keeping space and tools from the inners. We have three percent of Medina now set where security can't see it. We have support from the crew. We have transmission out to and back from Sol gate. Have to look at the margin of what we risk against what we'd get from it. All I'm saying."

"Well, sure," Holden said, and Saba tilted his head. In his peripheral vision, Bobbie leaned in. When he looked over at her, her expression was empty, but he had years of experience to tell him she was evaluating something. A threat, maybe, except that she was looking at him.

Holden shifted his legs again. "It's just that anything we do, we have to assume it's temporary, right?"

"Can't build on stone out here," Saba said with a grin, but Holden was pretty sure he hadn't understood the point he was getting at.

"Medina is our station," Holden said. "We know it better. All the niches and passages, all the undocumented features. All the tricks and doors and corners. And that's going to be true right up until it isn't. These people aren't dumb. They're busy right now, and maybe they'll stay that way for a while. But sooner or later, they are going to get to know the station. Our advantage only lasts for as long as it takes them to learn. So whatever we do here, it shouldn't be planning for the long term. We don't have a long term. We've got a short term, and maybe a medium term. Like, *maybe*?"

Saba shifted, sipped his tea, and nodded. "Good point, coyo," he said. "Maybe also, we start looking at evacuation plans. How not to spend a long life in a jail cell or a short one in an airlock."

"Whatever goals we pick," Holden said. "I just don't think we should spend the extra effort to make it something that's going to last a decade when we're probably looking at less than eight or ten weeks of freedom."

The way he said it, it sounded like an apology. Saba rubbed his palm across his chin. The room had gone so quiet, Holden could hear the hush of the man's stubble against his hand even over the whir of the fan. Eight or ten weeks of freedom. It was the first time anyone in the meetings had guessed at the time frame. Whatever little apocalypse took out the underground, Holden expected it would be less than a springtime back on Earth.

"Is fair point," Saba said as a noise came from the corridor. Voices. A thin-faced man with a scar over his left eye leaned into the room, looked around, and nodded.

"New reports from upstairs if you want them," Scar-eye said. "Doesn't look like much of anything new. Checkpoints still on the move, and they put some stupid coyo in their public prison for being out after curfew, is all."

"I don't think—" Saba began.

Bobbie interrupted him. "Maybe you should. We could take a break. Right, Holden?"

"Um," Holden said. "Sure."

Saba shrugged with his hands. "Bien á. Maybe bring in some lunch, yeah?"

The meeting shifted. It was all the same people in the same space, but the motion of it changed. Holden leaned in and kissed Naomi gently on the cheek. She leaned her head against his as if it were only affection.

"What the fuck is going on?" Holden whispered. "Did I do something to piss Bobbie off? Because I really try not to do that unintentionally."

Naomi shook her head so slightly, he only felt it. "You'll have to ask her what's up," Naomi said. "But you're not wrong. It's something."

The conversations in the room rose and shifted, swirling like birds. A word or phrase that passed between Amos and Clarissa got overheard by one of Saba's people, shifted what he was saying, and soon Saba mentioned it to Alex. *Controlling people is usually having stuff they want. Don't want nothing, and they're pretty much just down to hitting you until you do what they say* became *Was easier with the inners because they wanted to get rich and make rich-people toys* became *What do these Laconia coyos want, anyway? What do they think they do it for, yeah?* Everyone in conversation with everyone else, whether they were aware of it or not.

Holden watched it, listening and waiting for Bobbie to come over. If humanity ever developed a hive mind, it wouldn't be psychic brain links that welded it together. It'd be gossip and cocktail parties.

"Hey, Holden," Bobbie said, touching his shoulder. "Can I borrow you for a minute?"

"You bet," he said, hauling himself up from the floor. Bobbie slouched out toward the corridor, and he followed. The air outside the room was cooler and seemed less like it had just come out of someone else's lungs. The lighting was strung maintenance LEDs, harsh and bright. The walls were painted in a dozen different colors, guides to the pipes and conduits behind them. The map and the territory both.

Bobbie paused at the junction of a service crawl with the main corridor. Voices murmured behind them, too distant to make out, but present. As tight as the spaces were, she could have leaned against both corridors' walls at the same time, one with each shoulder. She flexed her hands like a fighter about to go into the ring. There had been a time, when they'd first met, that he'd found Bobbie's physicality intimidating. Over the years, she'd grown in his mind into a place where she was only herself. Every now and again, he'd be reminded that she was a professional warrior and well trained in violence.

Her expression was intense, focused. She could have been thinking her way through a hard problem or restraining herself from a killing rage. The two looked similar with her.

"Hey," Holden said. "What's on your mind?"

Her focus shifted to him, and she nodded like he'd said something worth agreeing to. "So are you here to help this or hinder it?"

"Well," Holden said. "I would have said help until you asked me that, but now it's feeling like a trick question. Am I missing something?"

Bobbie put out her hand palm first, like she was telling someone to slow down, but it seemed intended as much for herself as for him. "I'm thinking this through while I'm saying it, so just…"

"Got it," Holden said. "Whatever it is, take a swing at it. We'll work it out."

"Other people? People like me? We can show up and maybe not have an effect. That's not how it is with you. Either you're helping or you're holding things back. There's no middle setting."

A little discomfort tugged at him, and he crossed his arms. "Is this…Bobbie, is this about you being the captain of the *Roci*? Because that hasn't changed. Naomi and I—"

"Yes," Bobbie said. "It's exactly like that. Look, you've seen all those people who keep interrupting the meetings, right? They're all just swinging by to be in the room for a minute, even if it's something they could have done on hand terminals. Or not done at all."

"I know the ones you mean," Holden said. "But that's not me."

"That's *absolutely* you. James Holden, who led the fight against the Free Navy. And stopped Protogen from killing Mars. And captained the first ship through the ring gates. Brought people together on Ilus in the face of fifty different kinds of shit falling apart. You're in the center of everything just by walking into the room."

"Not because I like it," Holden said.

"When you showed up, Amos and I were getting ready to fight our way into all this. But then there you were, and you got recognized, and now we're all sitting in the absolute center of the conspiracy. Even if I'd pushed my way into this, there would have been days, maybe weeks, of proving to Saba and his people that they could trust me. You got that for free, and the rest of us drafted off you. I came in as the captain of the *Rocinante*, and it wasn't enough to be taken as seriously as you got for free."

Holden wanted to object. He could feel the denials welling up in his chest, but he couldn't quite bring himself to say them out loud. Bobbie was right.

"I have an idea how we gather intelligence on the Laconians," Bobbie said. "It's the first step that we need. But we have to move quickly. Saba and his people? They think this is like going back to before there were gates. No matter what they say, they think this is going to sustain and become a way of life for them the way it used to be. Did you notice how they've started calling the Laconians 'inners'?"

"Yeah, I did."

"But you were right in there. We're looking at a really small window. So if we're going to do what I think we really need to do? It has to be your idea."

"Okay, little lost here. Which idea of mine are we talking about?"

"I'm talking about you taking the operation I have in mind,

waltzing back in there, and presenting it like you just came up with it yourself."

Holden didn't know whether to laugh or scowl, so he did a little bit of both.

"No, I'm not going to do that," Holden said. "You say what you need to say, and I'll back you. But I'm not going to start taking credit for your proposals."

"If it's my idea, it'll be like when we showed up," Bobbie said. "I'll have to fight to prove it. If you do it, they'll just listen. Coming from you will give it weight that just being the right damn thing won't."

A clank came from behind them, a hatch being opened or a tool being dropped. He didn't turn to look. The unease he'd felt before shifted, changed its nature, but it didn't go away.

"I don't like that," Holden said. "I hate the idea that you're being treated as anything less than me. It's bullshit. I'll tell Saba that—"

"You remember the last time we went out to karaoke with Giselle? Right before Alex and she called it quits?"

Holden blinked at the non sequitur. "Yeah, of course. That was a terrible night."

"You remember the song she sang? 'Rapid Heartbeats'?"

"Sure," Holden said.

"Who was the singer? On the original, I mean. Who sings that one?"

"Um," Holden said. "The band is Kurtadam. The singer's Peter something? The guy with the one steel eye."

"Pítr Vukcevich," Bobbie said, nodding. "Now, who plays bass?"

Holden laughed, and then a moment later, sobered.

"Right?" Bobbie said.

"Yeah, okay. I got it. I don't like it, though. I'm not more significant than anyone else. Acting like everything important has to go through me or else it's not legitimate...I don't know. It feels like I'm being an asshole."

Bobbie put a hand on his shoulder. Her eyes were calm, and her smile was a straight line. "If it helps at all, I'm thinking about all of this as me using you as a tool to achieve my own ends. It makes me less angry that way."

They talked for another twenty minutes, Bobbie laying out her plan in enough detail that he could introduce it. He asked a few questions, but he didn't need many. The sense of working together with her had a weird nostalgia. As if the gap between arriving at Medina and now had been years instead of days.

Large, sudden events did that. They changed the way time passed. Not technically, maybe, but as a measure of who he and Bobbie were to each other. And to themselves. A month before, Laconia had been one background issue among thousands. Now it was the environment. A truth as profound as the EMC or the union. More, maybe.

Back in the meeting room, the food had arrived. Recycled wheatpaper bowls filled with rice noodles and chopped mushroom bacon and fish sauce. It smelled better than it should have. Bobbie went to sit by Alex and Clarissa, folding herself gracefully down beside them. Holden felt the impulse to go sit there too, to be part of the family again. And he could have, except he also sort of couldn't. Would he be doing it to help or to hinder? Because he couldn't do both. For the first time, he felt what stepping back from the *Roci* had cost him.

And still, he couldn't regret it.

"All well?" Naomi asked, snaking her arm around his waist. "You look thoughtful. Are there thoughts?"

"There were a few, yeah," he said. "Mostly that I'm a tool, but in a useful way."

Naomi sat with that for a moment. Saba caught sight of them and waved them over. Two bowls with forks and bottles of beer were waiting on the low table for them.

"Should I be offended on your behalf?" Naomi said.

"Nope," Holden said. "You should come eat."

Saba leaned forward as Holden sat. "This is good. One thing we can say about Medina, the ingredients are always fresh."

"True," Holden said. "But they're usually still fungus and yeast. Vat-grown bacon is…well, it's just its own thing. So, Saba, I had an idea I want to talk to you about…"

Chapter Twenty-Two: Bobbie

W e can't place a physical monitor on the data connection to the Laconian ship," Holden said, just the way she'd told him to. Saba had chosen the people to be briefed, selecting them by some means Bobbie didn't know and didn't care to guess. They were watching Holden intently. It felt weird that the role of the great James Holden, come to lead them to glory, was being played by the Holden she knew. Apart from the coincidence of naming, the two didn't have much in common. "We need to passively monitor incoming and outgoing signal without detection. Mirror the data."

"For for?" a tall, stick figure of a man said. His name was Ramez and he was in Medina Station's technical support department. According to Saba, he had the run of the ship, their insider on this mission. Bobbie didn't like him. "Alles la thick with encrypt. Better off reading their coffee grounds."

"Decrypting it is a later problem," Holden said, not giving too many details of the plan away to any one person. Bobbie had a decent idea, but she was still working out the details of how to get the decryption codes. The fewer people knew the details, the less likely it was to get out before she was ready. "Right now we just want to get as much as we can so that we can decrypt it when the time comes. The important aspect right now is that we get the signal without anyone knowing it's happening."

"Gotta look inside the pipe without touching the pipe. Que pensa?"

"I've brought along my team leader and technical expert to explain the how of the thing," Holden said, nodding to Bobbie and Clarissa. "Captain Draper?"

Bobbie gave him a wink only he could see. Say what you would about the man, he did take to the role of meaningless figurehead with panache.

Bobbie walked to the front of the room and pulled up a volumetric map of Medina on the wall display behind her.

"The *Nauvoo* was intended as a generation ship," she started.

"Fuck is a 'no view'?" a Belter woman asked. The others chuckled.

"Read some fucking history once," Saba said to her, then nodded to Bobbie to continue.

"They knew she'd be picking up signals from farther away than anything had ever needed to before," Bobbie said. She zoomed in on Medina's comm array. "So the comm system is massively overpowered, *and* much more sensitive than anything on a commercial or military vessel."

Ramez nodded and shrugged expansively with his long hands. "We don't even use most of that shit. No one talking from far away in here."

He meant inside the slow zone, and he was right. Nothing was ever more than half a million klicks from Medina. The physical boundaries of the space prohibited it.

"True, but the equipment is still there. And up on that comm array is a signal sniffer sensitive enough to track a single photon through a fiber bundle a meter thick," Bobbie said, zooming in on the technical map behind her. "But we can't just steal it. Claire?"

Clarissa pushed herself out of the corner she'd been hiding in and came to stand next to Bobbie. She wore a mechanic's jumpsuit with the name TACHI on the back, and had her hair pulled into a tight bun. With her gaunt cheeks and sunken eyes, it made her look severe and impatient.

"Even though this array isn't in use," Clarissa said without preamble, "it's still hooked to the primary comm system. If we start unplugging things, alarm bells are going to go off up in ops. So we need to put the circuits into a diagnostic shutdown before we physically yank the parts."

"Fuckonians all over in ops now, ninita," Ramez said. "Watching everything all the time, them."

Clarissa nodded her agreement, then said, "And that's where you come in. We need to get you onto the ops deck to shut down the panel long enough for us to do our work," she said. "And also if you call me 'little girl' again, I will hurt you."

"Is that right, *ninita*?" Ramez said, his grin turning condescending.

"No," Bobbie said, stepping toward him. "No, that's not right. Pulling that gear will be delicate work. I can't risk her damaging her hands before we get out there." Bobbie took another step into Ramez and stared down at him. "So *I'll* hurt you. Mao's my second on this. Don't make me beat some respect into you, *ninito*."

She glanced over at Holden. He looked shocked, and maybe a little sad. She wondered how he would have handled it, back before. It was so strange to be doing all this in the same room with each other.

Ramez threw a look to his buddies on the crates. No one stepped up to back him up. Saba was smiling and making a *Let's get on with it* circular motion with his hand.

"Sabe," Ramez said, looking to the side the way abashed primates had since the Pleistocene. "Just for fooling, que?"

"Sa sa," Bobbie replied, then switched the screen from the volumetric map over to her mission plan. "Here's the rundown, including precise times for each thing to happen. Mao and I will be on the outside of the station for most of this, and we can't afford to do any broadcasting out there, because the Laconian sniffers will almost certainly pick it up."

"I'll be calling up to ops using an unlocked hand terminal that Ramez here will get for me," Holden said, nodding at the man as an invitation for him to nod back. "We're picking a time when Daphne Kohl is the duty officer. She knows me now, and I'm thinking she'll understand what we're trying to do without me having to explain it. Comm discipline is in full effect, the assumption is everything is heard by everyone."

"So that call between Kohl and Holden is what we're all listening to," Bobbie said. "We'll pass out a list of code words Holden will use during the call as signals. This is our only method of coordinating the action, and there's no way for us to signal an abort or call for help. Our backup plan is everyone does this right the first time so we don't need a backup plan. Understood?"

"Lot of risk for a dump of gibberish we can't make sense of," Ramez said.

Bobbie felt a little flush of annoyance at the man. "The more we have, the more likely we find what we need in it when the encryption problem gets fixed," she said. "We start where we can, and that's this. Are we all clear?"

A murmur of *dui* and *sabe* and *sa sa* rippled through the room.

"Outstanding," Bobbie said. "Let's get to work."

The slow zone or *the ring space* or *the gate network*. No matter what you called it, it was fucking weird.

Bobbie and Clarissa exited the drum section of Medina Station using an old maintenance airlock that Saba swore wasn't monitored from ops. They were wearing emergency vac suits, the so-thin-they're-barely-there type whose only purpose was keeping the wearer from dying of asphyxia before help could arrive. They were bright orange and yellow to make the wearer easy to find in smoke or against the black of space. They had large flashing lights on the helmet and shoulders to aid rescue workers, but Bobbie had smashed those with a wrench before they put them on. Bad enough to be a brightly colored blob climbing up the outside of the station. No reason to flash a distress signal too. Under normal circumstances, going outside a ship or station wearing the emergency suits was asking to be cooked by radiation. The cheap throw-away suits had almost no shielding to them.

But the slow zone was fucking weird.

There was literally no radiation in the ring space that humans didn't bring in with them. No background radiation, no solar wind, nothing. Just a massive, unnaturally black void all around, defined only by the distant and faintly glowing rings equally spaced around it and the blue sphere of the alien station at the center where they'd had the rail-gun emplacements.

Bobbie and Clarissa rode the outside of the massive, spinning drum section of Medina inside the old airlock. The indicator of their motion being the occasional distant ring moving past the black window of the outer airlock door, and the fact that something kept trying to shove them out the door at a third of a g. Bobbie had them both tethered to a clip inside the airlock so they wouldn't be hurled into the strange non-space outside.

A large rectangular structure whipped past the outer airlock door. Bobbie pressed her helmet to Clarissa's and yelled so that sound would conduct directly. "That's one of the exterior elevators. We go for the next one."

Clarissa nodded, wide-eyed, and braced for the jump. Outside of the drum section of Medina, two structures ran the entire length of the ship from the engineering deck aft of the drum to the ops deck in the bow. They housed machinery, conduit, and a pair of elevators for moving from one zero-g section to the other without passing through the drum itself. Bobbie and Clarissa planned to use one of them to climb the station up to the comm array on the nose, and back down to the Laconian ship docked at the stern.

Bobbie opened the mesh bag at her hip, checking again that she had everything the same way she had a dozen times before. Spare air bottles for herself and Clarissa. They'd be outside for hours making the long climbs. A magnetic grappling gun with high-tensile cable and a winch. And finally, a fat black recoilless handgun that one of the Belters had managed to hide from the Laconian weapon sweeps. If they actually needed to use it, the mission was fucked anyway, but there was a dignity in going down fighting that appealed to Bobbie's romantic notions.

She hooked the emergency cable on her suit to a loop at Clarissa's waist, then unhooked herself from the airlock. The station tried to throw her out the door, but she grabbed the lip of the outer airlock with one hand and held on. In the other hand, she held the grapple gun. Behind her, Clarissa had one hand on her shoulder, and one hand on the bulkhead.

"Three, two, one, go!" Bobbie shouted, hoping enough sound would travel up Clarissa's arm. She launched herself out the outer airlock door by releasing her grip on it, and was shooting off into the void at 3.3 meters per second.

The massive rectangular structure of the maintenance shaft rushed toward her, and she fired the magnetic grapple into it as she passed. If the grapple failed to connect, they'd keep flying off into the empty space of the slow zone until they ran out of air and their lifeless bodies eventually flew into the eerie curtain of black at the edge of the alien space. Dangerous, but no more so than a challenging free climb back on Mars. She didn't even think about it. Her eye spotted the place she wanted the grapple to go, her hand and arm did the rest. The grapple landed less than half a meter from the spot she was aiming for. Like riding a bike.

The grappling line and the leash that connected the grappling gun to her suit snapped taut and pulled her in a fast arc around the maintenance shaft, dragging Clarissa helplessly behind. Bobbie started up the winch, pulling them closer as the speed of their arc increased. Just before impact, she bent her knees and activated her mag boots. The landing was going to hurt a bit.

She hit the metal surface of the maintenance shaft like the tip of a whip being cracked, and let the impact fold her knees up into her abdomen. Clarissa slammed into her back, and it felt like someone dropping a bag of cement on her from a couple stories up. Bobbie rolled with it, slapping the decking with her hands to activate the glove magnets, and hung on.

A few punishing seconds later, they were on the side of the maintenance shaft, all the violence of their motion gone, having been converted into lightly sprained knees and a collection of bruises.

"Ouch," Bobbie said, and floated motionless for a few seconds, tethered to the shaft by only one gloved hand.

"Yeah," Clarissa replied, faintly, through the helmet she had against Bobbie's back.

Bobbie pushed her helmet against Clarissa's. "It's a long climb, but at least there's no gravity to fight. You up for this?"

Clarissa answered by unhooking the tether, and pulling herself up the flat gray wall of the shaft.

"Alrighty, then," Bobbie said, and followed.

Two hours and an O2 bottle change later, they floated near the massive Medina comm array. A bewildering cluster of antennae, dishes, and radio broadcast towers, and at its heart sat a laser powerful enough to send messages back to Earth from a hundred light-years away. It had never been used.

"I remember when that almost ended all human life," Clarissa said, pressing her faceplate to Bobbie's. "It doesn't look so scary now."

"I've heard that story," Bobbie replied. "Wish I'd been here to back you guys up in that fight."

Clarissa shrugged. "The story's more fun than the actual experience was. You didn't miss much."

Clarissa pulled herself over the rigging of the comm array, coming to a stop next to an oversized receiver dish. She pointed at an access panel below it, then flashed the Belter sign for *This one.*

Bobbie nodded with one hand, then tapped the side of her helmet. *Now we wait for word from Holden.* She turned on the small emergency radio in her suit, already tuned to the channel Holden would be using to call Daphne Kohl up in station ops, and waited. Clarissa stared at her across the vacuum between them, motionless and patient as a hunting cat.

The minutes dragged. When her radio crackled to life, Bobbie found herself grinning. "Medina control, this is workcrew kilo alpha, do you copy?"

Bobbie could only hear Holden's side of the conversation, so there was a long pause and then his voice again. "Copy that. Can I get Chief Kohl on the line? Gotta route some repairs though her office."

Office was their code that meant Ramez was outside of ops, waiting for permission to enter, so the plan was proceeding, and waiting only on Kohl's cooperation.

"Hey, Chief. Good to *hear your voice* again," Holden said, hitting the words hard. He hadn't identified himself by name, and he wouldn't. If Daphne Kohl didn't pick up on what was going on, they'd scrub the mission. If she raised the alarm...Well, that would be an interesting problem. "Working with Saba down here in electrochemical. Tracking a grid problem that Laconian death ray caused, and we'd love to pull a panel up there to really nail it down."

And here's where the most dangerous part of the plan happened. It wasn't flying through space on a tether, or climbing up the outside of a massive station wearing the thinnest and crappiest vacuum suits. It wasn't even going to be later, when they climbed down to the Laconian ship to hook in their signal sniffer, hoping no one was watching the outside of the dock. It was here, where Holden was counting on his voice, Saba's name, and the mention of Laconians to signal Kohl that they were up to no good and needed her help.

And more than that, counting on her Belter pride being stronger than her fear of execution by their Laconian masters. Because if any of those things weren't true, Kohl could refuse them, and that was the end of the plan. Or worse.

Bobbie waited a very tense minute of radio silence, and then Holden said, "That's great. I've got a tech heading to ops to pull that panel, if you can let him in. He'll take a gander at our glitch and get out of your hair."

Gander. Code for *Go in five.*

"Copy that, Chief. We appreciate the patience while we sort this out."

Bobbie gave Clarissa a thumbs-up, then flashed her five fingers. Clarissa nodded with her fist, then started pulling tools out of the mesh bag at her hip.

First thing down, Bobbie thought. Just a two-kilometer climb aft and planting a bug on a Laconian destroyer without getting caught left to go.

With Medina Station functionally motionless in the slow zone, it was less of a climb than a mag-booted shuffle down the two-kilometer length of the maintenance shaft. Bobbie pulled the blocky module containing the field-strength sensor on a short leash behind her. It didn't have much mass, but she'd taken it without conversation when she'd looked through Clarissa's visor and seen the technician's complexion going a sickly gray. Other than jumping out of a rotating airlock, they hadn't done anything particularly taxing, but it was pretty clear that Claire was already running on fumes.

As they got closer to the engineering-and-docking-bay section of Medina, the Laconian ship came into view around the curve of the station. Bobbie couldn't help but whistle her appreciation of the beauty of the thing. Say what you would about Laconian authoritarianism, their engineering included a lot of aesthetic beauty in its design.

The destroyer—Holden had called it the *Gathering Storm*—looked like a natural crystal formation that someone had chipped into a knife. The colors were all translucent pinks and blues, faceted like a gem. She spotted something at the tail that probably served as the ship's drive cone but didn't look anything like the UN or Martian designs she was familiar with. The nose of the ship ended in a pair of sharp projections, like a dagger point with a channel cut down the center that left her almost certain it was a rail gun. If the ship had torpedo launchers or PDCs, she couldn't see them.

The ship was so strange, so unlike anything humans had ever designed or flown before, that if it had docked and green three-eyed aliens had walked off, it would have felt more appropriate than the humans that actually flew her.

Clarissa stopped and turned, so Bobbie yanked the sensor array to a stop on its leash, then pushed their two helmets together.

"There," Clarissa said, pointing to a maintenance access hatch that looked exactly like a hundred they'd already passed. "That's the router that feeds from the dock into the station network."

"You're sure?" Bobbie said, looking around at all the other hatches.

Clarissa didn't answer, just rolled her eyes and took the leash. She pulled the sensor array down and attached it to the hull, right next to the hatch. She pulled a few leads from the box and plugged them into slots inside the hatch, then stuck a hand terminal on the side of the array and spent several minutes going through what looked like menus. Bobbie replaced both of their air bottles while she worked.

A few minutes later, Clarissa stood up and gave her the thumbs-up. Bobbie looked over at the massive blade of the Laconian destroyer. If anyone on it had seen them working, the ship itself gave no hint. Clarissa walked over holding her hand terminal and touched it to the side of Bobbie's helmet. Her HUD snapped on, and a wall of text rolled past. The signal traffic between the destroyer and the local decrypt facility, complete with routing flags and timestamps. It was still locked behind military encryptions, but everything that the *Gathering Storm* sent down to Medina and everything it got back was here, and the underground was skimming a copy of all of it.

"Huh," Bobbie said to no one. "I honestly thought that would be harder."

Chapter Twenty-Three: Drummer

The ship came through the ring like an old video of a whale breaching the surface of the sea. The thousand kilometers of the ring gate was tiny in the scale of the solar system, huge by human measure, and the Laconian battleship fit between the two—too large to be comfortable in one, too small to fit well in the other. Its design seemed to come from the same uncomfortable place, neither the now-familiar eeriness of the protomolecule nor the history of human manufacture, but both and neither. Drummer watched the observations feed again and again, and it made her skin crawl a little every time.

She wasn't ready. Rock hoppers full of gravel were burning hard for positions that didn't matter anymore. The EMC fleet was consolidating around the inner planets and the Jovian system, but with days—sometimes weeks—left on their burns. The void cities were looping down to meet them. All of it preparation for tactical situations that weren't on the board anymore. Duarte and his Admiral Trejo had stolen the tempo. She had to make sure the price would be higher than they'd intended to pay.

"Madam President," Vaughn said. Drummer watched the *Tempest* emerge through the gate again before she spoke. It was astounding to her that something so large could make it through the gate at all. It looked big enough to break the safety barriers with its own mass and energy. Maybe there would have been a way to use that with Laconia the way they had with the Free Navy. Except that the fucking thing was already through the gate.

"Vaughn," she said, not looking back at him.

"Communications is asking for your decision on the repeater," Vaughn said.

She took a deep breath, let it out slowly between her teeth. There were thousands of radio signal repeaters scattered through the system, but she knew which one Vaughn meant. Their clandestine traffic to and from Medina—Avasarala's gift to her—ran through a low-energy repeater that was floating dark outside the ring gate. From Medina, its signal was weak and the wavelengths it jumped among similar enough to the gates' usual interference that it was easy to overlook. From normal space, it was more obvious.

And the closest ship to it right now was the *Tempest*.

She could order her communications forces not to use it. That was easy. But the EMC intelligence forces also had access to it. And Saba's underground. The more people who could make a mistake, the more likely that something would go wrong. And it was easy enough for her to shut it down. One signal packet would do it, like toggling a light off. It would go into a passive listening state, and someone would have to know where to look for it to register as more than a grain of sand floating in the unimaginably vast ocean of the void.

Going dark was the right thing to do. But she rebelled at it.

"What's the point," she said, "of having something you can't use? Functionally, it's the same as not having it." On her screen, the loop ended and began again. The *Tempest* rising up from the gate.

"Preserving something to use at the right time isn't nothing, sa sa que?" Vaughn said.

"Was being rhetorical," Drummer said.

"Apologies," Vaughn said.

"Tell them . . ." It was more than her window into Medina. It was her link to Saba. What if he needed to reach her? What if something happened, and his call for help died in silence because she was being too careful? Loneliness widened in her chest, stretched until it felt bigger than she was. Emptier. "Tell them to shut it down. Save it for a rainy day."

"Yes, ma'am," Vaughn said, and turned to leave.

"Have you ever seen rain, Vaughn?" she said, stopping him. Giving herself a few more seconds with the connection to Medina and Saba still there. Even if she couldn't use it.

"No, ma'am. Never been to Earth. Never plan to."

" 'Rainy day,' though. We still say it."

"Inner planet cultural imperialism is in everything," Vaughn said.

"Rain isn't just for inners. It rains on Titan too. It's methane instead of water, but you can see it if you're in the domes there. I spent my madhu chandra week there. A billion dots on the surface of the dome with the orange clouds behind it? They look like tiny dark stars. If you can see them. Saba's distance vision isn't good. He couldn't see them. But I could."

"If you say so, ma'am," Vaughn said. Either he was mildly embarrassed for her, or she imagined he was. *Well, fuck you too,* she thought, but didn't say it in case it was just her.

"All right," she said, turning back to her screen. "Send the order."

Vaughn didn't answer, just walked out and closed the door behind him. She watched the *Tempest* pass through the ring gate one last time, looking for a clue in it. Or a ray of hope. She didn't see one, and she closed the recording down and opened the other one.

This is Admiral Anton Trejo of the Laconian Imperial Navy, and high commander of the Heart of the Tempest. *I am presently on a mission to secure Laconian interests in Sol system. We recognize the deep cultural and historical importance of Sol system, and hope that this transition can be made peacefully and with the minimum of disruption. In the event that local forces resist, I am prepared and authorized to take any actions necessary to complete my mission. High Consul Duarte and I extend our best wishes to the local residents, and ask that you contact your governments to urge them to act in the name of peace. Violence is always a loss, and the measure of that loss is entirely in your control.*

The false gentility of the threat made her wish he'd just said he'd burn their cities and take their children. It would have felt more honest.

People's Home was on its braking burn to meet with the EMC's second fleet, where Guard of Passage already waited. Independence was already with the first fleet and Jupiter. The newest void city—Assurance of Peace—was half built at the Pallas-Tycho shipyards and wouldn't be ready for another year, assuming that they had another year.

The unspoken truth was that the union had commissioned the void cities as a permanent response to the colony worlds' interest in building their own fleets. A void city couldn't control a whole solar system, but it could command a ring gate. Or that's what Drummer and the union board had assumed. Now, People's Home was only a battleship. A massive one, with greenhouses and schools, children and common space, universities and research labs. But the prospect of violence meant that none of that mattered. People's Home was a delivery system for rail guns, missiles, PDCs. And she would drive it down to protect Earth and Mars, and be protected by their ships. She'd hate everything about it, but she'd do it.

And goddammit, she'd have to smile while she did.

The under-burn configuration of People's Home put the meeting rooms down near the massive array of Epstein drives. The

EMC was represented by Admiral Hu of Mars and Undersecretary of Executive Affairs Vanegas. Chrisjen Avasarala sat in a wheelchair at the back of the hall, eating pistachios and pretending to be dotty so that people left her alone. The lights had been set to a warm cut of the spectrum that was alleged to match a summer afternoon on Earth, and the air smelled of cut cucumber and soil. A reassuring environment that would hopefully affect the tone of the event, even if it was all engineering. The reporters and dignitaries on the formed bamboo benches all wore formal suits and dresses, as if a press conference were the same as going to church.

Maybe it was. Drummer had read somewhere that newsfeeds were where secular societies went to find out what cultural narratives were important and what could be ignored. There were thousands of feeds streaming right now, all around the system, with every variation of the ways to make sense of the history they were living through. In most, Laconia was an invading force to be resisted, but there were people who said Laconia was a liberating influence, an end to the oppression of the EMC and the Transport Union. Or that they were the true spirit of Mars, betrayed by the old congressional republic and now returned in triumph. Or that they were unbeatable, and capitulation was the only choice. Put a dozen people in front of their cameras, and you'd wind up with thirteen opinions. None of them would matter as much as hers, because she was the president of the Transport Union, and that, despite all her intentions and efforts, meant she was a war leader now.

In the green room, Vanegas was getting his makeup freshened before they went out to the cameras. Hu put down her coffee as soon as Drummer stepped into the room and hurried over to her, a grim expression on her face.

"President Drummer," Hu said, "I was hoping I could speak with you about the board's strategic cooperation documents?"

A steward led Drummer to a chair. A technician swung in beside her with a palette of cosmetics in his hand. She didn't have much use for makeup, but she didn't want to look sickly in the feeds either.

"I haven't seen the new draft yet," Drummer said, trying not to move her face.

"Santos-Baca is insisting on the chain of command passing through a joint committee," Hu said. "That's not coordination. That's making the EMC a branch of the Transport Union."

If they kill us all, Drummer thought, *this will be why. Not their technology, not their strategy, not the invisible cycle of history. It'll be our inability to do anything without five committee meetings to talk about it.*

"I haven't read the draft, Admiral. As soon as we're done here, I'll have them get me a copy. I don't want to get this muddy any more than you do."

Hu nodded sharply and smiled as if Drummer had capitulated. The technician touched her cheeks with a rouge brush and considered her like she was a painting. She had to fight the impulse to stick her tongue out at him.

And then it was time. Vanegas walked out first, and then Hu. They took the podiums to either side. Drummer took the center. The podium's screen threw up an image visible only to her, running through the lines of the speech. She lifted her chin.

It didn't matter how she felt. It didn't matter what she thought. All that counted right now was how she looked and sounded. Let those carry confidence, and she could find the real thing later.

"Thank you all for coming," Drummer said. "As you know, a ship originating in Laconia system has now made an unauthorized transit into Sol system. The union's stance is unequivocal on this matter. The Laconian incursion is illegal. It is a violation of the union's authority and the sovereignty of the Earth-Mars Coalition. We stand as one body in the defense of the Sol system and all its citizens."

Drummer paused. In the back of the group, Chrisjen Avasarala stood up from her wheelchair and dusted the pistachio bits off her sari. Her smile was visible even from here.

"And the union," Drummer said, "will dedicate all its resources to the defense effort."

Just like you told us to, you old bitch, she thought. She didn't say it.

In her dream, Saba was dead.

She didn't know how he'd died or where, and with the non-logic of sleep, she didn't question that. It was simply the truth: Saba was dead and she wasn't. She'd never see him again. She wouldn't wake up beside him. The rest of her life was emptier and smaller and sadder because of it. In the dream, she knew all of that. But what she *felt* was relief.

Saba was dead, and so he was safe now. Nothing bad could happen to him anymore. She couldn't fail him or abandon him or feel the weight of his disappointment. She woke into darkness, a moment's confusion, and then a wave of overwhelming guilt. The darkness, at least, she could control. She moved the cabin lights up a quarter. Dim gold, faint enough to leave everything in monochrome.

She could feel the thrust gravity when she turned. The absence of even trace Coriolis telling her what she already knew. She wanted to send a message out. To tell Saba she was thinking of him, and not quietly longing for the failures that would lose him forever. But she'd cut that line of communication, and having a weird subconscious wasn't a good reason to change that policy.

Instead she stretched in the near dark. Only half of her sleep cycle was done, but she wasn't interested in diving back into the pillow. Instead, she showered and ordered up a bulb of tea and a tortilla with fruit jam. Comfort food. Then she checked the system map.

The *Tempest* was still out in the vastness between the orbits of Uranus and Saturn. A billion and a half kilometers between the ring gate and the first human habitats of any real size, even if Saturn and its moons were at their closest. Having come through the gate so much earlier than she'd hoped, the *Tempest* wasn't burning hard for the inner solar system. At its present acceleration, it would take weeks to reach her. Drummer pulled on her uniform and went out into People's Home. The tube station was near her quarters. The void city knew where she was and arranged a private car for her without her even having to ask for it. Her security detail shadowed her with the practice of years. Even at the height of a shift change, she moved through the city like it was a ghost town. Only the litter and smell of bodies and old curry in the tube lingered as a promise that she wasn't as alone as she felt.

The arboretum was a restricted-access zone. Some of the trees were experimental, and being in a high-traffic area would have affected the data. But one person or a handful? That was within tolerance. It was warm there, the air thick with moisture and the novelty of oxygen that had just been breathed out by another living thing. It was a strange place, exotic and surreal. Like something out of a child's fantasy.

Usually, she was the only one there.

Avasarala sat in the shade of a catalpa. Her hands were folded in her lap. Her eyes were unfocused until Drummer stepped onto the black rubber walkway in front of her.

"The fuck are you doing here?" the old woman said. "Don't you sleep?"

"I could ask you the same," Drummer said.

"I don't sleep anymore. It's one of the things you lose at my age. I'm not incontinent yet, though, so I don't get to bitch."

Drummer leaned against one of the trees, folded her arms. She didn't know if she was pleased the old woman was there, or annoyed by her, or both. "Is there a reason you're still on People's Home?" she asked, but her voice wasn't biting.

"Thought I might need to firm up your resolve. But I didn't. Now I'm only here because I hate fucking space travel. You're going my way. I'll get out when the last leg of the trip home is shorter."

"So not just looking to stick your nose in my business?"

"Not until you fuck up," Avasarala said. "Sit down, Camina. You look exhausted."

"No one calls me that, you know," Drummer said, but she sat on the bench at Avasarala's side.

"Almost no one."

They sat for a moment with only the sound of dripping water and the tapping of leaves that moved in the artificially controlled breeze. The wisps of her dream haunted Drummer's mind like the afterimage of a strobe.

"One ship," she said. "They sent *one* ship. They didn't hold ground at Medina. They didn't fortify. They didn't build supply lines or prepare a flotilla. They sent one big-ass ship through by itself. Like a boast."

"I'm as surprised as you are," Avasarala said. "Though I feel like I shouldn't be. I actually read history. It's like reading prophecy, you know."

"All we have to do is deal with this one ship, and everyone will see that Duarte's not invulnerable. He's not infallible."

"That's true."

Drummer laced her fingers, leaned forward with her elbows on her knees.

"All we need is one lucky break," she said. "One thing to go our way, and your logistical mastermind who would never overreach loses his capital ship in front of everyone who's watching. And I think everyone is watching."

"They are," Avasarala agreed with a sigh. "But…"

"But what?"

Avasarala's smile was thin, hard, and bitter. Her eyes flashed with an intelligence poisoned by despair. "But it isn't hubris until he's failed."

Chapter Twenty-Four: Singh

Singh's monitor lay flattened on the desk in front of him. Above it floated a 3-D projection of Natalia and Elsa smiling back at him. It wasn't a great shot of them. He'd photographed it himself, and it was a little out of focus. But it was taken at the park where they'd had the monster's second birthday party, and his daughter grinned out at him with cheeks covered in vanilla frosting, and Nat positively glowed with happiness. It was one of his favorite memories.

Once the Typhoon *arrives, I will be able to move to the important work. It also almost certainly means this posting at Medina will be made permanent soon. I want you to start thinking about relocation. Your work was always about helping the colony worlds establish stable food sources, and this is the hub of everything. They'll welcome your research here with open arms. And I promise, the water issues should be fixed by the time you and Monster*

*would arrive. Nothing but clean water for you guys, or I'll tear the
station down one bolt at a time and rebuild it myself. I also—*

"Governor," a voice said from the monitor, startling him.

"Yes?"

"Major Overstreet is here, he says it's an emergency."

"All right," Singh replied, then shut down the image and saved
his letter to finish later. "Send him in."

Overstreet was almost the physical opposite of his predecessor.
Where Colonel Tanaka was tall almost to the point of rangy, he
was short, thick-necked and broad, with fists the size of boxing
gloves. His shaved head was the palest skin Singh had ever seen,
and his eyes were an icy blue. Among Martians, that combination
was fairly exotic.

"Governor," Overstreet said with a sharp salute.

"At ease, Major."

Overstreet shifted his feet apart and linked his hands behind
his back. Where Tanaka had been all arrogant insouciance, Overstreet was every bit the disciplined Marine. Singh liked working
with him.

"Governor, I'm sorry to report another terrorist incident.
Unfortunately, this one also included a loss of life."

Loss of life only meant one thing in this context: a Laconian
fatality.

"Thank you for keeping it off the wire, Major," Singh said. Following the assassination attempt, he'd ordered that any further
terrorist activity be kept as quiet as possible. They needed the
population of Medina to feel like they were safe under Laconian
control. "Who and where?"

"Second Lieutenant Imari, an enviromental support specialist.
She was tracking an air-filtration error and wound up in a crawl
space on the outermost level of the drum. A small improvised
explosive device was remotely detonated. Lieutenant Imari was
killed instantly. One of her techs received minor injuries and is
being treated on the *Storm*."

"Imari," Singh said, concentrating until he could place a face with the name. He'd only met her a few times. Pleasant and professional in all their interactions. And her skills with environmental systems would be sorely missed in Medina's refit. "Do we know who?"

"I had bomb techs on the site within minutes of the blast," Overstreet said. "The chemicals used to manufacture the explosive were traced to a storage compartment on drum level two. I pulled the logs. The majority of those with access have been identified. Marines have already begun rounding them up."

"That is excellent work, Major," Singh said. Overstreet brought him a solution with every problem he reported. It made his own terrible misstep with Tanaka feel like a blessing in disguise.

"The rules of engagement allow us to treat active terror cells as enemy combatants," Overstreet said. "But unless one of these idiots has a hideaway gun, I'm betting we'll bring them all in alive. So, it's your call, sir."

Overstreet looked like he had no opinion one way or the other. If Singh ordered him to go to the holding pens and shoot every single person in the head, it would just be the next thing he did that day. No lectures on how he'd fought Belter cells back in the day, no subtle digs at his lack of experience.

"We're going to need to start holding trials at some point," Singh said. "This seems as good a time as any. We'll need some time to form a civilian justice system for Medina and the colonies. Something less encumbered than the local habits."

"Yes, sir," Overstreet agreed with a nod. "I'll have my people put together all the evidence we've collected and forward it to the advocate's office. We're not police, but whatever we can do to expedite the trial process, we're happy to help out."

Singh leaned back and pointed at one of the visitor chairs next to his desk. "You're doing outstanding work, Major. You've slid into Colonel Tanaka's role without a hiccup. I appreciate it."

Overstreet stretched out, relaxing but without the aggressive informality of his predecessor. "Tanaka was a great mentor. She left me detailed files on...the duties of this post. Give her credit for the smooth transition."

"Mmhmm," Singh said. "Anyway, I've sent in my recommendation that you be promoted to the rank of lieutenant colonel, as befits the posting you now hold. We're just waiting on word from Laconia to make it official. You've certainly got the years in, and your record is exemplary. I don't foresee any difficulty."

"I appreciate that, sir," Overstreet started, then looked down at the monitor on his wrist. "That's fast work. The detachment reports that all seven of the suspects have already been rounded up and taken to a holding area, awaiting your orders. Shall I have them taken to the open-air cells, pending trial? Let everyone on the station see them locked up? Sends a message."

"Yes, I—" Singh began, then rethought it. "No. If that holding area is private, keep them there. I'd like to speak to them."

"Of course," Overstreet said. Into his monitor he said, "Triphammer oscar mike. We need transport and escort to level four, compartment one three one one echo bravo. Ready to move in five."

Singh had studied detailed files on the history of Medina, from its aspirational beginnings with an Earther religious faction to its outright theft by the OPA and conversion into the universe's worst battleship before finally settling in as the hub of human expansion through the gate network.

Singh found the idea of a generation ship fascinating, in a morbid sort of way. He could understand taking great risks for your children. He was doing that right now. Trying to help build the well-regulated human empire that his monster Elsa and her future children could thrive in. There was a romance in the idea of setting out on a journey you'd never see the end of so that your grandchildren might live a better life. But all the numbers he'd seen on how a hundred-year voyage like that would play out were fairly horrifying. It was, to say the least, a very high cost and very low probability of success. Singh assumed there was a faith element to the risk that he was just missing. In his opinion, faith was generally for people who were bad at math.

Compartment 1311EB turned out to be a former storage compartment for animal feed. Another of the many structures built into Medina Station back when it had been the *Nauvoo* and had interstellar colonization as its purpose. Medina was filled with these relics of the station's original purpose even as they had been converted over to new uses. Seven Belters sat on the floor, hands zip-tied behind their backs. Four men, two women, and one person who could be any gender or none and who looked far too young to already have decided on a career in terrorism.

Singh entered the room flanked by two Marines in power armor and Overstreet taking up a position by the door. The four Marine guards in the room snapped him a salute, then went back to watching their little gang of prisoners. With fifteen bodies in the room, it felt very cramped.

"I am the station governor, Captain Santiago Singh," he said, taking time to stare each of the seven prisoners in the eye as he spoke. The youngest stared back with a fierce rage that looked entirely out of place on their beautiful, genderless face.

"No one fuckin' cares," one of the men spat back at him. The Marine closest to him casually kicked him in the ribs. Singh waved him back.

"I need you all to listen to me very carefully," he said. "A bomb was made using chemicals from the warehouse you seven work in. That bomb killed a Laconian naval officer, and injured another."

"Good," said one of the women.

"Not good," Singh replied, without changing his tone. "Because the penalty for this criminal act will be death by firing squad. At this point, there is no reason to believe all seven of you aren't in collusion. You are either working with terrorist cells, or you are in fact the cell that planted that bomb."

"Better to die a free Belter than live a slave," the young one said. They had a singer's voice, high and clear.

He started to wonder if it might have been better to have seven different conversations with the prisoners rather than one with all of them. They were performing for each other now. Each of them signaling their loyalty to the others. It made it more difficult to know what their actual flexibility might be.

"We can debate the benefits of centralized government later," Singh replied. "For now, I have one offer to make, and only one. When I leave this room, I am going to ask that an appointed judge review the evidence from the bombing and find all seven of you guilty of terrorist acts. You will then be taken to a public place, and shot."

"Not much of a fuckin' offer," the first man said, rubbing his bruised ribs.

"While the judge reviews that evidence, I am going to have you held in private cells. The first one of you to cooperate in our investigation of terrorist activity on this station, lives."

"Turn traitor to save our own necks," the young one said. "You don't know Belters at all."

"I know humans. I know that staying alive and keeping one's family safe is not a trivial reward for valued service to the empire. It is the only choice you have left in your lives. Make the right one."

Before they could shout any defiance at him, Singh turned and left. As they walked away, he said to Overstreet, "Put them in separate cells, far enough apart that they can't hear each other. Then make sure there's a guard outside every door. Just in case someone decides to take me up on my offer."

"Copy that," Overstreet replied. There was a hint of skepticism in his tone.

Singh stopped. Overstreet turned to face him, a puzzled look on his broad face.

"Something troubling you, Major?"

"I didn't intend any disrespect, sir."

"Our mandate from High Consul Duarte is to win over the population of this station, as a first step in winning over the population of the colony worlds. We do that by entangling our interests.

By teaching them that what they think of as 'informing' is actually just good citizenship. This is just a first step in building what will hopefully be a network of cooperators to help us."

"Understood," Overstreet said. "Marines make terrible police, sir. We're not trained for this sort of job. If we could build up a security force made up of local cooperators and Marine elements, it would help a lot."

"Good. Make that part of your mandate going forward. You have full authority to offer amnesty to people you think might be useful."

"I'll pass it down the ranks," Overstreet said. He began gently pushing Singh back up the corridor toward their little convoy of carts.

"The other thing," Singh said. "I think it would be appropriate to make a complete audit of the security protocols. Call it a supplemental security review."

"I can do that if you'd like, sir," Overstreet said. "Can I ask what function the review would fill?"

He meant *Am I being called on the carpet?* This was also the fallout of letting Tanaka go. There would be a period where his people trusted him less. Suspected that he would blame them for failures in the system. Punish them for things that weren't their fault.

"We need—" he began, then caught himself. "I need to look over the complete system of security we have. Things are going to change simply because we are here, with these people, and not in a classroom at the academy. I don't know how yet, but I think it's inevitable. I am trusting you to tell me not only what we do but why. And whether you think it should be altered."

"Comprehensive, then," Overstreet said, but he sounded more pleased by the implied trust than put out by the extra work. "I'll see to it. Back to the office, sir?"

Singh almost said yes, but a thought stopped him.

"No," Singh said. "No, take me to Carrie Fisk's office. And notify her we're coming."

On the ride to the Association of Worlds' offices, Singh thought back to his letter home. The idea that being able to hold the ring space meant they'd won the war was optimistic. Or simplistic, at least. Laconia could absolutely control access to the worlds through the gates, but every single world could decide this didn't mean *they* were conquered. And even if they placed a Laconian governor on every world, and a Laconian naval ship in orbit and Marines patrolling the streets, every individual might decide they personally had not been conquered. Establishing the empire was an endless series of microscopic magnifications into greater and greater granularity, and every grain was a potential renegade. Medina was just a microcosm of the problem they'd be running into everywhere. Political opposition considered as fractal geometry.

He had been sent as a governor, and the more he saw, the more he came to understand what that assignment actually was. Not just a bureaucrat to oversee the smooth functioning of the station and the traffic it controlled. He was creating the template for making every other human world into a new Laconia. Seven Belters had decided that killing a single low-level officer was worth risking all their own lives. That wasn't a rational position. An enemy that bad at basic math might do anything. The colony worlds might decide that throwing a few hundred people with rifles onto a transport ship and trying a suicide attack on Medina made sense. He only needed to hold the station for a few more weeks until the *Typhoon* arrived and rendered any such foolhardy attack plan irrelevant. Carrie Fisk could help to carry the message that would dissuade any such error before it could happen.

The office complex occupied by the Association of Worlds sat inside the drum section of Medina, surrounded by farmland. It consisted of three blocky structures of prefab fiberglass sheets, painted a gentle off-white, and sporting the interlocking honeycomb banner of their organization. Singh suspected the design was intended to symbolize the interconnected rings of the gate network. For the headquarters of an organization whose goal was the centralized governance of thirteen hundred worlds, it looked cheap, shabby, and hastily erected. Nothing like the massive stone structures Laconia built to house the future government of mankind.

Carrie Fisk occupied an office on the third floor of the largest of the three buildings. She had a lot of empty space, a single desk with four chairs, and flaking light-green paint on her fiberglass walls. He wondered what their first meeting would have been like if he'd come to her office instead of bringing her to his. Seeing all of this, he might have recommended against working with her at all.

"Madam President," Singh said as he entered, taking her hand in his own. "I'm glad you could take the time to meet with me on such short notice. This is Major Overstreet, the Marine commander on Medina."

Carrie shook his hand, and gave Overstreet a baffled nod. "Of course, Governor, anytime," she said, and gestured to her chairs. Singh sat, Overstreet did not. "Tea?"

Singh declined with a wave of his hand. "I'm afraid I don't have much time to socialize. I have an important message for you to send to the association worlds, and to the local governments on those worlds that have at this point elected not to officially join you."

"Okay," Carrie said. She really was a frightened little mouse of a person, Singh decided. He found himself wondering how such a person could become the leader of anything, much less the nascent government for a galaxy-spanning republic. But she'd had a following before he came, so maybe there was more to her than he saw. Failing that, she could be made into the sort of person he needed.

"It occurs to me that while the *Heart of the Tempest* is engaged with the fleets in the Sol system, and additional Laconian forces have not yet arrived to secure Medina Station, some ill-informed members of your association or other prospective members who haven't officially joined you yet might view this as a moment of weakness for our occupation."

"I don't—" Carrie started.

"But it's important that everyone understand that such a view is both inaccurate, and dangerous," Singh continued over the top of her. "You will send a message, as the president of the new Laconian Congress of Worlds, to every planet in the network."

"The what?"

"The change of name will more closely join your group with the empire. It's important that they recognize you as a legitimate and trusted representative of Laconia. You will tell them that any hostile action taken through one of the ring gates, be that a ship full of soldiers or an angrily thrown rock, will result in the total sterilization of the inhabited planet on the other side of that ring."

Carrie went still for a moment. "Jesus Christ. Are you *serious*?"

"It's come to my attention that many of the social organizations of the old human power structures show a shocking inability to do risk analysis. They may foolishly attempt a doomed assault, thinking all they're risking is their own lives. Reason doesn't work with this kind of person. I need you to make them understand, on an *emotional* level, the price for such an attack. I will kill every single person on their planet. I assume even former OPA radicals have family members they care about, and whose lives they are less willing to risk on a romantic notion of a hero's death."

Overstreet's bright-blue eyes were on him. Singh felt the man evaluating him.

"I can't be part of something like that," Carrie said.

"You can," Singh insisted. "Because I'm making that the rule of engagement for our occupation here, whether you warn people or not. I think it's best if everyone understands that before they do anything with such a terrible price. Don't you agree?"

Singh stood up, and Overstreet opened the door for him. Carrie Fisk stared at him from behind her desk. Singh didn't see the fear he expected on her face. More a sort of simpleminded confusion.

"Please get the announcement out before the end of the day," he said. "I leave the wording to you, as long as all the details I laid out are included. Good day, Madam President."

He left the room with Fisk still reeling from the shock. Overstreet fell easily into stride behind him.

"Permission, sir?" Overstreet said, his tone reserved and formal. Distant, almost.

Singh felt a moment's chagrin. He should have called Overstreet by his given name. He'd forgotten that, and it seemed late to change their habits now. He needed to be more careful about that. "Proceed, Major."

"Are we going to order those attacks?"

"Only if we have to," Singh said.

Overstreet didn't reply at once, and when he did, his tone was flat. "Understood," he said.

Chapter Twenty-Five: Holden

Holden shifted in his bunk. If he lay on his side with one arm raised and his head resting on it like a pillow, he could block that ear, then put a hand over the ear that was pointed up at the bunk above him. It was almost enough to block out Alex's snoring. But it also made his shoulder ache after a while, and his hand fell asleep before he did. He could track down a set of earplugs, but that meant getting out of bed. Half-awake as he was, that seemed like a lot of trouble. Anyway, no one else in the bunks seemed to be bothered. He also knew—half knew—that if he woke up enough to fix the problem, he'd be too awake to sleep again. Admitting that age and anxiety had turned him into a light sleeper felt vaguely shameful in a way that probably wouldn't have stood the scrutiny of a fully conscious mind. Years of living with his crew had built habits and norms that they were violating in these new circumstances, and it was weird.

Clarissa made an uncomfortable sound halfway between a whine and a growl. In the bunk across from him, Naomi shifted. By the dim orange glow of the safety light, he could just make out the curve of her shoulder, the shape of her hair spilling out over her pillow.

Which meant his eyes were open.

Which meant he was awake.

He tried closing his eyes again, willing himself back down to sleep, but Alex coughed above him, and Holden shifted his arm. The pins and needles started in his fingers. The last wisps of dream and oblivion thinned and vanished out of his brain. As quietly as he could, he rolled to the edge of the bunk, let himself down to the deck, and slipped out the door, leaving the others to get the rest he couldn't.

The web of unmonitored space that Saba and his people had carved out of the flesh of the station was tighter than living on any ship Holden had crewed. Keeping the power low enough to avoid detection meant thick air and rationed water. The murmur of voices speaking in musical Belter Creole was as present as the hum of the air recyclers. Holden made his way to the head—an emergency cut-in to the processing system with a seat about the right size for a five-year-old. He had to wait for the woman already there to finish. By the time he stepped back into the access hall, he was fully awake, hungry, and a little grumpy.

Naomi slouched down the hall toward him. Her undershirt was stained with sleep sweat and use. The top of her half-undone jumpsuit gathered at her hips like humanity's worst bustle. Her hair and face still had the shape of her pillow to them.

She was beautiful. She made everything better than it would have been without her.

"You're up," she said.

"I am."

"Me too."

"Sucks, right?"

"Oh yeah," she said, then gestured toward the head. He shifted out of her way.

"Want to risk breakfast out in the world?" she asked as she passed him.

Holden let the question sit in his chest while he was alone in the corridor. When they were in the secret passageways of the underground, they were safe in that they were unmonitored. The Laconian-controlled station was dangerous, but it was also open. Fresh air, better food, and as far as Holden knew, they still weren't on security's shit list.

And there were things they could learn by being there that they'd never get if they only ever stayed where it was safe.

When Naomi emerged, he took her arm like they were stepping out to a formal affair, and together they walked to one of the security hatches, and from there into Medina Station. The transition points were the most dangerous. Moving from the unmonitored spaces into public without seeming to pop into existence out of nowhere meant timing their passage in places that were only intermittently watched, or else getting secondary entrances into showers, locker rooms, and toilets, where privacy gave them cover.

When they reached the open sections of the station, it was moving from one kind of oppressive environment into another. The halls were bright and open, the air fresh and if anything a little cool. Screens and monitors showed the locally produced Laconia-approved news: propaganda about the stability and security of the station mixed with whatever pop-culture feeds from outside the slow zone made it past their censors. Holden and Naomi walked through it like refugees at a shopping complex, trying not to blink into the too-bright lights.

They weren't alone. The crews of all the other ships and the citizens of the station all had the same dazed look to them, though at different intensities. People were still scrounging for quarters or camping on the inner face of the dome. The docks were still locked down, and that showed no sign of changing. Any normal hand terminals were still blocked from sending messages off Medina or gathering data that wasn't locally stored and vetted. There was a way that being in Saba's underground felt like being buried alive.

And there was a way that being outside of it made being buried alive seem like not such a bad thing. It was cozy, anyway.

They stopped at a café two levels below the open air of the drum's interior. He got a bulb of genuinely third-rate coffee—overroasted to hide the shitty beans in the taste of the char, and a chalky cream substitute—and Naomi got tea and a corn muffin that they could split. They sat at a little table as far away from the public passage as they could get and still have a good view of the foot traffic passing by. Two men, smoking pipes that looked like they'd been made of decking ceramic. A group of schoolchildren in matching gray-green uniforms. A busker with a marionette trying to amuse passersby with her antics. It could have been any station in human space. And as they watched, they talked about things that weren't dangerous if anyone were to overhear.

In the public corridor, a security team walked past. Two figures in the blue power armor bristling with weapons. The carts and foot traffic moved around the pair like a stream flowing around rocks. Their presence wasn't intimidating people as much now, or at least not in the same ways. On a screen across the corridor, Carrie Fisk of the newly renamed Laconian Congress of Worlds was being interviewed by a pretty young man with a military haircut. Holden wondered what she was saying, but the café had their system set to a light, friendly saidi list that shifted from one melody to the next without ever pausing in between. The same music, Holden guessed, that they'd played before Laconia came knocking.

It was all becoming normal. He could see it in the way the clerk served up the terrible, terrible coffee. He could hear it in the conversations at the nearby tables. It showed on the screens and in the gaits of the people walking by. Panic and alarm were exhausting. He was exhausted by them, and Medina was exhausted too. It was already shifting into its new routine. Checkpoints, yes. Armed security, yes. All the theater of dominance and control and nothing to undercut that narrative.

Just to look at it, you wouldn't guess there'd been a bombing.

Saba hadn't known it was coming either, and they'd only heard about it through him. A small explosion, but the unofficial reports said at least one Laconian had been killed. The official reports, apparently, were that it hadn't happened at all. That was a change. The assassination attempt had been used to justify the crackdown. Now the crackdown was just another day, and highlighting the attacks on the structures of power wasn't useful. Nothing had to be justified anymore. Governor Singh in his offices was trying to project a sense of normalcy and inevitability. And as far as Holden could tell, it was working.

"Kind of quiet," he said, meaning *They think they're winning.*

Naomi tugged her hair down over her eyes. "Right?" she said. It meant *I think they're winning too.*

Back in the underground, Holden found Saba sitting at a dumb terminal. Even in full light, Saba's hair and skin were nearly the same color. In the backsplash from the screen, he almost seemed like a cartoon of himself. He nodded at Holden and shifted a few centimeters on his bench to give him room. Holden sat.

"Checking on the *Storm* dump?" Holden asked, nodding toward the screen. The log entries spooled up. The information they were intercepting from the Laconians was encrypted on a variety of levels, and using more than one schema.

"Dui," Saba said. "Everything between the station and the *Storm* is coming in, but until we get access to the server that decrypts it, it's just noise. Plenty more irons in that fire, though. Medina comms got more compromised than we thought. Turns out Golden Bough bought a tech eighteen months ago, got a backdoor into the system we never noticed."

"Really?" Holden said. "How'd you find it now?"

"Coyo told us," Saba said, flashing a grin. "Patriotism is weird shit."

Holden chuckled. "Whatever works, I guess."

They sat for a moment in near silence. Saba scratched his arm and pointedly didn't look at Holden when he spoke again. "Big coya seems like she's got a little stone in her throat. Any trouble with your crew?"

"Nope," Holden said. And then, "I mean, yeah, but nothing that'll cause a problem."

"Don't guess you want to say what? Make me feel better to know."

Holden leaned forward. The logs spooled past, storage filling with traffic that might be everything to them. Or nothing. Bobbie wasn't something he'd talked about before. He wasn't sure he wanted to start now, but he was living in Saba's rooms, eating the man's food, coordinating on his operations.

"It's not exactly my crew," Holden said. "I had some trouble with the union before all this happened."

Saba's grin came again. "You're forgetting whose man I am, que no? Drummer spends a little time talking about you behind your back, and that means to me."

"Right, so...I was in the process of retiring when all this came down. Dropping off the Freehold guy was my last mission. Was going to be. The crew is really Bobbie's, only then history got in the way, and now I'm sort of back in charge and sort of not. It's awkward."

"Savvy," Saba said. "I'm there too."

"Something wrong between you and Bobbie?"

"No, no, no. Only that Medina's my home port, but the *Malaclypse* is my home. This came down, and I got put at the front because of my spouse and her job and the union. Plenty enough around here don't like that. Do their own thing because it's their own."

"Like the bombing," Holden said.

"Like that trap, yeah. Like the trying for the governor. Like a bunch of assholes I stopped who were looking to steal Laconian uniforms, beat up some of our own so they could start shit between, yeah?"

"That doesn't seem productive," Holden said.

"Not about productive," Saba said. "About reaching for what can get done. Plenty of old OPA on Medina. When the Alliance turned into the union, it didn't erase all the old factions. There's Ochoa OPA and there's Johnson OPA even when there's no Ochoa or Johnson. Voltaire Collective set that bomb like they'd just been waiting for the chance, and maybe they were. Oldsters going at it like they were young again. Young ones trying to live up to the stories of the bad old days. Like pumping oxygen into a fire."

Holden shook his head. "If we're going to manage anything, we have to—"

The dumb terminal chirped, and one of the entries came up highlighted. Saba pulled the interface pad closer and scrolled back to the flagged entry. He cross-checked and opened the file. All the things a real system would have done for him automatically, if they could risk using one.

Saba clicked his tongue against his teeth.

"What've we got?" Holden asked.

"Traffic control plan update," Saba said. "Got something slated as coming in through Laconia gate, but not right away."

"How far out?"

"Forty-two days?" Saba said. He moved through the data as carefully as he could, checking the distribution stamps and time codes. It didn't take him long to find the name and transit specs for the ship. The *Typhoon*. And from the mass and energy profile, it was huge. On a hunch, Holden had Saba match it with Laconia's first transit. The two were the same. The *Typhoon* was another *Tempest*. Holden felt a tightness under his rib cage wondering how many more like it there were.

Saba cursed under his breath. A man's voice came from behind them, somewhere in the warren of hidden corridors. A woman answered. The bulkheads, the exposed conduits and industrial decking, the thick air and the darkness. All of it was just the same as it had been when Holden sat down, except that now it seemed fragile.

Another warship from Laconia with more soldiers. The beginning of the permanent occupation. Not just the beginning of the end. The end.

Saba cracked his knuckles and smiled ruefully at Holden. "Well," he said. "Leaves me wishing I could tell Drummer and the union. Kind of thing she'd want to know."

"Yeah," Holden said, trying to gather his wits. There was more than a little of him jumping around behind his own eyes like a panicked monkey, but this wasn't the time for it. "All right. We still have some time. Whatever we decide to do, our obstacles are the *Gathering Storm* outside the station and something like two hundred, maybe two hundred and fifty power-armor-wearing Marines inside it."

"And loose-cannon OPA factions firing off without warning," Saba said. "When they hear about this, they'll get worse. Complicate everything if they won't coordinate."

"So that too," Holden agreed. His brain felt like it was stuffed with cotton ticking. He wanted to get all his people onto the *Rocinante* and run away. If there was anyplace that the Laconians wouldn't just follow them and shoot them down. If there was anyplace in thirteen hundred systems that would be safe anymore. For them, or for anyone.

"Okay," he said. "All right. Whatever goals we decide on, we have to take those three things into account. And we have to do it in the next forty-two days."

"Because after that," Saba said, "no more us, yeah?"

Chapter Twenty-Six: Bobbie

Bobbie, Alex, and Clarissa ate lunch together in a tiny compartment with ELECTRICAL SUPPLIES stenciled on the door in four languages. It had a few unlabeled crates in it that they could use as tables and benches, so they'd taken to calling it the Diner. The meal was the heavily spiced and deep-fried balls of bean paste that Belters called red kibble. On the side they had a few bits of dried fruit, and a thin seafood soup that tasted like the flavor came from having a fish swim through the broth.

"You know what I miss most about the *Roci* about now?" Alex said, poking at his kibble, which rolled around his plate. "My ship knows how to make Martian food. I'm so sick of this Belter shit."

He was exaggerating his Mariner Valley drawl the way he always did when he spoke of the ship. Bobbie laughed at him, then noisily drank off the last of her broth.

"It's good for you, boy," she said, mocking his drawl.

"It keeps body and soul attached, and that's about the best I can say for it."

Clarissa smiled at their banter, but said nothing. She was picking up a single ball of kibble at a time, then carefully chewing it. It was like watching a bird eat in slow motion.

"I wonder if the Laconians still eat Martian food," Bobbie said. "We could ask."

Alex tossed his plate down onto their crate-table in disgust. "You know, I think what chaps my ass more than anything else about this shit? The guys who came out of the gate and started wreckin' our shit and takin' over aren't some damn aliens. It's fucking Martians. I bet there're people on that Laconian ship I served with back in the day. Dollars to donuts, the top brass in the Marine detachment here are people you know, at least by name."

Bobbie nodded, chewing the last of her kibble. "That's actually an interesting idea. I mean, could that be useful? Find some people in their command structure that know us? Is that an in?"

"I ain't talkin' about how it's useful, Bob," Alex said, nearly knocking over Clarissa's water glass with his angry hand gestures. "I'm talkin' about the idea that people just like us, Martian patriots, picked up and ran off with this Duarte guy, and took about a third of the fleet with them."

"You ever wonder if it could have been us?" Bobbie asked.

Alex lowered his brows at her. "You lost your mind?"

"No, really, think about it," Bobbie said. "We were both out of the service when Duarte started making his move. You'd been retired for a decade at that point. I'd been out of the Corps for a couple years. But if we'd still been active duty, could we have fallen for his pitch? I mean, a lot of good people did."

"A third of the stars of heaven," Clarissa said, as if she were agreeing.

"Uh," Alex replied, cocking his head in confusion.

"A third of the what now, honey?" Bobbie said.

"From the Bible. Revelation. When the devil fell from grace, he took a third of the angels with him. It's described as the great dragon pulling a third of the stars of heaven down with its tail."

"Huh," Alex said like he had no idea what she was talking about.

"Why'd that pop into your head?" Bobbie asked.

"Whatever story Duarte was selling was compelling enough to get a big chunk of the Martian military to buy in. The devil's story was freedom from the oppression of God's rules, and it was good enough to win a lot of angels to his side. Whatever Duarte's pitch was, it's a good one. Don't be so sure you wouldn't have bought it."

"Oh, I'm pretty fucking sure," Alex replied with a snort.

Bobbie had to admit she wasn't. A galaxy-spanning human civilization run the way the Martians, at their best, ran things. Organized, focused on a single overarching goal. Efficient, well planned, not wasting anything. She could see why that appealed to a lot of people when Mars was watching its dream of terraforming die. Duarte could step in and sell them a new dream that used all the same skills and attitudes that the old one had, but was even grander in scope. Bobbie recognized that there was a version of her that was fighting on the Laconian side right now, and it made her itchy.

Alex had started to gather up the plates and cups from their meal when Amos walked into the room. "Hey, Babs. Cap wants to see us about that thing."

"Which thing?"

"The making-sure-no-more-bombs-go-off-we-don't-know-about thing."

"Oh, that thing. Be there in five," she replied, and he shrugged and walked off without another word.

"Still kinda chafes, don't it?" Alex said, his voice gentle.

"What? Hearing him go back to calling Holden 'Cap'?" Bobbie said, ready to shrug it off. But something caught in her throat. "Yeah. I gotta admit it does. I might have a word with him on that."

"Be gentle," Clarissa said. "He's fragile right now."

Bobbie had no idea what the word *fragile* meant when applied to Amos. She wasn't sure she wanted to learn.

Saba leaned against one wall in the larger storage space that they'd been using as their insurgent-cell meeting room. Someone had finally pushed all the crates and boxes up against the walls to serve as seating, and some enterprising thief on the crew had even managed to steal a few benches from one of the parks. About twenty members of their group were scattered around the space, including Holden, Naomi, and Amos.

On the wall screen behind Saba was a diagram of Medina, and a picture of a severe-looking woman with black hair and a lot of facial piercings. She stared at the camera with angry eyes, giving the picture a mug-shot feel. The name Katria Mendez floated beneath her photo.

"The Voltaire Collective," Saba said, pointing at her. "Bomb throwers from ancient days."

"Fighters," someone in the room replied, making the word a term of respect.

"Sa bien," Saba replied. "Now with Laconia? They go back to the old script."

"Apart from the fact that their strategy doesn't work anymore and it's fucking our shit up, they seem like people we want in our team," Holden said. "We should recruit them. Coordinate with them. Killing them or feeding them to the Laconians should be our last option." He sounded a little scattered. Distracted. She wondered what was up with him. He knew something or suspected something that was eating up all his spare cycles. Bobbie had seen it before.

Saba nodded with one fist. "If we can, we should." He pointed to a sublevel on the Medina map marked Water Reclamation. "Holed up here, them. I say we send our envoys to make them an offer of alliance."

Holden turned on his bench to look back at Bobbie. She gave

him a tiny nod. He stood up to take a spot next to Saba and said, "I think we should send Bobbie to speak for us. She can pass along our respects, tell them we need to join up, and if they get belligerent... well, she can handle that too."

"Agreed," Saba said. "How many you want with you?"

"Let's keep this small," Bobbie replied. "Just me and Amos for now. This should feel like natural allies reaching out. Not a war party."

"Sabe bien," Saba said. "But this ends with they don't plant more bombs unless we say so. Our house gets in order now. One way or."

"Yeah," Bobbie agreed. "One way or, that's where this ends."

The shortest path to Water Reclamation included a short jaunt through the inner drum. Bobbie didn't mind. Hiding out with her resistance-fighter buddies included an awful lot of sleeping and eating in tiny metal rooms. Getting out into the habitat space with open air and a dirt floor and the full-spectrum light on her face was a welcome change.

Even the ubiquitous Laconians didn't ruin the mood. For the most part, their conquerors were easy to get along with. They acted like people who'd lived on Medina for years: eating in the restaurants, browsing the shops, making use of the entertainment districts. If you gave them a nod, they nodded back like old neighbors. Even the Marine patrols moving past in their exotic blue power armor looked alert, but not particularly threatening.

Bobbie had seen the other version of them during the assassination attempt on the governor, so she knew they could go from friendly and professional to full rock-and-roll at the flip of a switch. Easy to get along with or not, the Laconians were a military occupation. You forgot that at your peril.

"How are you doing?" Bobbie asked as they walked through a particularly lush section of park. The lovingly tended path curved through grass, patches of flowers, and even past the occasional tree. Insects buzzed about, still the best-designed pollinating system there was. Technology did a lot of things well, but evolution had it beat when it came to environmental systems.

"My feet hurt," Amos said. "Kind of all the time now. Glad these Belters keep the rotation at a third of a g."

"It's quicker to list the shit that doesn't hurt, these days," Bobbie said. "But that's not really what I meant."

"Yeah?" Amos said. His tone didn't change at all, but Bobbie had flown with him for a couple decades now. She could hear the tension that had crept in.

"Claire thinks maybe you're having a tough time right now."

"Does she." Amos' voice had gone so flat, it might have been a badly written computer simulation of him. He was checking out of the conversation. Pushing it farther wouldn't help.

"Anyway," Bobbie said, keeping it light. "You need anything, I'm up for whatever."

"Yeah, I know, Babs," Amos said. "But these Voltaire guys are no joke. We better get our game faces on."

The Voltaire Collective occupied a dusty crawl space beneath and between half a dozen gigantic stainless-steel tanks. It was a good spot. Unless the piping sprang a leak, there was literally no reason for anyone to come down to the space. The Collective definitely still had some skill sets left over from their OPA resistance-fighter days. Katria Mendez in person was all hard angles and sharp edges, and her dark eyes burned with a constant low-level fury.

"You're actually coming here to lecture us on how to run an occupied insurgency," she said. Her voice was gentle and warm. The voice of a favorite teacher, or beloved aunt. A voice that asked if you wanted some lemonade with your cookies. It also had the precise diction and studied lack of accent that Bobbie associated with advanced education. Her Belter accent could have been measured in parts per billion.

"Not at all," Bobbie started.

"Because," Katria continued, "the Collective has been a militant branch of the OPA, resisting inner-planets control, for nearly a century."

"I understand," Bobbie said.

"Do you? Because it seems like you just showed up here and told us that we're not allowed to run any resistance operations without your consent. Or did I misunderstand what you were telling me?"

Bobbie heard shuffling feet behind her, and turned around to see five members of Katria's cell had taken up a loose semicircle at her back. None of them held weapons in their hands, but they all wore the loose-fitting jumpsuits of the Medina Station maintenance workers. Lots of big pockets that could be hiding anything from a hammer to a compact machine pistol. Amos, standing to her left, caught her eye without losing his smile. He took a half step back, managing to make it look casual.

"Look," Bobbie said to Katria, stepping up and looking down at her from their half-meter height difference. "We didn't come here to start a fight. As far as I'm concerned, we're all on the same team. But if you force it to go the other way, we're prepared for that, too. And I promise you it will not go the way you want."

"Honestly, I'm just not sure why Saba didn't come himself," Katria said, not backing down at all. "Or why he thought sending a Martian and an Earther to tell Belters how to fight was the right message."

Bobbie didn't know any answer to that other than *because we're the most intimidating soldiers he's got, now that walking through Medina with firearms has become a really bad idea.* She winged it instead.

"Because maybe that *is* the message. Because this isn't about Belters and inners and last century's bullshit. Because now it's about all of *us* versus the assholes who popped out of their gate thirty years into our game and decided they get to flip the table over."

Katria nodded and smiled. "That's actually not a terrible answer."

"Then let's ease down," Bobbie said, taking a half step back again to give Katria her space. "Let's find a place to sit and have a drink and chat about how all of us can work together to fuck these Laconian assholes up. Yeah?"

"You keep giving me that eye, boy, and I'm gonna pull it out of your head and hand it back to you," Amos said, his tone so mellow and conversational that it took Bobbie a moment to recognize the threat was real. He was looking back at the semicircle of OPA toughs at their back, directing his empty gaze at them. But Bobbie saw a vein at his temple throbbing like he was at risk of a stroke. The muscles moved under his skin like taut cable dragging over his jawbone.

"Amos," she said, and then she wasn't talking anymore because she was in a fight.

Amos threw himself at someone behind her, and she heard grunts and the meaty thud of fists hitting flesh, but she couldn't turn around to see what was happening because a long knife had appeared in Katria's hand and the woman was dancing toward her. *Fighters,* one of Saba's people had said. And like the Laconians, the Voltaire Collective folks also seemed ready to go from zero to a hundred at the flip of a switch.

Bobbie didn't have time to dance with Katria, nor did she want to get herself stitched up from a knife fight, so she straight-kicked the woman in the diaphragm and dropped her to the deck with an explosive *oof.* She took a second to kick the knife away, then started to turn when something heavy slammed into her cheek.

Through the explosion of stars in her vision, she saw Amos grappling with two men at the same time, choking one with his left arm while he slammed the second man into one of the water tanks over and over again with his right. A third man had climbed onto his back and was attempting a sleeper hold, but couldn't get his forearm under Amos' chin to lock it up. The other two OPA goons were flanking Bobbie, and one of them was holding the crowbar he'd just cracked her cheekbone with. In the sort of slow-motion clarity Bobbie always experienced during a fight, she saw skin and blood on the crowbar's edge.

Oh, she thought, *that's why my face feels wet.*

Crowbar was pulling back for another swing, while his partner tried to get behind her. Bobbie decided Crowbar was the more serious threat and lunged at him to get inside the arc of his swing. His arm went around her, and she felt the bar slam into her shoulder blade, which made her right arm go pins-and-needles numb. She threw a throat punch at him with it, and even though she couldn't feel it, her arm did what she told it to. Crowbar dropped his weapon and clutched his throat with both hands, gagging.

His partner kicked her in the back, twice. One kick hit her kidney, and the other her butt. While the kidney shot might have her pissing blood for a few days, it was the kick to the ass that almost put her on the ground. It felt like someone set off a small bomb in her lower back, and she felt a sharp crack that almost certainly meant he'd snapped her tailbone.

She turned to see him unleashing another kick, and managed to mostly sidestep it, letting it bounce off her hip and forcing him to stumble forward into her. She grabbed hold of his left arm and rotated through the hips to throw him face-first into a pressure-monitoring console a few feet away. He hit it with a thud and a crunch, and started to sag.

Then, just because he'd kicked her in the ass, she snapped his left arm before she let him drop.

Five minutes later, Katria and her five friends sat or lay on the floor, hands tied behind their backs. Amos had an eye that was already starting to swell shut, and four scrapes down his cheek that looked like he'd been clawed by a big cat. Bobbie had carefully avoided looking at her own face in anything reflective. But based on the volume of blood in her shirt, the wound on her face had to be pretty grotesque. *There goes my not-needing-stitches plan.* The pain in her backside also meant she wasn't going to enjoy sitting for the next couple of months. That thought made her want to kick the unconscious man with the broken arm again. Or maybe Amos.

"Katria," Bobbie said, leaning down over the Voltaire Collective cell leader. "Is it okay if I call you Katria?"

If Katria had any objections, she kept them to herself.

"Great. So, look. This could have gone better. We kicked your ass and you're pissed now, I get that. If you want to be part of the revolution, great, we'd love to have you. But you run all your ops through Saba's group. That's nonnegotiable. Anything else, and we're killing you and hiding your bodies in the fertilizer-recycling system."

Bobbie grabbed the front of Katria's shirt and picked her back up to her feet, then kept lifting until they were eye to eye.

"Do we understand each other?"

To her surprise, Katria laughed. There was a brightness in her eyes that looked like fever. "We do indeed," the woman said. It could have been a sparring partner's salute or the threat of retribution. Bobbie really wished she could tell the difference.

Chapter Twenty-Seven: Drummer

It was easy to forget sometimes that the void cities hadn't always been there. During the starving years, they'd been something like a dream. A promised land without the land. Homes for the Belt that could move through the gates to whatever system they chose. There had been a magic to them then. A sense of the unprecedented.

Time had worn that shine away. Drummer had spent more time in the last decade on People's Home and Independence and Guardian than on ships or asteroid stations. They'd become so familiar that they'd bled back in her memory until it felt as though the corridors and chambers had been present since her childhood, even if she hadn't been on them. Like a city often mentioned, but not visited until adulthood. She had to remind herself that war was always this way. Had always been. Cities had been falling under siege since the time there were cities. Mortars had fallen on schools. Soldiers had stormed hospitals. Bombs had set churches and parks and children on fire. Homes had been lost before now.

The tactical display floating over the table was off by orders of magnitude. If it had been to scale, Independence would have been too small to make out with a microscope. As it was, the identifying code was larger than the ship icon. A smear of light smaller than a crumb of bread that meant a city where two hundred thousand people, more or less, lived and worked, raised children, divorced and married, drank and danced and died. And then burning sunward from it, the evacuation ships—even smaller— that carried as many people as would fit away from the theater of battle. She looked at them and saw all the other times children had been carried away from a disaster that was approaching and that could not be stopped: London, Beijing, Denver. History, she reminded herself, was peppered with moments like this one. It only felt different because this was her city, a void city, and this had never happened before.

She had repurposed the central traffic-control station of People's Home for this. Military analysts and engineers, some of them union, most of them EMC, sat at the desks where civilians usually were. Feeds to the war rooms on Earth and Mars showed similar rooms with similar people, but considerably less light delay. The screens that usually listed incoming and outgoing ships with approach vectors and expected times were devoted to the incoming signals from all the active telescopy in the Belt. Images of the major observation stations showed when fresh data streams were coming in, where they were coming from, when People's Home was transmitting. Images from Independence and the dozen EMC ships included flags for time delay—an hour and twenty-three minutes—and a composite of the enemy claimed the central display. Pale as a bone, burning lazily toward the point where the battle would begin. Maybe had begun. Maybe had started and ended in the hour and twenty-three minutes it took light to bring the message to them.

"The, ah, the resolution will get better as we get the signal bounce," the EMC technician said. She was younger than Drummer had been when she started working on Tycho, with red hair pulled back in a bun and a wide, doughy face. On Earth and Mars, other technicians were probably having the same conversations with the prime minister and secretary-general. "It's a trade-off, of course, between immediacy of the direct signals and the better information density of delaying a few minutes to get the extra feeds."

"I just need to know what's happening," Drummer said.

Avasarala, who still hadn't made the passage back to Earth, and Vaughn were at the edge of the room. Admiral Hu was at one of the central control consoles, sitting forward like an overeager schoolgirl at the first lecture of term. She'd come as a forward observer, the military leader of the EMC nearest to the battle without being in it. A bulb of what smelled like green tea rested on a side table Vaughn had brought out so that the admiral wouldn't risk spilling on the control board. Drummer walked to her less because she wanted to talk than because she had to move.

"Madam President," Hu said, nodding to her.

"Admiral."

"Odd being on the same side of a shooting war, isn't it? I never thought the day would come."

That says more about you than the reality of things, Drummer thought. The EMC wasn't its own side any more than Ilus or Surabhi or Neue Ausland were. The dreams of empire faded slowly. It didn't matter.

"We've got a comm report, Madam President."

"Play it," Drummer snapped. The main screen shifted. The Laconian admiral appeared. His voice was patient and calm, but there was a glitter in his eye. An excitement. It made Drummer's gut ache to see.

"This is Admiral Trejo of the *Heart of the Tempest* to the approaching warships. I ask that you stand down. Any interference with our ship will be met in kind. Don't make this worse than it has to be."

"Fuck you," Drummer said to the screen, but not softly enough that Admiral Hu didn't chuckle. It was only ten seconds before the answer came. God, that's how close the distant war ships all were to each other. Light-seconds.

Emily Santos-Baca, the ranking board member who lived on Independence. Her hair was pulled back in a tight braid in preparation for null g. Or it had been an hour and twenty-three minutes ago.

"Admiral Trejo," Santos-Baca said, "on behalf of the Transport Union and the Earth-Mars Coalition, I am informing you that your presence in Sol system is a violation of territorial space and is being considered an act of war. Your ship will brake immediately and return to Laconia until appropriate contracts and diplomatic resolutions are in place."

They were reports from two competing realities. Drummer wished that Santos-Baca's sounded more plausible. The icons that marked the EMC ships were like dots drawn on the skin of a balloon, the *Tempest* moving in like a pin. It couldn't be long. Couldn't have been.

"The dispersal," Hu said. "You see that? The way they're spread out? That's based on the Medina data your people sent. The spread of that magnetic whatever-the-hell-it-was. We placed the ships so that no matter which one it aims at, it won't be able to get two. Good, eh?"

"Excellent," Drummer said. Her throat was dry, but the smell of the tea was a little nauseating.

"The range of it can't be good either," Hu said. "The science wonks say the power curve would be logarithmic. Remaining at range should force the bastards to use any other weapons systems they have. Assuming that the magnetic cannon even works in normal space. Because there's at least one idea that it's using special properties that only exist in the ring space. And if that's the case—"

"Gloria." The old woman's voice was like a knife. "You're doing it again."

Admiral Hu glanced back at Avasarala. Drummer hadn't heard her approach, but there she was. Her smile was indulgent and warm and, Drummer had to assume, utterly false.

"Gloria is a good warrior, but she gets chatty when she's nervous."

"We're seeing fire," one of the analysts said. His voice was as calm and businesslike as a surgeon announcing a bleeder.

The display shifted. The EMC ships and Independence were still there, but backgrounded as the focus changed to swarms of missiles pouring out toward the *Tempest*. Each one burned hard enough that a human body would have been pulped by the g forces, and they barely seemed to move. The distances they traveled were vast. Even at their speed, three million klicks was a long time. Verbal threats that took seconds at lightspeed followed by punches that would take minutes or hours. Even without the warheads, the kinetic force of the torpedoes would be massive. If they hit. The swarm crept forward, pixel by imperceptible pixel. Drummer waved a steward over and ordered a bulb of ice water and a bowl of hummus with bread. She had to try to eat.

The hummus was half gone and the tea tepid before the first of the missiles started winking out of existence.

"What are we seeing, please?" Hu said.

"It appears to be long-range PDCs," one of the analysts said. "We're waiting for the bounce feed so we can get higher resolution."

Another twenty minutes, and a much sharper image of the *Tempest* appeared with the timestamp to show it was just after the fleet's launch. All along the sides of the ship, tiny dark eruptions like the spots on a shark.

"The PDCs' housings appear to be covered by the hull. Telemetry from the *Michael Souther* is that the remaining missiles were redirected toward those structures." Were. An hour and twenty minutes ago.

"They're not using their magnet beam," Hu said. "That's good. If it was cheap for them to fire it, they could use it to knock down missiles. If it's expensive to use, we may be able to exhaust it."

Drummer thought that sounded like wishful thinking, but she didn't say so. She tried to take comfort in Hu's optimism. The data feeds shifted, more information coming in. The images of the *Tempest* sharpened. The PDCs came into clearer focus, but it didn't help Drummer understand them. The openings in the side of the ship looked like little mouths opening and closing. Like the whole side of the ship was singing. There was no mechanism she could see. She shuddered. The cloud of torpedoes was thinning. None of them would reach the body of the enemy ship.

A bloom of glowing gas erupted from the *Tempest*'s side, flinched, and then dissipated.

"Rail guns," an analyst said.

The chatter of voices went into a higher gear. Tracking the rail-gun round, examining the spectrum of the plasma that had accompanied it, identifying the particular torpedo that it turned to dust.

"Are their PDCs running low already?" Hu said, to herself as much as anyone.

"It was a warning," Avasarala answered. "They're showing us that they have teeth and giving us the chance to back away."

"Maybe we should," Drummer said.

No one replied. The markers for the EMC ships shifted like a school of fish moving together, and Independence with them. Their own volley of rail guns, the slugs raining down from all directions. The *Tempest* had no way to stop them. All it could do was dodge. Drummer counted the minutes, watching the *Tempest* pull back and corkscrew out of the paths of danger. Mostly.

"I'm seeing contact."

"Two impacts on the starboard. Waiting for confirmation from Pallas and Luna, but I think we did them some damage."

The knot in Drummer's gut eased a little. If they could hurt it, they could kill it. It was just a question of scale and tactics.

"The hull appears to be self-repairing."

"Matches the Medina battle," Hu said.

"Show me," Drummer barked, and the image on her screen shifted again. It was a fresh image, still fuzzy. The bone-pale skin of the *Tempest* rippled as a round struck it, and then again with a second strike. Waves passed through the ship like the surface of water. Nasty black-and-red welts glowed where the rail-gun rounds had hit, but the plating—or whatever it was—folded over the wound, closing it, then folded again, and the damage was gone as if it had never been there.

Another volley of rail-gun fire from the EMC ships, but as the *Tempest* flinched back again and spun away again, it erupted in a cloud of plasma, and then emerged from it. Drummer didn't understand until Hu spoke.

"Holy shit. How many rail guns does that bastard have?"

Now the *Tempest* shifted and swirled, leaving a trail of glowing gas behind it like an afterimage. It was beautiful in its way, a warrior's dance—power and intention and technique that were almost balletic. And then the EMC ships began to die.

"The *Ontario* is hit. Reporting reactor breach and dumping core. We are seeing impacts on the *Severin*, the *Talwar*, and the *Odachi*, but no system confirmation yet. Rounds arrived thirty seconds earlier than the model anticipated."

"Fuckers," Avasarala said. "That's why they took out the missile. Throw a changeup and let us think it was their fastball."

"Whatever they're using for predictive algorithms, it's really good," Hu said, awe in her voice. "That's almost a third of our attack group down. And if...Oh."

For a moment, Drummer didn't understand what she was seeing. Independence, the second void city to launch, the home to hundreds of thousands, seemed to bloom like a flower. Long petals of carbon lace and titanium peeled back, turning as they did. Something terrible and bright happened in the center of the city, but Drummer couldn't guess what it was. What she knew, what mattered, was that between one breath and the next, Independence was dead.

"We're counting eight simultaneous impacts on the void city," an analyst said from somewhere farther away than the control room. "They seem to have been placed to exploit resonance. We're seeing some structural breakdown."

Emily Santos-Baca was on Independence, Drummer thought, and she'd been dead already for over an hour. It didn't matter how much adrenaline was pumping through Drummer's veins, how tightly she gripped her bulb of old tea. She could shout the retreat order if she wanted to, but anyone in a position to hear her was dead already, or would be by the time her words could reach them.

The PDCs along the *Tempest's* side fluttered again. Another group of EMC torpedoes died, faster this time because it was a smaller attack. The *Tempest* seemed to pause, floating in the distant nothingness as if inviting the EMC ships to take their best shots. Taunting them.

An hour and twenty-three minutes before, the EMC ships shifted, lit their Epstein drives as hard as they'd go, and turned to whatever vector got them away from the theater of battle as quickly as they could. The *Tempest* didn't react. No new blooms from their rail guns. No more torpedoes. Drummer didn't believe for a second that the enemy's supplies had been exhausted. Trejo wasn't killing the other ships because he didn't need or want to. That was all.

Drummer put her tea on the little side table next to Hu's, turned, and walked out. She was aware in a vague, distant way of Vaughn behind her, calling her name. It wasn't something that mattered enough to attend to.

The decking of People's Home felt fragile under her feet, as if her footsteps might be enough to break them and spin her and everyone else in the city flying out into the vacuum. She passed her security detail, distantly aware of the men and women assigned to make sure she was safe in any circumstances scrambling to follow her.

It didn't matter. Because they didn't matter. Not when a whole city could die in a heartbeat.

She was in the lobby of the union's executive offices, sitting in an uncomfortable couch with her eyes locked on nothing in particular when Avasarala found her. The old woman steered her wheelchair across from Drummer like they were in someone's private quarters or a back porch back on Earth. There was no one else in the lobby. That was Vaughn's doing, more likely than not. In her imagination, the decking beneath her and Avasarala bucked and split open. What had Santos-Baca thought when it happened? Had she had time to think about it at all? She was trying to understand that she would never see the younger woman again, but the thought wouldn't take. She dreaded what came after it did.

"I'm sorry," Avasarala said.

Drummer shook her head.

"It won't help you," the old woman said, "but they all knew the risks going in. The chances that we would turn the *Tempest* back the first time we tried? Always thin."

"We should have waited," Drummer said. "We should have pulled them all back. Gathered everyone together and had every goddamn ship we have attack that fucking monstrosity at the same time. Wipe it out."

Her voice broke. She was crying, but it didn't feel like it was her doing it. Avasarala handed her a cloth. "You're mistaken, Camina. The cost was higher than we wanted. Higher than we'd thought. But we did what we came here to do."

"Die? Badly?"

"Learn," Avasarala said. "How quickly the deck healed itself? That's something we needed to know. But the places where a rail-gun round hit their PDCs, the weapons system there didn't grow right back into place? We needed those too, and we didn't even know to look for them. Maybe the ship can't fix more complex mechanisms. We have a map of the armaments now. Where the PDCs are. Where the rail guns are. Where the torpedoes launch from. Next time, you can target those specifically. Degrade its attacking power, push it in ways we couldn't this time because we just didn't know."

"All right," Drummer said.

"They didn't die for nothing," Avasarala said.

"Everyone dies for nothing," Drummer said.

They were quiet for a moment. Drummer coughed, blew her nose into the cloth, and then leaned forward, her elbows on her knees. Since the moment she'd taken the oath of office, there had been moments—not many, but enough to recognize—that she'd been certain that her place at the head of the union was all a terrible mistake. Saba promised her that everyone felt like that, like an impostor, sometimes. It was part of being human. His words had seemed comforting before. In her mind, Independence died again. She had the sick feeling that it would die a thousand more times before she got to sleep. More when she dreamed it.

"Did you do this to me?" she asked.

Avasarala frowned, papery forehead folding itself like a slept-on sheet.

"Did you manipulate me into sacrificing my people so that you'd get the data you wanted?" Drummer said. "Was this you?"

"This was history fucking us both," Avasarala said. "Live as long as I have? See the changes that I've seen? You'll learn something terrible about this."

"Tell me."

"No point. Until you see it yourself, you won't understand."

"Hey, you know what? Fuck you."

Avasarala laughed hard enough that her wheelchair thought something was wrong and bucked forward a few centimeters before she could stop it. "Fair enough, Camina. Fair enough. Here then. See if you can follow me. Last long enough, and you'll see that they're all our people."

"Independence and the *Ontario*," Drummer spat. "Union and EMC, all one big happy family standing against the blowtorch together. Wonderful."

"I told you that you wouldn't understand," Avasarala said, her voice cold and cutting. "The fuckers on the *Tempest*? I'm telling you they're us too."

Chapter Twenty-Eight: Holden

The artificially pretty man who acted as the news anchor for what everyone was calling the Laconian-state newsfeed sat in somber reflection, not quite looking directly into the camera. On a screen behind him, the first battle between the *Tempest* and the combined forces of the Sol system played out. It was all from the *Tempest*'s perspective, of course. Lots of telescopic zooms and torpedo-guidance camera footage. In one, a Martian frigate, one of the *Rocinante*'s next-generation cousins, died in a fireball as a rail gun shot cut through it from nose to tail. In another, a torpedo camera POV hurtled through space and into the flank of a UNN destroyer and ended in a flash of static.

One by one, the ships of the Sol fleet died. From the footage, it wasn't possible to tell if the *Tempest* was even damaged. And each time a ship died, a quiet gasp went through the air around Holden as he sat and watched the first act of the end of the world in a cramped metal room surrounded by the members of his little resistance group.

The screen behind the pretty man went blank. He turned his sober face directly into the camera and said, "To address Medina Station regarding what you've just seen, we are honored to bring you a statement from station governor, Captain Santiago Singh."

The camera pulled back to reveal Governor Singh sitting at the news desk next to pretty boy. Singh lacked his counterpart's carefully sculpted androgynous beauty, but he shared his look of quiet reflection.

"Greetings, Laconian citizens and residents of Medina Station. I come here in a moment of tragedy for us all. I will not gloat, or brag about Laconian military superiority. I have no wish to glory in the destruction you've just witnessed. Instead, I honor the brave warriors of the Sol system, who died believing they were defending their homes. There is no greater sacrifice a warrior can make, and I have nothing but respect for these courageous people. I ask that you honor them as well, as we have a moment of silence."

Singh lowered his head and closed his eyes. Pretty boy did the same.

"Motherfucker," someone behind Holden said. Next to him, Bobbie loudly cracked her knuckles and frowned so hard Holden worried she might pull out the fresh stitches holding her cheek together.

On the screen, Singh lifted his head, then a moment later opened his eyes. "Laconians, and I speak to everyone on Medina when I say that, as I consider all of you my fellow citizens and peers. Laconians, the stated goal of your military is always the defense and protection of life. When the Sol system fleet ceased their attack and began a retreat, the *Heart of the Tempest* immediately ceased firing on them. And no element of the Laconian military—ship, soldier, or station—will ever fire except in response to threat to life or property."

"Or in retribution against a whole fucking system you don't like," someone said from behind Holden. "Hypocritical dawusa."

Singh leaned forward, his dark eyes imploring all who watched him. "I urge everyone with family or friends in the Sol system to contact them, to urge their political representatives to meet with Admiral Trejo and discuss the terms of their entry into the Laconian Empire without further military action and loss of life. Those who died were heroes all, but Laconia wants live citizens, not dead heroes. It is our duty—yours and mine—to do everything we can to achieve peace and safety for all of us. To this end, I am temporarily lifting the communication blackout back to the Sol system for those with family there. Please use this freedom to help your loved ones make the right decision. Thank you for your attention, and good day to all."

Bobbie rolled her shoulders like a boxer stepping into the ring. To her right, Naomi was staring at the screen through half-lidded eyes, like she was solving a complex math problem. Holden was about to speak when Saba stood up and walked to the front of the room. The thirty or so people of the Medina Station insurgency became respectfully quiet. Holden held his breath.

"No reprisals," Saba said, and Holden released his held breath in a rush. That was *not* what he'd expected to hear. "You savvy, coyos? Not one *fucking* thing. Yeah, pissed off, you. Got reason. Got all the reason. Want to cut a throat, make somebody pay."

"God damn right," a skinny man everyone called Nutter said, standing up and toying with the knife on his belt. "Maybe a lot of throats."

"You do," Saba said to him, "and yours is next, and I'm doing the cutting. Mushroom food, you. Every Laconian throat you cut is ten of ours you're bleeding out. We stay angry, but we stay *smart*, sabe? Stay with your missions, stay with your plans."

A ripple of grudging assent moved through the room. People started getting up to leave. The mutters of conversation had an edge to them, but Holden didn't hear anyone actively planning a murder, so he'd call it a win.

Holden caught Bobbie's eye and then stood up to grab Saba's arm before he could leave. "Let's talk."

Fifteen minutes later Saba, Bobbie, and Naomi were sipping tea out of waxy cups in the Diner. Holden tried casually leaning against the wall for a minute, then gave up and paced around the room to give his restless energy someplace to go.

"The problem we've got right now is we're all rats in a cage," he said. "And we're spending a lot of time and energy figuring out how big the cage is and where the doors are and how we might open one. But we haven't got a single clue what we'd do if we actually got out."

"We don't start with just getting out?" Naomi asked.

"There was a time when I'd have said that was enough," Holden agreed. "But that was when I was still thinking of this as a war. When escaping to join up with our side of the fight might matter."

"This isn't a war now," Bobbie said, her voice low and dangerous.

"No?" Saba asked.

"No," Holden said. "The war's over. Sol might not know it yet, and a lot of people will die so that they can feel like they gave it a shot, but it's over."

"So what, then," Saba asked. "Good Laconians, us?"

"No," Holden replied. "At least not yet. But it does change the nature of what we're doing here. We're not looking to get the *Roci* free and join the fight. This is a jailbreak."

Naomi made a clicking noise with her tongue, her eyes distant, then said, "All the same problems. The Marines, the Laconian destroyer, Medina's scopes. But you're saying if we can solve those, we just get as many people and ships free as we can and make a run for it. Scatter."

Saba nodded one fist, then gave her the two-fingered OPA salute. Holden felt a little twinge of unease about that, but this wasn't the time to talk it through.

"It gives us a goal," Holden said. "Maybe we can keep everyone pulling the same direction if they understand what the end game is."

Saba tilted his head. There was no surprise in his expression. He'd been thinking along the same lines, so maybe he'd come to the same conclusions. "The decryption safe room."

"I don't like losing it," Holden said, looking more at Bobbie now than Saba. "We're still getting in a lot of data from the sniffer, and I know once we move forward with the plan, we lose that. We won't get it back. But until we can decrypt what we do have, we can't use it. And the *Typhoon*? It's due in thirty-three days."

"Thirty-two," Naomi said.

"I don't want to die with one still in the chamber," Bobbie said. "I'm good with the timing."

"Bien," Saba said. "I'm in."

"Great," Holden replied. "Get word to every cell leader and ship captain you trust. We need to have everyone ready when the time comes."

"This is gonna be some strange bedfellows," Saba said as he left.

"Find some lunch?" Holden said to Naomi.

"Give me half an hour," she replied. "I want to get a computer crunching the tactical data that video gave us. But after that, meet out front?"

"OK," Holden said, wondering how to waste half an hour in the cramped space of their little hideout.

"Hey, Holden," Bobbie said as Naomi left the room. "Can I hang on to you for a second?"

Holden shrugged and sat on a crate. Bobbie sat flexing her hands and staring at the floor so long that Holden started to wonder if he'd misheard her. He braced himself. He didn't know where this conversation was going to go, but he had a suspicion it was about her and him and the captaincy of the *Rocinante*, and he didn't know what to say about any of that. So it came as kind of a relief that he was wrong.

"Amos is going to be a problem," she finally said. "I had the Voltaire people talked off the ledge when he started that fight. He wanted to crack some heads, and he made it happen. That's fine for shore leave when he wants to blow off some steam, but it won't fly when we're under the radar like this."

"Huh. Okay. I'd wondered about that."

"It's a problem I don't know how to fix," Bobbie said.

"Me neither," Holden said. "But give it a couple days."

"Not sure we have them," Bobbie said.

"Why not?"

Bobbie pointed behind her back, meaning not what was physically behind her but backward in time. "You just gave us all a goal," she said. "Something to bring us all together."

"I did," Holden said. "And I'm thinking from the way you're looking at me right now that there's some aspect of that I've maybe overlooked?"

"Some of us are Katria Mendez and her mad bombers."

Holden felt a coolness down his spine. "Yeah. That could be interesting," he said.

"Right?"

He found Amos in a narrow side hall, a welding torch in his hand. The big man's arms showed little pocks of red where sparks had landed, but Amos hadn't done so much as find a long-sleeved work shirt.

"Hey," Holden said. "How's it going?"

"Doing all right," Amos said, gesturing at the conduits that textured the wall. "Saba's folks said we should reroute the power. Makes it a little harder for the cops to track down where they're losing it from if it keeps moving."

"Yeah?"

"Decent plan in theory," Amos said. "In practice, kind of an ass-pain, but whatever."

"I can see that," Holden said, then paused.

The truth was, in spite of decades flying the same ship, Holden still had very little idea what made Amos tick. He liked food, booze, meaningless sex, jokes. He seemed to like palling around with Alex, but when their pilot had decided to try being married again, Bobbie had been his best man. Amos treated every word out of Naomi's mouth as if it were gospel, but the truth was all of them did these days.

Amos found the conduit he was looking for, lit up the torch, and opened a six-centimeter length of it, exposing the plastic-sheathed wire inside it without so much as melting the insulation. It was a good trick. Amos killed the torch.

"So," Holden said again. "How's it going?"

Amos paused. Turned to look at Holden.

"Ah," the big mechanic said. "Sorry there, Cap. Were we having a conversation and I didn't notice?"

"Kind of, yes," Holden said.

"Babs ratted me out." Amos' voice was as calm as the surface of still water. Holden was pretty certain something big was swimming underneath it.

"Look," he said, "we didn't get where we are by me prying into things you didn't want pried into. I don't want to change that now. But yes, Bobbie's worried about you. I am too. We're going into some pretty dangerous times here, and if there's anything that you need to get off your chest, now is a better time than later."

Amos shrugged. "Nah, I get it. I got a little happy when we went on that last run. Opened up sooner than Babs would have liked. I'll rein in some if it makes her feel better."

"I don't want to make an issue of it," Holden said.

"It ain't an issue, then," Amos said, turning back to the conduit. He took a thick pair of pliers from his pocket, clamped them over the power cable, and started wrestling it out like he was getting crab meat out of a shell. It looked really dangerous. "I'll play nice. Cross my heart."

"Okay, then," Holden said. "Great. Glad we had this talk."

"Anytime," Amos said.

Holden hesitated, turned, and walked away. Bobbie was right. He didn't know what was going on in Amos' mind, but something definitely was. He was hard-pressed to think what the good version of that looked like. And if Amos was finally coming off the rails, he had no idea what would cause it or how to fix it.

Chapter Twenty-Nine: Bobbie

The representatives from the Voltaire Collective entered the meeting space like they were anticipating an attack. She would have felt the same if the positions were reversed. Three in the front with unencumbered hands, three in the back looking around like tourists coming to a casino for the first time in case something interesting or threatening would come from behind, and in the center, Katria Mendez. Her face was the expressionless calm of a player at a poker table. The kind that always left with more chips than she came with. Just seeing her made Bobbie's cheek throb a little. Psychosomatic pain, but pain all the same. She registered the sensation but didn't let it bother her.

Saba stepped forward, Holden at his side, and greeted them, waved them forward with smiles and Belter salutes. He let them check him for weapons first as a kind of social courtesy, and Holden did the same. The old phrase from back in the day came to Bobbie's mind: There's OPA and there's *OPA*. Same now as it had been then. It was always a little eerie to see how comfortably the men and women of the Transport Union fell back into being criminals. And how well she and the crew of the *Roci* fit in with them when they did.

Amos stretched his shoulders and neck.

"I know," Bobbie said. "I don't like it either."

"Don't recognize the one with the nose," Amos said, pointing with his chin toward Katria's bodyguard. "The other ones, I'm pretty sure we danced with."

Bobbie considered their faces. The one Amos was talking about stood in the rear, just behind Katria. He had olive skin, close-cropped hair, and a long nose that had been broken a couple times and not set right. A white scar marked one nostril like someone had slit it for him once. She was pretty sure she'd have remembered him if she'd run into him before. The others, she wasn't as certain. Katria, obviously, and two of her guards at the front all seemed familiar enough.

"Maybe we'll get to know him," Bobbie said.

"Now you're just flirting with me, Babs. Promising a good dustup when everyone else is here for talking."

"Yeah, well," Bobbie said. "A girl can dream."

The banter felt almost normal, but she wasn't easy with it. Not yet. She was plenty willing to play along for the moment, though. Katria caught her eye and nodded. Bobbie smiled, her cheek pulling at its new scab, and nodded back. It could have been respect between equals or the handshake at the start of a fight. Bobbie figured they'd all find out which soon enough.

The meeting space was new to her. A long, thin room that had been part of the water-recycling system recently enough that it still smelled a little bit of wet plant and sewage. Twice as long as it was wide, there was enough space for the *Roci* crew, Saba, and a half dozen of his most trusted crew. The ones who already knew the plan. It wasn't a pleasant spot, but the cartography of the underground's borders were shifting now, more and more often.

The Laconian surveys had been finding the holes in the system surveillance, denying them free access to the corridors and units they'd made their own. They'd been spending more and more of their time in the monitored public spaces. Part of that had been reconnaissance for her plan. Part of that had been that there were fewer and fewer spaces left on Medina where they could speak freely.

All through the station, there were soldiers and crowd-suppression drones. It didn't bother her, passing the people with haunted eyes, walking like the deck might be too fragile to support their mass. She understood them. The others, the ones who were laughing and talking and listening to music loud enough that she could hear the bass, bothered her more. They were acting like the open-air prisons and the power-armored Marines, the communications control and shift curfews were normal. And because of that, they were.

It wouldn't be long before the Laconians started shipping through the slow zone again. Maybe she and the others would be allowed back on the *Roci* when that happened, but Bobbie found it hard to believe there wouldn't be monitors placed in there too. It could take Naomi and Clarissa days or weeks to purge them all and make their ship fully their own again.

And by then, it would be too late anyway. Every day, every hour, brought the *Typhoon*'s arrival closer. And once it had cleared the Laconia gate, staying ahead of the occupying forces became orders of magnitude more difficult. Which was the optimist's way of saying "impossible." Bobbie felt the pressure of time slipping away like she was watching a door close, with her on the wrong side of it. If it hadn't been for the time pressure, she wouldn't have gone along with Saba's suggestion to reach out to the Voltaire Collective. Or at least not so soon after she and Amos had kicked their asses.

The only good thing was that Katria and her people were just as screwed as Saba and Bobbie and Holden, and by the same things.

"So," Katria said once the requisite sniffing was done, "I'm surprised at having so civil a meeting. I have to think you need something from me you can't manage by yourselves?"

Saba smiled, but waved his hand twice sharply. "Too many ears, sa sa? Come sit with me and mine, have a drink, and we'll talk about what we talk about."

Katria crossed her arms.

"It's not you," Holden said. "It's just that the fewer people know about this, the less chance someone gets picked up by security. You can't tell anyone what you don't know, right?"

Katria Mendez looked from Saba to Holden and then, pointedly over to where the *Roci* crew were sitting. Not just Bobbie and Amos, but Naomi and Alex and Clarissa besides. "So none of mine but all of theirs?"

"All of theirs already know," Saba said. "They're who wants to talk with you most."

"They have strange ways of showing it," Katria said.

"This is my house," Saba said. "My salt on it, yeah? Parley. And if it's nothing, it's nothing. But we're under the same thumb, you and me. Not asking you to love anyone. Just listen to."

For a moment, Katria hesitated. Her scowl bit into her cheeks like it was going for bone. Bobbie had a brief flash of certainty that the whole Voltaire Collective was about to turn and walk away without even hearing her pitch, and she was more than a little relieved at the idea.

"Esá es bullshit," the one with the nose spat. "They're just trying to get you on your own, que? Make you not be here, that's all. It's all of us or none!"

"It's my call, Jordao," Katria snapped. "Not yours."

The one with the nose—Jordao, apparently—stepped back, sulking. Holden was smiling like a salesman, as if his radiant goodwill could warm up every other interaction in the room. It left him looking more than a little ridiculous, but damned if Katria didn't consider him for a long moment and chuckle.

"If I refuse, then we all took a long walk for nothing," she said.

Holden beamed. Bobbie wasn't sure how he did it. The way he could disarm a situation with his almost palpable guilelessness astonished her every time.

"Thank you," Holden said. "I really appreciate this."

Saba lifted a hand and two of his people ghosted in from the corridor and led Katria's guard away. Standing by herself, she didn't seem any less imposing. The door to the corridor slid shut, and the bolt clicked. It was as near to privacy as anyone on Medina could have.

"So," Katria said. "What's on your mind?"

Bobbie took a long breath, let it out between her teeth. The idea had been hers from the start, and she'd been mulling it over for days. She hadn't slept as much as she'd wanted. Even when she hadn't been reviewing it and looking for holes in the plan, she'd felt too jagged and amped up to sleep. Part of that had been thinking about how to make the approach she was going for now.

"There's a single point of contact between the Laconian destroyer and Medina," Bobbie said. "And we have a bug on it."

Katria's eyes went a degree wider. She glanced over to Saba, who nodded. It was true. Katria didn't sit, but her weight settled into her hips a little. Bobbie had her attention. That was good.

"The encryption isn't breakable," she said. "Not from the outside. The Martian codes it's based on are solid. We might be able to crack them if we had between now and about a decade on, but we're down to a countable number of days. So we've got enough intelligence gathered to fill libraries that we can't read. But I think we can fix that."

She plucked her hand terminal out of her pocket, slaved it to Saba's local system, and pulled up the schematic of Medina that she'd been using. The cavernous center of the drum, command and control on one end, engineering and the docks and the massive but quiescent engines on the other. The elevator shafts that ran between them outside the surface of the drum. And also the ships in the dock, including—highlighted in red—the *Gathering Storm*.

"The longer goal is that we find a way to disable the *Storm*, here, shut down Medina's sensor arrays, and distract or isolate the security forces on Medina long enough to let all these ships get off station and out through the rings before their reinforcements from Laconia get here. The short-term goal"—she zoomed in on a small red mark inside Medina proper, near the docks—"is this."

"And that is?" Katria asked.

"It used to be backup power storage," Bobbie said. "But since our guests from Laconia got here, it's been repurposed."

"The thing is," Alex said, breaking in, "these Laconian fellas? They were all Martians to start, or their leadership were anyway. And they were serving just a little after me and Bobbie here did our tours."

He looked from Bobbie to Katria to Saba and then back. Bobbie nodded him on. Alex licked his lips.

"One of the things we trained on was how to go about securing an enemy station," he said, which wasn't true. It was something Bobbie had trained to do, not him. Storm and control the homes and communities of Belters. If there was going to be a sore spot, this would be it. It was why Alex was saying it instead of the woman who'd cleaned Katria's clock and left her zip-tied to her friends. It seemed less likely to rub on Katria wrong that way. "You heard of air-gap encryption strong rooms?"

Katria's eyes were brighter. She hadn't, but she didn't want to admit that. Alex licked his lips again, shot a look from Bobbie to Katria and back to Bobbie, then went on. "One thing that we did was maintain physical separation between whatever ship was taking control and the local systems. Lay in a pipe to one of our own boxes on the station, and send any commands we wanted for the base there. Communications, control protocols, everything. It gets unencrypted there, and set onto onetime physical media to walk over to the local system. No live connections at all."

"Bullshit," Katria said.

"It's standard," Bobbie said. "And it's part of why no one was ever able to hack back into a Martian ship from a controlled station. And since the Laconians are basing their protocols on Martian ones, this is where that machine is."

"But the lag time—" Katria shook her head. "That's impressive."

"The room is crewed by two people, always. The door is physically locked. Not connected to the security grid, no electronic interface. Old-school bolt and key, and no keyhole on the outside. Can't be hacked into remotely, can't be circumvented easily," Bobbie said. "And a full complement of guards at shift change."

Katria took control of the model, zooming farther in on the encryption vault. Her face was thoughtful, which was better than Bobbie had hoped. It made her nervous to talk about this.

"I see," Katria said. "You can't get in without making a lot of noise and calling in the cavalry. Is that why you need me? To blow the door?"

"No," Bobbie said. "We have a way in. We need your help to cover it up once we're done."

Katria traced a slow circle with her fingers. *Go on.*

Clarissa picked up the thread. "The room is still connected to the environmental system. But if we put a team here"—she pulled the model back to a larger frame and touched the power junctions near engineering—"we can shut down the fans and open the carbon dioxide scrubbers and recycling systems."

"Choke them out?" Katria asked.

Alex shook his head. "Make a path to pilot some little drones in. Half a dozen of 'em with point-blasting charges. Take down the two guards, then use the rest to pop the lock." He made a little boom sound with his lips and opened two fists in the physical cartoon of an explosion.

Bobbie pointed toward Naomi. "She has a snapshot cloning deck. I'll have a crowbar and a hammer. We get in, make a full-state copy of the encryption box, and get out to the hardened-radiation shelter"—Bobbie moved the model—"here. And then *you* come in."

"If los security coyos know we stole their codes," Saba said, leaning against the wall, "they change things up, yeah? Not just new crypt but new procedures. Everything we've got turns into a whole lot less. So they can't know what we do, even after it's done."

Holden pulled the model out to show where the *Storm* was docked against the side of the station. "We need to give them a different story. The *Storm*'s parked here. And the primary liquid-oxygen storage tanks are...right here. If that blows out, it will look like we're trying to blow up the *Storm*, but Tycho built this place well. Lots of redundancy and fail-safes. There's an explosion-relief route that'll vent the pressure blast out along this pathway here...which takes out the communications vault. And, y'know, a bunch of other stuff."

"You want to blow our air out as cover?" Katria said. "I think you may owe us an apology. We're usually the ones who are called extreme."

"Not our air," Saba said. "Theirs as soon as they came here. We're breathing on their grace, us. Plus, those tanks are docked-ship refills. Not for the habitat."

"And there will be plenty in the secondary and tertiary tanks," Holden said. "Remember, lots of redundancy, lots of fail-safes. And Tycho's original design remembers longer than the people living in it do."

Katria went quiet for a long time. Bobbie felt the anxiety growing in her gut. It had been a mistake to bring the Voltaire Collective in on this. It didn't matter how much Saba trusted them or how good they were with demolitions. She should have kept it just within her own crew, where she could control it. Where she was sure of everyone...

"I don't like it," Katria said, shaking her head. "A lot of moving parts. The more pieces there are, the more ways there are for it to break."

Bobbie shrugged. "If the time wasn't so short, I'd do something simpler."

"All we need is the right bomb, the right place," Saba said. "You give us those, and we take the mission from there."

"No," Katria said. "You need the charges, you need someone to put the charges in the right places at the right time. And need someone on the remote switch who doesn't panic and throw it a little too early and take out your team. And even if they don't, do you think someone in a rad shelter's going to live through that blow?"

Naomi cleared her throat. "They're rated for it. But you're right. We can't know until we try."

"What's the evac plan once your little Armageddon is over?" Katria asked.

It was more than Bobbie had wanted to say. There should be some parts of the plan that weren't being shared. Saba paused, weighing whether to bring Katria that far in. When he spoke, his voice was surly. He didn't like having his hand forced any more than Bobbie did. "Vac suits in the shelter. Go out through the hole. Same airlock we used to bug the line the first time, we use it to get back in."

Katria took control of the model again, turning it, moving through the lower reaches of Medina deck by deck. "It's going to kill people," she said. "When the engineering decks start breathing vacuum, not everyone's going to make it to the shelters."

"Savvy," Saba said. "Has a price."

"Is it one you'd pay?"

"Is," Saba said, but Holden's expression had a distance to it. Bobbie could tell what was in his mind. There could be innocent people on the decks when the time came. At best, their plan would risk them. At worst, some would be killed. If Saba and Katria were bothered by the idea, they didn't show it. Holden was bothered by it. She wondered if he'd stand on principle and scrub the whole thing. It was even money, knowing him.

"Demolition team goes here," Katria said. "Plant the charges, then fall back to the shelter and wait for the team with the stolen data to arrive, then blow it. Everyone leaves together, or no one does. It's not my first time on an op like this. You'll need a couple more vac suits, is all."

Bobbie didn't catch the important word until Clarissa spoke, her voice gentle and questioning. But Bobbie heard the sharpness under it. "*Your* first time on an op like?"

"Who else?" Katria said. "If you want it done right, you get the best to do it. I'm the best. I make the charges, I place the charges, and it's my steady hand holding the detonator."

The room was quiet apart from the soft hiss of the air recyclers and the soft, harmonic thrum of the ship. The hint of old sewage smelled a little worse. Saba had only wanted the Voltaire Collective involved for material support. They weren't looking for another player when the operation took place. But telling Katria she couldn't be active in the field...would it insult her? And if it did, would that be enough to get her to turn on them?

"Sounds good," Amos said. "You and me on the demo team, Miss Kitty."

His smile was placid and empty. Bobbie felt a shock of alarm. She met Holden's gaze and shook her head a millimeter. *This is a very bad idea.* Holden swallowed, nodded, forced himself to smile as well.

"All right, then," Holden said. "Clarissa leads the support team on environmental controls for Alex. Alex pilots in the drone swarm. Bobbie and Naomi take care of the server, and Katria, Amos, and I will set the charges to cover it all up afterward."

Bobbie leaned back, a lump forming in her gut. Adding Holden in was *not* a better solution.

"This'll be great," Holden said.

Chapter Thirty: Singh

Sol operation nearing completion. Prepare initial shipping authorizations.

Singh read Trejo's message over twice, joy blooming in his chest. He took a moment to send the order to his section heads and group commanders, and pulled up what everyone jokingly called the "occupation calendar." Even based on the amended projections from Laconia that included not pausing to rebuild the battery, the immediate transit of the *Tempest* to Sol system, and the early deployment of the *Typhoon*, they were weeks ahead of schedule. They'd built some flex into the schedule in the event that the Transport Union put up a more bitter fight to hold Medina, or the Earth-Mars Coalition Navy had revealed naval forces or technology significantly greater than their estimates. But neither thing had turned out to be true, and sooner than anyone expected, they could get down to the business of building the new human civilization.

The sad fact of the human species that High Consul Duarte understood so well was that you could never overcome tribalism and jingoism with an argument. Tribalism was an irrational position, and it was impossible to defeat an irrational position with a rational argument. And so, instead of presenting a logical plan for why humanity needed to give up the old national and cultural divides and become a single unified species, the high consul obeyed the old forms that everyone would understand, and went to war. Thankfully, a brief one.

The real work, the work that would let Elsa grow up in a universe that was safe for her, and for her children's children's children, was the work that came after the conquest of the rest of humanity. Work that required stability.

"Ensign," Singh said at his monitor, which was currently flattened out on his desk. He'd appointed a temporary replacement for Lieutenant Kasik, and he hadn't quite memorized her name yet.

"Governor?" she replied a moment later.

"Please send my compliments to President Fisk, and let her know we're sending a cart to pick her up. I need an immediate meeting to discuss some urgent matters. Do not take no."

"Yes, sir," the ensign replied. "I also—"

"Right away, Ensign," Singh said, then took a look around at his office. The flowers someone had placed in a vase on his corner table were dying, and the shelf that held his coffeemaker was a mess. "Also, send in someone to make fresh coffee and replace these flowers before the meeting."

"Yes, sir. I wanted to also let you know that you have an incoming message from Laconia. The *Storm* just sent it over."

"Send it through. And please let me know five minutes before President Fisk arrives."

"Of course, sir," the ensign said and then killed the connection.

Singh tapped on the glowing message button on his monitor and it projected a still picture of his wife holding Monster.

"Play message," he said.

The still image sprang to life. The recording must have started midway through her expression, because Nat's face went from an enigmatic Mona Lisa smile to her normal wide grin. Monster didn't seem all that interested in the camera lens, and instead was focused on something over her mother's shoulder. They were both beautiful, and Singh felt an emptiness in the pit of his stomach that was always there, but that he managed to ignore until he saw their faces.

"Hi, Sonny," Nat said to the camera. She held up Monster's hand and waved at the screen with it. "Say hi to Daddy."

"Hi, sweetie," Singh said to the recording like an idiot. He couldn't help himself.

"I know you're so busy right now, but we have some good news to pass along," Nat said. She put Monster down, and the girl ran off out of frame. Singh felt irrationally disappointed to see her go. "My work with sheep modification has been approved for the next round of live testing. We could go wide with it in the next thirty months. Which means a posting to Medina would actually help me move the project forward. No pressure, or anything."

She smiled as she said it, but he felt the loneliness echoed in her eyes. She continued. "Monster is doing well. She's a little bored, and *so* ready to move into the big kids' room at school. She spends most afternoons with your dad, and they're becoming the best of friends. She calls him Poompaw now, and he's started insisting everyone else call him that too. Most days he doesn't want me to take her when I get off work. We eat dinner at his place a lot of evenings."

Singh felt a swell of love and gratitude for his father that he'd never felt before he had a child of his own. He paused the video playback and took a moment so he wouldn't get maudlin and weepy. It wouldn't do to bring Carrie Fisk in and begin delivering his orders while his eyes were goopy and red. When he'd gathered himself, he started it again.

"So, that's it, I guess. Reply when you get a minute. The home monitor has figured out Monster's version of the word *play*, so she loves replaying your messages over and over again. Love you, Sonny. Be safe out there."

And that was it. Nat saying she loved him shattered whatever resolve he thought he had, and he spent the next several minutes blubbering shamefully to himself.

Someone tapped at his door, and he called out, "Give me a moment!" Then rushed off to his private bathroom. While he was washing his face, he heard the sounds of someone cleaning up his office, and by the time he'd put himself back in shape to see people, there was a fresh pot of coffee percolating on the shelf. A noncom was just finishing up by placing new flowers in his vase. The chief threw him a snappy salute, then faded out of the room like a cat.

Singh sat at his desk, composed himself, then started a recording to Nat. "Hello, my dear. Thank you for the lovely message. I'm so happy to hear things are going well there, and Monster looks very well fed, so my father is almost certainly spoiling her rotten with sweet rolls. Things are still ahead of schedule here. Living here will take some getting used to, but there's plenty of usable land for your sheep and lab, and we're working to get all the services up to snuff for my little girl. Talk soon. I love you, Nat. I love you—" He almost said *Monster*, but something felt wrong about using her pet name. "I love you, Elsa."

He killed the connection, and sent the file for processing to pass it down to Laconia with the next comm dump. He took a lot of pride in the fact that saying "I love you" to Nat hadn't sent him into another weeping fit. There were people who thought that sort of thing was unmanly. Singh didn't care about that. But it was undignified.

"Five minutes," Ensign Somebody said from his monitor.

"I'm ready," he replied.

Carrie Fisk sat in a chair in his office, drinking his coffee and looking twitchy and uncomfortable. She'd been picked up at her office by fully armored Marines and driven to the governor's offices in a convoy of three carts filled with other Marines. For her protection, certainly, but it could also be a little intimidating for someone who wasn't used to it. If that gave Singh a bit of a home-field advantage when dealing with the minor functionaries on Medina, he'd happily take it. He waited until she'd stopped fidgeting and started paying attention to him, then pulled up a list of the hundreds of ring systems that had habitable colonies and threw the list up onto his wall.

"Madam President," he said. "We've reached an exciting moment for us all, but especially for you as the first president of the Laconian Congress of Worlds."

"Are we married to that name change?" she asked. "Or..."

"The name of the legislative body is established in the documentation I gave you after our first meeting. Did you not read those documents?"

"I did," she said. "I just wasn't sure if that was a working title, or not. We haven't voted on adopting the new—"

"You do not vote on directives delivered from the executive authority of the high consul's office."

"I see," Fisk said. She stared at her lap and blew steam off her coffee.

"As I was saying," Singh continued. "This is an exciting time for us all. High Admiral Trejo has decided that our situation is now secure enough to allow limited trade to resume through the gates."

Fisk looked up at him with genuine surprise. "What?"

"Yes. *Limited* trade can be scheduled starting now. Put together a list of the worlds in the greatest need, as well as a schedule of deliveries that can meet those needs. Not from Sol system. Not yet. At first, we'll allow a single ship transit per week, and of course each transit must be approved by me personally at least thirty days before it's scheduled to occur."

"That's actually—" Fisk started, then stopped for a moment. "That's actually really good to hear. There are a lot of colonies barely hanging on by a thread. This will save lives."

"And that is, of course, always the first priority of our respective positions."

"Ah," Fisk said, then leaned forward to put her coffee cup on the edge of his desk. As Singh frowned at it and the disrespectful informality it denoted, she said, "On that topic I passed along your threat to every colonized world. I also extended your invitation to the planets that have not already joined the association—forgive me, the Laconian Congress of Worlds—to elect a representative to join our group once trade has resumed. I assume some of those planets will be asking to send their new reps along with the trade ships."

"That's good," Singh said. The Laconian Congress of Worlds was something High Consul Duarte insisted on to make the member worlds feel like they had a voice in government. As annoying as the idea of dealing with thirteen hundred Carrie Fisks would be, the high consul's opinion on this topic had the force of law, so he'd do his best to see that the new legislative body succeeded.

Fisk was still staring at him, waiting for some sort of answer.

"And?" he asked.

"And, if some of these transiting ships are carrying newly elected representatives, they'll need permission to dock or send shuttles to Medina. Does the lifting of the transit ban also include permission to dock with the station?"

Which was an excellent question, and Singh was annoyed that Carrie Fisk had thought of it before he did.

"Permission will be granted by this office on a case-by-case basis. Requests to be filed at minimum thirty days prior to the transit," he said, feeling like it came across as established policy and not something he'd just made up on the spot. He'd need to document that once Fisk left.

"Thank you, Governor," Fisk said.

"It's important that this feel familiar, stable, and safe as quickly as possible," Singh told her. "To the degree possible, you will use Transport Union ships and pilots. The union will also handle the pickup and delivery of goods using their existing policies. Other than the approval process for transits, everything should work the way it did before."

"I'll send out a notice to the union reps here on the station, and to the local leadership on each world."

"Excellent," Singh said, standing up and reaching out to shake her hand. "At the risk of sounding repetitive, these are very exciting times for us all."

Fisk didn't stand. She sat in his chair squeezing her hands and not looking at him. When the silence had become uncomfortable, he said, "Was there something else, Madam President?"

"There is," she replied, looking him in the eye for the first time. She showed no sign of standing up to leave, so he sat back down again.

"Then out with it," he said, immediately regretting the snappish tone. "Please."

"We're—I'm doing everything you asked. I've passed along your messages to the worlds. I've asked for reps to be sent from every planet that wasn't already part of the association. I've passed along President Duarte's—"

"*High Consul* Duarte," Singh interrupted her.

"Of course," she said. "I've passed along the high consul's very detailed documentation on convening the new Congress of Worlds."

"*Laconian* Congress of Worlds," Singh said.

"Of course. But so far, that's the only thing my office has done. Act as press secretary for *your* office. And, with all due respect, that is not what I was voted into my office to do."

She looked nervous saying it, and Singh gave her a minute to stew in her worry. If the mouse wanted to grow some claws, that was probably a good thing in the long run. The Laconian government had no use for those who wouldn't fight for what they believed. The high consul made it very clear that every conflicting viewpoint should have a vigorous proponent, so that everyone felt that the final decisions were made only after everything was considered fully. A planetary congress run by mice wasn't useful to anyone.

"And what," Singh said after he'd let her squirm enough, "would be a better use of your time, Madam President?"

"If we're to be the legislative body of this new government, when do we actually start legislating? You've brought me in here to deliver these directives for me to disseminate, but not once have we *voted* on them. I feel that very quickly we'll be viewed as a congress in name only, in place to rubber-stamp your orders."

"As the governor," Singh replied, "I am here as the direct representative of the executive branch, and the office of the high consul. You don't *vote* on orders from the high consul."

He couldn't help but laugh a bit at the very ridiculousness of that idea. As if the high consul might change his policies because of a vote.

"Then," Fisk replied, "what do we vote on?"

"When the high consul's office has decided on this year's legislative agenda, you will be the first to be notified, Madam President. Until then, please continue working with the member worlds to ease their transition into the new government. And I assure you, that will be an *excellent* use of your time."

"Okay," Carrie Fisk said, and stood. "I'll just go make sure my rubber stamp is all warmed up."

Singh didn't stand to shake her hand. "You are dismissed."

Singh was still mulling over the deeply unsatisfying meeting he'd had with Carrie Fisk when his monitor buzzed and Overstreet's voice came over the speaker.

"Sir, I have a…gentleman who says he has important information for you."

"Can't he give it to you?"

"He's reluctant to, sir. Says it's for the top man only. I think it might be worth the interview."

That was interesting. Even if the alleged information turned out to be nothing, he was curious to see what sort of thing Overstreet thought important enough to engage him.

"Do we know this person?"

"No, sir," Overstreet replied.

"I assume he's already been searched for weapons."

"Yes, sir."

"Give me two minutes, then," and Singh closed the connection. His office was still neat and tidy from Fisk's visit. He sat up straighter in his chair, and pulled his uniform jacket tight. He turned on his monitor's front-facing camera and examined himself. Secured and shipshape. The very picture of a military commander.

There was a discreet knock, then two Marines walked in with Overstreet and a tall, thin man of the generic Belter variety. The only feature this one had that seemed different at all was his comically large nose. It was misshapen from repeated breaks, and had a large scar on one nostril. Clearly a man who'd been in a few fights, and who did a poor job of keeping his hands up while boxing.

"You asked to see me?" Singh said. He did not offer the man a chair.

"My sister in one of them cages you got out there," the man said, clearly working to keep his accent as Belter free as possible, and only sort of succeeding.

Singh glanced at Overstreet.

"Not one of the people involved in the bombing, Governor," Overstreet said. "Petty theft from a merchant."

"A military tribunal has been formed, and the cases will be adjudicated promptly and in the order they were filed," Singh replied. "Is that all?" It couldn't be, or Overstreet wouldn't have brought the man to his attention, but he was willing to let the Belter do some of the work here.

"All that shit you said, about we help you, you help us? That just the merde or what?"

"It's the truth," Singh said, feeling a glimmer of interest. Overstreet had what could have been the ghost of a smile on his lips. "Are you here to help me?"

"Let my sister go. She's just stupid, caught stealing, no threat to you. Let her go, I know something you want to know." The man rubbed his big, lumpy nose nervously as he spoke. "Something coming, and I know the coyo behind, yeah? Deep in with Voltaire Collective, me."

"You're in contact with the forces behind the bombing?"

"Maybe," the broken-nosed man said. His bravado was barely thick enough to stretch across his fear. "If there's enough in it. You tell it to me."

Singh paused for a moment, letting the silence stretch. A network of locals loyal to him. Dependent on his generosity. It was all coming together so well.

"I think you and I are about to become friends," Singh said.

Chapter Thirty-One: Drummer

Sleep and Drummer had developed an uncomfortable relationship. Its worst aspect was the time it left her to read the public comment boards and newsfeeds.

THIS SENSE OF PURPOSE IS EXACTLY WHAT MARS LOST WHEN THE GATES OPENED. THIS ISN'T AN INVASION AT ALL. IT'S THE RETURN OF THE REAL MARTIAN SPIRIT TO ITS PROPER PLACE, AND I AM HAPPY—FUCK, *DELIGHTED*—THAT I HAVE LIVED LONG ENOUGH TO SEE IT.

The way it played out was predictable. During her days, she felt like People's Home was turning too fast on its axis. Only it wasn't just her body that was getting spun. Her mind was too heavy to lift. She was controlling herself with a bad lag, like driving a mech with choppy software or running a waldo at the edge of its range. Meetings with the union board, with the EMC admiralty, with her own staff. Interviews and speeches in which she declared the independence of the union. She got through all of them with a physical sensation like her brain was evaporating. All she wanted to do from the start of her shift to the last moment before bed was close her eyes.

And then, as soon as she did, they opened again, as if by themselves.

THESE ASSHOLES SHOULD HAVE BEEN CUT OFF BEFORE THEY COULD GET THROUGH THE GATE. THIS IS EXACTLY THE PROBLEM I'VE BEEN TALKING ABOUT FOR YEARS. A TRADE UNION DOESN'T MATTER FOR SHIT WHEN AN ARMY COMES KNOCKING. IF YOU EVER NEEDED ANY PROOF THAT THE TRANSPORT UNION ADMIN-ISTRATION WAS INCOMPETENT, THERE YOU GO. IT'S RIGHT HERE FOR YOU, AND IN SPADES.

She'd try to rest. Try to lure sleep back. Her eyes felt gritty. Her mouth felt dry. She wanted to eat, even though she wasn't hungry. Wanted water, even though she wasn't thirsty. It was like her body knew it needed something, and all it could do was run through the list of possibilities over and over, hoping that some-thing would give her solace that hadn't the last time. She found herself craving a pipeful of marijuana, even though she hadn't smoked in decades.

She waited an hour, maybe two, then got up and spooled through the feeds and networked discussions with a dummy account she'd made for the purpose. She told herself it was research, that she was gauging the morale of the populace. It was easy to pretend that she was somehow learning something that would help. It felt like tearing off a scab and pressing salt into the opened sore, but it was better than paging through the names of the dead. Emily Santos-Baca...

From Ganymede, an independent journalist's twenty-minute recording on the importance of solidarity in the face of the enemy. An old Earther's open letter about surviving the terrible years after the rocks fell and why this time was different. A roundtable discussion by an open salon on Ceres about how the union was or wasn't able to rise to the occasion and address the Laconian threat. A dozen languages, a thousand faces and voices and rhetorical styles. If she was looking for clarity there, she didn't find it.

MY WIFE IS ON MEDINA STATION. I JUST GOT A MESSAGE FROM HER SAYING THAT THE LACONIAN GOVERNOR IS OFFERING BETTER TERMS THAN THE TRANSPORT UNION DID FOR EVERYONE WHO WORKS FOR THEM. AND SHE SAID THE TECHNOLOGY THAT'S COMING THROUGH LACONIA GATE IS GENERATIONS AHEAD OF ANYTHING WE HAVE. I KNOW IT'S NOT A POPULAR OPINION, BUT IF THEY'RE GOING TO TREAT THE WORKERS BETTER, BRING BETTER EQUIPMENT, AND STAY OUT OF OUR BUSINESS OTHERWISE, I THINK OUR REAL ENEMY IS THE BUREAUCRACY IN THE TRANSPORT UNION OFFICES!

There were other voices—many more of them, really—that saw the attack on Medina for what it was. She read essays on defiance in the face of tyranny, listened to music designed to rally the patriotic against the enemy. A school on Luna had started a campaign where the children were dyeing their right hands red in defiance of Laconia. The symbolism of it escaped her, but the trend spread far past the school, and half of the interviewers and journalists on the feeds had some version of it. Red gloves or finger sleeves or rings.

If she'd wanted to feel hopeful or resolved, it would have been easy to find those people and spend her insomniac hours only with them. But like a tongue prodding a sore tooth, she kept reaching for the others. Laconia is the future. The conquest is inevitable. Stop the war.

Capitulate.

There were also whole subfeeds devoted to speculating on the strategy of the EMC and the union. Some of the conversations there were eerily like briefings from the EMC admiralty. Others were desperation-fueled optimism dressed as military theory. None brought Drummer any more hope than she'd had before, and some left her mood darker.

And she hadn't heard from Saba. Even when Medina lifted its comms blackout for propaganda, there'd been no message from him. From the others fighting against the occupation. She imagined that he was still there, sneaking between the decks like a rat made for gnawing through steel. That Medina would fall, and she'd hear his voice declaring their victory. Or failing that, that she'd hear his voice at all.

And behind it all, pressing down on her soul like a suffocating hand, the *Tempest* made its vast, stately way sunward. Already past the halfway point. Already braking. She understood their strategy perfectly. A single ship, making its way for everyone in every system to see. It was a demonstration of authority. Of inevitability. A piece of theater designed to humiliate, to subjugate, to control.

It was what she had done to Freehold.

That, as much as anything, kept her at the table in her quarters as the hours of sleeplessness slipped by. When she'd made the call, it had seemed like the obvious thing to do. Hard, yes, but in the service of a greater peace. A more orderly universe. Someplace where there'd be some respect for the rules.

The colonists on Freehold had made their choices. They'd broken the rules she and the people before her had set down. She'd felt justified when she sent the *Rocinante*. Now she wondered whether the colonists there had sat up in their beds in the night. Wondered how they would feed their children. Whether there was some way to finesse their way out of the future that was bearing down on them. Probably they had.

Maybe this was the way the universe showed her the errors of her ways. Taking the evil that she'd committed so offhandedly and turning it around to point at her. Her and Santos-Baca. All the refugees of Independence. All of the void city's dead. If it was, then the universe hadn't embraced the idea of proportional response yet.

The small, quiet part of her mind that watched all the rest knew that she wasn't right. That there was no way for her to be right, not in a situation like this. If she'd been able to sleep, maybe. But the fear was eroding her bit by bit and taking away all the things that let her recover. Like a recycling pond with a plugged drain, she was filling with shit, and sooner or later, she'd overspill. It wasn't a source of anxiety. It was just something she knew about herself, as if she were thinking about some different woman.

She drew her robe closer around her chest, spooled through the feeds. Watched a few seconds of the news from Loundres Nova, a few seconds out of the shipyards at Tycho-Pallas Complex, Ceres, Luna, Earth. Never enough to hear a whole story.

Weirdly, not all of it was about Laconia. There was a fire at an arcology outside Paris. A popular musician Drummer had liked as a girl had died. It was as if not everything were defined by Laconia and Duarte and her own failures. And then the top traffic on the feed would re-sort, and there was an image of the *Tempest* in all its threat and glory.

Holden had been right. Her plan for Freehold had been cruel, and she'd done it for the convenience of not being a government, not really. So that she could be unprepared when a navy no one knew existed arrived in force. She should have been kinder, wiser, more cunning. She should have been something other than what she was. There had to have been a moment when she could have chosen something different, when all of this could have been stopped. She couldn't think when it had been.

Her system made its tock. If she'd been asleep, her lights would have come up.

"Ma'am?" Vaughn said. Not even his nighttime staff. Whatever it was, they'd woken him up for it first, and he'd made the decision to wake her. That couldn't be good.

"I'm awake," she said.

"We've had a message for you from the *Tempest*. It came in on tightbeam an hour ago. Signal intelligence says it's genuine."

"Not broadcast?"

"No, ma'am. Unencrypted, but not broadcast."

Something the enemy wanted her and her people to see, but not as a press release. The switch in her mind flipped, and she wanted nothing more than to crawl into bed and sleep forever. "I'll take it in my room," she said.

Her screen went dark, and then Admiral Trejo was on it, looking out at her as if he could actually see through the screen and light delay. His expression was almost rueful. That would be a pose, of course. A decision he'd made about how to appear. She hated that, even knowing that, she felt herself hoping he could be reasoned with. Wanting to like him, because then maybe he'd like her. Stockholm syndrome's first, pale roots. She pushed the gentle impulse away and summoned up her hatred.

"President Drummer," he said. "I hope I find you well. On behalf of High Consul Duarte, I'm asking again for the Transport Union's ships to stand down and accept administration by the Laconian Empire. But I understand if that answer is still no. I'm going to keep asking until you change your mind, though. The sooner that comes, the less loss of life your people will suffer. Their fate is entirely up to you.

"If we do not have your unconditional surrender within eighteen hours, though, then I'm afraid things will become less pleasant. I have been ordered to deny you the use of the shipyards at Pallas Station. I'd rather get through this with the least loss of life and infrastructure. Again, entirely in your control. You can end this at any time.

"I am tendering a similar offer to the EMC, and I imagine you'll all want to talk this over. I urge you in the strongest possible terms to do the right thing and lay down your arms. The high consul has given me a certain amount of latitude in how we bring this unpleasantness to a close, but the longer this drags on, the less freedom I'll have. And the worst-case scenario isn't something I relish.

"Confer with your colleagues at the EMC, and reply back to me as soon as you can. If I don't hear from you, I'll assume you've chosen to protract this a little farther. The blood of Pallas Station will be on your hands. I sincerely hope and pray that you'll be wiser than that."

He gave a little nod, and the message ended. Drummer's rage was sluggish and muddy from lack of sleep, but it was hot. She made the connection request, and Vaughn picked it up immediately.

"How many people have seen this?"

"The comms officer on duty, my assistant, me, and now you. Only four."

It was two people too many. Maybe three. Still it might not find its way onto the nets, depending on how well the EMC controlled information in its house. It was the nature of bad news to spread, and once it was out, it was out forever. She had to assume that she didn't have much time before it did. One more chance to try being the person that the situation called for instead of just herself.

If she were the person who should be here, if she were the leader that the union and the system and humanity needed, what would she say now? How would she say it?

"Wake Lafflin up, and get Admiral Hu on the horn. We're going to need a talk."

Pallas Station, Trejo had called it. Not Pallas-Tycho Complex. One of the strange things about Laconian language was the decades of linguistic drift. No one had called it Pallas Station since before Sanjrani had been in charge of the union. He'd overseen the update of Pallas' refineries and the semipermanent installation of Tycho Station as the primary shipyard of the metals and ceramics, lace and nanolaminates produced there. It had been more efficient than leaving Tycho independently on the float. There were generations of work that would need to be done, and putting everything in the same place made it all go faster.

People's Home had been assembled there. And Independence. The void city Assurance of Peace was half-together now, its vast carbon-silicate ribs still bared to the vacuum. Thousands of families lived and worked there, and would for another few hours, unless Drummer capitulated.

"The loss of building capacity would set us back by decades," Admiral Hu said. "Any chance we have of rebuilding and fortifying a navy relies on that station. This would cause a bottleneck that would radically change our projections."

Drummer shifted in her chair. It wasn't the first time she'd listened to the message.

"Deploying the full force of the EMC-and-union-combined navy can't be accomplished in the time frame described here." Hu's face was replaced by a schematic of the system, each fleet marked with its time to engagement. They'd been keeping the ships scattered to deny the *Tempest* a single target-rich environment. Here was the trade-off for that...

"And furthermore, only three-quarters of our ships have completed resupply with the torpedo modifications based on our first engagement. Our strategic analysis is that a decision to sacrifice Pallas-Tycho Complex in order to fully prepare the combined fleet will degrade our long-term readiness, but increase our chances of making a decisive blow against the *Tempest* in the short term. Of course, any decision requires full coordination between the union and the EMC."

Whatever she chose, they would do the same. In the midst of the apocalypse, the military brass on Luna were still playing cover-your-ass. That seemed like the most optimistic thing about the whole report. They still thought they might have careers worth losing when this was over.

Drummer could remember living on Tycho Station. She could still walk through the corridors in her memory. The layout of the engineering decks the way they had been before the refit. The smell of the habitation ring. The office she'd inherited from Fred Johnson after his death. He'd had a personal cabinet there with a few things—an old book, a bottle of brandy, the physical copies of some of his personal initiatives that had foundered after he'd gone. She'd been the head of Tycho Station for three years before she'd cleared that out, and she still remembered how it had felt when she had. Like a widow finally selling off her dead husband's suits.

When she looked at Pallas-Tycho Complex, she felt the same way again. She wanted a way to save it. She kept looking for the clever move that would put it out of the enemy's hands, only there wasn't one. It was already too late. She could hand it and any chance of freedom away, or she could see it destroyed. One or the other. And she had to choose.

"Vaughn?"

"Madam President?"

"We need to put out an emergency evacuation order for Pallas-Tycho. Everyone who doesn't have their own craft, put on Tycho and break it away from the complex. No one is to be left in the Pallas structures, and the highest possible burn for all ships and Tycho Station is recommended."

She looked over at him. His face was grayish. His eyes were dead as a shark's. He didn't argue, though. He only braced, turned, and left the room to carry out her order. Even if he disagreed with her, he was probably glad he hadn't had to make the call. She would have been.

She set her system to Record, considered herself on the screen. Her eyes were sunken with exhaustion and despair, but not as badly as she'd thought they would be. Her skin had a waxy look in the bright light of her private office. She'd want to have the communications staff get her some powder and rouge before she made the public announcement. God, there would have to be a public announcement. But that was later. That was next.

She keyed in the reply code, and the high-security link to Luna showed Ready. She coughed and looked into the camera.

"Admiral Hu, I have given the evacuation order to Pallas-Tycho," she said. "Even if we can't save the station, we can make it harder for the *Tempest* to kill the population there. And seeing whether they feel the civilian targets are worth hunting down may also give us greater insight into the character and aims of the enemy. I advise the EMC forces to refrain from any premature engagement with the enemy at this time.

"It is my opinion that attempting to save Pallas Station would have been an error," she said. "It would be better to prepare the forces we have at our disposal for a full, coordinated, and unrestrained engagement under circumstances more nearly in our control and to our advantage. And with the modified torpedoes and munitions available to all ships. Whatever gives us the best chance in that battle is worth the sacrifice."

She paused. She was thinking this all through as she said it. The implications of the choice she'd made and the future of the war.

"We only have one shot at this," she said. "There isn't room for half measures. We're going for the kill."

Chapter Thirty-Two: Holden

The electric cart they rode on seemed almost as old as the station. The magnetic wheels gripped the ramp and kept them on track even as the spin gravity of the drum fell slowly away. If Medina Station had followed its intended path, it would have been well away from Earth by now, gone into the vast depths between the stars where spare carts were pretty hard to come by. The Mormons had built everything about the ship to last for generations, to grow and renew itself, to recycle with the least possible loss. Medina Station would outlive them all.

Except that he was going to blow a hole in it.

Amos rode shotgun, his hands splayed wide on his knees, his head freshly shaved. From his place in the backseat, Holden mostly saw the back of the big man's neck—white skin flecked with age spots but still muscular and hard. He didn't need to see the amiable smile to know it was there, and how little it meant. A massive conduit wrench clanked at Amos' feet. Katria drove with the studied boredom of someone who knew the consequences of drawing the attention of station security. Her hair was already in a tight bun, prepped for the null g of engineering. She tapped her palm against the side of the cart as if she were listening to music, so maybe she already had her earpiece in. Holden tried to lean back against the seat, but in the lower g, it just scooted him forward. The bomb rested on the bench beside him like a fourth person.

It wasn't big. A square box, safety orange with scratches at the edges and corners, the marks of long use. He didn't know exactly what was inside it, only that Katria was certain it would blow the right kind of hole into the pressure tanks and that the ruptured pressure tanks would blow the right part of the station apart. She also said that, in its present form, it was both hard for security to detect and stable enough to play football with if you didn't mind a square ball. Still, Holden didn't rest his elbow on it.

They were nearly at the top of the ramp when a line of carts stopped them, all heading the same direction as they were and all stuck waiting. At the entrance to the transfer point, three Laconian Marines in power armor were talking to a dark-skinned woman in a green jumpsuit.

"Checkpoint," Holden said.

"Inconvenient," Katria said. She sounded like it was an annoyance more than an immediate threat to all their lives and the safety of everyone in the underground who was counting on them. He really did admire the way she did that.

The raid had come two shifts before, when Holden had been in his sleep cycle. Between the time he'd curled up in the bunk and put his head on the thin pillow and when he'd opened his eyes again, a quarter of Saba's people had been snatched up and a man named Overstreet was on all the screens in the station telling the rest of Medina about it. And the *Typhoon* was already past its flip-and-burn, braking now toward the other side of the Laconia gate. They weren't saying exactly when it was supposed to arrive, but their data placed it at around ten days. And the news from Sol looked grim, even correcting for the fact that it was all coming through the state-run newsfeed.

The noose was drawing tight. And in order to have any chance of escaping it, they were about to at least risk the lives of, and most probably kill, a bunch of people who were on the engineering decks at the wrong time.

"Holden. Do you have to do that?" Katria asked.

"Do what?"

"Grunt."

"Was I grunting?"

"Cap does that when he's thinking about something he don't like," Amos said.

"He has a wide variety to choose from," Katria said.

From the way they talked, Holden could almost believe that they wouldn't kill each other, given the chance. Almost, but not enough that he was sorry to be there. Maybe Katria really didn't hold a grudge about the fight that Amos had started. And maybe Amos wasn't spoiling to start another one. Or maybe the bomb was the most stable thing in the cart.

"I'll think happy thoughts," Holden said. "Butterflies. Rainbows."

"What the fuck is a butterfly?" Katria said.

The cart ahead of them shifted, and they followed. It took fifteen minutes to get to the guards and then a minute and a half to get past them. Their cover story—Holden and Amos were applying for on-station work permits since their ship was locked down, and Katria was taking them to an on-site test—never even came up. Katria drove the cart to its queue, strapped the bomb to her back, and led them into the engineering decks, moving from handhold to handhold with the unremarked grace of someone who'd spent a good portion of their life on the float. Amos followed with the conduit wrench in his fist like a club.

Once the drum was well behind them, Holden pulled the earpiece out of his pocket and turned on the contact microphone.

"—is clear," Clarissa said. "Can you confirm?"

"Yup," Alex replied, his voice slow in the way that meant he was concentrating. "I'm moving my little pixies through now. Gimme just a...All right, I'm through."

"Turning the recycler back on," Clarissa said.

Clarissa and her team were in the drum, tapped into the environmental controls through a back door that, if they were found out, Saba would never be able to use again. Alex was back in the underground's galley, flying the drones with his hand terminal and several layers of encryption. Naomi and Bobbie were, he assumed, loitering outside the secure server room, ready to force their way in. It was strange hearing their voices as if they were with him. It made him feel like he was back on the *Rocinante*.

The engineering decks of Medina were a lesson in the way ships learned and changed over time. If he squinted, he could still see the bones of the original, unmodified space, but years and mission drift had altered everything. Here, a section of floor had a slightly different color where a bulkhead had been taken out. There, a set of conduits had been rerouted with the three-point welding style that Martians favored. The pipes along the walls were labeled in half a dozen languages and safety-regulation styles. History made physical. Even where the walls were had changed over the years, added extra reinforcement from when the docks had been built or taken away when the new generation reactors had been put in place. Katria led the way down a side corridor, moving from handhold to foothold to handhold. Amos followed close behind her, only crowding her a little, and she seemed not to notice. Or at least not to care. Their little triumvirate. Katria to place the charge, Amos to keep an eye on her, and Holden to keep an eye on him.

A young woman floated past them, coming the other way. She had an electrician's rig strapped to her arm, and her hair was the same texture Naomi's had been when they'd first met. She passed Katria, then Amos. When she and Holden landed at the same handhold, she smiled an apology and pushed quickly off. He wondered whether they were about to kill her. Seemed possible. He hated the thought.

"Alex?" Bobbie said. "You're awfully quiet there, buddy. Everything all right?"

"Yeah, sorry. Just…there's a little lag. It's not bad, but it makes me paranoid. Last thing I want is one of these charges to go off in a vent someplace. Take the whole group out."

"That would be bad," Bobbie agreed.

"Jim?" Naomi said. "Are you on yet?"

"We're here," he said softly. "Past the checkpoint. Not at the pressure tank yet."

"There was a checkpoint?" Bobbie said.

Amos' voice was calm. "Nothing we couldn't handle, Babs."

"I'm coming up on the last turn here," Alex said.

"There's a carbon dioxide scrubber intake," Clarissa said. "Don't get caught in the draft. I'm accessing it now."

Katria started whistling between her teeth, a tuneless sound that her mic didn't pick up. They reached an access panel with caution placards in a dozen languages and half the colors of the rainbow. CAUTION HIGH PRESSURE SYSTEM. Katria plucked a knife from her boot and pried the panel open as casually as if she did it every day.

"Make sure no one's coming," she said.

"You got it," Amos replied, sailing on a little farther down the corridor and slipping to the center of the narrow space so that anyone coming the other way would have a hard time getting past him and his massive wrench. Katria pulled the bomb off her back and popped the case open. The workings inside didn't look like much. A cone of carbon-silicate lace, the same as a ship's plating. A hand terminal. A pair of standard wires. It didn't look like enough to do much damage. Certainly not enough to blow out the side of the station. But of course, it wasn't. That was all coming from the pressure tanks on the other side of the bulkhead. This was just the pin that popped that balloon.

"Okay," Clarissa said. "You're good to go."

"Heading through," Alex said. "And we're past. The vent for the server room should be just ahead. Looks...looks a little higher grade than I was expecting."

"Do we have a problem?" Bobbie asked. He could hear the tension in her voice. The electrical technician he'd bumped into intruded into his memory, and with it the faint and compromised hope that maybe it would all go wrong and they'd have to abort the mission.

"I think we'll be fine," Alex said. "My little pixies here are armed for bear. But I'm pulling five of them back around the corner here so they don't get mussed up when the vent goes."

Katria closed the case, set it in behind the access panel, squinted at it, shifted it fifteen degrees. What was it like, Holden wondered, being able to picture blast cones in your mind? What kind of life did you have to lead to have that come naturally? Katria rubbed her throat, and when she spoke, her voice had doubled, coming from the air they were breathing and through the earpiece. The reverb gave her words a weight.

"We're done here. We'll see you in the place."

Meaning, the shelter. Where, when Naomi and Bobbie joined them, they could trigger the blast and wipe out the evidence.

"Hey," Katria called down the corridor. "You coming?"

Amos floated back toward them as Katria slid the panel back into place and slipped her knife back into her boot. They were skimming along through the air together when it all fell apart.

"Um," Alex said. "I think we've got a problem here."

"What's up, Alex?" Bobbie asked.

"Well, I got my little pixie looking through this vent. I've got eyes on both of these Laconian fellas, and one of them's got his hand on something that sure looks like a dead man's switch."

"That's not protocol," Bobbie said.

"It ain't Martian protocol," Alex agreed. "But I'm pretty certain that's what I'm seeing here. If I move forward with this, I won't even have the door open before the Laconian fellas know about it. You're going to be ass deep in alligators pretty damned quick."

"We knew we were going to have to move fast," Bobbie said. "This just means we move faster."

"It means more than that," Clarissa said. "It means they'll log the alarm. The whole point of blowing out the pressure tanks was so they wouldn't know we'd compromised them. If the secure room shows an alert right before the explosion, they'll know what we did. They'll change all the procedures. The data we recover won't be worth anything."

The silence lasted one long breath. Then another. Holden felt something in his chest loosen, it was almost like relief. And almost like dread too.

He knew what had to happen before anyone else did.

"All right," Bobbie said, and Holden could see her clenched jaw as clearly as if she were there with him. "Let me think."

"You'll be fine," Holden said. "Just wait until the...I don't know. The tenth alarm goes off."

"The tenth what?" Alex said, but Holden plucked out his earpiece and the mic and tossed them to Amos. The big man caught them in one wide hand.

"You going somewhere, Cap?"

"Yeah," Holden said. "Can I borrow that wrench?"

Amos pushed it gently out to him. It was massive enough that Holden had to readjust his grip on the handhold to stop it.

"Am I getting that back?" Amos asked.

"Maybe. You get Katria to the shelter. Everything goes forward, just like we planned."

Amos' face went still as a mask for a moment, and then he smiled his empty smile. "You got it."

Holden squared himself on the wall's footholds and launched down the corridor. In an instant, Amos and Katria were behind him. *It'll be okay,* he told himself, but he didn't dig into why that might be true. He was pretty sure it wouldn't hold up.

It only took about twenty seconds to find a panel with a manual fire alarm. He flipped the case open, pulled the switch down, and a Klaxon started screaming. *One.*

In the next corridor, he picked a thin copper pipe, set the wrench around it and pulled until it popped. Green fluid that stank like vinegar and acetate spewed out into the hall. Somewhere, the system would register the pressure drop and raise a flag. That was *two.* He heard voices shouting from the main deck. They weren't raised in panic, not yet. More like they were trying to be heard over the alarm. He passed a radiation alarm and tripped that too—*three*—then headed toward the voices.

Naomi would understand, even if the others didn't. She knew him well enough to follow his mind without so much as a question. There were two ways to hide something. Either put it where no one could see it or leave it in plain sight with a thousand others just like it. If the alarm went off in the secure room, that would mean one thing. If a bunch of alarms went off all through the engineering and dock levels, and it was only one, maybe the guards had panicked. It would just be more noise in the chaos. Unremarkable.

In the wide space leading to the transfer hub, half a dozen people were clinging to a wall, each of them talking over the others. He recognized the electrical tech they'd passed going in.

"Hey," he shouted, waving his wrench. "Can't you people hear? Get to the shelters!"

It was enough to start them moving. He picked another corridor at random and launched himself down it. He broke three electrical conduits, tripped another fire alarm and another radiation. If he could make his way down closer to the reactors, there'd be more he could break, but there would also be guards there. The wrench was unwieldy and massive enough that cracking the conduits and pipes open was starting to leave his shoulders and palms aching. He ducked into an access crawl and pulled two power exchanges out of the wall. That had to be good for at least one alert. He floated out into another hallway. The engineering deck was drowned in a cacophony of blaring alarms. He pulled himself toward a ladder. When the station was under thrust, it would lead down toward the drive cones.

It took the Laconians about two minutes to find him, but it felt like longer. Holden was trying to fit the wrench behind a support strut when two Marines in power armor came around the corner, their suits clicking as the actuators fired. Holden started to raise his hands, but the first one slammed into him before he had the chance. The impact knocked a few seconds off his awareness. The next thing he was sure of, there was a barrel pressed just above his left eye and his ribs hurt badly when he tried to breathe.

"You just fucked up, old man!" the guard growled.

Holden blinked. "I surrender," he said. Breathing really hurt. There were bones broken. He was sure of it.

"You don't have that option," the guard said. Holden realized his life was now based on whether a Laconian Marine who looked like he was maybe in his early twenties had the self-control not to shoot his brainpan empty out of anger and excitement. Holden nodded.

"I understand, sir," he said, and hoped that submission and respect would be enough to keep that one critical neuron from firing. "I am not resisting. You got me. I'm no threat."

"CJ," the other Marine said.

The one with the gun snarled, pulled back a few centimeters, and hit Holden along the side of his face hard enough to split the skin. Bright red globes of blood flew in a cloud and painted the pale anti-spalling cloth of the hallway. The pain was dull first, and then bright.

"You are an ungrateful piece of shit," the Marine—CJ, apparently—said. "If we were someplace civilized, your sad ass would be in the *pens.*"

"What are the pens?" Holden asked, and the guard hit him again, hard against his right ear. He had the impression that CJ enjoyed this kind of thing. Holden wasn't frightened so much as resigned. He'd known that he'd be trading his freedom for the chance that Bobbie's plan would work. And for the electrical tech's life. He was past the good part of his plan now, and the bad part might last a very long time or a very short one. Either way, probably the rest of his life.

CJ hauled him out into the free air where there was nothing for Holden to grab onto. A drop of his blood smeared the Laconian's faceplate.

"What the fuck do you have to say for yourself now, asshole?" CJ said, shaking him just enough to make his teeth rattle. Holden took a deep, painful breath.

"We should probably get to an emergency shelter," he said.

Chapter Thirty-Three: Bobbie

Tenth what?" Alex said. His voice was reedy and distant. Not all of that was because of the tiny speaker it was coming out of. Alex understood what Holden was doing just as much as she did. One alarm was significant. One alarm out of a dozen meant less. Holden was giving them cover, and Alex was asking Bobbie to say that Holden hadn't just decided to sacrifice himself to keep the mission on track.

Her mouth was dry.

"You heard him," she replied, keeping her tone all business. "As soon as that tenth alarm goes off, blow the vent, take out the guards, and get us into the room."

"Am I getting that back?" Amos asked, but not to them.

Naomi was staring at her, wide-eyed. She was on the radio, too. She knew what was happening. But she tightened her grip on her tools and pressed her lips together, then gave Bobbie a nod. *Good to go.* The *Roci*'s former XO would finish her mission. Then she'd worry about Holden afterward. They both would.

The sound of the alarms had started close to them, and grew more distant as new sirens joined the cacophony. Holden was moving away from them. Which was good, considering what was about to happen.

"Chief," Alex said. "That was ten."

Bobbie took one last look at her surroundings. She and Naomi floated alone in the narrow corridor. The door to the computer room was five meters away, and she had her improvised battering ram in one hand. As it always did in the calm seconds before a mission began, her mind ran through the checklist of things that were about to happen. Nothing popped up as a red flag, so she said, "Go, go, go."

For three long breaths, nothing happened.

There was a distant thump, like a firecracker going off inside a locker. *The first drone just blew itself up to take out the venting cover.* This was followed by a shout of surprise. Bobbie could picture the two men in the room looking up in shock as the vent turned into shrapnel behind them, and five tiny drones flew into the room. Then two more bangs, close together like firing a double tap with a pistol. This time louder, and closer. *Two more drones going off to take out the guards.*

The alarm in the room started screeching as the man with his hand on the dead man's switch went down. But now, instead of drawing every guard in the area, it was just one of over a dozen alarms going off, and new ones coming up every few seconds. Holden had been busy.

"I'm getting smoke in the vents," Clarissa said. "I'm turning up the recyclers."

The last explosion was the loudest yet, right on the other side of the door. *The last three drones clustering around the latch and detonating.* Alex said, "My guys are done. Me and my team are cleaning up the logs and shutting down."

Bobbie planted her feet on the corridor wall and launched

toward the door. The heavy length of ceramic-filled pipe she was using as a ram was gripped in both hands, and she slammed it into the door just above the latch. The door exploded open so violently that it bounced off the bulkhead and swung back hard enough to clip her knee as she flew by. It hurt, but not enough to think about.

She had a split second to clock the room: workstation and two dead men with blood soaking their suits floating next to it, server rack bolted to the deck in the center of the compartment, plain metal walls. She slammed into the server rack and bounced off into an empty corner of the room.

"Ouch. Fuck."

"What's that, Chief?" Alex asked.

"Nothing. Just went a hundred kph when twenty would have done," Bobbie replied. "We're good, Naomi. Do your thing."

Naomi's lean form slid through the opening with Belter grace, tapped one foot against the bulkhead, and came to a perfect stop next to the server rack. Watching her slide through the air like a fish in water made Bobbie feel overlarge and clumsy.

"I'll be in the hall, watching for gawkers," she said.

"Mmhmm," Naomi replied, already ignoring her. She was pulling panels off the server rack, and a variety of gear floated in the space around her like a high-tech cloud.

Before she left, Bobbie pushed over to the two Laconian guards and checked their pulse. Up close, it was hardly necessary. Both men had massive head injuries, and bits of bone, blood, and drone parts floated around them. It was a shitty way for a soldier to die, ambushed like that, and Bobbie pushed down the feeling of guilt and regret. It was war. Right now, her brothers and sisters in the Martian fleet were fighting and dying in the Sol system in that same war. And a lot more blood was being spilled on their side than on the Laconian one so far.

Still, as a person who'd stood a watch in enemy territory, the sightless eyes of the two dead men made her scalp crawl the way she'd always imagined it would when a sniper had you in their sights for the kill shot.

"Your turn now," she told the dead man. "My turn later."

She pushed out into the corridor to keep watch. The shrill electronic screech of alarms echoed down the hall and all around her. So far, no one had come to check on the computer-room alarm. Why would they? Holden had made sure that the only important alarm was drowned out. She had to hand it to him, as an improvised element of the plan it was a pretty good idea. Probably something they should have included, just in case.

Next time, she thought, knowing there would never be a next time.

"Got it," Naomi said from behind her. Bobbie nearly elbowed her in the face before her brain could override the startle response.

"Great," she said instead. "Let's get to the shelter before Katria gets itchy and blows us all to hell for the fun of it."

"Jim won't be there," Naomi said.

Amos and Katria were floating in the cramped space of their chosen radiation shelter. It was nothing more than a four-meter length of hallway with heavy pressure doors at both ends. Netting hung on both walls with rebreathers, first-aid kits, emergency vac suits. Bobbie had stowed a gear bag with the less-standard equipment.

As soon as she and Naomi climbed in through the one open door, Katria slapped her hand to the panel and it slammed shut.

"What the fuck?" Amos said, rounding on her.

"We need that closed when the bomb goes off," Katria replied, pulling the detonator out of her pack. "You know, to live."

"Nothing happens without my direct order," Bobbie said to her and put a restraining hand on Amos' chest. He reacted by mag-booting himself to the deck, so she kicked on her own boots and clamped them to the bulkhead to keep her leverage.

"Babs," Amos said, "I'm going to go get Cap, and it'd be nice if you held off on the boom till I'm done."

Bobbie waited for Naomi to voice her agreement, then Katria to argue against it, and for their tiny shelter to turn into shouting and chaos. But to her surprise, everyone just looked at her. It was an interesting fact of her brief captaincy that the only time anyone seemed to want her to make a decision was when it was one she didn't want to make.

Amos was staring at her, his expression as blank as always. But he held his fists with the ease of long use, and Bobbie knew how fast the old man was in a fight. With his feet clamped to the deck for leverage, he'd be tough to restrain if he decided to start swinging.

"Our window is closing," Bobbie said, raising her hands, making it about the logic of her words instead of a threat. "At some point someone checks that alarm and finds two dead guys. We don't have time for a rescue."

"She's right. So let me blow this fucker and get on with it," Katria added. Bobbie winced at the cold disregard in her words, but didn't take her eyes off Amos.

Naomi still hadn't weighed in, but Amos' eyes kept cutting to her, waiting for the go sign. If Naomi said, *Yes, go get him,* Bobbie knew the only way they'd keep Amos in the room was to physically restrain him. Bobbie couldn't see what Naomi was doing behind her back, but whatever it was, Amos wasn't getting the signal he wanted, because he didn't make a move.

"Those alarms were moving away from us, fast," Bobbie said, still only looking at Amos. "Holden knew the schedule. Either he's made his way to a shelter or he's told whoever has him now to get to one."

"You don't know that," Naomi finally said.

"No, I don't. But I hope. And right now, that's what I've got. Because we have to blow that bomb now, or this whole operation fails and we still don't get Holden back."

"Yeah, so let's get on with it," Katria said.

"Stop fucking helping me, lady," Bobbie snarled at her without turning around.

Naomi spoke, and her voice was as calm as it was empty. "Bobbie's right. This can't all be for nothing."

Amos flicked his eyes to Naomi, then locked on Bobbie. His face had the same meaningless half grin it always wore, but his shoulders were tense, and his fists were white-knuckled. A flush of blood darkened his neck. Bobbie had never seen him like this before, and she didn't like it now.

Not that it changed anything.

"Katria, get ready to blow on my signal," Bobbie said. "Let's get into these emergency suits for evac immediately after. You've got one minute to dress."

Bobbie heard the Velcro ripping sounds of vac suits being pulled off the walls and hastily donned. Amos wasn't moving.

"Put your suit on, big man," Bobbie said.

"You're really gonna blow it," Amos replied. He didn't sound surprised. Or like he was issuing a challenge. He didn't sound like anything. Bobbie involuntarily braced for violence.

"Yes," she said.

Without changing his expression, Amos squared up on her, hands at his sides.

"I guess you really want that captain's chair back, huh Babs?"

Before she knew she was going to do it, Bobbie had already grabbed his collar and yanked him up hard enough to pull his mag boots off the floor, then slammed him against the bulkhead.

"If we had more time," she hissed at him through her teeth, "you and I would be dancing right now."

Amos smiled at her. "I got time."

"Katria. Blow it," Bobbie said, and the world ended.

When Katria's charge went off, it demolished the control panel and ripped a seventeen-centimeter hole in the oxygen storage tank. Bobbie didn't know the exact size of the tank, but she had a vague memory that liquid oxygen compressed down to about eleven hundred kilograms per cubic meter, and now all of it was trying to become a gas again, all at once.

The initial blast of expanding gas was deafening. The shock

wave ripped apart bulkheads and piping. All the liquid oxygen in those pipes joined the explosion as additional expanding gas. From inside the relative safety of their reinforced emergency compartment, it sounded like someone had set off a tactical nuke in the next room.

And then, as was inevitable, something oxidized fast enough to produce a flame, and the initial blast of air became fire.

The entire emergency shelter shuddered, then canted over onto its side. The reinforced and blast-hardened bulkheads didn't break, but the mounts holding the compartment to the deck were sheared off by the force of the blast. It took seconds that lasted for hours.

The inner walls and the pressure doors at each end of the compartment got hot enough to start smoking. Bobbie shared a look with Amos, then let go of him and they both scrambled to get into the emergency vacuum suits.

When the exterior bulkhead blew out, there wasn't another deafening explosion, but rather a sudden drop in the sound level. The roar was replaced by the hiss of rushing air, then a high whine, then nothing. The seals on their shelter stayed intact, so afterward all they could hear was their own panicked breathing.

"Okay, we're getting massive alarms," Clarissa said, her voice the only calm thing in the universe. "The station's going into shutdown. I'm pulling out too. I'll see you back at the place."

"God *damn*," Naomi said.

"Told you," Katria said. "My shit always works."

Bobbie finished pulling on her vac suit, and saw Amos was sealing up his own. They traded a look. "We need to get out of here," she said to him, and he nodded his agreement. Whatever was going to happen between them, it was on hold for now. They'd come back to it, she was certain of that. And it would need to get settled.

If I just killed Holden, this probably ends with one of us dead.

Whatever she'd imagined when she heard the blasts from inside the shelter, the reality was worse.

They opened the door to an entire deck that had been dropped in a blender, then spun up in a centrifuge. Bulkhead panels, control stations, equipment, decking. It had all been torn, twisted, burned, and then thrown out against the outer walls at high speed. A long piece of pipe was embedded in a wall, still quivering like an arrow shot into a tree. Something that looked like a metal desk had been slammed into a support beam so hard that the metal had actually fused. And in one corner, a single boot had been pinned to the ceiling and then melted into a stalactite of rubber. She hoped there wasn't a foot in it.

They floated silently through the wreckage looking for their exit. It wasn't hard to find.

A hole gaped in the exterior bulkhead of the drum nearly five meters across. The nearly circular rim of it was all bent outward, like the metal wall had been breached by a giant's battering ram. Which, Bobbie supposed, it had. Only instead of concrete and steel, it had been oxygen and fire. Outside, she saw the faint twinkle of light on the ejecta as it raced away from the station and toward the curtain of black at the edge of the ring space.

"*Exactly* where I said it would be," Katria cackled. "Damn near half a meter from the exact spot I marked as the weak point. I should charge money for this."

"Do you think anyone survived?" Naomi asked.

"We kept everyone we could out of the affected area," Bobbie replied. "Only should have been Laconians down here…"

"And anyone who didn't get our fucking memo," Amos added.

"Jim would have warned anyone he ran into," Naomi said. "He wouldn't be able to stop himself."

"Yeah, by then it wouldn't matter much," Amos agreed. "No time to track the bomb down before it did its business."

"And fuck any Laconians who were here," Katria said in a tone that sounded like she'd have spit if she weren't wearing a helmet. "I hope they fucking saw it coming."

"Kat," Bobbie said, "please shut up now."

"This is going to work," Naomi said, pointing out the hole toward the docks. "They're going to think that was our target."

The *Gathering Storm* sat a few dozen meters away. The nose of the ship and its port-side flank showed significant hull damage. Debris from the blast had punched holes in the landing clamps and dragged long gouges down its side. A large cluster of objects that looked like a sensor or communication array had nearly been ripped off the side of the ship, floating now at the end of a tether of cables.

It was an eerie ship. The angles of it were like something cut from crystal, and the curves felt like something grown more than built. It was like looking at a venomous snake. She had a hard time pulling her eyes away.

"Too bad we didn't kill it," Katria said, ignoring Bobbie's request.

"Yeah," Bobbie agreed. "Too bad."

Amos pulled a magnetic grapple gun out of the gear bag he was carrying and fired a line over to the elevator shaft exterior. They'd need to climb up to a point not far from the maintenance hatch on the outside of the drum she and Clarissa had used earlier. The hard part would be getting a grapple onto the drum, then hanging on while the station tried to hurl them away at a third of a g. After that, it was an easy climb up to their secret entrance back into the station. Up into Medina from the underworld, and mission accomplished.

Unless something else went wrong. The only thing worse than losing Holden would be losing him for no damned reason.

"Laconians are gonna find this hatch," Amos said. "Shouldn't plan to use it again after this. No way the crews that come to fix that hole are gonna miss it."

"Yeah," Bobbie agreed. "If we thought the sweeps before were bad, they're about to get a hundred times tighter."

"Yeah, fuck 'em," Katria snorted.

"No," Naomi said. "It'll be worse than that. We stung their

pride before. But today we hurt them. Hurt them bad. And they're going to try to make it better by hurting us back. Not just us either. Anyone who they think might be like us."

While Amos hooked his grapple line to the edge of the hole so that they could climb up to the elevator housing, Naomi remained staring at the damaged Laconian ship.

"We killed a lot of people today," she said. "Some of them just don't know it yet."

Chapter Thirty-Four: Drummer

The battle will be here," Benedito Lafflin said, indicating a space between the curve of the asteroid belt and the orbit of Mars. The place where physics and geometry calculated that the paths of the *Tempest* and those of the fleets of the EMC and the union would cross. There was nothing there now—no port, no city, no outpost of any civilization. Only a hard vacuum wider than worlds, an emptiness of strategic importance. "We're calling it Point Leuctra."

"Luke-tra?"

"The Spartans were decisively defeated there by Thebes," Lafflin said. "I mean, they call their planet Laconia. Psy ops thought it might speak to their sense of their own invincibility."

They stared at each other a moment. *That's the best we've got? Intimidate them with classical allusions?* floated at the back of her throat. Lafflin shrugged uncomfortably.

"All right," Drummer said. Because what else was there to be said? It wasn't as though her will was going to change any of the factors involved. The timetable was listed at the side of the display, days and hours as ticks of red and gold.

"The eggheads have a good model of the *Tempest*," Lafflin went on, swapping out the map of the system for a schematic of the *Tempest*. The weird, organic shape of it made her feel like she was looking at a detail from an autopsy. *Here is the vertebra where things went wrong. You can see the malformation.* She smiled at the absurdity of the thought. Lafflin smiled back reflexively. "The only hard data we have is where the PDCs and torpedoes came out, but we also got a lot of good heat data from the last engagement."

"The death of Independence," Drummer said. The death of the first void city and everyone who hadn't fled their home.

Lafflin looked down. "That, yes, ma'am. The data's given us some idea about the internal structures too. Enough that we feel confident that we can target the right places on that bastard. Take it out before it reaches Earth."

Because that was the point, Drummer thought. That was always the point. Protect Earth and Mars. Keep the inner planets safe and independent, even at the cost of more Belters' lives. And she'd known that. From the moment Avasarala had stepped into her meeting, she'd known. Some part of her expected to feel some kind of outrage, some betrayal. Resentment that the wheel of history was still rolling over the backs of her people first.

She didn't. There was a term she remembered from her years in the OPA. *Saahas-maut*. She didn't know where the term came from, but it meant something like *the pleasure you take in hardship*. It was supposed to be a peculiarly Belter emotion, something that the inners didn't name because they didn't feel it. She looked at the *Tempest* now, the guesswork lines of her superstructure and drive, the target points along her hull. Drummer wasn't angry at the inners for using the union to protect Earth. She wasn't even angry at the Laconians for being another iteration of everything the inners had been before the union existed. War and loss, the prospect of the oppressor's boot. There was a nostalgia to it. A bone-deep memory of what it had been to be young.

She couldn't help wondering what that girl, riding rock hoppers and taking gigs at Ceres and Iapetus and Tycho, would have thought of the woman she'd become. The leader of her own oppressions. Not much, probably.

Lafflin cleared his throat.

"Sorry," Drummer said. "Didn't sleep well. Vaughn? Could you get me some tea?"

"Yes, ma'am," Vaughn said. "Also, Pallas."

"Thank you," she said. She didn't mean it.

She'd placed the strategic update with Lafflin on her schedule on purpose. The *Tempest*'s inexorable flight sunward was slated to reach its point nearest to Pallas Station within the hour. The evacuation was complete, or as near to complete as it would be. There was always some old rock hopper with a gun and an attitude who'd stay behind out of spite and rage. It wouldn't help. One of humanity's oldest homes in the Belt would be dead before she went to sleep again, or if it wasn't, it would be because Admiral Trejo had seen fit to grant his mercy. She was pretty sure that wasn't going to happen. At least she could go into the terrible, predictable tragedy with all the vulnerable points of the *Tempest* firmly in mind. She had some hope of retribution.

There was a certain peace in the impossibility of subterfuge. Sure, there were stealth ships and long-range torpedoes. The cloak and dagger of vanishing into the vastness between worlds. They worked for a ship here and there. For the small and swift and furtive. But on this scale—the scale of war on the battlefield of the abyss—everyone knew more or less where everyone else was. Their drive plumes and heat signatures announced them. The hard laws of orbital mechanics and time placed every base, every planet, every person predictably in front of their own personal firing squads. Situations like this one, they could see death coming, and it didn't matter. Death still came.

"Did you…" Lafflin said. "We can continue this after. If you'd like."

Drummer didn't like. She didn't want to see it happen. Didn't want to hope that Pallas might survive. But she was the president of the union, and bearing witness was part of what she was supposed to do. She wondered where Avasarala was, and whether the old lady was going to watch too.

"Yes," Drummer said. "That'll be fine."

Lafflin nodded, rose from the table, and made his way out of the meeting room. Drummer stood, stretched, and switched the display to the tactical service's analytics. The image wasn't real. It was a composite of visual telescopy and Pallas' internal data cobbled together into a best guess that was five minutes old from light delay before it reached her. Without Tycho beside it, Pallas looked…Calm? Still. The curves of the bases' structures didn't spin against the starscape. Pallas was older than that. By the time they'd learned how to spin asteroid stations up, Pallas had been in business for more than a generation. It would die without changing. A countdown timer showed the minutes to the *Tempest*'s closest pass. Seven minutes and thirty-three seconds.

The door slid open again, and Vaughn ghosted into the room, a drinking bulb in either hand. The smell of tea wafted to her seconds later. He didn't speak as he reached out to her. The bulb warmed her palm and the tea was rich and sweet.

"Hard day," Vaughn said. It was strange. She didn't like Vaughn or dislike him, but she'd come to rely on him. And now, in this traumatic hour, it was this crag-faced political operative at her side instead of Saba. The universe was tricky, and its sense of humor came with teeth.

"Hard day," Drummer agreed.

On the display, the *Tempest* fell slowly toward the sun. Pallas Station would pass on the ship's starboard, and too far away to see with the naked eye. Admiral Trejo would be watching the show on a screen of his own. The death of Pallas would be one of the most observed events in history. Five minutes and fifteen seconds. Which meant, in Pallas' frame of reference, now.

She took another sip of tea, feeling the hot water against her tongue and the roof of her mouth, Brownian motion making it seem to fizz against the soft flesh of her palate, beat against the individual taste buds. Molecules of sugar latched to contact sites, and the nerves ran through the meat of her tongue, back into her body like she was drinking twice, once with the liquid and once with electrical fire. A sense of vertigo washed through her.

She tried to put the bulb down, but the surface of the table was distant, visible, but through a distracting cloud that was the air— atoms and molecules bouncing against each other, striking and spinning away and striking again. Thicker than bodies at a tube station.

She tried to call out to Vaughn. She could see him, right there before her, the jagged territory of his skin fractally similar at every scale. She tried to make out his expression, but she couldn't bring her focus back that far. It was like trying to see the face of God. Something hummed and throbbed, ticking faster than she could quite be aware of. The pulse of her own brain, the tempo of her consciousness. It sang like a chorus, and she heard herself hearing it.

She dropped the bulb. It clattered against the table, rolled, and dropped to the ground, falling closed so that it kept even a drop of tea from escaping. Vaughn took a step, then sank down to his knees. His eyes were wide, and his face pale as death and covered by sweat. Drummer sat slowly. Her knees felt weak.

"God," Vaughn said. "Besse God."

Drummer couldn't tell if it was profanity or prayer.

The timer on the display read two minutes and twenty seconds. Whatever had happened, it had taken almost three minutes out of her life. It hadn't seemed that long. Maybe she'd passed out?

"I need," she began, and her voice felt strange. Like she could still hear overtones fluting up from her vocal cords. "I need to know what that was."

"I don't," Vaughn said. He was weeping. Wide, thick tears dripping down his cheeks.

"Vaughn," she snapped, and it sounded more like her own voice again. "Come to! I need to know what that was."

"I saw everything," he said.

"How widespread. What happened. Everything. Get me reports."

"Yes," he said, and then a moment later, "Yes, ma'am." But he rested his head on his knees and didn't move.

On the display, the timer came to twelve seconds, and the *Tempest* fired. Not missiles, but the magnetic beam that Saba had reported. The thing that had stripped the defenses from the slow zone and burst gamma radiation out all the gates. Pallas Station vanished like a blown-out candle with eleven seconds to spare. They were roughly five light-minutes away, so it had happened... the two things had happened together in the *Tempest*'s frame of reference.

"Tur," she said. "Get me Cameron Tur."

"The thing you have to understand is that the technology of the ring stations doesn't break the speed of light," Tur said, his Adam's apple bobbing like a ball on a string. "The one thing we can absolutely say is that the protomolecule is bound by the speed of light. Everything they designed got around it with a different understanding of locality. That's not the same thing at all."

He was talking fast and, Drummer thought, more than half to himself. That she was in the room let him think out loud, but he didn't have his science-advisor voice tuned up. This was one step short of a chimpanzee shrieking and pointing at the charred spot where lightning had struck.

"If you look at it, the gates themselves are clearly bounded by lightspeed. The strategy the protomolecule employs is to send out bridge builders at subluminal speeds to environments where there are stable replicators to hijack and employ to...to poke holes into a different space. Going from Sol gate to Laconia or Ilus or wherever, we don't accelerate ships past lightspeed, we just take a shortcut because the slow zone is a place outside locality where very different places in *our* reference can be very nearby in *that* frame."

"That's great," Drummer said. "Was it a weapon?"

Tur goggled at her. "Was what a weapon?"

"That—" She waved her fingers in front of his eyes. "That whatever the hell that was. With the hallucinations and the missing time. Was it a weapon? Can the Laconians turn us off like that anytime they want?"

"It was…it was associated with their weapon," Tur said. "I mean it happened at the same time, but that's the thing. Time doesn't actually work like that. 'The same time' is a weird linguistic fantasy. It doesn't exist. Simultaneity doesn't act like this."

He waved his arms, flapping them out toward the sides of the room. *This.*

The whatever-the-hell-it-had-been hadn't just happened in Drummer's meeting room, or on People's Home. It had been spread throughout the system—Earth and Mars, Saturn's moons and Jupiter's. Even the science stations on moons around Neptune and Uranus, and the deep labs in the Kuiper Belt. The reports were startlingly similar—hallucinations and lost time that began uniformly at the moment the *Tempest* had fired its magnetic weapon at Pallas Station. Or, more accurately, the moment in the *Tempest*'s frame of reference. Tur seemed very specific about that. Like it was important.

"But it didn't happen when they fired it in the slow zone," Drummer said. "Why didn't Medina have this happen?"

"What? Oh, no, we don't know. The ring space and the station there and the gates, we don't know what their relationship is with normal space. The rules of physics may be different. I mean, it's clearly an active system, and the energy output from the magnetic weapon there was smaller than the gamma bursts that came from it, so it was tapping into an energy supply that didn't have anything to do with the *Tempest* per se. But the thing is I'm not sure that was a propagating event. If it wasn't a propagating event, then maybe it didn't violate lightspeed."

"I don't know what that means," Drummer said between clenched teeth.

"Well, I mean when you drop a pebble in a pond, there are ripples. They propagate, and all propagation is limited by lightspeed. But instead of a pebble, imagine you dropped a sheet of plating. So that the surface of the plating hit the surface of the pond everywhere at once. It doesn't matter that the trigger that dropped the plate was in one place, because it happened everywhere. Not a point location, but a nonlocalized location."

"Nonlocalized. Location," Drummer said, pressing her palms into her eye sockets. Annoyance and fear curled in her throat. *So you're telling me you don't know shit* floated at the back of her mouth.

"Everyone would experience it as if the effect began exactly with them and then propagated away in every direction at the speed of light, but in reality—"

"I don't care," she said. It was still harsh, but less than what she wanted to do. Tur reared back from her anyway. "What it is, what it means about the way you understand the universe or physics? I don't care. None of that matters to me."

"But—"

"They just demonstrated a weapon that at its minimum ripped Pallas Station down to hyperaccelerated dust. I am preparing to lead thousands of soldiers on hundreds of ships into battle against this thing. You need to tell me was that a glitch in consciousness because of their attack, or can they make that happen again anytime they want? Did they know it was going to happen? Did they suffer all the same high weirdness that we did? Because if they can turn our brains off for a few minutes at will, I'm going to need some *very different strategies*."

By the end, she was shouting. She hadn't meant to shout. Tur had his hands up, palms toward her, like he was afraid she might attack. Fine, let him wonder. Maybe it would focus him up.

"I…that is…" Tur took a deep breath, let it out slowly. "I feel comfortable saying that the glitch, if that's what we're calling it, was associated with *Tempest*'s attack on Pallas. Given that it didn't happen in the slow zone, I can't say whether it was a controlled effect or an artifact of the weapon with some quality of local space around Sol."

"All right," Drummer said.

"Whether the enemy anticipated it or not, I can't say."

"That's fair," Drummer said. The first pricks of regret were forming at the back of her mind. She shouldn't have yelled at him.

"And I can't say whether they suffered the same effect…but I would guess they did. If I'm right about the mechanism, there isn't any sort of shielding against it. You can't block something that's already there. That's what *nonpropagating* means. It doesn't come from anyplace. Everywhere it is, that's where it came from."

Drummer leaned back. That, at least, was interesting. If the Laconians had to go through the same things she had every time they fired their big gun, it would make a gap when automated systems might be able to penetrate their defenses.

"We're also seeing the increased quantum creations and annihilations much more broadly," Tur was saying somewhere nearby. "Like *system-wide* broadly. And there's early suggestion that some experiments on Neptune and Luna that were working with controlled entanglement structures collapsed. So maybe—"

Drummer leaned back in her chair, folding her hands together. Her eyelids fell to half-mast. She knew—they all knew—that this was the first time one of the Laconian ships had left its home system. This wasn't only an invasion, it was also a shakedown cruise. And nothing ever went completely as expected on a shakedown. The question was whether the Laconians knew what had happened. Whether they'd been anticipating it. If they'd been taken by surprise as well, they might not risk using the magnetic beam again.

Tur wouldn't be able to tell her that. Or Vaughn or Lafflin. Admiral Trejo could say it, but not to her. Which meant there was only one plausible way for her to find out.

Her heart leaped at the idea, and she waited for the joy to fade before she risked thinking about it again. It was always dangerous when the universe fell down in a pattern where the thing you wanted and the wise path were the same.

Somewhere, Tur was still talking. He might as well have been on another ship. Drummer's mind pressed through the possibilities, the dangers, the possible profits, and the certain loss. Each time, she found herself at the same conclusion.

She thanked Tur, using the social conventions of conversation to signal him it was time for him to go. She even shook his hand to make up a little for losing her temper before. As she walked him to the door, he was still talking about locality and signal loss. She closed the door behind him and went back to her desk.

Vaughn answered the connection request like his finger had been hovering over the button.

"Ma'am?"

"The *Tempest* is going to make a report. It may go back to Medina, or route through Medina back to Laconia," she said. "We're going to find out what it says."

"Yes, ma'am. And how are we going to do that?"

"Saba," she said. "The risk is worth it now. We're reopening communications with Medina."

Chapter Thirty-Five: Singh

An improvised explosive device punctured a liquid-oxygen storage tank on deck four of the engineering section," Overstreet
said. He was reading from a report that scrolled by on the monitor
wrapped around his thick forearm. "We've recovered very little
of the device itself, but what few pieces we have indicate it was
made with material common to this facility. It'll be difficult if not
impossible to track the exact source."

Singh sat and listened to the report and tried to look present
and thoughtful. But the truth was, his mind was bouncing around
like a tiny animal trying to escape a predator. He found he only
processed about half of what Overstreet was saying. His hands
were shaking so badly that he didn't trust himself to pick up the
glass of water on the desk in front of him. He kept them under the
desk, where Overstreet wouldn't see them. The sense that he was
in immediate danger was inescapable because it was true.

"The damage to that deck was significant. Total loss of the primary liox storage. The thrust from the breach caused the station's maneuvering thrusters to fire, and the shaking knocked down several structures in the habitat cylinder. The network-traffic station for the *Storm* was completely destroyed. A backup environmental-systems plant was significantly damaged, and will probably not be repairable."

"The *Storm*," Singh said. *My first command. The symbol of Laconian power at Medina.*

"This is preliminary, of course," Overstreet replied, flicking one finger to skip down the report on his arm. "It does seem like that might have been the target of this attack, so minor hull damage and the loss of one sensor array feels like we got off light."

Singh's hands felt like they were shaking hard enough to be visible, even under the desk, so he gripped his thighs with both hands and held on tight.

"Preliminary casualty reports?"

"Again, light," Overstreet said. "At this time, we have five confirmed Laconian fatalities, three from the engineering detail, two from security. Seven injuries ranging from life threatening to minor. Only two locals confirmed dead at this time. But we also have another dozen missing, so that number will probably go up."

"To be willing to do so much damage to their own station, to their own people, just to try to hurt us..." Singh said, then trailed off.

"We have several persons of interest in custody," Overstreet said. "One of them was setting off alarms immediately before the blast. It's possible he wasn't involved, but the coincidence seems unlikely. I will be debriefing him once we're done here."

"Is he a local?"

"Former captain of a Transport Union ship. James Holden."

Singh frowned. "Why do I know that name?"

"Apparently he's something of a celebrity, sir. He was involved in the Io Campaign and the defeat of the Free Navy back in the day."

Both things that had happened when Singh was a child. The old guard still playing old-guard games.

"We will need to make the strongest possible response to this," Singh said.

Overstreet nodded, his face grim. The hesitation meant something that Singh didn't understand. "Sir, the radical factions of the Outer Planets Alliance fought a guerrilla war with Earth and Mars for nearly two centuries. The veterans of that war are almost certainly in leadership positions in this insurgency. That means we have some difficult decisions to make. About the scope of response."

"I'm sorry," Singh said. "I'm not following..."

"Insurgencies are historically nearly impossible to eradicate, for a few very simple reasons. The insurgents don't wear uniforms. They look just like the innocent populace. And, they're the friends and family of that populace. This means that every insurgent killed tends to increase recruiting for the insurgency. So unless you are willing to rack up a sizable civilian casualty count, we can't just shoot everyone we suspect. If we take the strongest *possible* response, we stop calling it counterinsurgency and start calling it genocide."

"I see," Singh said. He'd studied counterinsurgency and urban pacification at the academy, of course. Afghanistan had been impossible to conquer going all the way back to Alexander the Great. Ireland in the twentieth century. The Belter troubles for the last two centuries. It was different reading about it, but now he saw how this cycle of violence could go on and on for him too. "I'm not prepared to execute every Belter on the station."

Overstreet seemed to relax without visibly moving at all.

"I agree, sir. All we can do is make it harder for them to operate," Overstreet said. "We're going to have Marines enter every compartment on the station. Anything we don't control or have immediate use of will be sealed and the atmosphere removed. It won't end this, but it'll make it harder for them to plan and execute with no spaces under their control."

"Agreed," Singh said. "You have authorization to conduct this operation, and shut down any sections of the station you see fit. Let's see if these people can work in daylight, not hiding in the sewers."

Overstreet stood and saluted, then headed for the door. But just before he left, he turned back as if suddenly remembering something. "Sir, you might consider putting more pressure on your civilian informants. This is exactly the sort of thing they should be doing for us."

"Yes," Singh agreed. "That's next on my list."

The Belter with the badly broken nose—Jordao, Singh thought he called himself—was ushered into the office by two Marines. They held him by the arms, his feet barely touching the ground. His expression was somewhere between angry and sniveling.

"Put him down," Singh told the Marines. When Jordao moved toward a chair, he said, "Don't sit."

"Sabe, bossmang."

"You know about the attack?" Singh's hands had mostly stopped shaking after Overstreet left, so he took a sip of his water. It was all playacting. Look calm, casual, in control. Make Jordao feel like Singh already knew the answer to every question he was asked. Make him afraid to lie. It seemed to be working. Jordao rubbed his hands together and bobbed his head like a supplicant.

"Sa—I mean, yes, boss, I heard."

"It shook the station hard enough to knock down buildings in the drum section," Singh said. "So, of course, everyone knows about it. I'm not asking that. I'm asking if you *know* about it."

"Knew the underground was up to something, them, but details? I don't—"

"Because, you see," Singh continued, "I released your sister from our lockup as a down payment for future services rendered. Services like letting me know when a bomb was going to blow up half the engineering section of my station, for example."

All the servility left Jordao's face. Singh watched it happen, like a switch had been flipped in the man's head. He was a man who would grovel only so far and no farther. It was a useful fact about him, though it did seem to diminish his value.

"Old OPA, them, sa sa que? The ones the inners couldn't kill," Jordao said, not attempting to hide his thick Belter accent now. "The ones like me? We never get to know."

"Before you leave this room, you will give me a list of every name you think might be involved in this underground so we can add them to our surveillance list. You will also make sure that whatever happens next, you are part of it, so that we can catch the conspirators in the act and bring the full force of the law against them."

Jordao was shaking his head. "Kenna nothing, you—"

"Or," Singh continued. "I will have your sister rearrested, tried for larceny and crimes against the empire, and hanged in a public space as a warning to others."

Before Jordao could respond, Singh nodded at his Marines, and they picked the Belter up off the floor again. "He doesn't leave until his list is delivered and verified."

"Copy that, sir," one Marine said, and saluted with the hand that wasn't holding Jordao.

The Belter looked from him to the Marine and back again, understanding blooming in his eyes. Understanding and fear.

When it was over and he was alone in his office, Santiago Singh found that he very much wanted to send a message to his wife. Tell her how afraid he was. Tell her that maybe accepting this assignment had been a terrible mistake. That walking the line between the man he had always thought he was and the ruthless authoritarian ruler the job required of him wasn't something he could do and remain whole. That the man who could order civilian deaths as a reprisal could not share the same space with the man who loved his wife and played with his daughter and couldn't wait for her to get old enough so he could buy her a kitten.

But he couldn't make that call, because the explosion had cut the *Storm* off from the station, until they could replace the network encryption node. Which was probably a good thing, because he suspected that everything he would have told his wife was a lie.

The truth—the one that he didn't think he'd ever be able to admit to her—was that he could be both men at once. He'd already delivered the ultimatum to Carrie Fisk that any colony world that joined the resistance would be destroyed. He understood that, should it become necessary, he could order Overstreet to execute every person on the station that hadn't come through the gates on the *Tempest* and the *Storm*. The Marine commander would do it. And that when Natalia and the monster arrived, he would be able to hold them and kiss them and be the man he'd always been around them. And know that he'd made them safe.

That was what terrified him. Not that the job would force him to be both of those men but that he was capable of being both. That all it would take is a bit more pressure, and Santiago Singh would be a man who loved his daughter with all his heart and who also ordered genocides.

He tapped at his desk. "Chief."

"Sir," came the immediate reply.

"How long until we have the network back up so I can send traffic back through the *Storm*?"

"It's on the priority list. I've been told eleven hours until the replacement system is in place."

"Thank you," Singh said. "Please let me know the instant it's done. I have priority traffic for Laconia."

"Yes, sir. Sir? On that topic, the *Storm* reports traffic incoming from the Sol gate, marked highest priority. They have a courier bringing it over now."

"Very well. Bring them directly in," Singh said, then killed the connection.

It seemed too early for the *Tempest* to be reporting the Sol system's surrender, but he was open for a pleasant surprise. According to his tactical map, they would barely be crossing the asteroid belt now. Their projections placed the earliest expected surrender point at the Mars crossing.

Singh needed a distraction to pull himself out of his self-pitying and introspection. Whatever Admiral Trejo needed to tell him so urgently, it was bound to be interesting.

The petty officer who was ushered into his office half an hour later was a tall woman with pale hair that had been turned dark by sweat. She was breathing heavily, and her uniform was damp.

"Sir," she said, then held out a small black wafer to him.

"You look terrible, sailor," Singh replied, taking the chip. "Are you all right?"

"The Marines are using all the carts for patrol duty, so…"

"Did you actually run this over all the way from the *Storm*?" Because of the attack, traveling from the ship to his office meant donning a vacuum suit, moving through the damaged sections of the station, then removing the suit and running down the long spiraling ramp that went from the center of rotation down to the drum floor. And after that a kilometer-and-a-half run across the drum to reach his office complex.

"Yes, sir," the petty officer said, starting to get her breathing under control.

"I'll be sending my compliments to your senior chief. Outstanding effort, sailor. Take a moment to clean up, and we'll round up a cart to drive you back."

"Thank you, sir," she said, then gave him a sharp salute and left.

Part of the self-pity trap that Singh had realized it would be easy to fall into was the terrible sense of being utterly alone in his job. He needed more interactions with his fellow Laconians. With his ship, and the sailors under his command. He needed these reminders that he wasn't working alone. That hundreds of like-minded and dedicated professionals shared the dream of the empire. Singh made a mental note to spend more time on the *Storm*.

He rolled his monitor out onto the desktop and dropped the small black chip on it. "Transfer all files and wipe," he said, then when the monitor blinked its acknowledgment, snapped the little black chip in two and dropped it in the recycler.

Admiral Trejo's face appeared on his monitor. Singh found he was a little excited. Trejo was a man with even greater responsibility than his own, and one who handled it with dedication and grace. He was a man who always knew the right thing to do, and did it without hesitation. If Singh wanted to spend more time with the Laconian sailors like himself, he wanted to *be* Admiral Trejo. He told the monitor to play the message.

Trejo's face blurred into motion, and his expression became one of puzzlement, and maybe even fear. "Sonny. Something's happened, and we have no idea what it is or what to do about it. We need some help."

He paused, and something like dread took root in his expression. "It seems we've taken on a passenger of sorts."

Singh watched the message play out in fascination and then horror and then fascination again.

The object—there really wasn't any other word to describe it— was a floating sphere of light and darkness hovering about three feet off the deck in a corridor on the *Heart of the Tempest*. Just looking at a recording of it on the monitor's small screen made his head hurt. Someone passed a length of pipe through it and back again on the recording. The pipe did not seem to interact with the object at all. And in fact Singh had the sense that he saw both the pipe and the object at the same time with equal clarity even when that should be impossible. It made his head hurt even worse.

Mercifully, the person with the pipe stopped doing it, and Trejo began speaking.

"As you can see, the anomaly doesn't seem to exist as a physical object. It doesn't appear to radiate on any wavelength, except for visible-spectrum photons. Not one sensing device we've aimed at it can even tell that it's there, but we can record it and see it just fine. Being in the same room with it, looking at it, it's quite disorienting and causes double vision and severe headaches."

As if in response to this, four sailors set up a curtain around it using poles and blankets. While they worked, Trejo continued. "It's moving with us. With the ship, because we're still under thrust and it hasn't moved a millimeter since it first appeared. I've tried making some minor course adjustments, but it keeps us as its frame of reference. I've included all the data we've collected on this file, but I can tell you that its first appearance almost exactly matches the moment when we destroyed Pallas Station. It also includes a nearly three-minute blackout shared by every single person on this ship."

The sailors had finished setting up their curtain, and left. Trejo pulled his monitor close, so his face filled the screen. He lowered his voice, as though telling Singh a secret.

"If this is some new weapon of the inner planets, we need to understand it and now. Blacking out a crew for three minutes, the *right* three minutes, would create a serious tactical advantage for them. I need you to pass along this information to Laconia through our most secure channels. Get me answers fast, Sonny. I'm about to engage with the combined might of the inner planets' navies, and this is the first thing that's made me wonder if I can win."

Singh sank back in his chair, and rubbed his face with both hands. What if everything, including the attacks on Medina, had just been a distraction? What if the inner planets needed time to bring some new superweapon to bear, and feints and jabs from the Sol fleet and his own insurgents were just to create confusion and buy time?

"Major Overstreet?" Singh said to his monitor.

"Yes, sir."

"I'll need a cart with an armed guard. I'm going to the *Storm*."

"Copy that, sir,"

Singh took another data chip out of his desk, laid it on the monitor, and copied all the files Trejo had sent. He then told his monitor to wipe everything. He placed the chip into a lockable metal briefcase, and waited for his ride to arrive.

While he waited, something tugged at his mind. Some memory,

from the academy, maybe. Another mention of a sphere of light and darkness. It had to do with the first wave of colonization, even before the high consul had led his people to Laconia...

He took a moment to have his monitor search the local network for any mention of such an object with the properties Trejo had described.

The search took less than a second, and what it found was a minor colony world named either Ilus or New Terra. In among the list of names connected to what the article was calling the "Ilus Incident" was one that his monitor underlined. When he tapped it, he understood why.

In the report, Captain James Holden of the *Rocinante* had reported seeing the exact object that was currently residing on Admiral Trejo's ship. The same James Holden who was now in their security lockup, under suspicion of terrorist acts.

Chapter Thirty-Six: Bobbie

The public prison was full, but not with her people. Laconian guards stood at the corners with weapons drawn, watching the crowd watch the prisoners. Drones buzzed overhead, scanning constantly. On the far side of the steel mesh, men and women sat disconsolately waiting for trial or judgment. Bobbie stuffed her fists deep into the pockets of her plain gray jumpsuit. A man at the back of the lowest cell on the left looked a little bit like Holden, but not so much she could talk herself into thinking it was him. Even if they had him, Holden probably wouldn't be put here. This jail was more than half for show—public stocks for a new generation. Anyone with real value to the security forces would be somewhere else.

Still. She had hoped. It never hurt to hope, except when it did.

"Pinché schwists, alles la," the man next to her said under his breath. She'd been around Belters long enough to translate it in her head. *Lousy kids, all of them.* The man who'd said it had long brown-gray hair and an expression as sour as old lemons. She only smiled her agreement. This wasn't a place where she wanted to say anything aloud against the Laconians.

It turned out it was just as good she didn't.

"Esá all the fucking underground, yeah?" he said. "Things aren't hard enough, now they're killing our goddamn station?"

Bobbie felt her smile grow tighter, less sincere. The rage in the man's eyes wasn't for the invaders who'd swept in, destroyed their defenses, and taken over. It was for the people fighting against them. It was for her.

"Hard times," she said, because the drones might be listening.

She walked away, heading north along the drum. The straight line of sun above her, the ruins of the engineering decks far away at her back. Being out in public like this left her feeling exposed. The Laconians were everywhere, the checkpoints twice as thick as they'd been before, and everywhere she looked, faces shaped by fear. The Laconians' fear that their control over the station hadn't been enough to stop the underground. The locals' fear of Laconian reprisals. Her fear that she'd be found out, or that she'd broken something she wasn't going to be able to mend.

Saba's network had managed to get the warning out pretty well. The death toll in the explosion was low. She'd heard a dozen, and most of them Laconian, but it was hard to know what was true. It was as deep in the culture of the Belt as bones in their bodies that you didn't fuck with the environmental systems. She hadn't thought about the symbolic meaning of her plan, or what it took for Saba and Katria to agree to it. To Bobbie, they'd been getting important intelligence and covering their tracks. To the Belters, they'd been saying that they would be free of Laconian rule, even if the only freedom was death. If not everyone on the station signed on for that, she couldn't blame them.

A swath of green grass lawn on her right had a classroom's worth of children, a teacher talking about insects and soil. A man on a bicycle rode past her, whistling to let people know he was coming, and to clear the path. All the things that had happened before Duarte and Trejo and Singh. She couldn't guess how many of the people she was walking past would have turned her in to the authorities if they'd known. How many would have applauded her. There was no way for her to ask.

That was the trick of living under the thumb of a dictator. It broke every conversation, even the private ones. The invasion had wounded everyone, one way or another. Herself very much included.

Her hand terminal chimed, and she plucked it out of her pocket with a sense of dread. The message was from Alex, and all it said was WHEN YOU HAVE A MINUTE. The underground was still using encrypted back channels. The security forces wouldn't see the message in their logs. But if Bobbie got picked up, or someone looked over her shoulder, the words would be innocuous. Saba's cramped halls and corridors were the only place they could speak freely. Everywhere else on Medina had become the land of subtext.

She found an escalator and let it carry her down into the body of the drum. It wasn't far to the entry to Saba's alternate station, but they all had to be careful to see they weren't followed. Their bubble of freedom was fragile, and once it popped, it wouldn't come back.

Alex was waiting for her when she ducked into the access corridor. The flesh under his eyes looked ashy and his shoulders slumped like he was under a higher gravity than they were. He smiled, though, and that her friend seemed pleased to see her counted for a lot. For more than it should have, even.

"How's the weather out there?" he asked as they made their way down toward the makeshift galley.

"Stormy," she said. "Get the feeling it'll get worse before it gets better too."

"That was a given."

In the galley, half a dozen of Saba's people sat at the tables, talking. The air smelled like noodles in black sauce, but the food was gone. Bobbie wasn't hungry anyway. One of Katria's men, a crook-nosed guy named Jordao, nodded to her, smiling a little too widely. She nodded back with a sense of dread. This was not a time she wanted someone hitting on her.

"Any word?" she asked, her voice low even though security wouldn't hear her. She wasn't afraid of being found out here, but the wounds were fresh. Some things didn't need to travel outside the family.

"On Holden, no," Alex said.

"Okay," Bobbie said. It cut her a little every time there was nothing, and she welcomed it. If it came back that she'd killed him, the hurt would be a million times worse. Every little wound was a good thing because it wasn't the killing blow.

"That stuff Naomi pulled off the encryption machine? It's working. Saba's folks are able to dig through a bunch of stuff we intercepted before. Of course, the *Storm*'s not talking to Medina anymore since we blew the channel, so we're not getting anything new. But it makes it rough for the bad guys that they can't have their ship talk to the station without radio or tightbeam, so..."

He trailed off like his words were running out of pressure.

"So we won," she said. "Go us."

"Doesn't feel like it, does it? I keep asking myself what the hell happened."

"We lost Holden."

Alex shook his head, tapped four fingertips on the table. "Yeah, and that's hard, but something happened before that. We've faced all kinds of bad before now, and it never split up the family. It was always everyone else, never us. Now Naomi's off in her room, and Amos is wherever the hell Amos is. You're going for long walks. We used to be a crew. Now it's me and Claire playing cards and worrying about everyone." She heard the accusation in his voice, and she wanted to push back at him. Only he was right. Something deeper was wrong. Had been wrong.

In the hallway, Saba's voice. A woman replied. It was all too quiet to make out the words. The people at the other table laughed about something. Bobbie hunched forward, her scowl deep enough to ache.

"Holden's not just Holden," she said, knowing it was an evasion but saying it anyway. "He's the face of the *Rocinante*. He's been on newsfeeds since before I joined up. He's the special man. We pulled this thing off, and we lost one person in the operation. That's a win. If it had been you or me or Claire that got caught, we'd still be celebrating, but it was Holden. Now it feels like we lost our good-luck charm."

"Feels like that to them, sure," Alex said, pointing to the others with his thumb. "But we lost him before, and it didn't break us. Him and Naomi retiring was sad. And then he didn't go away, and that was weird."

"Yeah. The whole Captain Draper thing might have worked if he'd actually been out of the picture—"

Alex leaned forward, talking over her.

"But we know better. Whatever's going on with Amos and you, it didn't start when Holden left. Or when he came back. It was when that big-ass ship steamed through the gate from Laconia and fucked everything sideways. And now Naomi's curling up in her bunk while everything's still on fire."

"She's not helping with the decrypt?"

Alex shook his head once, sharply.

"She can't pull back," Bobbie said. "She's the best tech on the station. Saba's people are fine, but she's better. She can't just stop working because…"

Because her lover's dead. Or worse. Bobbie felt the hurt and the guilt again.

"We need her," Alex agreed. "I'll have a talk with her if you want. Unless you want to be the one who kicks her butt?"

"I really don't."

"Good, because I don't want to be the one who tells Amos to get his shit together. So that one's on you."

To Bobbie's surprise, she smiled. For a moment, she could pretend the cramped little galley was the *Rocinante*. That she and

Alex were burning between the gates and the stars. She put a hand on his arm, grateful that her friend was there. And that however shitty things got, the plan was still to fix them.

Alex's smile was enough to show he understood everything she hadn't spoken. "Right?" he said.

"You're Naomi. I'm Amos. Then if Holden's still alive, we find him, crack him loose, and get the hell out of Dodge before the next big-ass ship comes through that gate."

"See? Now you're talking sense," Alex said. He sighed. "Which is good, because I thought I was going to have to tell you to stop sulking, and I really wasn't looking forward to the part where you punched me in the mouth."

Saba stood at the wider part of the hallway where an access panel had been taken out and never replaced. He held his arms above his head, bracing against the ceiling with the unconscious ease of someone ready for a ship that might move unexpectedly. He lifted his chin as Bobbie came close.

"Hey, I'm looking for Amos," she said.

"Problem?"

"Tell you when I find out," she said. "He's not answering his comms."

Saba's brow furrowed. "Que shansy que he's after Holden?"

"I wouldn't put the odds high that he'd go on an extraction by himself," Bobbie said. Then, a moment later, "I mean not zero, but not high."

"See it stays, if you can," Saba said. "We're carrying plenty enough already, and more rolling down, yeah?"

Something in his voice caught her. "More news?"

Saba hesitated, then shifted his head. *Come this way.* "You looking for yours, me looking for you. You want the good word first, or the worrying?"

"Good," Bobbie said. "I'm looking for good."

"Word from a coyo on the cleaning crew is Holden's alive. Locked down tight, but not dead."

A tightness released in Bobbie's gut. Whatever else happened, she hadn't killed him. And more than that, when she found Amos, she'd have it on her side. She felt a deep gratitude that she'd run into Saba before he'd found him. She had to let Alex know. And Naomi. And everyone. The relief was profound.

"That's...Okay. What's the worrying?"

"Message from the union. From the spy repeater."

"Wait," Bobbie said, following him as he walked toward his cabin. "We've got communications lines open? I thought we shut that down."

"Turned it back on for this," Saba said. "It ate a missile right after. Drummer thought it was worth burning the channel for."

"Something big, then?"

"Come see."

Saba had Drummer's message up on his cabin's monitor. The change in her face was shocking. It wasn't only that the president looked tired and thinner. She looked older, like the last few weeks had been measured in years instead of days. Saba didn't speak, but started the message from the beginning. Bobbie listened until the end, then played it again, making sure she understood. The loss of Pallas, and the loss of time.

"Well," she said. "Holy shit."

"Yeah," Saba said. "Got my people going through all the information we intercepted. All that's finished decrypting, anyway. Nothing about lost time or boiling up the vacuum."

"Even if we found something, it's not like we can sneak a message back if the repeater's dead."

"Not sneak one, no," Saba agreed. "Can shout, though. If it was the right time. Medina's not home anymore. Not for us. When we scatter, maybe send something back down to People's Home. Tell them what we've got to tell them. If we get anything."

"Fair point," Bobbie agreed. "And that is the plan now, right?

Clear a path and evacuate as many as we can before the new ship gets here?"

"Already putting out the word to the underground," he said. He sounded as tired as she was. "Just the ones we trust. Saying to get ready. Window opens, and get to the ships and go. Everyone someplace different. Harder to kill us if we're not in one place."

"Even better if they don't know who went where," Bobbie said. "I'd love to find a way to take out Medina's sensor arrays when we go."

"Would be sweet," Saba said, his voice dull.

"You holding up okay?" Bobbie asked.

Saba shrugged toward the image of Drummer still on the screen. "That woman is my heart, and I lost her. Lost my ship. Lost my place for my people. Got an enemy ship killing my cities and stations, and now it can turn off minds in a whole system at once. Got another one like it braking toward me. Got all those Marines in power armor ready to shoot me and mine through the brainpan, and the loosest mouth on a thousand worlds is in the enemy's jail. So given so, I'm all right."

"Holden won't rat us out. He's given a lot of unvetted press releases over the years, but that's not the same as this."

"They have him, they'll have us. Not talking him down, but these people were Mars before they were this. Ask anyone in the OPA from the old days. Martian interrogation, it's a question of how long until the break. Never if. Better that he'd died."

"We can move," Bobbie said. "Do you have any holes that Holden didn't know about?"

"Few," Saba said, reluctantly. "But fewer now. My people are moving now. Still room for you and yours, but there won't be. Not for long. And..."

He shook his head.

"And what," Bobbie said. "If there's something more, I need to know."

Saba shrugged and nodded at the screen. "When it comes, if it comes, the one system we can't go to? Sol. Anyplace else, I can try for. Anyplace else, I can go. But no matter where it is, she won't be there. Wasn't so bad when the repeater still was, but with it gone, it feels…"

A tear tracked down Saba's brown cheek. Bobbie looked away.

It was so easy to forget all the others. Not just Saba, but all of them. The crews of all the ships trapped in the dock beside the *Roci*. The children in Medina's schoolrooms, the medical staff in the clinics. The artists playing music live outside the cafés out of love of doing it. Medina Station had been the nearest thing to a void city before the void cities were built. It was a home for a generation of people, and every one of them was carrying something now that made their days harder. She thought of the prisoners in the public jail, the angry man who'd come to watch them. Who had he lost back on Sol? What was keeping him awake in the nights?

There were so many families, so many crews, parents and children, lovers and friends, whose lives had been changed past recognition since Laconia gate had opened. It wasn't just her and the *Roci* crew. It wasn't just Saba. Everyone was dancing on this same landslide, and no one knew how to make it end well.

She wanted to say something comforting, but she couldn't bring herself to lie. The best she could think of was to change the subject.

"When we get out," she said. "Not if. When. We're going to need a plan. If every ship just bolts off on its own, we'll lose contact. *They* shouldn't know where we went, but *we* should. At the very least, we should have a record of who went where. This everyman-for-himself-and-God-against-all shit's romantic, but we have to plan for something past just this."

Saba nodded. In the distance, voices and footsteps.

"Not just encrypted but in code," Saba said. "Something where only we know what it means."

"We?"

"Ou y mé," Saba said. "Leaders of the underground, us. First among dissidents."

Bobbie chuckled. "Well, there's a fucking job title."

The footsteps came faster now, and coming closer. Saba looked up like an animal smelling smoke. *Fuck,* Bobbie thought. *Not something else. It's too much already. We can't carry something else.*

The woman who appeared in Saba's doorway was older, white hair pulled back in a tight braid. Her body was long and thin, her head a little too large for her shoulders. The classic build of someone who'd grown up without gravity to hold her down. She even had the split circle of the OPA tattooed on her arm. She should have looked ancient, but the brightness in her eyes belonged on a woman a third her age. She looked from Saba to Bobbie and back with something like triumph in her eyes.

"Maha?" Saba said. "Que?" And then to Bobbie, "Maha one of our best communications techs. Had her hands in the codes since before I was born, yeah?"

"And I know all their secrets," she said in a weirdly accented voice. She held out a dumb terminal that wasn't connected to Medina's system. "The new decryption run turned over some stones. And look you what was squirming under one."

Bobbie was closer. She took the handheld terminal and flipped through the file there. It was titled MEDINA STATION SUPPLE-MENTARY SECURITY REVIEW AS REQUESTED BY GOVERNOR SANTIAGO SINGH. The file's creator was listed as Major Lester Overstreet. She checked the file length and whistled.

"Que?" Saba said.

"This is way too long to just be an incident report," Bobbie said. "It's…"

The section headings were Materials, Procedures, Personnel, Protocols, Audit Summary, Recommendations. She recognized the style of paragraph marking from when she'd trained back on Olympus Mons. It looked like an MMC security report, but twice as long. Maybe three times. She shifted through one after another, her head starting to swim a little.

"I think…Saba, I think this is *everything,*" she said.

Chapter Thirty-Seven: Alex

His back hurt. Of all the thousand things that were jacked up and wrong in his life right now, the one that chose to make him crazy was that. His back hurt, just below his rib cage where it clicked for a couple days after they'd been on the float for a while. Now it clicked and ached a little. Just time and age catching up with him, but it made him crazy. Probably anything that he couldn't fix was going to make him crazy right now.

He walked down the tight hallway, his shoulder brushing the conduits and pipes, and told himself that things were getting better. Not losing Holden. That was still a long way from better. But the rest of it. The rest of them. Whatever else happened, he still had Bobbie.

And for him anyway, Bobbie counted double.

Taking care of their little family had been his job damn near since the day the *Canterbury* died, back in some other lifetime.

And usually, he felt like he managed it pretty well. The only time things had really come apart, he'd been married to Giselle and preoccupied with trying to pump air into that leaking sack of a relationship. But all the times he hadn't lost focus, Alex felt like he'd kept the crew of the *Roci* working together, mostly. It wasn't big things. The powerful stuff was always small. A kind word when Clarissa was feeling unappreciated, a little elbow in the ribs when Holden's outrage on someone else's behalf threatened to eclipse the person in question, a cordon around Amos when the big man was in the bad part of his head. Every crew that lasted more than three runs together had someone who kept a weather eye on the balance. For decades now, he'd been that man on the *Roci*.

Only they weren't on the *Roci* now. And that, so far as he could see it, was more than half of the problem. Not the whole problem. But more than half.

"Hoy, hoy, hoy," one of Katria's people said, trotting up behind him. Alex recognized him from the galley. Young guy with a nose that had gotten bent sometime back and never put straight. "Passé alles gut?"

"Sure," Alex said. "Everything's fine." It wasn't true, but he wasn't looking to talk about family business outside the family.

"Bist bien," the crook-nosed guy said. "Just. We're alles busted about Holden, yeah? Whatever Voltaire can do, help out, yeah?"

Alex clapped the crook-nose on the shoulder, and looked deeply into his eyes. "Thank you. Seriously. That means a lot."

The kid was just another someone who wanted to get close to the action. There had been a million like him over the years. Holden had always been the one who soaked up the fame and celebrity, because for the most part he didn't notice it. He just kept on being himself, and got vaguely surprised when anyone recognized him. The rest of them had to build up their routines and diversions, ways of being polite to the people who wanted to insert themselves into anything that the *Rocinante* did so they could tell their friends and feeds that they knew James Holden. Shaking Crook-nose's hand and sending him away didn't cost

Alex much, but it didn't cost him nothing. Part of him wanted to ignore the guy or yell at him. But this was easier in the long run. He had enough experience to know that, and he was pretty good with patience when he needed to be.

After a well-calculated moment, he turned away and resumed walking toward the makeshift bunkroom. And Naomi.

It had been hard when Holden and Naomi pulled the ripcord, but it hadn't been unexpected. Part of him had been braced for it since his own second divorce. He'd been ready for the blow when those two packed up their things and retired. When Duarte's forces blew through the gate and changed everything, part of him had thought that getting Holden and Naomi back was going to be the silver lining.

He'd called it wrong, though.

They treated it like Laconia was the only problem because it was the one most likely to get them all killed, but there was more than that. Now that Holden was out of the picture, the only one in a position to fix it was Naomi.

Fix it. That was optimism. The only one who could fix as much of it as was fixable. He hoped she was able to rise to the occasion. He hoped he was too. But no matter how bad it was, things had gone pretty well with Bobbie. He still had Bobbie.

The smuggler's cabin was dim. Golden light spilled from the toolkit light they used for illumination when the built-in fixtures were too harsh. The air was warmer here, and it had the vague smell of bodies and old laundry. They hadn't changed out the sheets since they'd gotten here. Some things slipped when you were hiding from authoritarian police squads and trying to topple a conquering army. Linens appeared to be one of those things.

Naomi sat against the back wall, her stool tipped back so that she could rest against the bulkhead. She smiled when he came in and put a finger to her lips. Alex paused, and Naomi nodded toward the bunk to his left. The lump under the blanket was the curve of Clarissa's back. It rose and fell slowly. She was asleep. Alex turned back to Naomi, gestured to the door behind him in invitation, but Naomi shifted her stool to one side, making room for Alex to sit on the lower bunk beside her. *Come sit with me. I will not go outside.*

With a sinking sensation in his gut, Alex sat. His back popped like a bolt shearing off, and the ache went away. In the shadows, Naomi seemed like someone just waking up from sleep or just falling into it. On a borderline, regardless, between one state and another.

"Hey," Alex said softly.

Naomi made a little wave with a smile behind it. "I've been sitting with her for the last couple hours. Amos is trying to get something to take the edge off in the short run, but we need to get her to the med bay. That sludge in her blood is building up. It's making her jittery."

"Soon as we're out of here," Alex said. "First thing. How're you holding together?"

She shrugged with her hands.

"Yeah," he said.

"You coming to tell me that I need to put my big-girl boots on? Stop sulking in my tent and rejoin the battle, quick before Patroclus does something rash?" There was a warmth and a humor in her voice he hadn't expected. It almost undercut the sorrow that he had expected.

"Yeah, I don't actually know who Patroclus is," Alex said.

"Greek kid, got in over his head," Naomi said, waving it away. "I'll be fine, Alex. I'll be out there. Just I needed to be away for a little while. It's just the down cycle."

He went through all of the things he'd planned to say, all the arguments he'd prepared to make. None of them seemed to quite fit the situation.

"Yeah, okay," he said instead. And then, a moment later, "Down cycle?"

"The part where I don't know if he's dead or alive. The part where I don't know if I'll ever see him again. The part where I think how much I want him to be here and safe and not hurting. And telling me not to hurt either."

"I know it's…that's got to be—"

"Alex, I live here," Naomi said. "I can't tell you how many times he's put me here. How many times he's seen the right thing to do and rushed off to do it without thinking about the price. Without letting me or you or the *Roci* scare him into being less than his conscience demands. He doesn't even know he's doing it. It's natural to him. Who he is. It's the only thing about him I'm really angry about." The buzz in her voice wasn't sorrow.

Alex took a deep breath and let it out slowly. "I may not have really understood the whole situation."

"You remember Io? When he went off to a ship with active protomolecule all over it because maybe he'd be able to save Mars? Or Ilus, when he vanished with whatever that weird version of Miller was because maybe he'd be able to keep you and me from falling out of orbit? Or on Marais, when he went into the cliffs so we wouldn't run out of water? So this time he went to keep Amos and Katria playing nice, and instead, he saved the whole operation and maybe opened the way for all of us to get away safely. All it cost was *him*. And he paid that price without hesitating. Same as *fucking* always."

A tear tracked down her cheek, and he felt his own eyes stinging.

"We'll get him," Alex said. "We'll always get him back."

"Sure we will. Until the time we don't," she said. "It's like this for everyone. There's always going to be a last time, eventually. I just wish with Jim there could only be *one* last time, and not all of them, over and over and over."

He took her hand. Her fingers were warm, but thinner than he remembered them being. He could feel the little bones beneath the skin, and her skin was dry.

"He's exhausting," she said.

"But we love him."

She sighed. "We do."

They sat in silence for a moment before she drew her hand back from his and wiped her cheeks dry. She leaned forward, setting the legs of her stool down against the deck. Her sigh came from a thousand klicks away. "Let me get cleaned up, and I'll get to work," she said.

Alex stood when she did, but waited behind as she walked out. He'd been traveling with Naomi for a lot of years. It was amazing how easy it was to forget how much she knew herself. He didn't know if that said more about her or him.

Probably him.

Clarissa made a soft sound, somewhere between a grunt and cough. She turned toward him. Her skin was pale, sheened with sweat, but her smile was strong and unforced. "Hey," she said. "What did I miss? Did we hear about Holden? What's news?"

"No, it wasn't that. I was just getting a little pep talk," Alex said. "How're you doing?"

Clarissa's eyes drifted closed and then open again, like a blinking in slow motion. "Living the dream," she said, and chuckled. "Have you seen Amos? He was going to get me...something."

"I think he's still out doing that. He'll be back, though. Don't worry."

"I never do," Clarissa said, and shuddered like she was cold. The room wasn't cold. "You think they could fix me?"

"Who?"

"The Laconians," Clarissa said. "I keep thinking about how their tech is all levels and levels above ours. And I wonder if maybe their medicine is too. Maybe they could get these fucking implants out of me. Plaster over the worst of the damage."

"I don't know. Maybe."

"Kind of ironic that I'm working to fuck them all the way up, isn't it?" She made a single, low sound. If she'd strung a few like it together, it would have been chuckling.

"I guess it is," he said. And then a moment later, "If you want to go to one of their clinics? I mean it would probably mean getting out of this underground business, but if you want to, we can work something out."

Her smile was love and pity. "You really think that's true? That we could work something out?"

"Hell yes," Alex said.

"Well, I'll keep that option in mind," she said. "You're a good man, Alex Kamal."

"You're not too bad yourself," he said.

"I am not presently at my best," Clarissa said. "But I appreciate the thought. I really do."

Her eyes fluttered closed again. Her face relaxed. She looked like a wax model of herself. *She'll be better when we get the* Roci *back*, he thought. *Not* better-*better. Just improved, but better than this.* And once he was back in the pilot's seat, he wasn't ever going dockside again if he could help it. Being on the *Rocinante* was being home.

Everywhere else was where the trouble came.

Bobbie came with the news about Holden, and something else besides. It felt almost like something foreordained. As soon as he had told Naomi that they'd save Holden, Holden appeared in the station brig and the document outlining how to free him fell into their hands. It was perfect enough to make him very nervous.

"This is astounding," Naomi said, paging through the file.

Alex leaned over her, trying to see the screen of her terminal and not interrupt her at the same time, and doing a middling job of both. If there was any sure sign of Naomi's relief, it was that she was back on the job.

The room was small, the door firmly closed, and Saba had set the monitor to the local newsfeed with the volume high. A young man he didn't recognize was interviewing Carrie Fisk about the war in Sol system and the traffic between the colony worlds that was just about to begin. *The colonies don't care who's running*

Medina, so long as we're running it well. The Transport Union was fine, and Laconian oversight will be fine too. Better, even, because the Laconian model respects self-rule. The Laconian Congress of Worlds is a real voice for its members. That's never been the case before. Alex tried watching her, just so he'd have something to do besides hover. It didn't work very well.

Bobbie paced along the wall behind her, three strides one way, then turned, then three back. Saba was more subdued, his body held still and only his eyes flickering. The two of them had the same sense of barely restrained action. Like a boulder on a mountaintop that's just starting to shift toward the slope.

Naomi made a small, satisfied sound at the back of her throat and followed a linked passage to a schematic of a ship that looked from the outside like the *Gathering Storm*.

"Who knows about this?" Alex asked. "I mean, who's seen it?"

"One of mine broke the encryption," Saba said. "She brought it to me straight. Didn't read it, even. Maha, she solid like stone. Not everyone of mine is, but her? I tell her she didn't see it, and it never got seen."

"This has the operational plans for the *Gathering Storm*," Naomi said. "Whatever else you want to say about these Laconians, they are thorough."

"Most of it's MRCN and MMC protocols and practices," Bobbie said. "Five-sixths of it are the operating procedures Alex and I trained on, word for word."

"You should both read the thing, then," Saba said. "Alles la. Mark down where it's changed. There's reasons to change things. Might point us the right way. Know what's behind it, maybe even better than this on its own."

"I don't know," Naomi said. "This on its own is pretty damned good."

The excitement in Alex's chest felt like champagne bubbles. Bright and dancing. He'd forgotten what a good break felt like after all the dread. It was astounding to think how close he'd come to scrubbing the mission, leaving the waldoes abandoned in the air duct, and calling it impossible. And if this was the key that let them get themselves and everyone else in the underground off Medina before the *Typhoon* appeared, his balking would have pissed their best chances away.

Holden's gambit had worked. He'd thrown himself to the wolves so that they'd have this, and it was everything they'd hoped for. Everything but having him back, and maybe that too.

"Is there anything in there about where the prisoners are held?" he asked.

"There is," Naomi said, her inflection landing on the words in a way that meant it was the first thing she'd looked for. All the rest of it was important, but that part—where Holden was, how to get him out—was a settled issue in her mind. That was enough for Alex. He could hear the details later, so long as there were details to hear.

"Problemas son," Saba said, shifting his weight. "Maybe is too good, yeah? Maybe is designed to look like something it's not."

"You think it's fake?" Naomi asked.

Saba made a ticking sound with his tongue and teeth. "No. But can't make the assumption without risking everybody's ass, yeah? Hoping more than not. If it is what it is, it won't stay secret for long. Too proud a victory, yeah? Someone finds out, gets a little drunk, then everyone knows."

"You don't trust your people's discipline?" Bobbie asked.

Saba pointed at the closed door. "My people are the crew on the *Malaclypse*. These others weren't mine until they stopped being Drummer's. And she's had five or six layers of bureaucrats between. It's not I don't trust, it's that I don't trust blind. People are people. Fucked up like we all are, it amazes me when we can even make a sandwich."

"A man of infinite cynicism," Naomi said, but Alex could hear the calm behind the words. Whatever she was seeing there, it soothed her more than he'd been able to. And then, "Bobbie, when you were active Martian Marine Corps, did your Goliath suits have a command override?"

"A what?" Bobbie said.

"Command override. Something that let your commanding officer shut the suit down?"

"Sure, we called it a radio. CO said stand down, and we did. What are you seeing?"

Naomi leaned back so that Bobbie—and since he was right there, Alex—could see better. Back when he'd been in the service, there had always been a clear chain of command, and procedures in place for when someone bucked it. Most of the time it involved MPs dragging someone off for a little summary roadside attitude adjustment followed by a court-martial. Maybe it was different in the Marines, but he was pretty sure he hadn't seen anything like what was outlined on the screen.

"They can...they can turn them off?" Bobbie said, her voice caught between outrage and laughter. "Because that right there looks like it's saying the governor can push a button and turn all those pretty suits of power armor into a couple thousand sarcophagi."

"Life-support functions stay in place," Naomi said. "But disables the weapons and comm systems, and freezes all the joints."

Alex whistled appreciatively. "These folks must really be scared of mutineers."

"Well," Bobbie said. "Think about how they got here. Duarte managed to build a schismatic faction inside the MCRN big enough to start his own navy. Going on with the assumption that no one would ever try the same thing on him would seem stupid. He's not stupid. This solve in particular, though..."

"Seems a mite overaggressive," Alex said.

"And it's always the aggressor who exposes their weakness," Bobbie said. She put her hand on Naomi's. "What are the chances we could spoof that lockdown signal?"

"Get me one of their powered suits," Naomi said, "and I'm pretty sure we could manage it."

"The *Storm*, Medina's scopes, and the Marines," Bobbie said. "This looks like we can build a plan that's three for three."

"And the prisoners," Naomi said. "Freeing the prisoners."

She meant Holden, Alex knew. Bobbie did too.

"Goes without saying," Bobbie said.

Chapter Thirty-Eight: Singh

Singh found it unsettling to think of a time before Laconia. He'd been young enough when his parents made the crossing that he had virtually no memories of anything *but* Laconia as home. And yet, Laconia wasn't even the first of the thirteen hundred worlds to be colonized. First, there had been a ball of mud and water that the settlers called Ilus.

The government of Earth, faced with the daunting prospect of surveying, studying, then exploiting the potentially vast riches of these new worlds, did what it always did. It gave out a government contract to a civilian company to do it for them. But when the prospecting vessel from Royal Charter Energy arrived at what the UN was calling New Terra, they found a couple hundred squatters already there digging up mineral resources and calling themselves an independent government.

A lot of violence later, RCE left the planet, Ilus had its own charter from the UN, and it was, up until recently, a founding member of Carrie Fisk's Association of Worlds and an exporter of lithium and heavy metals.

James Holden had been there during the worst of that initial violence. Now he was in an observation room with his ankles shackled to the deck.

Singh considered the man on his monitor. Holden was older than he'd expected, his temples gone white. The images he'd pulled from the public archives going back decades showed that same open, serious-eyed face on a man very nearly Singh's own age.

Now Holden sat with his head bowed forward. Blood streaked the chest and sleeves of his prison uniform. Round drops of it spotted his paper slippers. He cradled one hand against this belly, and his cheek was swollen and bruised. The stool he sat on had a single leg bolted to the deck, and he swayed forward and back like a man nodding himself to sleep. The restraints on his wrists looked like wide black ribbon, but Singh knew they were strong enough that the man's bones would break before they did. He wasn't a person so much as a distillation of human misery.

"Should I ask how many of those wounds came from the explosion?" Singh said.

Overstreet didn't smile, but a subtle merriness came to his eyes. "If that's important to you, sir, I'm sure I could find out."

After the prisoner had set off false alarms throughout the engineering deck, he had been captured. Five minutes after that the real alarms had begun. In other circumstances, Holden would already be dead. All that had kept him alive until now was his connection to the mechanisms and people involved in his terrorist group and his own stubbornness.

But if this was going to work, Singh knew he would have to somehow reach this man. Make a human connection with someone ready to kill Laconians out of prejudice and hatred. If he was going to find something that he could exploit, he had to believe there was good in him, even if he only maintained the illusion

for a little while. If he could reframe Holden in his own mind,
if he could see some other version of the man than the obvious
one, it might be possible. "He did warn people. The alarms before
the detonation? They let more people get to safety. When he was
taken, he warned the security forces to take shelter. If he hadn't
done what he did, the loss of life would have been worse."

"That's true," Overstreet said. "He could also have chosen not
to bomb the air supply."

What was this man? A patriot to his government? A man so
frightened of change he'd resort to violence? A rabble-rouser who
took Singh's governorship as another opportunity to start trouble
that he would have been making under any circumstances?

What he came back to—what he brought himself back to—was
that point: Holden had let himself be captured in order to save
lives. It wasn't much, but it was all Singh had.

"Well," he said. "Let's see what happens."

Holden looked up as he entered the room. The older man's left eye
was nearly shut and his upper lip was split and scabby. He nodded
to Singh as a guard brought a light chair for the governor to sit on.

"Captain Holden," Singh said. "I'm sorry we couldn't meet
under better circumstances."

"Me too," Holden said. His voice was low and graveled. Singh
had the sense that it wasn't always that way.

"Can I get you anything? A cup of water?"

"Coffee," Holden said. "I could stand a cup of coffee."

Singh tapped his wrist monitor, and a moment later the same
guard reentered with a bulb. Holden accepted it with both hands
and sipped it. His smile seemed genuine.

"This is actually pretty good."

"I'm glad you approve. I'm more of a tea man myself."

"It'll do in a pinch," Holden said, then lifted his gaze to meet
Singh's. He had surprisingly clear and focused eyes, considering
all he'd been through. "Just to clarify, are you trying to build rap-

port with me, or am I trying to build rapport with you? I'm a little hazy on it."

"Both, I think," Singh said. "I haven't done this before. I'm a novice."

"Yeah, well. No offense, but you look like a teenager."

"I'm the same age you were when you were thrown out of Earth's navy."

Holden laughed. It was a warm, rueful sound. "I'm not sure you'll do yourself any favors comparing yourself to me back then. I was kind of an idiot."

Singh found it was easy to chuckle. He could imagine coming to like this man. That was good. It made the next part easier.

"So why do you hate us? If you don't mind my asking."

"You personally? I don't. But this conquistador bullshit? It's true I don't think much of it."

Singh leaned back in his chair, cocked his head. "This is all a conversation about politics for you, then? It matters to you that much whose vision guides the government, no matter what that vision is?"

"Not that academic," Holden said. "I've spent a lot of years trying to get people to get along without anyone's boot being on anyone's neck. Your plan A is what I've spent a lifetime pushing against."

"Do you really think we're so bad? Look at what we've done, how we've done it. We haven't opened fire on a single ship that didn't attack us first. In all of history, when has a conqueror been able to say that? We have embraced local rule. Any of the colony worlds that submits can make their own local government, keep their own local customs—"

"Unless they conflict with your rules."

"Of course."

Holden sipped his coffee. "That's the thing. The people you're controlling don't have a voice in how you control them. As long as everyone's on the same page, things may be great, but when there's a question, you win. Right?"

"There has to be a way to come to a final decision."

"No, there doesn't. Every time someone starts talking about final anythings in politics, that means the atrocities are warming up. Humanity has done amazing things by just muddling through, arguing and complaining and fighting and negotiating. It's messy and undignified, but it's when we're at our best, because everyone gets to have a voice in it. Even if everyone else is trying to shout it down. Whenever there's just one voice that matters, something terrible comes out of it."

"And yet, I understand from Ms. Fisk that the Transport Union was condemning whole colonies that didn't follow its rule."

"Right?" Holden said. "And so I disobeyed that order and I quit working for them. I was all set to go retire in Sol system. Can *you* do that?"

"Can I do what?"

"If you are given an immoral order, can you resign and walk away? Because everything I've seen about how you're running this place tells me that isn't an option for you."

Singh crossed his arms. He had the sense that the interrogation was getting away from him.

"The high consul is a very wise, very thoughtful man," he said. "I have perfect faith that—"

"No. Stop. 'Perfect faith' really tells me everything I need to know," Holden said. "You think this is a gentle, bloodless conquest, don't you?"

"It is, to the degree that you allow it to be."

"I was there for the war Duarte started to cover his tracks. I was there for the starving years afterward. Your empire's hands look a lot cleaner when you get to dictate where history begins and what parts of it don't count."

"So you and your friends decide instead?" Singh said, trying to keep his tone light. "You know that sooner or later, you're going to tell us who they are."

Holden took a long drink from the coffee cup and set it down gently on the floor beside his feet. "I'm hoping for later," he said. "But I see we're already done with the part where we make friendly with each other."

Singh felt the warmth he'd cultivated toward Holden slipping away into frustration. He'd started in too quickly. He should have spent more time building up the relationship, and now they'd both fallen into adversarial stances with each other. It was time to change tack.

"Tell me what you can," Singh said, "about Ilus."

Holden frowned, but not angrily. "What do you want to know?"

Singh waited without answering.

Holden shrugged. "All right. It was the first contested colony. I went out there to try to mediate between the different claimants, and it all pretty much turned to shit. People shooting each other. Old artifacts coming to life and blowing up the ocean. Local ecosystem trying to mine us for fresh water. And there were death slugs. It wasn't great."

"Artifacts coming to life?"

"Yeah," Holden said, shifting on his little stool. "We had a trace of active protomolecule on the ship. We didn't know about it. It was trying to report in about the Sol gate being complete, but everything it wanted to report to was dead or turned off. So it started turning things on. Only part of it was this guy I used to know, and... It's kind of a weird story. Why do you want to know about Ilus?"

"What about the *other* artifact?"

Holden shook his head, opened his hands. *What other artifact?*

Singh pulled up the image from the *Tempest* on his monitor. A bright-black nothingness. He enlarged it and held it out for Holden to see.

"Yeah, the bullet," Holden said. "It was the thing that turned everything off again. Deactivated the protomolecule."

Singh felt a chill in his heart. The calmness and innocence of the way Holden said the words was deeper than any threat.

"It did what?"

"The guy I used to know? The dead one? He was a detective, and it was using him to look for where to report in. Only he—the reconstructed version of him—noticed that there was this place that killed off protomolecule activity. He said it was like a bullet that someone had fired to kill off the...the civilization...that... Bring that where I can see it better?"

Singh enlarged the image. Holden blinked. The weariness seemed to fall away from him, the pain of his injuries forgotten. When he spoke, his voice had a firmness and command Singh hadn't heard there before. "That's not Ilus. Where is that?"

"It appeared in Sol system. On one of our ships."

"Oh. *Fuck* that," Holden said. "All right, listen. There's a woman you need to find. Her name's Elvi Okoye. She was a scientist on Ilus. I don't know where she is now, but she spent years researching the artifacts there, including that one. She went through it."

"Went through it to where?"

"Not like a door. Like she carried part of the protomolecule's network into it, and it killed off the sample. Turned it all inert. And she said it turned her sort of off while it did."

"Turned her off. Like she lost consciousness?" Singh said. "Lost *time*?"

"Something like that," Holden said. "I don't know. I didn't go through it. But I did see the thing on the station. I saw what happened to them."

Singh found he was leaning forward. His blood felt like it was fizzing. And what was more, he saw the same feelings echoed in Holden's battered face.

"There was a station on Ilus?" he asked.

"No. The one here. The station that controls the ring space. The first time anyone came though the ring, that same dead guy took me to the station. It was part of how the rings turned on. But I saw things there. Like a record of the old civilization? My friend, the dead guy, was looking through it for something, and because he was using me to do it, I saw it all too. Whatever made this? All of this? They were wiped out a long time before you and me got here. Billions of years, maybe. I saw whole systems going dark. I saw them trying to stop it by burning away entire solar systems. And it didn't work. Whatever they tried to do, it failed, and they were all just wiped away with just their roads and their old machines left for us to stumble across. That thing that showed up on your ship? That's them. The *other* them. That's the thing that killed everything before Earth and Mars were part of the gate network."

"But why would it appear now?"

Holden choked on a laugh. "Well, I don't know. Have you people been doing anything different recently?"

Singh felt a little stab of embarrassment. It was a fair point. For the first time, the *Tempest* had employed the magnetic-field generator in an uncontrolled environment both here and in Sol system. Maybe this was a side effect. Or something else about the battleships built on the platforms. Or...

"Look," Holden said. "You and me? We're not friends. We aren't going to be friends. I will oppose you and your empire to my dying breath. But right now, none of that matters. Whatever built the gates and the protomolecule and all these ruins we're living in? They were wiped out. And the thing that wiped them out just took a shot at you."

Singh couldn't sleep that night. He was exhausted, but whenever he closed his eyes, Holden was there, squinting through his injured eyes, pointing with his broken hand. And the enigma of the bullet, the threat and mystery it represented. They defied him to sleep.

In the middle of his sleep shift, he gave up, put on a robe, and ordered a pot of tea delivered from the commissary. When it arrived, he was already searching through the station records for other documentation of Holden's ravings. He was hoping to find something to suggest that the man was either insane or playing a game to deflect attention from his terrorism. But file after file, report after report, confirmed him. Even when there was no other witness to what he'd seen, there was at least a history to show that his claims had been consistent.

It would have been so much easier if James Holden were only a madman.

Your empire's hands look a lot cleaner when you get to dictate where history begins, and what parts of it don't count.

He knew the story of Laconia's founding. He'd been there for it, though he'd been a child at the time. The gates to the thirteen hundred worlds had opened, and the probes had gone through. They'd brought back reports of the different systems, the stars and planets, and the stranger things that they'd seen. All humanity had seen the opportunity of new lands, of new worlds to inhabit, but alone of them all Winston Duarte had recognized the terrible danger that expansion would bring. The chaos and violence as humanity pressed out past the limits of civilization. The choke point of the slow zone and the endless wars it would generate. The unanticipated environmental collapses made worse by the lack of a central response. And he alone had the will to solve the problem.

From among all the planets on the far sides of the gates, he chose Laconia because of the orbital construction platforms. He found the live culture of the protomolecule that he could use to harness Laconia's power. He found Dr. Cortazár to lead the research and development. And he took a third of the Martian Navy as the seed that would grow to become the world tree. The fraction of humanity that would rebuild on Laconia and come forth to bring order to humanity's chaos. To bring the peace that would last forever. The end of all wars. Singh doubted none of it. Holden's version wasn't incompatible, even if it chose a different emphasis. Holden himself had used the protomolecule on Ilus—or been used by it—to turn on the ancient mechanisms. Only he had done it haphazardly, and with terrible results. Duarte had done it carefully, and to glorious effect.

He sipped his tea. It hadn't quite gone cold, but it wasn't as warm as he'd expected. Holden was a problem. He was the key to breaking the terrorist network on Medina. He was also the key to the mystery of the thing that had appeared on the *Tempest*. His was the only report on the visions from the ring station. He was singular in all humanity because he'd bumbled into being in so many of the right places at so many of the right times. If there was one thing Laconia's history taught, it was the power of the right person at the right moment.

Singh had always known that the history of Laconia and the history of Sol system were connected. He'd never felt those common roots more deeply than now. The sense that his world and Holden's were part of a single, much vaster story. The makers of the protomolecule were also a part of that larger frame. The things that had killed *them*, and then vanished.

The things that had returned.

Chapter Thirty-Nine: Amos

I was thinking about the recyclers," Peaches said. She sounded tired. She always sounded a little tired, but this was more.

"Yeah?" he said.

They were alone in the bunk. She was sitting up, paring her toenails with a little knife he'd found for her. Something about her meds made them thicker and yellow. He knew it was important to her to keep them short, even though she never said anything.

His hands imagined what it would feel like to snap her neck. The tension first, then the grinding feeling of cartilage ripping as it gave way. He saw the look of betrayal in her eyes as the life went out of them. It was as clear as if he'd actually done it.

"The returns aren't as good as they ought to be," she said. "We've been able to get eighty-eight, ninety percent recovery, but I don't think we broke eighty-five on the Freehold run."

"Worth looking at," Amos said. "You got any suspects?"

"I want to take a look at the water filters. I know they're supposed to be the best there is without retrofitting to a straight gel system, but I don't think they're doing what's on the label."

He closed his eyes and the *Rocinante*'s recycling system appeared in his mind. If the filters were underperforming…yeah, could throw off the pressure going into the recyclers. Might be enough to drop the reclamation percentages. He pictured what else it would do.

"We should take a peek at the feed lines," he said.

"Look for distention?" she said.

He grunted. Peaches scowled and nodded once, the way she did when they'd come to an agreement. There were still a few things about the *Roci* that he knew better than she did, but those were few and far between. And mostly about the weapons systems. She didn't like those, and it had an effect on how much she thought about them. There were conversations he had with her that he couldn't have with anybody else.

That didn't keep the thoughts from coming. It didn't do anything about the thing in his throat. "You think Holden's okay?" she asked.

"Is or he isn't," Amos said. The thing in his throat got a little bigger. A little tighter. He wasn't sure why.

"I wish there was something more I could do," she said.

"Naomi'll come up with something. Whatever needs doing, we'll do it."

She finished the last nail and tossed him the knife. He caught it in the air, folded it closed, and put it under his pillow, where it would stay. Peaches got another couple of her pills and swallowed them dry, then lay back on her bunk. There wasn't room enough between her bunk and the one above her to get a decent punch going, but he knew what it would feel like to do a straight-kick to her ribs. Or her head. Push her back against the bulkhead, then the next kicks, she wouldn't be able to avoid. He wasn't going to do it, but the thoughts came anyway.

"You need some sleep?" he asked.

"Little."

"You should try to eat some afterward."

"I'm not keeping much down right now."

"That's why they call it 'try,'" he said. "Worst case, just smear it around your face like a little kid. Absorb some nutrients through your skin."

She chuckled. "You talked me into it, big guy. After I rest."

"I'm going to get a jump on it," he said. "You need anything, you just say it."

"Thank you," Peaches said.

He made his way down toward the galley, his shoulders brushing against the conduit and pipes on both sides. In the galley, one of Saba's people was drinking a cup of coffee. Nice-looking guy, always been pleasant. The thing in his throat moved a little, and Amos felt the coffee cup slamming into the other guy's face. The edge of the cup folding against the guy's upper lip. The coffee burning them both. He felt what it would be like, bending him back, trapping his legs under the table so he couldn't writhe away, pulling until his back snapped. There'd be others by then. The guy's friends. He thought about how to kill them too.

Amos smiled amiably and nodded. The guy nodded back. Amos got a bowl of oatmeal and honey flavoring. He sat by himself to eat. Saba's guy finished his drink and walked away. There was a moment when his back was turned, Amos felt his own foot driving into the back of the man's knee, knocking him forward and down where he'd be in the right place for a choke hold. Amos only sighed and took another spoonful of grain mush. The stuff on the *Roci* was better, but this was warm anyway. It soothed his throat.

"Hey there, big guy," Babs said from the doorway.

She stepped over, sat across from him. Her jaw was set and her gaze was firm and straight-ahead. Looking right at him like she was playing at being Holden.

"Got a minute?"

Amos took his half-empty bowl, dropped the spoon in it, and threw them all away as he walked out the door.

There was an environmental-control station about seven doors down. Saba'd been using it to store food, but they'd all been eating at a pretty fair clip, and it was mostly empty space now. Only one entrance, so no one spent much time there. Thick walls filled with insulation foam. The kind that just ate up sound like it was nothing. If the Laconians came, it was a death trap. He shouldered the door open. Babs' footsteps came from behind him, hard and fast and authoritative. Like a schoolteacher about to chew out her students.

The room was dark, but he found the switch. Too-bright utility lights. They were down to half a pallet of textured protein and some tubs of grain and yeast. The walls were all steel plate except for a patch in one corner where they'd used carbon-silicate lace. A pipe ran along the corner where the ceiling met the left wall. The actual environmental controls were all in locked cabinets and behind security doors that would take a crowbar, a welding torch, and a couple hours to get through. The whole place was maybe three meters by four, and a couple high. It wasn't perfect, but it was pretty good. He didn't have anyplace better.

Babs stepped in behind him and closed the door. Her nose had the two little half-moons beside the nostrils that she got when she was pissed. The thing in his throat throbbed like a tumor. For a second, he thought it was maybe going to rupture.

Babs crossed her arms, blocking the door.

"Look, Amos. I understand you're pissed off at me. And honest to God, I'm more than a little pissed off at you right now too. But we're a crew. We're friends, and we can work this out, whatever it is. I'm here, okay? So whatever it is—"

"When did you turn into such a fucking pussy, Babs?" he said. His hands were tingling like they had too much energy in them. Like he was about to ground out. "Did you really come in here to talk about your feelings?"

Her face went blank, her eyes flat. She uncrossed her arms. Her weight sunk into her hips. Her knees bent a little. He figured she was good for maybe one or two more rounds of insults, but he'd gauged wrong.

She shifted her shoulders, swung at the hips, her right arm unfurling. A few years earlier, he might have been able to slip it and get inside. But a few years earlier, she might have been faster. Either way, all he managed was to turn his head away and pull back a couple centimeters before her knuckles slapped into his cheekbone. If he'd been slower, it would have splashed his nose across his face. Her next punch was already coming, and he turned so that it got his shoulder at an angle. The pain was sudden and wide and familiar as an old song. He felt this thing in his throat blowing up like a balloon, expanding out bigger than he was.

He kicked straight, hitting just above her hip with his knee still bent. It wasn't to break her but to push her back, then with the room he'd opened between them, he rushed her. Right fist to her face, left swinging up into her ribs. She lifted her arms into a boxer's stance, but a fraction of a second too late. He finally got inside her guard, his right elbow across her throat, and he had her back against the door. Pushing against her windpipe. She shifted under him, looking for a way to get a breath. His legs and back ached with the effort of closing her throat for her. He gritted his teeth until they creaked.

The pain in his balls started with a thump like hearing someone drop a brick, then a second later the brightness came, spreading out through his whole body. He felt himself stumble back. Bobbie turned out from under his arm, hitting him once with each fist on exactly the same rib. He felt it give.

She wasn't pulling her punches. She meant it. He let go of the last shred of restraint, and surged forward, roaring. Ready to kill or get killed. The tiny part of him that was still watching him, still thinking and aware, expected her to flinch back. Instead, she jumped in toward him. They hit like a wreck, her hand on his neck, her hip against his, and he was in the air. He hit the bulk-head hard enough that sound faded away for a second. He pushed off just as she swung a knee into his gut, grabbed her around the thigh, and lifted, swinging her up over his head, and then both of them down to the deck as hard as the spin gravity would take them.

Someone was shouting, and it might have been him. It was all ground game now, and her hands were on his head, fingertips dig-ging into his skin, looking for a grip. If she got his ear, she was keeping it. He reared back, grabbing for her arm, trying to get her elbow where he could bend it back. Snap it. For a second, he was almost there, but she twisted, got a foot against his waist, pushed him back. He caught her ankle and tried the same move on her knee, but the muscles there were too strong, the joint too solid to break. And while he was trying it, he couldn't move as well.

Her other heel came down on his left eyebrow, popping it open. He pushed in toward her, driving her back. The blood stung his eye, but he moved fast and with a lifetime of practice. He had his hands around her throat, squeezing as hard as he could. Her windpipe was between his thumbs where he could crack it like a walnut—

Except she was already bringing her arms up inside his, roll-ing her shoulders and shrugging off his grip. She'd planned it. She wasn't lost in rage haze. She was still thinking.

She locked her legs with his, and rolled so she was on top. The heel of her left hand pushed his chin up and away so her right fist could land on his throat. Amos coughed, tried to roll away. His breath was a thick wheeze. The air that made it into his lungs felt pressed thin. He struggled to get to his feet, but she was already up, kicking his knee out from under him. He hit the deck hard. She was over him, kicking down. Curb-stomping him. He tried to curl away from her. Her heel hit his shoulder, his back. She was going for his kidneys, and he tried to shift away, but he couldn't. The pain was exquisite and vast. He was helpless. He was fucked.

She kicked him again, the whole weight of her body behind it, and he felt another rib go.

He wasn't going to make it up. The violence was going to go on until she decided it was over, and there was nothing he could do to make it stop. He curled against blow after blow after blow, felt the damage in his body getting deeper. There was nothing he could do to defend himself. If Bobbie wanted him dead, he'd die.

He endured, helpless. The pain smeared into itself until it wasn't any part of him that hurt. Until it was bigger than his body.

His mind slipped, shifted. Images flickered through him like a memory too deep to bother being coherent. A perfume smell like lilacs and bergamot. A white blanket so used that the cotton fibers were shattering, but soft. The way the cheap ice pops they sold at the shitty little bodega at Carey and Lombard tasted. The sound of a feed in the next room, of rain. It had been a long time since he'd thought about how the rain sounded in Baltimore. Violence, helpless pain, but cheap ice pops too.

A deep peace welled up in his gut, flowing out through him, lifting him up and out of his body. He relaxed into it. The thing in his throat was gone. Or no. That was never going to happen. It was sated. Back in the deep place where it belonged. He felt like the moment after orgasm, only better. Deeper. More real.

Eventually, he noticed Bobbie wasn't kicking him anymore. He rolled onto his back. Opened his eyes. There was blood on the bulkheads and the deck. His testicles felt like soccer balls made of agony. Drying blood glued his left eye closed. His throat ached and burned when he swallowed, but the thing was gone. Something was weird about his breathing, though. It took him a second to figure out what. It was that he wasn't the only one wheezing.

Bobbie sat with her back against the door. Her legs were spread a little, taking up the space. Her hands were on her knees. The little bleeding divots where the skin over her knuckles had split looked like art. Her hair was plastered to her neck. Mostly by sweat.

He looked at her looking back at him. Neither one of them spoke for a while. The hum of the station was the only sound.

"So," Bobbie said, then took another couple breaths before she went on. "The fuck was that?"

Amos swallowed. It hurt a little less this time. He tried to sit up, then thought better of it. There were even a few spatters of blood on the ceiling. One of them looked a little like a cartoon dog face.

"I don't," he said, then gulped in another breath. "I don't want things. You know what I mean?"

"Nope."

"People...people want things. They want kids. Or they want to get famous or rich or something. And then they get all screwed up trying to get it. So I just don't want anything. Not like that."

"All right," Bobbie said.

"Only I fucked up. Didn't even know I was doing it, but it got where I wanted a thing." He waited for the lump to come back to his throat, and when it didn't, he went on. "I want Peaches to get to die at home. With her family."

"On the *Roci*," Bobbie said. "With us."

"Yeah, I want that. Only ever since we got back from Freehold, it's all coming apart. It wasn't so bad when it was just Holden and Naomi peeling off on their own, because they picked that."

"And also they never actually went away," Bobbie said.

"But then that big bastard came through the Laconia gate, and now we're locked off the *Roci*, and it's like the chance to do it right's just slipping too far away to get a hold of it, you know? I see her acting like it's not much one way or the other, only it is to me. And then...then everything gets harder. I get cranky. Start thinking about shit I don't want to think about. You know."

They were silent for a long moment. Amos tried sitting up again, and managed it this time.

"All right," Bobbie said. "I get it."

"You do?"

"Close enough," she said. "I get it close enough."

She levered herself up to standing, then held a hand out to him. He took it, his hand on her wrist, hers on his. They pulled together and got him to standing. Her face was almost unmarked, but there were some bruises starting to show around her neck. "You really beat the shit out of me," he said.

"Would have been easier to kill you," Babs said, and grinned with bloody teeth. "But I feel like we still need your dumb ass."

He nodded. She was right about both things.

"We should get you some ice," he said.

"Fuck you," she said. "If I did half my job, you'll be stuffing your jock with every cold thing we have."

"Yeah. You can have it when I'm done, though."

She managed another bloody smile and turned toward the door.

"Hey, Babs," he said. "No hard feelings, right?"

"Just next time you need to beat someone up, how about you don't insult me first."

He chuckled. It hurt. "If I need to beat someone up, I've got a whole station full of possibilities. But if I'm looking to *lose* a fight, I'm pretty much down to just you."

She took a second. "Fair point."

It took him about five minutes to get to the head. He washed up the best he could, but he was going to need some fresh clothes, and washing his eye pulled the clot a little bit loose. It started bleeding again. He'd talk to Saba about getting someone to stitch it closed. But clothes first.

"Jesus Christ," Peaches said when he stepped into the room. "What happened?"

"Huh? Oh, you mean this? Me and Babs were doing a little sparring. I put my face where it shouldn't have been. It ain't nothing."

Her face balanced between not believing him and choosing to, despite the thinness of the lie. He looked at her collarbone, waiting for the thing to come up with some way to break it, but nothing came. So that was good.

"You need to be less rusty," she said at last.

"That's not wrong," Amos said. "What're you up to?"

"I was going to go smear some food on my mouth like a toddler," she said.

"Sounds good," he said. "I'll go with you."

Chapter Forty: Naomi

W ake up. We have to go," someone said. "Now. Go, go, go."
Naomi forced her eyelids open. Her feet hit the decking
before the dream she'd been in loosed its grip on her mind. There
had been a fire. She'd been talking to it...she felt herself forgetting, the dream dissolving like sugar floss in water.

Amos rolled off his bunk with a grunt of pain and went to help
Clarissa up. Alex was tugging his jumpsuit up over thin, brown
legs. The new voice belonged to a girl too young for the split-
circle tattoo on the back of her hands.

"What's going on?" Bobbie said. "We got a problem?"

"Saba got word we need to go, so we go. Now go."

"Where is he?" Bobbie asked.

"Gone," the girl said, and then she was gone too. Light spilled
into the bunk from the door she hadn't closed. The voices and
sounds of metal against metal were loud and panicky, but they

weren't battle. There wasn't gunfire. The fear and the urge to motion that grabbed Naomi's heart were still as violent.

"You good, Peaches?" Amos asked. Clarissa nodded, and pulled her hair back into a ponytail like she was getting ready to go to work. There was more color in her cheeks since she'd gotten the new medicine. If Amos hadn't found a supply, they'd have been carrying her right now. Heaven. Small favors. Like that.

They piled out into the corridor, and Naomi paused, looked back. There were no tools, no terminals, nothing left behind but traces of hair and DNA. Which would be plenty enough to identify them.

"Naomi?" Alex said from the hall. "Everyone else is getting out mighty quick here. We should maybe—"

She moved quickly, decisively, pulling blankets and pillows and sheets up in her arms. They were cheap, so they pressed down to almost nothing. Another small favor. She shoved them into the makeshift recycler feed at the end of the hall. Maybe it wouldn't make a difference. Maybe she'd been foolish to take the time. It didn't matter. She'd done what she'd done.

A lot of her life was like that now.

Saba was at the service doorway that led out to the rest of the station. The vast body of Medina that the underground didn't control. His jaw was tight, and there was a darkness around his eyes that the brown of his skin couldn't hide.

"What's going on?" she asked.

"Had word from one of ours in system logistics. Laconia's slated this section for survey. If they're going to find our holes here, best we not be in them."

"Well. We knew it would come."

He pressed a hand terminal into her palm. "This is yours. Cooked profile. Got one for alles la along with. Rooms, jobs. Don't scratch the chrome, it'll come off, but it's what I could do fast."

"Thank you," Bobbie said as he passed one to her.

"Messages too. Just text. And just to me. Your circle is your circle."

Naomi nodded. It felt like being young again, in all the worst ways. Amos, Alex, and Clarissa were already moving toward the common corridor, Bobbie trotting to catch up to them. Naomi put her hand on Saba's arm. "The false identities don't have to hold up long. We're close to doing this. No despair."

Saba's eyes softened. "My lady wife is back in Sol leading the fight against these bastards. And I will move worlds to wake up beside her again. Just once more."

Naomi thought of Jim, and the ache of fear in her stomach. Saba touched her shoulder, and pushed her gently away toward her friends. Her crew. Her family, less one.

The inner layer of Medina's drum could have been any of the old spin stations. Wider, common corridors with room for carts and foot traffic both, ramps that led up toward the soil and false sun of the inner face or down toward the vacuum beneath her feet. She hadn't stepped outside Saba's hidden dens since they'd lost Jim. Now, walking with the normal inhabitants of Medina, trying to fit in with the midshift patterns, she kept noticing how open everything felt. In another context, it might have been a relief. Now it left her feeling exposed as a mouse in cat territory.

She plucked up the terminal that Saba had given her, trying to look bored as she checked who she was, where she lived, all the answers she'd need to give the Laconians if she was stopped. She'd seen plenty of faked identities before, and this one was decent. The real question was how deeply Saba's moles had been able to get into the Laconian datasets. With the link between Medina and the *Storm* severed, they'd be working from local copies. Corruptible ones. Odd to think that without Jim's sacrifice, the underground might have ended right then. Her gratitude was complicated by anger.

Wide screens showed the station newsfeed. Laconian propaganda, but maybe true, some of it. They were playing images of Sol system and the war there. She didn't watch that, but when it shifted, she paused. A young woman with olive skin and a wide jaw in Laconian blues. The text below her said, ADMIRAL JAE-EUN

Song of the Eye of the Typhoon. And on the other side of the screen, a young man. Santiago Singh, governor of Medina.

"What are your hopes for your arrival at Medina Station?" he asked, the subtitles in Spanish, Chinese, and—unnervingly—Belter Creole.

The woman nodded seriously, and answered. "The important thing is that we ensure the safety of the people on the station. High Consul Duarte has made it very, *very* clear that—"

Naomi didn't realize she'd stopped until Amos prodded her.

"Should probably keep moving, boss. Less attention."

"Yes," Naomi said.

"It's editing," Clarissa said. "They do it all the time. That's not what the light delay really is. There's still time."

Naomi nodded. She didn't trust herself to speak.

Her name, according to Saba's faked ID, was Ami Henders, and her address was listed as refugee housing on level four. She was supposed to be the pilot of the *Blue Genius*, a water hauler presently burning somewhere on the far side of the Athens gate without her. She wondered whether Saba had been able to scrub Naomi Nagata from the station records. He wouldn't have been able to get her out of decades of newsfeed footage, standing behind Jim and wishing the cameras were elsewhere.

She was walking on the surface of a soap bubble and hoping it wouldn't pop.

The refugee quarters, when they reached them, were a little better than living in the underground had been. A little suite of five rooms with a narrow common hall and a shared head at the end. She could have touched one wall with her elbow and the other with her shoulder. It was tighter than their quarters on the *Roci*, but with doors, so they could sleep without breathing each other's dreams. A little monitor in the wall was set to the official newsfeed, but the captain of the *Typhoon* was gone, replaced by a sober-faced man in a security uniform.

"The base was exactly what we thought we would find. These rat holes are what allowed the terrorists to function and plan in secret. Without them, they'll be forced out into the light. That's where they can be stopped.

"We don't know how many people were using the secret base, but we've cordoned it off and we're making a full investigation. We feel certain that the threat to the station is reduced, but we can't be complacent. These people are willing to risk the integrity of the environment for their ideological purity. Risk the lives of the whole station. It's important that we isolate and disarm these terrorists before another attack like the one on the oxygen tank.

"With that in mind, the governor has authorized a limited amnesty for anyone who—"

Clarissa turned the monitor off with her thumb. She met Naomi's eyes, and the determination and exhaustion in them was clearer than words could have been. *Let it go. We have work to do.*

Alex cleared his throat. "Well, since there's no galley anymore, I guess I'll head down the hallway and see if I can't find a coffee shop or something. Anybody else need breakfast?"

There would be guards. There would be drones. There would be the risk that trying to pay for something would collapse Alex's false identity or flag his real one. She wanted to grab him and lock him in his room. She wanted to make sure no one left the uncertain safety of their cabin.

"Tea," she said. "Maybe some protein cakes."

"All right," Alex said. "I'll be back." The way he said it made it a promise. As if he could keep it.

"I'm gonna..." Amos said, gesturing to Clarissa.

Naomi nodded. "I'll get some work done."

"That leaves me for watch," Bobbie said with a lopsided smile. "Not much of a plan, but it isn't nothing."

"I'll get you a plan," Naomi said.

Sitting alone on her new, thin bunk, she built a list on Saba's terminal. If she thought too much about the dangers, the time pressure, she knew the dark thoughts would start coming. There wasn't time for that. If she could focus, though, problem-solve, she'd be okay. She'd known herself long enough to learn that. The care and feeding of a well-used mind.

The final goal was to get out of the slow zone and find someplace safe to hide and regroup. So the last step was at the top of the list:

REGROUP

She didn't have the details of what that would look like. Probably keep her head down and see what happened. Wait for the enemy to stumble or new allies to appear. The old, old strategies. But whatever shape it took, that was the final goal. In order for that to happen, they would have to manage some other things...

REACH SAFETY

Before that...

IDENTIFY SAFETY

After all, they'd need to know where they were fleeing to before they fled. It had to be someplace that they could land the *Roci*. Someplace that wasn't likely to fall in line with Duarte and turn them in. So none of Fisk's association worlds, and not Sol either. That was tricky, but she felt the beginnings of some ideas for it. So all right. But there was more than one dependency for that, so she split the column and added the other track.

BLIND MEDINA AND GATHERING STORM

If the Laconians knew where they'd gone, they wouldn't stay hidden long. So that would be important. And it would be the last thing they did before they left, so the enemy wouldn't have time to fix whatever they chose to break. She'd have to have everyone ready to go before the sensor arrays went down, so...

GATHER EVACUATION GROUPS

And in order to do that, they'd have to get the word to everyone in Saba's networks. All the underground. All of them. And there it was. The sorrow and the fear. And the tightness at the back of her throat. It was all right. She just had to put it on her list. It was just part of the plan.

SAVE JIM

Saba sent a message an hour before "Ami Henders" was supposed to get off her shift. Bobbie got the same message, though none of the others did. It was a restaurant just one level under the drum's inner surface and a route to reach it that would, if everything went well, avoid any checkpoints. Naomi washed her face in the little sink no wider than her two palms together and tugged her hair into something like order. When she got home to the *Roci*, she was going to spend a day in the showers. A whole damned day.

Alex and Clarissa were waiting for her in the public hall. Bobbie and Amos were a few meters down, pretending to talk, but actually keeping watch. They were both bruised, and there was a cut over Amos' eye. They looked like they'd been caught in the explosion, which was technically true, but the tension that had been showing in the way Amos held his gut and shoulders was gone.

No, not gone. But lessened. That was good.

"We ready to paint the town red?" Clarissa asked, taking Naomi's arm. It had the form of a playful gesture, but the need for support was there too.

"I hope this place serves margaritas," Alex said. "It's been a long time since I had a good margarita."

"Trust me when I say you've never had a good margarita, Martian," Amos replied. "Still some things only Earth does well."

Bobbie caught Naomi's eye, gave a little nod, and started off along the route. Amos walked at her side, his steps rolling a little in the fractional gravity, like something hurt with each step. Naomi gave them a few seconds, and then started after them. There was a story behind those bruises, and she had the impression she'd never know what it was.

James Holden had shipped with five others on his crew, but they weren't five. They were a couple up ahead, and a different group of three behind. As ways to avoid pattern recognition, it was thin. But it was something.

The restaurant was a wide, white ceramic bar open to the corridor. Billows of steam came from the back, rich with the smells of fish and curry. The design didn't fit into the aesthetic of the original ship. This space was a modification, the *Nauvoo*, which became the *Behemoth*, which became Medina Station in the process of learning what it was and would be. Looked at that way, Naomi liked the restaurant, even if it was a little ugly.

The man behind the counter nodded, greeted them all in a dialect Naomi didn't recognize, and waved them back into the steam. The kitchen was small, with two women—one very old, the other hardly more than a girl—who looked at them curiously as they passed through.

The old man opened a thick metal door and nodded, smiling, at the walk-in freezer beyond it. Saba was already there, a blanket over his shoulders and a thin, black cigarette in his mouth. His cheeks were ruddy with the cold. The old man closed the door behind them, and a golden emergency light came on, throwing shadows across them from crates of vat-raised fish. Amos' gaze cut over to Clarissa, but if anything she seemed to be enjoying the cold.

"Not perfect," Saba said, "but hard for them to hear us."

"You think they're listening?"

"No," Saba said. "But here, seems less likely I'm wrong. Perdón for the fast change. I didn't have much warning."

"Shikata ga nai," Naomi said, and Saba nodded ruefully.

"We have a plan," Bobbie said. "Well, Naomi does."

"The outline of one anyway," Naomi said. "I don't love it, because a lot of things have to happen in a very small time frame. But the *Typhoon* arrives in less than a week, and slowing that down isn't something I can do."

"I have people," Saba said. "You tell me, I'll tell who needs telling."

"There's just a lot of moving parts," Naomi said. "Lots of ways for things to break down."

"Tell me a story," Saba said through a cloud of smoke and visible breath.

Naomi did. She went through step by step, detail by detail. As she talked, the whole operation solidified in her mind, letting her speak with a clarity and authority she only halfway felt. It was a terrible plan, open to a thousand different failures, and some of them wouldn't be things they could recover from. If the assault team couldn't get onto the *Storm*. If the kill code was changed or unhackable. If the Laconian repair crews could get the sensors fixed more quickly than she expected.

But with every word she spoke, with every detail she provided, she felt the *Typhoon* looming behind her. Coming close. Ending any chance they had.

"Gonya need two bombs," Saba said, pulling up his hand terminal. The one that didn't connect to the station's legitimate network. He talked as he composed a message. "One for sensors, one for the jail. Katria's good for one. Have to see who she likes for two. Which one matters more?"

They both matter, Naomi said at the same moment Clarissa said, *The jail.*

"I worked on this station, back in the day," Clarissa said. "Get me access to the secondary power junction that feeds them and a way to reset the primary. I can keep the sensors down."

"Claire," Bobbie said, concern in her voice.

"I'm good for it," Clarissa said. "It will work."

And then that was decided. Saba was already putting a message into his hand terminal.

"Bist bien alles," he said.

"Amos and I are dealing with the *Storm*," Bobbie said. "You give us a team, but we're point or no deal."

"Deal," Saba said. "I'll put me and mine on the *Malaclypse* as soon as the signal goes. If the muscle here has trouble, at least there can be two against the one. Plan B, sa sa?"

Alex raised his hand. "No one's flying the *Roci* on this but me. We all knew that, right?"

"I'll take the jail," Naomi said. *I'll get Jim.*

Saba's terminal chirped, and he looked at it with pleasure. "Katria has someone. Coyo with experience in demolitions. He'll need to know what we're doing. Just his part, though. Inner circle, us."

"Inner circle," Naomi said. "Claire and I can meet with him."

"Good," Saba said as he trundled to the freezer door and pounded on it with a blanket-wrapped fist. Then he pointed to Bobbie and Amos. "You come with me. We'll see Katria. Talk about how to hunt Marines."

Something flickered over Bobbie's face. Hardly even an expression, but Naomi saw it.

"You lead, we'll follow," Amos said, smiling his empty smile.

"Any thoughts on how to get me onto my ship?" Alex asked as the door opened.

"Several," Saba said. "You should come with." Then he shook his head. "Too many things. Not enough time."

They stepped out into the suddenly burning air. Naomi hadn't even noticed she was getting cold until suddenly she wasn't anymore. Saba led them out to the kitchen, and then they slipped through the steam and into the civilian world two by two until she and Clarissa were all that remained.

They sat at the counter and watched people go by. The fish was unremarkable, but the curry and mushroom rice actually were good. Across the corridor, a monitor spooled out the newsfeed until it repeated. Clarissa ate, drank tea, talked about everything and nothing. Naomi almost didn't notice the tremble in the other woman's hand or the way her eyes jittered sometimes. *If she thinks she can do it, she can do it,* Naomi told herself.

The man arrived, sliding into the chair beside them. Dark, handsome eyes and a bright, excited smile with a crooked nose between them. "Namnae na Jordao," he said. "Seen you both back at home, yeah?"

"I remember," Clarissa said.

"Katria, she sent me," he said, then leaned forward. "So what is it we're going to do?"

Chapter Forty-One: Singh

He had trained on ships back home, as anyone at his rank would. He'd spent weeks sleeping in a tight cabin and eating elbow to elbow with his fellow officers, but at the end of training, he went home, back to Laconia and Natalia and the monster. The weekends after a training run had been some of the best he'd ever had, waking up late with Natalia beside him. Before the monster came, they'd had quarters with a bedroom on the third story and a folding wall that they could pull back to get fresh air and the view. He remembered lying in that bed, looking out over the city as twilight fell. Vast clouds turning gold and violet on the horizon, and the alien construction platforms glittering among the stars.

He'd laid his head against Natalia's as-yet-unoccupied belly and thought about the ships being made up above the planet's atmosphere. How one day, he might command one. It had seemed glorious at the time.

He'd known without checking the dates when his exile on Medina Station had lasted as long as a full training tour. Something in the back of his mind had been anticipating the end of low ceilings and false skies. Each day, he found himself growing more anxious, and it wasn't only the threat from local terrorists or the mounting pressure he felt to reopen the traffic through the gates. It was his flesh itself, grown accustomed to these long isolations having an end, expecting relief and not getting it. Wanting his wife and his child and their sky, even as his conscious mind knew the first two would come much later, and the last...perhaps never.

It was possible that he would live his whole life and die as the governor of Medina Station and never see a real cloud again. He'd known that from the moment he'd met with the high consul, all those months ago. It hadn't started chafing until just now.

The draft of his monthly report was open on his monitor, his personal journal inset in a smaller window. Everyone above him in the chain of command could see his journal if they chose to, but his report gave him the chance to summarize his experiences. To say what, from his perspective, was important. His fingers hovered over his keyboard, where they had been since the memory of Natalia and their old bedroom and the clouds had intruded on his thoughts. He wished he could pause longer.

Many of the locals persist in referring to the transfer of control in Sol system as a war. This kind of rhetoric has emboldened dissident factions on Medina Station. Given the escalating violence employed by the dissidents, I have elected to maintain the closed-gate policy until the arrival of the Typhoon. *Ships coming in from colonial systems have too great a potential to smuggle in relief supplies and reinforcements for the recalcitrant elements here.*

He paused again. A small, angry voice in the back of his mind said, *In the event of another large-scale attack on the station, I recommend pulling Laconian forces back to the* Storm *and venting Medina Station.* He pushed the thought away without writing it down. It wasn't only that it was immoral, though that should have been enough. It was also a statement of weakness. An admission that he could not cut the rot out of this tree without burning it all. And still, the elegance of it made it hard to turn away.

If Holden and his allies had been held to truly Laconian standards, they would be dead. It was that simple. If Singh treated them with the respect and dignity with which Duarte treated him—to which Singh held himself—removing them all from the equation would just be proper discipline. But he had grown to understand that they weren't Laconian. Not yet. They hadn't had time to understand the necessity of the empire. Holden's arguments were more than proof of that.

He had to be patient with them. Firm, but patient. He had to keep them from hurting themselves or others until the ripples of this admittedly vast change had calmed. Until the new patterns of life had become normal for them.

While I am certain that James Holden knows more of the local dissident factions than he is presently admitting, he is not our only resource on that matter. His experience and expertise in the anomaly that Admiral Trejo reported make him a genuinely unique asset on that issue. For that reason, I have chosen to break off his interrogation here and remove him immediately to Laconia for debriefing in whatever context the high consul considers most appropriate.

Meaning that the terrorist figurehead would see Laconia before he did. Might even come across Natalia and the monster before they came out to Medina, if the high consul chose to treat him gently. Holden would smell the rain. See the sunrise. And Singh would be here, in this spinning can in an eerie non-space that didn't even have stars to make it feel like home. It was a deep irony that being a prisoner and being in power could be so mismatched.

"Damn it," he said to his empty office, then leaned back, running one hand across his scalp. There was so much more to put into the report. The preparations he'd made—was making—for the stationing of the *Typhoon* and the additional personnel that it was bringing to Medina. The victories he'd had in rooting out the bombers and repairing the damage they had done. His schedule for coordinating and controlling the traffic between the worlds. The empire would succeed or fail on the back of its logistical planning, and his implementation of the high consul's vision was actually quite detailed. Only just now, something itched in his soul, and he couldn't concentrate.

He wondered whether Duarte ever suffered the same base animal distractions. It seemed he would have, but Singh couldn't imagine it. He closed the draft report, opened his personal journal wide enough to edit, and then closed it too. The walls themselves seemed to push the air at him. It was like an optical illusion of something falling that never quite fell.

"Damn it," he said again, less forcefully this time.

The reports coming in from Sol were distracting too. Trejo's private reports tracked through the *Gathering Storm*, but they were meant for Duarte. Singh wished he could read them himself. There were so many questions—whether the *Tempest* had taken any lasting damage in its first foray against the enemy. Whether anything had changed with the anomaly that had appeared after Pallas. When Trejo anticipated the next battle would come. And if he believed it would be the last one.

There were the public feeds, of course. The positions of the combined navies were, for the most part, a known thing. The larger cruisers were impossible to hide, and the massive union ships they called void cities. But there might be stealth ships lying in wait or fields of torpedoes launched into a quiet orbit, counting on the vastness of space to conceal them until they burned to life. Just looking at the declassified tactical map made Singh's flesh crawl. The vast cloud of the enemy shifting through the gravity-bent space of inner planets, like a swarm of insects with a single, hated enemy. And the *Tempest* alone in its simple course. Trejo wouldn't evade and he wouldn't retreat. He had his orders, and he would follow them.

Singh reminded himself of how powerful the *Tempest* was. How resilient. The high consul wouldn't have committed the ship to a path that led to embarrassment for the empire and death for

Trejo. And yet, what if he'd miscalculated? Or what if Earth or Mars or the union had been behind the wave of lost time? Or...

This speculation was pointless. Worse, it was self-indulgent. Even if he knew everything else he needed to put into his official report, it was going to have to wait. He had to get out of his offices, if only for a while. He had to collect himself.

Overstreet answered the connection request almost at once. "Governor?"

"I will need a security detail to my office at once."

Overstreet's silence was less than a heartbeat. "Is there a problem, sir?"

"No. I want to inspect the docks. When will there be sufficient security for that?"

If Overstreet was surprised or annoyed, there was no sign of it in his voice. "I'll have a detail to you in five minutes, sir."

"Thank you," Singh said, then dropped the connection.

The *Lightbreaker* was a cargo ship that had been in the union's fleet. A small vessel, but fast and with an efficient drive. All of the ships and their crews were guests of the empire until the *Typhoon* arrived. But not the *Lightbreaker*. Of all the ships on the station manifest, that was the one best suited to act as a prisoner transport. It was slated to push off in half an hour's time with James Holden in its brig and a crew Singh had chosen from the *Gathering Storm*. And Singh found he very much wanted to be there when the first ship left Medina Station for Laconia. The first transit to happen while he was in charge of the ring space. His watch.

He straightened his uniform and checked himself in the mirror before stepping smartly into the outer offices. He heard the change when he walked into the room. The men and women under his command making certain that he saw them busy. Eight Marines in armor were waiting outside, along with a driver, who wasn't in power armor but did carry an assault rifle beside her in the cart.

"The docks, sir?" the driver asked.

"Berth K-eighteen," Singh said, then sat back as the cart started off.

The Marine escort loped along as fast as the cart could drive and with the sense that they weren't anywhere near an uncomfortable pace. The hallway had been cleared, and guards stood at the intersections with weapons drawn. It was like traveling through the dream of a tube station that had grown out in all directions until there wasn't even the promise of finding a way up to the surface. A woman with a heart-shaped face peered past the guard's shoulder, straining to catch a glimpse of him, and Singh waved at her. Let the civilians see that their governor was here, not hiding away in his office. If he wasn't scared of the terrorists, the loyal faction of the population wouldn't be either. Or less so, anyway.

And still, he did wonder how many of those people he passed would have been as happy to see him dead. He wondered if the girl with the heart-shaped face would have shot him if she'd had the chance. There was no way to be certain. Would never be a way to be totally certain. Or at least no way other than…

At the end of the drum, they left the spin gravity behind. The Marines shifted gracefully into a protective star formation with him at its center. He had seen images of the terrorists' attack— twisted metal and shattered ceramic. Flakes of carbon lace floating in the air like black snow. Passing through the space now, what struck him was the stink of it. Welding torches and burning lubricant oil, overheated wiring and the back-of-the-throat bitterness of exhausted fire suppressants.

They did this to their own station, just to spite me, he thought. And then *No, not their own. Mine. This more than anything else proves they can't be trusted with the future. This station is mine.*

They passed by the crowd of people waiting for permission to visit their ships, the Marines alert for any sign of violence, and passed by without so much as a scowl. At the berth, the guards held Holden at the airlock, assuming that Singh had come because he wanted to inspect the prisoner before he left. On the float, Holden looked younger. The lines in his face softened, and his hair stood wildly out from his head. He could see what the man had looked like as a boy.

Singh nodded.

"Governor," Holden said. He made it just polite enough to make it clear he was impatient without actually demanding offense be taken.

"Captain Holden. I wish you a safe journey."

"Thanks."

"Laconia is a beautiful place."

"Not sure I'm going to be seeing the nice parts of it, but I'm open for a pleasant surprise."

"If you cooperate with the high consul, you will be treated well," Singh said. "We are an honorable people. No matter what you think, we were never your enemy."

Holden's smile was weary. "Okay." *That's bullshit, but I'm too tired to fight about it.*

Singh nodded, and the guards guided the prisoner away. The airlock closed behind him.

Fifteen minutes later, the *Lightbreaker* left dock and burned hard for the Laconia gate with Holden aboard.

Singh heard Overstreet's report in the security office rather than his own. The walls were a pleasantly neutral gray-green that matched everything. The only decorations were a small potted fern and a framed piece of calligraphy in red, black, and gold that listed the high consul's Nine Moral Tenets.

Overstreet himself sat behind his desk with a physical solidity that made it seem like he'd grown there. Singh stood looking down at the man rather than take the seat and posture of a visitor. It might be Overstreet's office, but it was all Singh's station.

"I'm expecting some unrest after the news comes back from Sol," Overstreet said. "People don't like seeing their team lose. I'm trying to get ahead of that. Channel it into something we can control. Not let it turn into something that can gain momentum."

"That's wise. Are you seeing a reaction to the news about the underground losing their hiding place?"

"Not among the general population, no. But it meant a lot to the security force. We knew it was here someplace, but actually finding the hub and shutting it down? It's a major step forward. Without a physically isolated space, it's harder for the terrorists to coordinate. And it lets us move into the next phase. Identification."

"How many have you found?" Singh asked.

Overstreet spread his massive hands. "Fifteen for certain. Maybe twenty. The level of internal corruption within the local population can't be understated. My best estimate is that a third of our operating personnel are at least open to working against us."

Singh let the assessment sit for a moment, watching his outrage at the ingratitude and arrogance of the locals flare like it was happening outside himself. When he was sure he wouldn't curse, he spoke.

"That's unacceptable," Singh said. "Changing that has to be a top priority."

"Didn't mean to suggest I was accepting it. Just reporting in on where it stood. I've put in double and triple checks, random audits, all the internal security procedures I can, but this is going to be something we struggle with until we start getting regular commerce open again. Once we can start breaking up the old guard here, I expect to see these problems fall away. Wash out the bad, bring in the new. Like that."

Singh made a small sound of acknowledgment, neither approval nor condemnation.

"The dock attack was what led us to their nest," Overstreet said. "But even there, I'm fairly sure some information isn't getting passed up the chain to us."

"And where do we stand on that investigation?"

Overstreet's ice-blue eyes looked away.

"Permission to speak freely, Governor?"

"Granted."

"It'd be going a lot better if you hadn't shipped my best resource back home. Holden was central to the conspiracy. The man's a murderer. And I'm still not a hundred percent certain what the aim of the attack was."

"To damage the *Storm* while it was still in dock," Singh said.

"Maybe," Overstreet said. "But why? In preparation for something? Or was it to degrade the oxygen supply and force us to open shipping before we're ready? Or was it to destroy the air gap server, or the secondary power storage, or one of the eight warehouses that got scraped out by the blast? Or was it just a propaganda move to make Laconian rule look weak? Or provoke a crackdown as a way to recruit new insurgents?"

"It did all of those things," Singh said.

"But which ones it *intended* matters, sir. Understanding the mind of the enemy is what lets me do my job."

Singh heard the frustration in Overstreet's tone. That was fair. Part of his error in removing Tanaka had been putting Overstreet into position without the training and preparation time he should have had. And with the underground running circles around them, the man couldn't feel he was doing a good job. Nothing degraded morale like the sense that the potential for excellence was being denied.

Happily, Singh was in a position to address that point right away. He took out his hand terminal, opened the message that had occasioned this particular visit, took off his personal security encryption and passed it to Overstreet. The young man appeared on Overstreet's monitor. Wide, slightly feverish eyes, unruly hair. The lens and the perspective made the bent nose seem larger than it actually was.

"Hoy, bossmang. Something big going down," Jordao said, "I only got my part, but it's about the sensor arrays. Parley, tu y mé, aber keep it quiet. Voltaire finds out I know you, and you'll see my water in your faucets, yeah?"

Overstreet's eyes narrowed to slivers of ice. His lips had thinned to a single dark line.

"Well, that's interesting," he said.

"The Belters aren't the only ones with a network," Singh said. "Not anymore. See that your debriefing isn't observed. This time, we'll be ahead of the bastards."

"May mean pulling personnel off the engineering investigation," Overstreet said.

"This is the most important thing now," Singh said.

Overstreet nodded slowly, lost in thoughts and calculations of his own. When he sighed, it was like a dying man's breath. "We're holding this station with just the crew we carried out here on the *Gathering Storm* and a few extras that Admiral Trejo could spare us. And this station is a damn lot bigger than our ship was."

"Is that a problem for you, Overstreet?"

"It's just that we do have a great selection of number-one priorities. Don't we, sir?"

Chapter Forty-Two: Drummer

"...and if you fail to turn back," Secretary-General Li said, "we will be forced to respond with force. There will be no further warnings."

"He looks good," Lafflin said. "Statesman-like."

Drummer thought he looked sad, which actually came off pretty well, all things considered. It made it seem as if it was the impending loss of life that had dragged his spirits down. She was fairly certain that if she'd done the announcement, it would have come off as anger. Or fear. Or a near-psychosis-inducing lack of sleep.

She went back in the spooled message and watched it again. The line had been drawn where everyone had known it would. Point Leuctra, 2.1 AU from the sun. By conventions of mining law and centuries of precedent, that placed the *Heart of the Tempest* inside the asteroid belt. An invisible line in space, unmarked by anything more than what people believed about it. And that was enough.

The combined fleet of the EMC and her union hadn't played coy. They had burned and braked to reach this position. Two hundred and thirty-seven ships, ranging from the void cities to traffic-control skiffs. Anything with a gun was spread across the surface of a modified parabola with one focus on the *Tempest*'s flight path. The ships on her side might shift and evade, but everything the secretary-general had said was for the newsfeeds and posterity. Anyone with a map and half a semester of military history could have drawn accurate conclusions without him.

She wondered if Saba would see it, back on Medina. She wondered if he was still alive. There hadn't been a reply to her desperate question about the time slip, and the *Tempest* showed every sign of ignoring the EMC's warning. Drummer went from optimism that Cameron Tur was right—that the Laconians wouldn't dare use their magnetic matter-ripping beam for fear of its mysterious side effects—to expecting time to stutter, stop, and come back with the fleet already in ruins.

If she died here, would Saba see it? Would the official Laconian newsfeeds be how they said goodbye?

Lafflin changed the display to the tactical map—the hundreds of green dots that were their fleet including the one that was People's Home. The single orange blip that was their doom. As a piece of abstract art, it looked like something a student would have come up with at lower university. If she'd ever thought to put together a visual display that said *destined to fail*, it would have been that small, glowing bit of orange.

But still…

Somewhere, when she'd still been working security contracts, she'd seen an interview with an old, smiling imam, whose name she didn't remember. The one thing he'd said that stuck with her was, *I am a human being. Anything that happens to human beings could happen to me.* One time and another in the years since, she'd taken comfort from that. Or warning. People fall in love, so maybe I will too. People get jobs, so maybe I will too. And people get sick. People have accidents. And now, she supposed, people are divided from their families by war and history. And so that could happen to me too. Even when they won, would it mean she would wake up beside Saba again? There were so many variations of victory and loss.

"They're confident, aren't they?" Lafflin said, leaning back in his chair. "It's astounding."

"I suppose it is," she said. She didn't know where his mind had been, but it had clearly been somewhere different from her own. "You should probably get to the transport."

Lafflin's smile was rueful. "Is there anything you'd like me to pass on?"

"No," Drummer said. "Anything that needs saying, I'll say after."

Or, she didn't say, *not at all.* That part was understood.

As with Pallas Station and Independence, the plan was to evacuate the civilian population before the violence began. Ships had been docking with People's Home for days now, hauling off families that had lived there for years and taking them to Mars and Earth, Luna and the Lagrange stations, or any of the thousand little holes in the Belt that could still hold air. Going to the docks with Lafflin now was like walking through a graveyard. The wide, curving halls should have been filled with people. Music and voices should have echoed down through the common parks, the transfer tubes, the docks. Even the air smelled different—closer and musty as the recyclers shifted down to match their reduced loads.

She gave Lafflin points for waiting until near the end. Most of the EMC political types in his staff had been among the first out, just after families with children. The lines of refugees waiting to leave were all older people now. The staff and citizenry that didn't have the skills to help in a battle, all with small bags floating beside them. Overnight bags, many of them. As if they might be coming right back. There was a lot of laughter in the line, and a sense of anticipation that bordered on feverish.

Part of her wanted to stop, to shake hands, to take a little of that bright, jittering energy for herself, but Drummer and Lafflin didn't pause. There was still some decorum that came with rank. The executive waiting area was well appointed with bulbs of coffee or liquor, living plants in wall gardens, soft music and LEDs that matched the spectrum of the morning light in early spring. Or so they told her. It wasn't as if *spring* were a concept with any practical existence in her life. It was nice, anyway.

Avasarala floated in a white sari with a golden sash. Drummer admired the old woman's ability to wear it and remain decent. It wasn't something a lot of Earthers could manage.

She touched Lafflin's shoulder. "You'll excuse me?"

"Of course, Madam President," he said. "I look forward to seeing you at the post-action debrief."

"You too," Drummer said.

Avasarala nodded as Drummer slid close, braced on a handhold to kill her momentum.

"You're leaving too?" Avasarala asked, her voice carefully neutral.

"No," Drummer said. "I live here."

"You're a fucking idiot," the old woman sighed, "but you'd be one if you left too. It'd be a better world if there was always at least one right answer instead of a basket of fucked."

"Are you all right?" Drummer asked.

Avasarala waved the comment away, then reached out to the handhold to steady herself. "I'm trying to decide if we're absolutely certain to lose or absolutely certain to win," she said. "I change my mind every ten minutes or so."

"It's one ship that hasn't been able to resupply in weeks," Drummer said. "It's already been through a battle. And that turning-off-people's-minds-for-a-while thing it did, we're ready for it this time. The automated systems have their governors off. We may have to get clever before the next one shows up, but no matter what happens, we'll keep firing until *that* thing is a cloud of complex molecules and regret."

"And because it's this ten minutes," Avasarala said, "I find that argument persuasive. Next one, I'm going to remember that Duarte sent it, and then I'll get scared." She shook her head. "Who knows? The son of a bitch has been off in his own private system since before the Free Navy got their nuts handed to them. And it's pretty clear he's been rubbing up against whatever artifacts he found there. Maybe it made him stupid."

"Doesn't change what we have to do," Drummer said.

"It doesn't," Avasarala agreed. "I hate this part. You have a clear succession? Santos-Baca went down with her ship too, and even if you turn that ugly motherfucker of a ship to slag, one of the EMC bastards is as likely to throw something the wrong direction. If this goes badly, the last thing we're going to need is a long, angry committee meeting with everyone saying they've got the conch."

Drummer felt a blaze of annoyance, but pushed it down. The old woman wasn't trying to be insulting. She was just flailing around trying to find something she still had control over.

"We have bylaws," Drummer said. "And it won't matter. If I eat a stray torpedo, Albin Nazari takes over."

"That whiner? He's just gotten used to Santos-Baca's chair, and then to get yours too? He'd be like a five-year-old driving a mech loader."

"I'll be dead," Drummer said. "So I won't give a fuck."

Avasarala's laugh was short, surprised, and joyful. "I don't hate you, Camina. I hate almost everyone these days, but I don't hate you."

"I'm not planning to put Nazari in charge," Drummer said. "I'm planning to win."

In the scheme of the battle, People's Home was many things: battleship, medical facility, port, and resupply. It was all the things a city could be. In the display, it was slightly paler than the other green dots that were its fellows. Guard of Passage had a position that mirrored it. The two great cities of the union with their drums spun down, burning into the fight as anchors for the fleet. Cities that had become battleships.

"Coffee?" Vaughn asked, and Drummer waved him away.

The control room was lit like a theater—dim and warm with the tactical display in a multinetworked holographic output. Drummer had been in other battles. She had studied more than that. She had never seen more firepower leveled at a single target. She was fairly certain it had never happened before.

She strapped herself into her crash couch, checked the juice. The chances were very slim that People's Home would go on the burn, but if it did, she'd be ready. The whole sphere of battle was less than three light-seconds across. Eight hundred and fifty thousand kilometers from the two most distant ships in the EMC fleet, a balloon holding three hundred quadrillion cubic kilometers of nothing, with a few hundred ships dotting its skin. If she'd been in a vac suit, the drive plumes of the navy would have been invisible among the stars. It was the most tightly formed major battle in decades—maybe ever—and she wouldn't have been able to see her nearest ally with her naked eye.

"The enemy's crossed Leuctra Point," the weapons tech said, his voice calm.

"Are the EMC ships opening fire?"

"They are, ma'am."

"Then let's do too," she said.

She wanted there to be a throb of rail guns, the chatter of PDC fire, but People's Home was a huge structure. Even as her display told her that the rail guns were firing, the room was silent. Hundreds of other ships were doing the same thing at the same moment. Tens of thousands of tungsten slugs moving at a nontrivial fraction of c. It would be less than a minute before they converged on the *Tempest*, staggered and spread to make dodging difficult. But not impossible.

"And the enemy is evading," the sensor tech reported, her voice sharp.

"Do we have visual?"

In answer, she put up the live feed. A second's delay. Maybe two. Hardly anything at all. They were so close, they could have spoken in real time. It made her feel uncomfortable to be so near the *Tempest*. But there it was, its weirdly organic shape bright in the enhanced colors. Jets of reaction mass gouted from one side, pushing the ship to a slightly different course.

"Correcting for new vector," the weapons station said. "And firing. EMC forces are also launching torpedoes."

"Do the same," Drummer said. She checked the time. Three minutes had passed. She took control of the visual display, zooming in on the skin of the enemy ship. It didn't look like it had plating so much as a single, textured surface. She threw on the tactical overlay, and a dozen points appeared that weren't visible in reality. The high-value targets, the vulnerable places on the *Tempest* that didn't grow back, or at least not quickly. A dozen carefully placed dots that Emily Santos-Baca and Independence had died to find.

"Come on," she said, willing the missiles to strike.

"The enemy is firing PDCs," the sensor tech said.

"Show me," Drummer said, and the *Tempest* almost vanished in a cloud of tracers. The data field was too rich to comprehend— missiles, streams of PDC fire, the straight-line paths of the rail-gun rounds.

"EMC Battleship *Frederick Lewis* is reporting damage," Vaughn said.

"Are you working comms now?" Drummer asked. "Who's going to get me my coffee?"

"They're dropping core," Vaughn said, ignoring her.

A little cheer went up, and it took Drummer half a second to see why. One of the hardpoints on the *Tempest* was blinking— the system reporting a missile strike that had connected with the target. The cloud of PDC fire grew a degree thinner. Any ship Drummer knew, any station she'd ever heard of, would have been reduced to slivers of metal and flakes of lace by now. The only thing she could think of that would withstand that barrage was a planet. Even then, cities would have been pounded to dust by what had been launched in the last fifteen minutes. Sixteen now. It was so fast. There should have been hours between launch and response. But this wasn't that kind of battle. There was no finesse to it. Just brutal, constant violence.

The tightness in her throat was the memory of Pallas. The harder they pushed the *Tempest*, the more Drummer feared the magnetic beam. If the Laconians used it on People's Home, she wouldn't live long enough to notice she was being ripped apart. And if the glitch happened again... well, the observatories on Earth and Mars might get more data about how long it took the enemy to recharge the damned thing.

But they hadn't used it yet. Maybe the time slip had been the fucking thing breaking. The universe owed her a little slice of luck like that.

Another two hits on the *Tempest*. It shifted, plumes of steam appearing from its thrusters as it evaded incoming fire. Five more of the EMC ships took crippling damage or turned to bright dust, too far away to see. The *Tempest* veered and danced. Dark streaks marked its sides where the missiles and rail-gun rounds hit, and while most of the marks faded, not all of them did.

"We have expended two-thirds of our rail-gun ammunition," the weapons tech announced. "Shall I maintain fire?"

"Yes," Drummer said. "Then start putting chairs in the launcher. We hit that thing until we're down to pillows and beer."

"Understood, ma'am," the weapons tech said. She could hear the smile in his voice. She felt it too—the giddy sense that even if they were winning ugly, they were at least winning.

On the display, the *Tempest* shifted and dodged like a fish in a tank. The organic curves of its design made it hard not to think of it as an animal. An apex predator surprised to find itself outmatched by its prey. And there was something...

"On the aft. By that third contact point. Is that a gas plume?"

The sensors tech shifted through half a dozen slices of the spectrum in less than a second. "That is correct, ma'am. The *Tempest* appears to be venting atmosphere."

"EMC *Governor Knight* is launching high-yield nuclear torpedoes," Vaughn said.

Drummer sat back in her crash couch. Anticipation was a tightness in her throat and her hands. The *Tempest*'s PDCs weren't all disabled. There was still the chance it might kill the nukes before they got close enough to detonate. Seconds stretched into minutes. Her neck ached from straining toward the display.

The light of the explosion whited out the sensor array. A ragged cheer came from all around the control room.

"One down," she said to herself. "And fuck you all along with it."

It wasn't over. Laconia would send another ship after this one. A fleet, next time. The union and the EMC would have to get much more clever. But they knew more now—about how the enemy ships functioned, how they maneuvered in battle, and most important of all, how they could be killed.

And she had to expect reprisals. By deciding to send her one last, desperate message, she had as good as told the Laconians that she still had allies on Medina. The choice had seemed like the right and obvious thing at the time. She'd pointed at Medina and said, *Look for my people here.* It might be the thing that killed Saba and his crew.

It was a problem for another day. A tragedy she'd face when she could do something about it, and not before. There was too much that had to be done here and now.

"Send the return signal to all the transport ships and get the docks ready to bring everyone home," she said. "It's going to be a long couple weeks, people. We may as well get to it."

Another cheer, this one louder. They'd all been so hungry for a win, they were drunk with it. She was too.

"Ma'am?" the sensor tech said, the word like a drop of ice in a sauna.

The sensors had finished their reset. The *Tempest* was still where it had been, not scattered into atoms. An eerie blue mottling danced in lines like veins under the ship's skin, bright but fading. The EMCs' nukes might not have made contact before they detonated, but the fireball should have been enough to kill anything. Or at least anything that Drummer knew of.

"It's firing missiles, ma'am," the sensor tech said.

They'd known. Laconia had known they'd be facing nuclear torpedoes. And now everyone on all the colony worlds would see that even that wasn't enough to kill their ships. Maybe that had been the point all along.

"Tactical," she said. "Get me tactical."

The display jittered and shifted. The orange dot was now deep in the cup they'd created to destroy it, and it was still not destroyed. Even with its tactical maneuvering, its course toward the inner planets hadn't shifted.

All around it, bright-green dots were blinking out.

Chapter Forty-Three: Naomi

The scratch came in the middle of the third shift. If Naomi had been able to sleep, it would have been her midnight, but she was in her bunk, staring into the darkness and waiting for something she knew wouldn't come. So she heard it—fingernails against the access door that led to the corridor. It was softer than a knock, but it meant the same thing. *I'm here. Let me in.*

She sat up. Her body ached like she'd worked out too hard, but it was just stress and fatigue. She pulled herself up, opened her door as Bobbie, across from her, opened her own. Bobbie was wearing a tight jumpsuit. The kind you'd put on under a vac suit. Or, she supposed, power armor. She nodded to Naomi, but didn't speak. They were both being quiet for the others—Amos and Alex and Clarissa. The ones who could sleep, maybe. Someone ought to.

Bobbie opened the door to the public corridor.

Katria wore the uniform of the Medina maintenance crew. Green with a station logo printed on the shoulders and back. A ceramic toolbox rested on the deck by her left foot. Gray where it wasn't scratched white by long use. Naomi guessed there was enough explosive in it to kill all of them so fast they wouldn't know they were dead until the funeral. Katria's nonchalance with it was like a boast. Voltaire Collective had always been like that, even back in ancient days when Earth and Mars had ruled the solar system and no one had ever heard of Protogen. Every revolution needed its mad bombers, apparently.

"Tag," Katria said to Naomi. Then to Bobbie, "You ready to play a game?"

Bobbie put her hand on Naomi's shoulder. "Take care of the kids until I get back."

"I will," Naomi said. "Good hunting."

"Thanks," Bobbie said. Katria stood aside and let the big woman pass. The emptiness on Bobbie's face could have read as indifference to someone who didn't know her. To someone who didn't understand the kinship that Bobbie felt to Mars and its military, and to those who had served once and then been forced by conscience or circumstance to walk away.

"Bobbie," Naomi said. "I'm sorry."

Bobbie nodded. That was all. An acknowledgment that they both understood the situation, and would do what needed to be done. Katria plucked the toolbox up, and the two of them walked away down the corridor. Naomi closed the door behind them.

Back in her bunk and sleepless, she wondered what Jim would have done. Something idealistic and impulsive that would lead to more complications, probably. Certainly. And he would have done it in a way that kept that expression off Bobbie's face if he could. Even if it meant doing something terrible to himself. Like languishing in a Laconian brig. An image came to her mind of Jim being tortured, and she pushed it away. Again. Feeling fear and sorrow would come later, when they were done. When he was back. There'd be time for it then. She didn't manage actual sleep, but she was able to drift a little before the shift change. It was enough to let her feel rested, but not deeply.

She met Saba at the same public counter where they'd used the freezer, but this time they sat at the front like customers. The girl behind the counter turned up the music playing from her system speakers loud enough that they could barely hear each other, their words drowned in drums and strings and ululating voices. Saba looked as tired as she felt.

"Something happening back in Sol system," he said. "Looks like the big fight. Not sure how it's going to play."

Half a dozen possibilities flashed through her sleep-starved mind ranging from the miraculously good to the catastrophically bad. It didn't matter. Nothing that happened there changed what they were doing here. But Saba's wife was there, back in the empty spaces where they'd all lived, once upon a time. She knew too well what that fear felt like.

"You have the list?" she asked.

Saba nodded and pressed a silver memory chip into her hand. "All the ships we could make contact with," he said.

"How many?"

"Twenty-one."

Naomi nodded. Twenty-one ships docked on Medina and waiting for their chance to load up and fly. It was more than she'd hoped for. It was also enough to pose some problems. "I don't like having this many people knowing what's going on."

"It's a risk," Saba said, as if he were agreeing with something she'd said. "How does it make us for time?"

"If you don't mind half of them vanishing in transit, we can go pretty fast," Naomi said, more sharply than she'd intended. She shook her head, apologizing, but Saba ignored both the snappishness and the regret for it.

"Say we don't. Everyone through the gates safe and sound. What does that look like?"

"I can't know that until I look at the ship profiles. Mass, drive type, cargo. All of that's going to make a difference."

"Ballpark."

"A hundred minutes. That's conservative. I can probably find a way to make it less."

The girl at the counter swung past, pouring fresh tea into their glasses. Tiny bits of mint leaf swirled in the reddish amber. Naomi took a sip while Saba scowled. "That's a long time for the station's eyes to stay blind. And a lot to lose if they find a way to put it back together."

"Truth," Naomi said.

Saba scratched his chin with the back of his hand. If they ever played poker together, it was a gesture she'd remember. His tell.

"Your technician. The one to break the system?"

"Clarissa."

"Her, yeah. If she doesn't do the thing and do it well, everyone on those ships is going to die from trusting me. Not disrespect, but it's mine to say. Not sure she's good for it."

"Clarissa knows what she's doing," Naomi said. "She's smart, she's studied, and she knows this station. She broke it once already."

"She's as thin as wire," Saba said. "I could blow her over from whistling."

There was no humor in his face.

"I trust her with my life," Naomi said. "No hesitation."

"You're asking me to trust her with more than that," Saba said. "I don't. Not that she doesn't know, not that she's unwilling or not to trust. But straight between us, sister. Putting all of us on one girl just this side of hospital? It's not prudence."

"I think you're asking me for something."

"You go with her," Saba said. "Leave the prison work to me and mine. We'll do that. You back up your crew."

Naomi shook her head. "The prison's mine," she said. "Clarissa will do whatever needs doing. She's got backup already. Jordao. Katria's man. Unless you don't trust him?"

"I don't trust anyone," Saba said. "Not him, not her, not you. But I work with what I have to work with, and I know you're not going to run when things go harsh. Maybe Katria's people will, maybe they won't. You won't. And...the sensors are more important than the prisons. We lose the prisons, we only lose the prisoners, savvy sa?"

He was right, and she knew it. Putting the success or failure of the mission in the hands of a medically fragile woman—however competent she was—and then not giving her the backup to deal with an emergent problem was bad practice. But in her imagination, Naomi saw the letters on her list as clearly as if she'd been reading them afresh. SAVE JIM. She shook her head. "Prison's mine. Sensor arrays are hers. Won't be a problem."

Saba sighed as the music shifted key and tempo. A man's voice growling like a bearing going bad lamented his own failings in a mix of Hindi and Spanish that she could almost follow. She looked Saba in the eyes until he looked away. "Work up a schedule, then. All the ship data's on there. But do it fast. We have to distribute it by hand before we pull the trigger."

"Two hours," Naomi said. "I'll have it ready."

An hour later, there was still no word from Bobbie. No way to check in. They waited in their bunks, the doors open on their little common hallway. Amos stood in the head, leaning against the sink with his arms crossed. Alex sat in the doorway of his cabin. Clarissa stretched out on the deck like a bored teenager waiting for the hours to pass until she could begin living. Her skin was unnaturally smooth and tight. It helped the illusion. Naomi sat on her bunk, hand terminal in her lap, and arranged the flight schedule while they talked.

"I don't know," Alex said. "I mean, sure, it's a risk that there'll be ships waiting on the other side of the gates. There have got to be some queuing up to get to Medina when they don't think they'll get shot at. But if we're only looking at twenty-one ships?"

"I'm only lookin' at one," Amos said.

"So let's say there's two hundred ships waiting to come through,"

Clarissa said, ignoring him. "High end of plausible, but what the hell, right? That's eleven hundred gates with no one standing by close enough to get a really good look at whoever came through. That's still a fifteen percent chance of getting seen."

"That high?" Alex said. "You sure? I thought it'd be less than that."

Naomi went through the data Saba had given her. The *Old Buncome*, a recent-generation transport ship with a high-capacity Epstein drive and a cargo hold full of refined titanium. The *Lightbreaker*, a three-generation-old yacht salvaged by a semigovernmental courier service. The *Rosy Cross*, a rehabilitated prospecting ship with five previous owners and a drive that leaked enough radiation to cook with. The *Han Yu*, a privately owned coyote with authorization to carry settlers to the colony worlds.

Each ship had its own specs, its own limitations. And each one would have an effect on the ring gates that could make the ship leaving after it vanish into wherever ships went when they went dutchman. Naomi knew the curve as well as she knew her name, and the hand terminal—limited as it was—had enough native computing power to lay that in. Writing a program to weigh all the variables, evaluate each ship, and create a best-speed model wasn't hard, but it took time and focus. Neither of which she had in great supply.

"It ain't that high if you're only looking at one ship," Amos said. "You can bend the odds pretty good. I mean, no one's going for Sol gate unless they're tired of life. And there's not going to be any ships waiting to come through from Charon or Naraka."

"If we're down to hiding out in dead systems..." Alex began.

Clarissa interrupted him. "We should go to Freehold."

"You feeling okay, Claire?" Alex asked. "You remember we didn't leave on good terms, right? It was even money for a while that they were going to shoot Bobbie and Holden before they could get back to the ship."

From where Naomi was sitting, she could see Clarissa's ankles shift around each other as she rolled onto her belly. "No, I'm serious.

They're fiercely independent. They were willing to stand up to the Transport Union, and I don't see them rushing to wave the Laconian flag either. They're underdeveloped enough that there won't be complex local politics. No factions within factions that we don't understand. Or at least fewer than you'd get somewhere like Gaon Complex. Plus which, we know there aren't any ships observing the other side of their ring, because we were the only ship in the system, and no one's gone out there since the occupation started."

"That Houston asshole *was* pretty smart," Amos said.

"Ah! I see what you're doing," Alex said. "You're trying to make flying out to Charon and dodging radiation flares sound like a good idea. It's that whole 'I'll put a shitty idea next to a *really* shitty idea so the first one looks shiny by comparison' thing."

"I think we should go to Freehold," Amos said. "Naomi? You think we should go to Freehold?"

"Sure," she said, starting the data run.

"Seriously?" Alex said.

"Her points are all solid," Naomi said. The data run stopped a third of the way through. She ended the process and opened the run logs. "We have to get small for a while. Be hard to see. Wait for Laconia to show us where its weak spots are. We'll have to be someplace while that happens. It might as well be there."

"But the shooting-us part?"

"Is something we'll need to work through," Naomi said. "Hey, those paper uniforms people can get out of the station kiosks? Do you think we could get that to print out sheets?"

"Like bedsheets?" Alex said.

"Something to write on so we can distribute this when I'm done. Can't put it on the system."

"Maybe," Amos said. "Be kind of weird, though."

The run log looked decent until it started the confirmation routine. Then it hung on something. She grabbed the code reference and went back to the original script.

The others were still talking, but her focus on the screen lowered the volume on them. She was aware of Amos' low, gravel-strewn voice. Clarissa, higher and more musical. Alex with the ghost of a Mariner Valley drawl that was more habit than accent. Her family. Part of her family.

There was a zero result where there should have been a berth number. That was where the code was choking. It probably made sense to just chuck the routine entirely. Reaching beyond Saba's secret network—even if it was only for passive information like reading docking records—was a little risky. But building a schedule on unconfirmed data could screw them up as well.

She hesitated, pulled the code, then put it back and reopened the logs. The bad entry was the twelfth ship in the logs. The *Lightbreaker*. She tapped her fingers against her thigh. Dig deeper and risk being noticed by security or ignore the error and move ahead as if everything was as expected. If she'd gotten a little more sleep, it would have been easier to make the decision.

"Bárány o juh, son toda son hanged," she said to herself and opened a low-level request to the docking records. It only took seconds for confirmation to come through. The *Lightbreaker* wasn't in its berth. It had shipped out two days ago. The flight plan listed the destination as Laconia with a service code that looked military. Well, that was one less for the evacuation plan. It would make things faster, but Saba would need to know. The crew, if they weren't on the burn for the heart of the enemy, would need other bunks.

She looked at the service code. Touched it with a fingertip.

"Alex? Did the MCRN have a code eighteen twenty-SKS?"

"Sure," he said from the hall. "Did a few of those myself, way back when. Priority prisoner transfer. Why?"

When she'd been about eleven, Naomi had been working in a warehouse on Iapetus. A steel support beam had popped its welds and sprung out, clipping the back of her head. It hadn't been pain, not at first. Just a feeling of impact, and her senses receding a little. The agony had two, maybe three seconds to clear its throat and straighten its sleeves before it crashed over her. This felt very much the same.

Her hand trembled as she looked for a manifest. Something

to say who'd been on the *Lightbreaker*. Who'd been important enough to the empire that they'd commandeered a ship just to take them away. There was nothing. Of course there wasn't. Why would the Laconians announce that to anyone? She checked the dates, the times. It didn't have to be Jim. It could have been someone else. But it wasn't. She took a moment for herself and the pain. Five seconds. She could let herself hurt for five seconds. Then she had to get back to work. The rest would be for later.

She sent a message—text only—to Saba. The missing ship, the service coding, her suspicion that James Holden was already past the ring gate and into Laconian space. Did Saba have any contacts who could confirm that? After the message sent, she took a deep breath. Then another. She pulled the *Lightbreaker* out of her dataset and ran her code again. It didn't hang this time.

She got up, surprised by how steady she felt, and took the two steps to the door.

"What's the matter, boss?" Amos asked.

Naomi shook her head. When she spoke, she spoke to Clarissa.

"I had a talk with Saba. I'm going with you on the sensor-array leg of this."

Clarissa's brow was bent by whatever she saw in Naomi's face. "Okay. Why?"

"Risk management," Naomi said. "If the prison break fails, we don't get as many people out. If the sensors come back up and they're able to track which ships went through which gates, the whole mission fails. Better that we spend our resources where they matter the most."

"But if Holden is…" Clarissa began, then went quiet. Naomi watched her understand. "The prisoner transfer."

Alex's face was grayish. And pale. "Fuck," he said.

"And we need something to write down the evacuation plan on," Naomi said. "Something small and portable, and not connected to the computer networks at all."

Amos pushed himself up from the sink. "You got it, boss. Give me twenty minutes."

"And something to write with," Naomi said as the big man walked out into the public corridor.

Her hand terminal chimed, and she went back to her crash couch. The run was finished. Twenty ships, in the order that would get them through the gates and gone at the min-max point of risk and speed. Optimal was eighty-seven minutes, even with the *Rocinante* looping back to pick up Amos, Bobbie, Clarissa, and her. It was a solid plan.

She had a solid plan.

She pulled up her organizational notes and sat for a moment, looking at the words she'd put there.

SAVE JIM.

She drew a line through them.

Chapter Forty-Four: Bobbie

"Tag," Katria said, then turned to look at her. A ghost of a smile touched the other woman's lips, and Bobbie wondered just exactly how much of the violence of their first meeting was really forgotten and forgiven. "You ready to play a game?"

After half a beat, Naomi's gaze tracked over to her. Exhaustion had yellowed her sclera, and her skin had an undertone of ash. She put a hand on Naomi's shoulder to steady her as much as anything.

"Take care of the kids until I get back."

"I will. Good hunting."

The words were a little punch in the gut. *Hope you kill someone. Some other Marine who had the bad luck to be born on the wrong side of this. Who's as loyal to his people as you are to yours. Whoever they are, I hope you get them before they get you.* The truth of it was, despite everything, there was a joy in this. She'd

spent some of the most important years of her young life training for moments like this one, and as much as she wanted to have
grown and matured, aged into a woman of peace, part of her still
really liked it.

"Thanks," Bobbie said, and stepped out.

"Bobbie...I'm sorry."

Bobbie nodded as Katria scooped up her toolbox. They walked
together toward the intersection with a larger corridor. The door
closed behind them with a soft click and the whir of the lock.
Katria chuckled under her breath, but Bobbie didn't ask why. She
didn't much want to know.

Most of the people in the corridor were walking, but there were
a few carts loaded with containers. At one intersection, a man
was driving a loading mech, moving it from one warehouse to
another. It was a four-point harness. If she got in by his side, she
could loop one arm around his neck and choke him out while she
unbuckled him from the controls with the other. Drop him out,
swing around, and strap herself in. It would probably take thirty
seconds. Maybe less. Easy peasy.

As they walked, she felt herself relaxing, sinking down into her
hips as she walked. Lowering her center of gravity. She whistled
a little, softly. Katria raised an eyebrow, but didn't comment. The
screens along the walls announced that the security forces were
closing in on the terrorist cell that had blown up the oxygen
tanks, but Bobbie didn't see anyone giving the pair of them a second glance, much less closing in.

There was a sparseness about the halls. Even with the carts and
the people, there was an emptiness showing through. Part of it
had to be that, with no ships coming in or out of the station, there
just wasn't as much to do as there would have been. But part of it
was also fear. People staying in their holes. Staying out away from
the checkpoints. Out of trouble.

They took the ramp down, away from the inner surface of the
drum. There weren't many places on the drum that came close to
the skin of the station. Most of the outer layers had been designed

with radiation shielding in mind. Water tanks, storage for ceramic and metal and steriles. Service halls with anti-spalling covered in paint and conduit and pipes. But there were a few junctions near service airlocks where only a few layers of steel and ceramic and foam separated their feet from the outside. It reminded her of being on one of the old *Donnager*-class battleships. The bare functionality of the design belonged to a different generation from the residential levels or the inner face of the drum.

The hallway where Katria stopped looked just like the sections they'd been walking through, but she checked the section identifiers painted on the walls and the pipes, then stamped her foot on the deck like she was listening for something in the way it rang.

"Here?" Bobbie asked.

"This is the place. Boost me up."

Bobbie locked her fingers together into a cradle, and Katria put her foot into it. She didn't weigh much. Bobbie hauled her up toward the ceiling. Could have kept her there for hours, she thought. Katria caressed the ceiling with her palm, then found what she was looking for, pressed hard enough that Bobbie felt it, and slid a panel aside. A little gap, hardly more than a decimeter, between the panel and the structural beam above it. Katria hoisted her toolbox, checked its orientation, and slid it into place. She pulled the ceiling tile back and tapped Bobbie on the shoulder to be put down.

"That's it?"

"No," Katria said, and pulled a bit of black tape from her pocket. After a moment's consideration, she curled it around a bit of pipe just beside the bomb, then took her hand terminal out and shifted to a screen Bobbie had never seen before. A rough, grainy image of the hallway appeared on it, including her and Katria from the tape's perspective.

Katria stood directly under the bomb, then tapped her own image on the screen. Red script came up—LOCKED—and she put the terminal back in her pocket.

"*Now,* that's it," she said.

"Okay," Bobbie said. "Let's go outside."

The maintenance airlock was uncrewed. Two vac suits hung in the lockers, a large gray transport box with its lid open and unsealed, and inside of that, a yellow ceramic box beside them with ZEMÎ TOR stenciled on it in black.

The transport box's wheels were retracted, the steering handle stowed on its side. The walls and lid were only a little thicker than the real thing. Whatever they were using for shielding, it was thin. She hoped it was light too.

Bobbie put on the environment suit, checked her seals and air supply. She and Katria checked each other. The suit had a magnetic tether built into it, a ribbon as wide as her hand and thick as her pinky, dirty from years of use. The airlock itself was set into the floor. The little platform to carry them out to the drum's surface, and hopefully not fling them out into the emptiness of the slow zone. With both of them and the box, it was a tight fit. Bobbie watched the suit's sleeve puff out a little as the lock cycled out the air.

Katria pressed her helmet against Bobbie's and shouted. With only physical conduction to carry the sound, her voice was distant and muffled. "Last chance to back away."

Bobbie smiled and made an obscene gesture. She could see Katria laughing, but she couldn't hear it. The lock cycled, and the platform descended.

The body of Medina's drum curved away above her to the left and right, extended ahead of her and behind. She felt like she was hanging on to the belly of some massively vast whale. The gates were only pinpoints of eerie and erratic light, as regular as a printed pattern against the surreal darkness below her. The gates and the tiny dot of the alien station in the center of ring space. It wasn't her first time outside a ship in the slow zone, but she shuddered all the same. Falling off a spin station in normal space meant drifting out at whatever velocity the station had given her until someone came to haul her back or she ran out of air. Losing her connection here meant falling into the blackness between the gates and vanishing into whatever existed—or failed to exist—on the other side. Normal, star-strewn space could feel like an infinite ocean, vast and glorious and uncaring. The slow zone felt like being in something's mouth.

Katria put her safety tether on the surface of the drum, then lay on her back and pushed her feet up until her mag boot locked to the station. Bobbie waited to follow until she'd taken a couple of awkward, swaying steps. And then she was also hanging upside down from the turning station. The crate in her hand wanted to fly up like the loop of her safety harness. Blood rushed into her head, filling her ears with their own distant roar as they walked— release, swing, push up, and reconnect to the station—back along until they found the stretch of plating that would become the breach point. Katria gestured to the crate—two fingers pointing, the Belter's gesture for *opening or deploying*. Bobbie nodded yes with a closed fist.

The mining net was a square of woven steel cable reinforced by carbon fiber. Rock hoppers and subsistence miners had been using things like it since humanity had first crawled up the well and started harvesting the near-Earth asteroids. The primary piton was thicker than Bobbie's thigh. She fastened it to the skin of the station, then waited for a moment as the external elevator shaft that ran along the drum from engineering to the command center passed overhead. She and Katria took different edges, pulling and stretching the net as they navigated around the target, placing the secondary pitons until the whole thing lay like a low, black blister on the side of the drum.

The trap set at last.

Katria dropped the box, and it flew up and away into the darkness, gone in an eyeblink. She led the way back almost to the airlock platform, then turned off one mag boot, and then the other, and swung on her safety harness, feet to the void. Bobbie did the same. It felt better to be right-side-up again, and worse to know that only one failure point was keeping her alive. Trade-offs. There were always trade-offs.

Katria slaved her hand terminal to the suit's arm display, copied the output to Bobbie's, and set up a low-power radio connection between them. The corridor where they'd set the bomb appeared in the same grainy, muted colors as before. Empty for now, but not forever.

"Now we wait," Katria said through the radio. "The patrol puts their foot in our trap, or someone notices that we're out here."

"Yeah," Bobbie said.

"Don't worry. These Laconians are just like Earthers. They only think of ships and stations as inside. Comes from growing up in free air."

" 'The predictable limits of a conceptual framework,' " Bobbie said. A phrase from her classroom on Olympus Mons. "It's always where to hit the enemy. Whoever they turn out to be. When I learned how to do things like this, we were thinking about Earthers and pirates."

Katria laughed. "When I taught myself how to do this, I was thinking of people like you. Strange how the wheel turns."

The elevator passed above them again, the glowing orb of the alien station at the slow zone's heart appearing like a moon on her left, vanishing again on the right. Bobbie turned to look toward the docks. The *Rocinante* was down there somewhere. Her home and her ship. Or Holden's. Or neither of theirs.

Strange how the wheel turns.

The minutes stretched. Became hours. Twice, people passed through the corridor. A pair of electrical technicians. A sketchy-looking young woman pulling a child by the hand and looking over her shoulder as she walked. Bobbie wondered what the story was there, but it wasn't hers. Her anxiety slowly faded into a kind of dull anticipation, and then to both at the same time. The void passed beneath her feet again and again and again. She switched her air to the secondary bottle.

"Ah," Katria said. "Here we go."

On the monitor, two people walked down the hall toward the camera. Bobbie couldn't mistake the Laconian power armor for anything else. The patrol they'd been waiting for. The enemy approaching. Without a word, she swung back, set her feet against the station, and reengaged her mag boots. The spin gravity would try to straighten her legs, but that was exactly the wrong thing. She bent double, put her hands behind her knees, and held herself there. Katria did the same. Bat-brace position. It was hard to relax like that, especially knowing what was coming. She took a deep breath starting in her belly and moving through her whole chest, then let it out. Shook her shoulders to get out the tension. Smooth and loose. That was the way to be.

She remembered the young Marine she'd flirted with when the Laconians had first taken the station. She wondered if he was on one of the patrols walking above her now, the soles of his feet unknowingly against her own. *Your turn now, my turn later,* she thought. The seconds stretched. The temptation to shift her arms so she could look at the screen was almost irresistible.

The station hit the bottoms of her feet like a hammer. Her legs slammed into her chest, blowing the air out of her. One mag boot threw an error, but only for a second. Then it was done. She turned, walking fast toward the net. It wasn't a low blister anymore. It was a hemisphere of debris and cables. Bent plating, shredded foam, and at the heart of it, trapped like two fish hauled out of a tank, human figures. Above her, the debris small enough to escape the net seemed to fly away from her, though it was really her spinning away from it.

"Hurry," Katria said. "They'll already be on their way."

"I know," Bobbie said.

At the net, they undid one of the pitons, opening it like the mouth of a tent. The gaping hole that led up into the station leaked water and coolant out, flying down past them as they hung. The nearer of the two bodies had taken the worst of the explosion. A crack along the collar and chest assembly. The inside of the helmet was a soup of blood. Bobbie wrestled the corpse closer, holding the arms and waist in a rescue hold while Katria fastened grips to the Laconian suit.

"Hold still," Katria said. The low-power radio made her voice seem farther away than she was.

"I'm doing my best," Bobbie said through clenched teeth.

"All right. He's solid."

"You're sure?"

"Positive," Katria said, and disengaged the primary piton. The net pulled free and fell away below them into nothing. Bobbie turned, forcing herself back to the airlock. Her muscles were burning from the effort. Twenty years ago, they wouldn't have been. The spin of the station made it feel like the dead Marine was pulling her down toward the depths, or else up into the emptiest sky in the universe. The power-armor helmet knocked against the back of hers. The dead arms and legs hung loose. Blood leaked from the crack in the chest plate.

"I hope this suit's not too fucked up," Bobbie said.

"Hope later," Katria said. "Walk now."

At the platform, Bobbie shifted her weight and the dead Marine's with a cry of effort loud enough that Katria turned off her radio. She hung from her safety tether and motioned Bobbie up. There wasn't room on the platform for all three of them. Bobbie didn't even nod, just turned the controls, and the platform rose. While the air cycled in, she sat across from the armor. Her heart was pounding. Her muscles ached. She'd just killed two of the enemy. There would always be a little something—that tug on her humanity that came from doing violence. There was a satisfaction too. It didn't mean she was a good woman or a bad one. It meant she was a Marine.

Somewhere in the station right now, security forces and maintenance techs were scrambling to figure out whether the hole in the station or the possibility of rushing into more bombs was the greater threat. By the time they came to a decision, she needed to be as far away from here as possible.

The inner airlock door cycled open, and she hauled the corpse up into the locker room before she cycled the airlock again for Katria to use. When she popped her helmet seals, the dead man

stank of blood and overheated metal and the same kind of lubricant she used on Betsy's joints.

She pulled the body into the large gray transport box, closed
the lid, and triggered the seals. Whatever alerts, whatever alarms
the power armor had been sending out were blocked now. Or if
Saba was wrong, she and Katria would find out soon enough.

The airlock cycled open while Bobbie was pulling off her environment suit. Her jumpsuit was drenched in sweat. Katria undid
the seals of her own helmet and slung it into the locker.

"You get the package to Saba," Katria said.

"I know the plan. I'm on it," Bobbie said. "And thank you. I
know we didn't get off on the right foot, your crew and mine."

"No need for that," Katria said, popping the seals on her suit
with the speed of long habit. "Just get the work done."

"Copy that."

"You know, this is the second time we've played the same trick.
Use the blast to hide what we really meant? The data center. Now
the missing power armor they'll all think is out there in the black?"

"If they think we have it, they'll change the shut-down code
before we can reverse engineer it."

"I know why," Katria said. "I'm saying don't count on doing it
again. Patterns get people like you and me killed. This strategy's
played out. If Saba thinks otherwise, he's a fool."

Bobbie popped the wheels on the transport cart out, extended
the handle. It rolled easily. She wasn't looking forward to pushing
the damned thing through the public areas of the station to Saba's
rendezvous, but she also wanted to get out of here as quickly as she
could. She forced herself to take one long, slow look at it before
she opened the doors, though. In case there was blood on it.

"There won't be a third time," she said.

"You sure of that?" Katria asked.

"Positive," Bobbie said. "You get your people, and you tell
them to be ready. Cracking the code on this suit is the trigger.
Two minutes after that happens, we're all getting the hell off this
station."

Chapter Forty-Five: Drummer

Bright-green dots were blinking out. Not all at once, but enough to notice. A wave of darkness moving through the cloud of attacking ships. Drummer checked the timestamp, but there was no gap. Whatever the *Tempest* had done at Pallas, it still hadn't repeated here. So what the hell was going on?

"Is it the *Tempest*? Is it firing?"

"Yes, ma'am," the sensors tech said. "The missiles are coming from the *Tempest*. Yes."

"How fucking many of them?"

The cloud of green, the orange dot, and now a new form. Red threads blooming out from the enemy, thick and ropey as a capillary map. The ship itself was lost in them. They reached out toward the EMC vessels. The union fighters. The void cities.

"That isn't possible. That's wrong," Drummer said.

The *Tempest* hadn't resupplied since it had come through the ring gate. It had been in a major engagement already. There was no way for what she was looking at to be real.

"The data is confirmed," the sensor tech said. "Guard of Passage is reporting the same thing."

"Get me Cameron Tur," she said. "Or Lafflin." Anyone who might be able to make the incomprehensible make sense.

"Should I continue to fire?" the weapons tech asked.

"Are we still in a fucking fight? Then yes, you should keep firing."

Vaughn made a small, disapproving sound in his throat, but she was far past caring about the delicacy of his sensibilities. The red threads swam through the void. They only seemed slow on the display because the distances were so vast...

Here and there a thread died, a PDC round or a missile destroying the *Tempest*'s attack. But there were so many, and when even one slipped past the guard, another green dot blinked out. The green dots shifted, swirling in the display as the ships did in the darkness. A few dove toward the *Tempest*, moving almost at the same speed as the torpedoes. As gentle as it looked on the display, it was a killing burn. A suicide run for the crews of every ship that did it. More followed suit until dozens of ships were driving down toward the enemy.

It was a tactic of unspeakable bravery and desperation. Drummer didn't notice that her hands were in fists until the ache caught her attention. She made her fingers open, looked at the little flaps of skin she'd carved off with her nails.

The suicide attack reached its peak. It reminded her of pictures she'd seen of cloudbursts over the deserts of Earth. Huge, angry clouds with numberless tentacles of gray falling from them. A torrent of water racing toward a parched landscape, and evaporating again before a drop could darken the soil.

On the visual display, the bright, dancing veins on the *Tempest* were fading, and now that she knew to look, Drummer could see tiny openings along the sides of the ship opening and closing like pores. The lights of the missiles' drive plumes were like blue fireflies.

"How can they *do* that?" she whispered past the tightness in her throat.

"I have Cameron Tur," the communications tech said. The camera made his face even longer than it seemed in person. The light shone in his eyes.

"Where the fuck are you?" Drummer snapped. "Are you seeing this?"

There was almost no lag before he answered. He was close, then. One of the escape ships. "I don't understand. The number of missiles they've fired...that they're *firing*. These can't be normal devices."

On the display, the last three suicide attackers blinked out. If the *Tempest* moved to avoid the debris fields, it wasn't enough to register at this scale. It looked as though the enemy wasn't even bothering to evade anymore.

"The first battle, we wanted to learn from them," Tur said, talking fast and not looking directly at the camera. "I mean, we wanted to win. Of course we wanted to win, but we didn't expect to. The data—*how* we lost—was as important as stopping them."

"Tur?"

"Maybe they were learning from us too. Maybe they recalibrated something about the regrowth of the ship. Or the missiles."

"They survived a direct nuclear strike," Drummer said. "Are you telling me that's something they can just *do*?"

"Apparently?" Tur said. He licked his lips anxiously. "We knew from the moment they stripped the rail guns off the ring station that they are capable of focusing and directing incredible sources of power. Things we've only ever seen on celestial levels. Collapsing stars."

"Collapsing stars? We're fighting a supernova in the shape of a ship? Why the hell didn't you see this coming?" She was shouting. Her throat hurt with it.

Tur blinked and his jaw shifted forward. He would have looked like a man spoiling for a fight if it hadn't been for the tears on his cheeks. She didn't think those tears had anything to do with her raising her voice. "Ma'am, that ship stripped Pallas Station down to something less than atoms. It shut down *consciousness* throughout the system in a way that I don't have the structural language to explain, and it seems pretty fucking unimpressed by the idea of locality. It's affecting the nature of vacuum through the whole solar system. If you didn't know we were punching above our weight here, I'm not sure what I could have said to clarify that."

"There is a way to beat them," Drummer said, "and we are running out of time. Find me how to win this, and do it now."

She cut the connection before he had the chance to reply. Silence filled the control room. No one was looking straight at her, but she felt their attention like a weight. All the time she'd spent resisting the pressure to make the Transport Union into a police force—into a military—and here she was anyway.

"Mister Vaughn?"

"Yes, ma'am?"

"Find me whoever is in command of the EMC wing of the fleet. I need them now." *Whoever's still alive,* she thought, but didn't say.

"Yes, ma'am."

The weapons tech's voice shook. "Should we—"

"*Keep firing,*" Drummer said.

Drummer felt a heat in her chest. A rage and a certainty. This was the moment that tested everything she'd meant to be. This was what it was to be a leader in a time of crisis. She felt the power of it, the raw will to succeed. To devastate and end the people who would destroy her and the systems she embodied. She rose to her feet, her hands behind her, and she knew that everyone in the control room who looked at her would see nothing beyond her superhuman resolve. Not even Vaughn.

And she knew it for the hollow mask that it was. How fragile.

"Guard of Passage is reporting a missile strike that got past their PDCs," Vaughn said. "They're requesting permission to withdraw."

"We can't run away," Drummer said. "If we break now—"

People's Home shuddered. A sound like the wail of a demon rattled up from the deck, bellied out from the bulkheads, rained from the ceiling. She waited for the wide, low hiss of escaping atmosphere. The fading of screams as the air became too thin to carry them. Instead, Klaxons blared.

She held her voice as steady as she could. "Report?"

"We're hit," the sensors tech said. "Something hit us."

"Do we know what?" Drummer said.

"Rail gun," Vaughn said. "Appears to have impacted section twelve, just spinward of the medical facilities."

"How bad's the damage?"

"I'll let you know as I have reliable information," he said. "Still trying to identify the chain of command with the EMC."

Which meant they were in disorder. She wondered whether the band of suicide ships had been led by some admiral bent on making their last stand count for something. People's Home bucked again, then twice more.

"Engineering's been hit," Vaughn said. "The reactor's...I can't tell. Something's wrong with the reactor."

If the magnetic bottle failed, it would be like a low-yield nuke going off. Even if it didn't crack the city open like an egg, the systems that kept them all alive would be melted and fused. And the prospect of aid ships reaching them in the chaos of the battle were low enough to pass for never.

"Drop core," Drummer said.

Vaughn didn't reply, but the thrust gravity stopped. Drummer grabbed the edge of her crash couch and dragged herself back into it, strapping down with the ease of a lifetime's habit. The automated emergency report showed long swaths of the city under lockdown, pressure doors isolating levels and halls. Keeping the air in the city as best they could. If she hadn't sent away as many nonessential personnel as the ships would hold, it would have been worse. As it was, it still meant deaths. People who'd trusted the union elections to put someone in charge who would protect them. How many of them were dead now who'd been alive an hour ago? And how many more seconds before the next round came? It was like someone else's thought dropped into her own brain.

A sickly calm washed over her. This was what it felt like to see death. To know that the worst was coming, and there was nothing she could do to turn it aside.

"Keep firing," she said. *If we're going down, let's go down swinging.*

The weapons tech coughed out something between laughter and despair. "We are dry on rail-gun rounds. We are at six conventional plasma torpedoes, and five percent on PDC."

Fire anyway, Drummer thought. *Throw everything at them.* Except that if the *Tempest* threw a missile at them, there would be no defense. Drummer closed her eyes. The temptation was still there. If it meant that she died—that all the men and women under her command died with her—at least it would be over. She wouldn't wake up in a wave of dread. She wouldn't watch the structures she'd sworn to protect be peeled away by a threat she hadn't considered worth thinking about until the *Tempest* had flown through Laconia gate.

Come on. There has to be a way. Think of it. Find *it.*

"Should I maintain fire?" the weapons tech asked.

Drummer didn't open her eyes. The moment stretched. "No," she said. "Shift to defensive fire only. We can't shoot down rail-gun rounds, but we can hold their missiles off."

"Yes, ma'am," the weapons tech said. She could hear the relief in his voice. She wondered if he would have thrown away the last scrap of protection on her order. And she wondered whether she'd have done it, in his position. Maybe.

"I have a connection to Colonel Massey," Vaughn said.

"Who?"

"Commander Fernand Massey. Of the *Arcadia Rose*, ma'am. He's in command of the EMC ships."

"I've never heard his name before," Drummer said.

"No, ma'am," Vaughn said. All the admirals were dead. All the people she might have known. As ruined as People's Home was, the fleet was in tatters. Her tactical display listed the ships disabled or dead. There were so many. A quarter of the combined fleet incapacitated or destroyed. They'd thrown everything at the *Tempest*. A wall of tungsten and explosives. And the enemy was still under thrust. Still firing.

It had all been a show. She'd known that. The *Tempest*'s intentionally predictable approach to Earth and Mars. Letting the EMC and union prepare themselves. She'd thought it was just a way to erode their morale, but it was more than that. She saw it now. They'd known that they would win, so they'd invited the enemy to make the strongest showing it could. That way, when victory came, it would be unequivocal.

"Ma'am," Vaughn said.

"Yes, fuck it. Fine. I'll talk to him."

"No, ma'am. There's a new message for you. A tightbeam from the *Tempest*. It's listed as 'command to command.'"

Something twisted in her gut. Part despair and part relief. If they were sending messages, maybe they weren't sending nukes. At least not until she'd had the chance to hear what they had to say.

She undid her restraints and launched herself to a wall handhold. Her crash couch hissed and spun on its gimbals. "Route to my office, please," she said, as if it were a normal message on a normal day and not the dividing line between living under a conquering boot and dying before the end of shift.

Anxious curiosity shone in every expression—even Vaughn's— as she passed. She could have played the message there, in front of all of them. Maybe she should have. Nothing in it would be secret for long anyway. But she didn't want anyone watching her when she saw it. Except Saba, and she wanted him there badly.

In her office, she closed the door, then locked it. The little fern in the corner held its fronds high in the null g. A few things she hadn't stowed—a drinking bulb, a printout on plastic flimsy, a clump of potting soil—floated in the air. She'd spent too long in spin gravity. She'd come to assume it would always be there, a few years' habit enough to erase generations of experience and Belter identity.

She was aware that her brain wasn't functioning normally. She felt more like she was piloting her body than living it. She knew it was shock and trauma, but knowing it changed nothing.

She strapped herself into her chair, took control of her personal interface, and opened her pending messages. Three were listed as unread. One was from the commander of one of the refugee ships, one from a captain of one of the EMC ships, and the last was listed as Admiral Anton Trejo of the Laconian Imperial Navy. Somewhere in a different universe, the Klaxons stopped their wailing. She wished now that she'd brought Vaughn at least. And maybe a whiskey.

She started the message playback.

Trejo sat at his station, his uniform immaculate and pressed. His thinning black hair was in place and his eyes a bright green. He didn't even have the good taste to look disheveled. His smile radiated warmth and sympathy. She half expected him to start talking to her about his relationship to God or a business opportunity she should keep quiet about for fear of starting a rush.

"President Drummer, I hope." He drawled like someone from the Mariner Valley. "If not, then please accept my condolences for her passing. I am Admiral Trejo of the Laconian battleship *Heart of the Tempest*, but you knew that. I'm reaching out to you now because I don't want to be misunderstood. Despite all the hostilities the Transport Union and the Earth-Mars Coalition have greeted me with, we're not enemies. Not you and me. Not the union and the empire. Not Sol system and Laconia. The high consul knew that there would be resistance to this change. We all did, and we respect that you had to do the things you've done.

"When people like you and I enter into a new phase of history, there's...I don't know what you'd call it. Birth pangs? There's a time when you have to expect violence, even though you don't celebrate it. When the high consul first explained to me the parameters of this mission, I wasn't pleased. One ship, no backup, against an entire system? But he brought me around. And this moment, this message, is part of why I felt that his approach was the only moral way forward.

"I have tried to reach Secretary-General Li, but he isn't returning my messages yet. You're here, and you are at least equal in dignity to anyone on the inner planets. You can end this. I understand that you had to fight. You had to try to destroy me. I don't blame you for this. But I am permitted at this point to accept your surrender. Do this, and the inner planets will follow you. You will be treated fairly by the new administration. I promise you that.

"If you are not yet willing to accept defeat, then I would ask you, out of what I hope is mutual respect, to tell me one thing. What is the number of dead that you need in order to show history that your choice to end this was wisdom? That carrying on the fight would not have been bravery but foolishness. A hundred more. A thousand more. A million. A billion. Only say how many more corpses will make this possible for you, and I will provide them." He spread his hands. "Tell me the number. I await your reply."

The message ended. Drummer floated against her restraints and thought about whether to play the message again, if only to give herself a few more moments before she went back to the command center. She could feel her pulse in her throat and in her wrists—a throbbing exhaustion. Released herself, pushed toward the door, down the short hall.

They were all silent when she arrived. She looked at her crash couch, there before the display. The moth-eaten wave of green. The tiny, indomitable dot of orange.

"Vaughn, I'll need you to send a message to the *Heart of the Tempest.*"

"Ma'am," Vaughn said, nodding crisply. *I could order him to his death. I could tell them all to fight to the last breath.*

"The message is this: 'The number is zero.' Send that, and then order all union ships to stand down."

She looked for some reaction in Vaughn's face. Rage or relief or disappointment. It was like expecting emotions from a stone.

"Yes, ma'am," he said. "Is there anything else?"

"No," she said.

There is nothing else. No way forward. Her fight was over. If there was any hope to stand against this empire, it was someplace else now.

If.

Chapter Forty-Six: Singh

He didn't see the catastrophe coming. Even when the scope of it became clear, he struggled to understand it. Blindsided.

The talk in the station—the talk everywhere—was about Sol system and the surrender. Singh watched it play out in newsfeeds and discussion forums, taking the role of official censor more for the joy of being present in the unfolding of history than from any immediate need. The combined fleet of the Transport Union and the EMC beaten and standing down. The newsfeeds from the local sources in Sol system were anguish and despair, with only a few outlets calling unconvincingly for the battle to continue.

For their own side, Carrie Fisk and the Laconian Congress of Worlds proved to be an apt tool for the job, praising the Transport Union's capitulation as a moment of liberation for the former colony worlds. *The rules and restrictions on trade are no longer being dictated by the generational politics of Sol. By being outside the*

system of favoritism, nepotism, political horse-trading and com-
promise, Laconia is positioned to bring exactly the reforms that
humanity needs. He noticed that she shied away from mentioning
High Consul Duarte's name. It was always just *Laconia.*

Which was fine. The two were essentially the same.

But it was the conversation beyond her and other specifically
recruited allies that made him feel best. Governor Kwan from
Bara Gaon Complex issued a statement of support for the new
administration so quickly that Singh was almost certain it had
been recorded in advance. Auberon's local parliament also sent a
public message to put themselves in place as early supporters of
the new regime. New Spain, New Roma, Nyingchi Xin, Félicité,
Paradíso, Pátria, Asylum, Chrysanthemum, Ríocht. Major colonies, some with populations already in the millions, had seen the
battle at Leuctra Point and drawn the only sane conclusion. The
power center of the human race had shifted, and the wise were
shifting with it.

The imminent arrival of the *Typhoon* also helped. He had
known Rear Admiral Song since he'd entered the service. Not that
they'd ever been close, but she was a face and a name that carried
a weight of familiarity. He'd only traded a handful of messages
with her, mostly to arrange the piece for the newsfeeds, but speaking to her had reminded him powerfully of home. The routines
he'd had on Laconia, the taste of the tea, the little part where he
would sit with Elsa when she was newborn and Natalia was sleeping. Watching sunbirds dive into the pond. Sending James Holden
back had begun it, and the coming of the *Typhoon* would complete it. Traffic to and from Laconia. Proof that the great roads of
space were open.

The longing it called forth in him was vast and complex. The
open sky that he wouldn't see as long as he remained governor of
Medina. The touch of his wife's skin against his, which he could
look forward to. His daughter's laughter and the soft sounds she
made at the edge of sleep.

There was a way in which every day since he'd stepped off the

Storm had been a pause, like holding his breath. And soon, soon, his real work could begin. With the *Typhoon* in place and Sol system conquered, the empire would be unassailable, and humanity's future assured. He'd ignored his own anxiety and impatience, and now that he could almost relax, he felt them straining for that release.

Taken together, all the good news nearly made up for the bad.

"By comparison, the attack was minor," Overstreet said, walking beside him as they went to the executive commissary. "We lost two Marines, but the infrastructure damage was trivial compared with the previous attack."

Singh wasn't sure whether they had come off the patterned time for the executive staff or if word had spread before him and cleared the commissary, but only four people were seated at tables enough for fifty. The door attendant ushered them to a small table set apart from the rest, where they wouldn't be casually overheard. He and Overstreet made their requests—green tea for Singh, a local drink called black castle for Overstreet—before they went on with the their conversation.

"We have them on the run," Singh said. "Smaller attacks, targets of convenience instead of strategic ones? This underground is running out of steam."

"That is certainly possible, sir," Overstreet agreed. "Still, I'll feel better when we have them all in custody."

It probably wasn't another dig at his decision to send away Holden, but Singh felt a little sting all the same. The drinks arrived with a small plate of pastries. Overstreet held back until Singh had taken one. A small point, but one that Singh appreciated.

"What is the status of our friend's operation?" he asked.

Overstreet leaned forward, folding his hands around the cup of black castle. His mouth narrowed. "We should know in about half an hour now. If your informant is what he claims to be, he and his co-conspirators will be walking into the power-routing station. I have five officers and five Marines waiting for them."

"Do you expect a fight?"

"I'm hoping for one," Overstreet said. "There's nothing the troops would like better than an excuse to break a couple heads."

"I need those brains intact."

"Fingers, then," Overstreet said with a chuckle. "No one loves a mad bomber."

"Fair enough. The informant, though. He goes free."

Overstreet nodded, but he looked like he'd tasted something bitter. Singh leaned in a degree and let the silence ask the question for him. Overstreet met his eyes, looked away, and shrugged.

"I'm not sure that's a good idea, sir. If we take the others and he slips away, his people will know he's working for us. They could turn him back."

Singh felt a stab of annoyance, but he pushed it down. He had to remember what he'd learned with Tanaka. Better that he be patient.

"You think he may be a triple agent?"

"It wouldn't be the first time something like that had happened. The one thing you know about someone who's willing to compromise his allies is that he's willing to compromise his allies."

"What do you suggest?"

"Question him, the same as the others," Overstreet said. "When his trial comes up, put a word in the judge's ear."

Singh sipped his tea. It was still a little too hot. It scalded. "I'm not certain that helps us build a network of locals who will work with us."

"If I do my job right, we'll be able to put a replacement in his spot. And a little clemency come sentencing time is more than he deserves."

It felt like a betrayal. The man, compromised though he was, had done his part. He'd brought the information to prevent the sabotage of Medina's sensors to Singh. Handing him over for trial didn't seem like a just reward for loyalty. But Overstreet had a point. Jordao was a member of a conspiracy against the station and Laconia. He likely had blood on his hands, and there was a greater loyalty that a governor owed to his own people than any-thing a local thug could command.

"Fair enough," Singh said. "A normal interrogation. But tell your people just that. If they need to take their frustrations out on someone, make it the ones who weren't working with us."

"I can do that," Overstreet agreed. And a moment later, "It'll be good having this wrapped up before the *Typhoon* gets here. I was hoping this wouldn't drag on."

"To a degree," Singh said, "it's to be expected. Periods of tran-sition invite a certain—"

Overstreet started. He put his black castle down fast enough that it sloshed onto the table, then he checked the monitor on his wrist. The red of a priority alert glowed there like a little flame. He tapped it with a scowl. His eyes went dead. Singh's breath went shallow.

Something had happened. Another terrorist attack.

"What is it?" Singh asked.

"We have an unauthorized launch," Overstreet said, standing up. Singh stood with him, drinks and baked goods forgotten. Adrenaline surged through him. A ship—even a small one—crashing into Medina could do terrible damage. Could crack the drum, destroy the station. Overstreet was already walking for the security station, fast, scissoring steps that weren't quite running and weren't quite anything else. Singh had to trot to catch up.

"What ship?" Singh asked.

"Old Martian gunship," Overstreet said. "Name's the *Rocinante*."

"James *Holden*'s ship?" What did that mean? Was his crew making some kind of doomed bid to catch the *Lightbreaker* and bring him back? Or take revenge for his loss?

"It has capacity for twenty missiles and a keel-mounted rail gun. Not to mention a fusion drive that could melt the station to slag if it chose to," Overstreet said, "but it hasn't opened fire. It's staying close to the station with maneuvering thrusters."

"Can we take them out?"

"We destroyed Medina's defenses when we took it," Overstreet said. "We have a few that were repairable, but without the supplies from the *Typhoon*, our abilities are limited."

"The *Storm*, then," Singh said.

Overstreet took a deep breath, turning smartly at the intersection. Surprise and anxiety made the security office seem kilometers away. "I don't like the idea of having a close-quarters battle between those ships right near the station. If the *Rocinante* is just trying to escape, there's an argument for letting it go."

"We can't rely on the enemy's goodwill to protect us," Singh said, and opened a priority connection to the *Storm*. Commander Davenport, his executive officer on the journey out, answered like he'd been waiting.

"Davenport, this is Governor Singh. I am formally instructing you to leave dock immediately and protect the station from the gunship *Rocinante*."

"Yes, sir," Davenport said, then hesitated. "We are presently at less than full crew, sir—"

"A little short-staffed now is better than a full ship too late. Try to chase them away from the station before you engage."

"Yes, sir," he said, and he dropped the connection.

Ahead of them, security was clearing the corridor. An emergency alert sounded and a gentle voice began. *This is an emergency alert. Report to shelters immediately and await official instructions. This is an emergency alert.*

The security center was buzzing like a kicked hive. Voices raised in alarm thickened the air. The feeds from drones and surveillance cameras filled every screen. Singh assumed it was all in response to the *Rocinante*'s launch until an older woman in security uniform barked at them. "Major Overstreet, sir! We have reports of a riot in the detention cells."

"What?" Singh said.

Overstreet's voice was level and calm. Like a pilot whose ship was coming to pieces around him. "What do we know?"

"Someone overrode the containment on the cells. There was some kind of explosion. The guards have retreated to the security lock, but I'm getting reports of gunfire from the civilian side too. I have two fire teams on their way."

"Good," Overstreet said. He turned to Singh. "Sir, it is my opinion that the sabotage effort your friend discovered is part of a much larger operation, and whatever the enemy has in mind, it's happening right now."

Singh shook his head, not as disagreement, but like a drunk man trying to clear away the fog. Some part of him was still thinking that because they had the guard force ready to keep the station sensor arrays up, things were under control. That he was prepared for whatever was happening, even as it bloomed out around him.

"I understand," he said.

"As your chief of security, I recommend that we get you and any other essential personnel in lockdown until the situation is better controlled."

"Of course. I'll return to my office."

"Might not want to stay that near an obvious target, sir. I have a secure position prepared. I'll have a fire team escort you and stay there until we understand better what we're looking at," Overstreet said. He turned to the older woman and gestured toward Singh. "He needs an escort."

"On their way, sir."

Belay that, Singh thought. *I'll stay here.* Except that it was a stupid impulse, based in pride. A leader should stand with his team in a time of crisis, but—as much as it galled him—Overstreet was that leader in this moment. He would only get in the way. And even so, part of him wanted to remain. To be *seen* to be in control.

"I will expect updates," Singh said. "When you need my authorization, I will be waiting."

"Thank you, sir," Overstreet said without missing a beat, then turned away. A moment later, four Marines in power armor stepped in through the main door and saluted.

"Governor Singh, sir."

"You're my escort, then?" Singh said with a smile that he hoped looked confident. "Let's be on our way."

As they walked, Singh consulted his own wrist monitor. There was too much happening—too many individual groups coordinating on the fly—to have a complete picture of the situation. The *Storm* was maneuvering, and the *Rocinante* hadn't yet made an aggressive move. The riot at the detention cells was growing more violent, and the Marine fire team was requesting permission to escalate to lethal countermeasures. And Overstreet's words came back, haunting with their implications: *My best estimate is that a third of our operating personnel are open to working against us.*

The hardest thing was to trust his own people to do their jobs well, but it was what he had to do. He wondered if the high consul suffered the same thing—knowing that all the critical action would be taken by others who were guided by his orders, but in conditions he could only guess at, and in places where his intervention, even if it were possible, could only muddy the waters. It was a subtle and terrible insight. The powerlessness of control.

The warning echoed through the station. A man ran through an intersection ahead of them without pausing to look. Singh's legs burned a little from his pace.

"Where are we going?" he asked the head of the fire team.

"We have a hard shelter at the end of this corridor, sir. It's a bit away from the main offices to be a less obvious target, but it has independent environmental controls and—"

The Marine froze in midstride. Singh felt a rush of fear, looked down the corridor to see what danger the man was reacting to. There was nothing.

"What's the matter?" he said. It was only when he got no answer that he realized all the Marines had stopped. Their visors were opaque, their radios silent, their power armor in lockdown. Singh stood, suddenly alone and terribly aware of his own vulnerability. The back of his head itched at the idea that someone might be targeting him right then, and he had no protection.

For a moment, he saw Kasik again, dying before him. Was all of this a distraction to pull him away from safety? Hands trembling, he strode fast down the corridor to the first door. A public restroom. He stepped in, made certain he was alone, and locked the door behind him. His heart was beating hard enough to feel the ticking of it in his neck. Leaning against a narrow sink, he pulled his monitor and keyed in his security codes. His Marine lockdown hadn't been triggered. The Marines shouldn't have been disabled. Someone was putting out a false shutdown signal.

Overstreet answered his connection request at once.

"My fire team is disabled," he said.

"Yes, sir. I'm seeing the same with all the powered teams. Stay where you are. I am sending a conventional escort to your location."

"What the hell is going on out there? I need a report!"

Annoyance flickered across Overstreet's face, gone almost before Singh could register it. "The loss of functioning fire teams has let the situation at the detention cells deteriorate. I have initial reports that something's happening at the dockmaster's office. I'm waiting for better intelligence on that, but I am seeing what looks like several ships getting ready for launch. The *Storm* has engaged with the *Rocinante*, but not conclusively as yet."

Now, may I please go do my job instead of talking about it? He didn't say it, but Singh heard it anyway.

"I will wait for the second escort," Singh said. "Carry on."

He dropped the connection. In the mirror, he looked small. Frightened. He stood, straightened his uniform, and composed himself until his reflection looked more like a man confident in his control of the situation. It was important when his people came that he give the right impression. That was all he could do now.

Something thumped deep below him. A strike on the station drum, maybe. A sign of the battle going on all around him while he hid in a public toilet.

The underground had caught him unprepared. To give them their due, he'd underestimated their coordination and their numbers and their will. He had been told that the Belters of the old regime had a culture of violent resistance. After the sabotage of the oxygen tank, he had thought he understood what that meant, but he hadn't appreciated the depth of it until now.

Their plan was unfolding right now all around the station. All he could hope was that the one place he knew that he was ahead of them would prove decisive. If disabling the sensor arrays was critical to their plan, he could still bring all the rest of it crashing down.

Chapter Forty-Seven: Bobbie

Bobbie's harness consisted of three magnetic locks about the size of her palm and two bands of woven nylon that looked like they'd been green sometime in their past. Basic safety equipment, standard on any ship, any dock, any station outside a gravity well. Wondering whether they worked was like wondering if her next footstep would sink through the atoms of the deck.

"You think these things are going to hold?" she asked. Her radio was set to a broadcast strength so low a thick T-shirt would have jammed her. Amos, beside her, looked up the long curve of the *Gathering Storm*'s exterior. His helmet hid his expression, but his tone was fatalistic.

"If it doesn't, this'll be a weird day."

The surface of the ship wasn't like anything Bobbie had ever seen. Faceted like a gem, without the protrusions of PDC cannons or sensor arrays. The pinks and blues seemed less like the color of the material itself and more like some kind of refraction. Something that it did to light that was much weirder than selective absorption. The darkness of the slow zone was profound. Her helmet had to enhance everything with what it picked up from the glow of the ring station. It even stretched the edges, pulling ultraviolet and infrared into the visible range, just to have more to work with. It was always like this, but waiting—exposed and uncertain—made it seem ominous.

While the surface of the ship looked like crystal, it was soft in a way that she wanted to think of as foam. What it really reminded her of was skin. The magnetic locks bound her to it in a rough, uncomfortable cradle, or would once the ship was under way. Provided that the magnetic locks held on. The red glow that said they were clamped was solid, except that every now and then she thought she caught a flicker of amber. The other ten members of the insertion team besides her and Amos were all using the same equipment. Their suits were all low-level environment suits. None of them had better than welder's padding as armor. They looked more like a cleaning crew than a crack military force. It worried her how true that might be, but that was for after the locks held. If the *Storm* pushed off from the dock and left them all floating behind it like a snake's shed skin, it would be up to Alex to solve the problem of the enemy destroyer. And they'd probably all die. There was no upside.

"*Really* hope these hold," Bobbie said.

The encrypted alert came. Bobbie tapped her forearm controls. When Alex's voice came through, it had the thick Mariner Valley drawl that meant he was scared shitless but also a little euphoric on the fear. "This is Alex Kamal of the *Rocinante* calling out to my friends and family and all ships at sea. We are about to start this rodeo. Breaking loose from the docking clamps in ten. Nine…"

"Brace," Bobbie said. "We don't know how fast this is going to happen."

She took the nylon cords, tracked them in tight, and waited for the *Gathering Storm* to leave port.

In order to get there, they'd crawled out from the elevator shaft that ran the length of the station from the command and control at the bow down to engineering at the stern. They'd moved quickly, skimming along centimeters above the station. The others had been laughing until Bobbie reminded them that low-power radio wasn't radio silence and politely suggested they all shut the fuck up instead of getting the team killed. After that, she'd been alone with the sound of her own breath, the smells of old rubber and someone else's sweat. Alex had been on her right, Amos on her left, and the dock spiked with ships a quarter of a klick before them. Past that, just the blackness of the slow zone, and the killing nothingness beyond the gates.

The drum had spun beneath them. The scars and damage from the brief battle with the *Storm* still showed in blackened streaks and bright patch foam. Medina had taken more than her fair share of licks in her life, and today wasn't going to be any better.

They'd pulled out every trick that any of Saba's underground had up their sleeves. Stealing the welding rigs, uncrating the hidden caches of weapons, compromising the access shaft that let them through. Ever since the Laconians had come through the gate, smart people familiar with the station had been planning for this moment. Maybe since before that, if some of them were smugglers.

As they passed over the last of the drum, Alex split off. He had to make his way almost a third of the way anti-spinward from the *Storm* to reach the *Rocinante*. She told herself it wasn't the last time she'd see him as if she knew it were true. Then with a flick of her fist, she'd directed the insertion team toward the dark, looming form of the destroyer.

The plan was to lure the *Gathering Storm* off the station. As soon as its docking clamps were off and no new soldiers could get on, Bobbie and Amos would breach the hull and lead an insertion and take the *Storm* off the playing field. Whether they did that by blowing its reactor, sabotaging its controls, or steering it out toward the nothingness between the gates was going to be a game-day call once she was inside. Without better knowledge of the ship's internal workings, improvising was a better option than pretending she could make a solid plan.

The secondary objective was to get her people off the *Storm* and safely picked up by one of the fleeing ships. The tertiary objective was to get away herself.

Alex reached zero, and Bobbie thought she felt a little tremor through the *Storm* as the *Roci* blew her clamps and spun out away from the docks using the body of Medina as cover. Two of her magnetic locks flickered amber, and then safely back to red.

It was a day with a lot of ways to die packed in it. Like Alex, she couldn't keep from grinning. Maybe it was a Martian thing. She stayed braced, her feet against the hull, knees bent. The minutes stretched. The blower in her helmet felt cold against her forehead. That meant she was starting to sweat.

"How you holding together there, Babs?" Amos asked. The radio made it sound like he was half a klick away and whispering.

"I'll be fine once they get this ship out of dock."

"Yeah. Not really leaping into action, are they?"

"We were hoping to catch them flat-footed."

"That's true," Amos said. "Still."

"Maybe they didn't notice," one of the others said.

Or maybe they're waiting for more troops to get on board, Bobbie thought, and the *Gathering Storm* surged out to the black, snapping the nylon bands taut.

They were on maneuvering thrusters. Fifteen meters down from them, a blast of superheated steam vented, pushing the destroyer into a fast rotation. It didn't seem to come from anyplace, as if the thruster were hidden under the weird not-metal of the hull until they wanted it. Good thing they hadn't set up their camp there or at least one of them would probably have been blasted off the ship and cooked to death already.

The *Storm* lurched. The rumble of the thrusters translated itself up her legs. Medina fell away like someone had dropped it. The drive plume of the *Storm*'s main drive flared, and the ship jumped forward. Only about a quarter of a g. They weren't going to risk melting Medina to slag. Still, it was a little eerie seeing her shadow stretched long ahead of her on the body of the ship. A reminder that if she fell, she'd die in fire.

"Amos," she said. "Make us a hole."

"I see you coming after me," Alex shout-sang. "You ain't catching the *Roci*, friend. We're just too damned pretty for you."

"Alex, get off this channel," she yelled, then remembered that her signal was intentionally too weak to carry. She shook her head and hoped he wouldn't be too distracting.

Amos had the welding kit out, power supply strapped to his side. With two broken ribs, she figured the rig had to hurt like hell, but nothing about his movement betrayed the pain. Her own cracked tailbone wasn't making it any more comfortable either. They'd done themselves a lot of damage getting this far. She had to make sure it didn't make a difference. Pain was just her body telling her something. She could choose to ignore it. Amos held the torch to the hull, and everything went bright. Sparks seemed to stream away behind them, curving down and vanishing against the hull like gravity was pulling them and not just the turning of the ship.

"Weapons ready," she barked, and the others acknowledged. If the destroyer had the double-hulled design that all Martian ships had, cutting their way through here would only be the first step. But it was a critical one. There was damage they could do there, but it was also difficult to defend, and with none of the *Storm*'s crew there, tactics like flooding it with hydrogen and oxygen could take out her whole team without risk to the enemy. Tempting as it was, she had to get into the ship proper, and—

"Ah, Babs? This is weird as shit."

Amos stood braced. The cut from the welding torch was a line of brightness in the hull half a meter long. Half a meter long and shrinking fast.

"What have we got?"

"Remember how it looked like the hull could repair itself? It's doing it now too."

"That going to be a problem?"

"Yeah," Amos said. "I'd say that'll make this hard."

The *Storm* lurched under them. The drive plume brightened below them, and the *Storm* gathered speed. The acceleration pulled the straps taut as the thrust gravity made the nuclear-powered flames of the plume more definitively *down*. The bow-most of Bobbie's magnetic locks flickered amber and slid a few centimeters before it went red again and stopped. The little moment of give shot adrenaline through her body. Her heart was thudding in her ears. Her voice was so calm it sounded like someone else.

"Got any bright ideas?"

"Lemme try something," he said, and hunkered down.

He cut again, but in a tight curve, not making a hole they could breach through, but something smaller. When he got around it, he punched in, pushing the little core of hull material into the space within the ship. The circle he'd made instantly began closing, but Amos was carving slivers off its edge. He pared the hole wider and wider, even as it fought to narrow. His motions were fast and efficient. He didn't slow down even as the ship bucked and turned under them, the proof of a lifetime's physical labor made into elegance. Bobbie knew that if she'd tried this, she'd never have been able to keep up, but with Amos, the hole grew wider.

"Edges are going to be toasty," Amos said. "Nothing I can do about that."

Saba's voice murmured in Bobbie's ear. *Marine fire teams have reached the detention cells. Time to turn our little friends off.*

"Sooner would be better than later," Bobbie said.

"You ain't wrong about that," Amos said. He started whistling tunelessly between his teeth. "I'm not going to be able to stop this while folks go through."

"Fuck that," one of the others said. "Not winding up half in and half out, me."

Bobbie turned to the solider. "You'll do as you're told, or I will shoot you in the head as an example to others," she said, she thought more politely than the man deserved. "Get next to the hole. You're going in on one. Three...two..."

The man dove through, Amos cutting through the nylon bands as he went. The hole didn't close over him, but only because Amos kept carving the sides.

"Next up," Bobbie said, pointing at the nearest soldier. "You. Three. Two. One."

Again and again, Bobbie shoved one of her team through the molten hole of the hull. The abandoned magnetic locks clustered around it like wildflowers in a garden, the cut tethers shifting as the ship shifted. Like seaweed in an unsteady current.

Medina swam above them, and twice Bobbie caught glimpses of the *Rocinante*'s drive plume limning the station like a sunrise that never came.

"Gonna be tight, Babs. This is taking a lot more fuel than I budgeted."

"Keep going," she said.

He did. Eight. Nine. Ten. And then it was just the two of them.

"We're good," she said. "Give me the rig. I'll get you in."

"I appreciate that thought," Amos said. "But just between you and me? You're not that good a welder. Head in. I'll make it."

"No heroic gestures."

"Oh, I'm not dying out here," Amos said, and pointed toward the interior of the ship with his chin. "Worst-case scenario, I'm dying inside there."

Bobbie shifted her magnetic locks to the edge of the burning hole, then launched through, tucking her legs in. Arms caught her and pulled her to the side. The suits' worklights filled the space between the hulls with blue-white radiance.

It was eerie. It was familiar as a well-loved face, but wrong. Where spars of titanium, ceramic, and steel should have been, crystals grew. Lines of fracture shot through them and then disappeared like watching lightning discharge in a bottle. Where sheets of metal and carbon lace should have been, seamless blankets of something that she tried to think of as lobster shell and then fabric and then ice defined the spaces.

It was unmistakably a Martian destroyer. And it was like nothing she'd ever seen before.

"Coming through," Amos said, and she turned to pull him safely to a handhold. The hole where they'd breached squeezed tight. It didn't completely close, but the opening ended up five centimeters across. In the worklights, Amos smiled his empty, amiable smile.

"Well, that part's done," he said. "Hope the next hull's a bit more familiar, if you know what I mean."

Alex was keeping the chase consistent. It was the only reason they weren't being bounced through the space between the hulls like rats in a dryer. The entry into the ship proper was always the most dangerous moment. Bobbie had known that from the start.

They moved quickly, bracing at the hand- and footholds, until they found a stretch of bulkhead. Amos checked the fuel on the welding rig and shook his head, but he didn't speak. The smoke shook and fell away with every turn of the ship like water falling from a faucet. The hull didn't heal itself, but that was the only good thing.

"That's going to be small," she said.

"It's going to get done," Amos said. "Any more, and we'll be trying to bend it to get through."

Amos cut, and air and light spilled in from the other side. The ship's interior was still pressurized. That was odd, for battle conditions. If the crew of the *Storm* hadn't realized they were being boarded, they were finding out now. Bobbie squeezed through first into the back of a bunk room. Two rows of gel-mattress bunks, not that different from the quarters on the *Roci* where the

Marine fire teams were meant to sleep. These beds were empty and neat. She took a position by the doorway while the others pushed in. Amos came last, slapping a plastic patch over the hole that bellied out into the space between the hulls like a balloon before it hardened.

"I don't want to shoot you bastards," Alex shouted through the radio. It was a code phrase. The *Storm* was getting close. The *Roci*'s evasions were going to fail, and soon.

Bobbie popped the door open, ducked her head out and back, and a bullet tore a streak out of the frame where her skull had been.

"How many?" the man beside her asked.

"At least one." She looked around the bunk room for something—anything—that would give them the edge. "This place is a death trap, and we're out of time. You three, with me. You two go in firing left, you to the right with me. If you see a grenade or anything that might be one, duck back in. Everyone else, into the bunks, on your backs. Set up to shoot between your feet if the bad guys rush the door. You have four seconds. Go."

She picked high when they went out. The woman crouched down beside her could have been anyone, but their lives depended on each other now. Down the corridor, Bobbie saw the intersection where the fire had come from before. A single head bobbed out and back. She aimed for it, but she couldn't tell if she hit.

Another doorway stood across the hall. She pointed and gestured. They made the crossing in a rush. Another cabin. Bunks for twelve, but no sign that they'd been used. No one fired at them. Whoever had tried before was down or fled. Going for whatever reinforcements the ship had. Surprise had gotten them this far. Skill had to take it from here.

"Amos?" she said into the radio.

The walls of the ship attenuated his response, but she could still hear him. "Babs? How do you want to play this one?"

It had been too many years since her ship tactics, but this one at least was easy. The ship had two points of vulnerability to boarding attack—engineering and command. The enemy had the home-field advantage, but if they were understaffed, they'd protect whichever one they thought she was making a play for. So the smart thing was to feint at one and hit the other.

"I'm taking these five and heading for ops. Wait two minutes, then take yours for engineering."

"You got it. Are we looking to disable or blow up?"

The *Storm* lurched again. A smooth rattling sound echoed through the ship like a chain slipping off a shelf. It was different enough from what she was used to that she almost didn't recognize it as PDC fire. They were going for the *Roci*.

Before she could speak, Saba's voice came through on the radio. *Evacuation teams are at the docks. Waiting for clear sign, yeah?* And then, almost overlapping, Naomi's answer. *Message received. We're going in.* The underground's ships were ready to launch. Medina's sensor arrays were going down soon. The window was opening. It wouldn't stay that way long.

"The first thing you find that kills this ship, do it," Bobbie said.

"What about evac?"

She knew what he meant. If he could blow the reactor, should he? Was the mission more important than living through it?

"Use your judgment, big guy," she said. "I trust you."

Chapter Forty-Eight: Clarissa

There were only two ways that she felt anymore. Either she had the shakes or she was exhausted. The shakes part had been nasty when it started because it felt like being scared—jittery and heart racing. And because it felt like fear, she kept thinking she was afraid, and then becoming afraid without any focus or reason. Once she understood it was just her shitty aftermarket endocrine system leaking into her bloodstream, it helped. At least she understood that it wasn't just her going crazy with amorphous anxiety. She still shook, though.

In the worst of it, she'd go back to her old mantra, the one from prison. *I have killed, but I am not a killer. Because a killer is a monster, and monsters aren't afraid.* She felt like she was afraid all the time now, and in that frame, it was almost comforting.

The superstitious part of her kept thinking that she'd invited this shape to come into her life with the sympathetic magic of her words. The rational part thought she'd invited it by paying a shitload of money to have illegal body modifications as part of an insane adolescent revenge fantasy. That and the part where she'd killed a bunch of people.

"You okay?" Naomi asked.

Clarissa lifted her hand in the same Schrödinger's answer she always had, no matter how she expressed it. Always yes, and always no. Yes, I'm fine in that I am not presently in medical collapse. No, having that be what *fine* meant didn't ratify her early life choices.

"You?"

"Fine," Naomi said in a tone of voice that probably meant the same thing. Ever since Holden had been taken, a light had gone out of Naomi's eyes. After discovering the *Lightbreaker* was gone and Holden with it, Naomi wasn't catatonic from grief, and so sure. Fine.

They were waiting on a bench at the edge of a field on the inner face of the drum. Wheat stretched out to their right, curving up and away from them, ripening in the light of the false sun. A woman in a systems control uniform walked along the path holding a little boy's hand. He stared at Clarissa as they passed. She could practically hear, *What's wrong with that woman, Mommy?* he was thinking it so loud.

It felt a little weird being out among the normal inhabitants of Medina. All of the people going about their lives like they were trying to forget that the Transport Union had ever existed. Picking their kids up from school, eating dinner with their friends, working their jobs and performing their duties as if they'd always done this at the wrong end of a gun. As if Laconian rules were normal. As if there weren't already things in play that were going to change everything before night.

"I'm sorry about Holden," Clarissa said. She hadn't meant to, but she did.

Naomi took a quick breath, let it out. Like someone ripping off a bandage that had adhered a little too much to her skin. A quick pain, and then over with. "Thank you. It's not...what I was expecting."

"Yeah," Clarissa said. "It seems like there's always the way we wanted things to go, and there's what actually happens."

A warning tone sounded through the drum, echoing with the distance and the free air. An artificial voice reassured them with its tone while it repeated, *This is an emergency alert. Report to shelters immediately and await official instructions.*

"Listen," Naomi said. "They're playing our song."

"Oh my," Clarissa said, laughing. "We have lived our lives wrong, haven't we?"

Naomi took her arm, half as a joke and half to give her support if she needed it, and they started toward the rendezvous. Clarissa's body twitched and shuddered as she walked. Once they went below, into the corridors and halls of the drum, the traffic thickened. The alert sounded from every corner. Businesses closed their doors. Kiosks shut down. Everywhere, people moved quickly, some shouting and angry, but most with a kind of deathly focus. They'd had too many explosions and too much violence for any joking around. The illusion that life was normal for any of them vanished.

She and Naomi waited for a gap in the flow of bodies, then ducked into a public restroom. Clarissa sat on the couch built into the wall. She felt a little nausea haunting the back of her throat, but it wasn't bad. Naomi went to the sink and washed her hands slowly, not to make them clean but to make it look like they weren't just loitering in the place should anyone from station security come in.

The plan—their part of it anyway—was simple enough. Or at least it was from Clarissa's perspective. She'd tried to walk Alex through it once, and she was pretty sure he'd only followed about half. The sensor arrays on the Medina were all linked to the main system, but they all had their own backup batteries. Shutting down the power would keep Medina from seeing where the ships went in real time, but it wouldn't clear the local caches in all the sensor arrays. As soon as the power grid came back, the arrays would check in, reconnect, and deliver everything they'd saved.

And that process right there had a vulnerability in it. When the arrays checked in to reconnect, the system could request a diagnostic run. The arrays would take about twenty seconds to cycle through their diagnostics and return the results with a fresh check-in. During those twenty seconds, no new data came in. And if the array check-in requests got routed to a false system that only replied with diagnostic requests, they could keep doing that until some poor bastard figured out where the false route was coming from or else physically went out to the arrays and ran a new dedicated line.

When she'd gotten to about this point in the description, Alex's eyes had lost their focus, and she'd simplified. Make a fake traffic card. Put the fake traffic card in at the secondary power junction. Blow the primary power junction to reset all the arrays. Arrays don't come back on without a lot of tedious work. She'd gotten a thumbs-up from him then. It had been cute.

It was always strange to remember that she knew things that other people didn't. Not just about power- and signal-routing protocols. What it was like to murder someone who'd only ever been kind to you. How it felt when the people you'd dedicated your life to killing took you in as family. Even though she knew better, she always defaulted to the idea that her life wasn't singular. That whatever she'd done must not have been that odd, because after all, she'd done it.

The door opened and the bomb guy came in carrying a ceramic toolbox. Jordao. He nodded to Clarissa and then to Naomi. Between the hunch in his back and his ashy skin, he looked like a sample picture of "furtive possible terrorist." *If we're going to pull this off, that guy's going to have to calm the fuck down.*

"Hey," Clarissa said.

"Hoy," he responded. "Bist bien?"

"No problems so far," Naomi said. "But we've been out of touch. You heard anything?"

"Unauthorized launch," Jordao said as he set the toolbox beside the sink and opened it. "Nos ew bû?"

"Yes, that's one of ours."

"Perdíd," he said, forcing a grin. "How many plays playing in one day?"

"One less if we don't move," Naomi said.

Jordao opened the case and tossed earpieces to her and Naomi before fitting his own. "Katria, she didn't parle ero que la, right? They're going to be down on us hard after this. Alles la preva? Look like we were in a kids' school."

"If this works the way it's supposed to, that won't be a problem," Clarissa said, shifting the earpiece so it was a little more comfortable. "Just stick with us, and you'll be fine."

Naomi dried her hands, pulled her hand terminal out of her pocket, checked it, put it back. "We should go," she said.

Jordao closed the toolbox, hoisted it onto his hip, and followed Naomi out. Clarissa brought up the rear. The shakes were a little better. A little less. That was sort of a good thing, because she hated the shakes. It was sort of bad, because the exhaustion came next, and she needed to get through the mission. At least enough not to slow Naomi down.

Outside, the halls were emptier. *This is an emergency alert. Report to shelters immediately and await official instructions.* Naomi turned toward the ramp leading down toward the outside of the station. Clarissa put her hands in her pockets and tried to look bored. Her mind divided itself gracefully between rehearsing the steps that she'd need to take to swap traffic cards and watching for security patrols. When Saba broke the silence, it startled her.

"Evacuation teams are at the docks. Waiting for clear sign, yeah?"

Naomi put a hand to her ear. Hearing her through the earpiece and in person at the same time gave her words a little echo. Like they had more weight than they should have.

"Message received," she said. "We're going in."

It would only take a couple of minutes to swap the card and set the charges. After that, they'd get to the docks if Saba's people could hold them that long, or if Laconian security retook them, an airlock. Naomi paused at an access panel, checked her hand terminal, and nodded. This was the one. Jordao was sweating and pale. He looked worse than she did.

"It's going to be okay," she said. "We have a surprising amount of experience with weird situations."

Naomi leaned against the access panel. A security drone passed through the intersection behind them, but didn't turn their way. Clarissa felt a little surge of adrenaline, but it only served to highlight the growing torpor in her muscles. *Do this*, she thought. *Get this done. You can rest when you're dead.*

The access panel clicked and slid down.

"What are we doing here?" Jordao said. "Got to go, us."

"We're doing the thing that makes the next part matter," Naomi said, then stepped aside. The guts of the ship would have looked chaotic to anyone who didn't know the things she did. For her, there was a simple logic in every weld, every conduit, every connector. She took the doctored traffic card out of her pocket, plucked the old one out, and slotted hers in. The fault indicator barely blinked to amber, and then went back to a flickering, happy green.

"Okay," she said, sliding the panel back into place. "Let's go set the charges."

But when she started walking, she knew it was going to be harder than she thought. If they moved fast enough, they'd be done before she ran out of energy. That was why Naomi was here, after all. Because none of them thought she could do it by herself. Because they weren't necessarily wrong.

The worst part was that she'd done it to herself. The damage to her body, the wear and the weariness, were all products of conscious, determined choices made by a girl she hadn't been in decades. She carried the weight of those decisions like a sack of bones. Like a toolbox full of them.

Some sins carried their own punishment. Sometimes redemption meant carrying the past with you forever. She'd gotten used to that over the years, but it was still pretty fucking inconvenient.

"Down here," Jordao said, waving them on.

"I know," Naomi said.

The door to the primary power junction was reinforced. A red border was painted around the frame, with warnings in half a dozen languages that all meant *Please be careful. There's a lot of things in here that we'll have to fix after they finish killing you.*

Jordao opened the door, and Naomi stepped past him into the maintenance way beyond—

And then stepped backward, her arms rising. Running footsteps came from behind her, sudden and loud. A young man in the blue uniform of Laconian security stepped out from the red door, a pistol leveled at Naomi's stomach. Rough hands grabbed Clarissa by the shoulder and threw her to the floor. Jordao leaned against the wall and sank down to sitting.

"There a problem, sir?" Naomi asked, her voice the perfect echo of innocence.

"Knees," the pistol man said. "And keep your arms up while you do it."

Naomi looked down at her. Clarissa saw no sorrow in her eyes, only calculation. And then a conclusion. Naomi sank to her knees. Jordao's head was leaned back, looking at the ceiling and taking deep gulping breaths. He still had the toolbox under his arm, and she thought he might be about to set off the charges and turn them all to paste, until he started laughing. It wasn't mirth or gloating, but it was relief. Even before he spoke, Clarissa understood they'd been sold out. She laid her head against the rubber matting on the deck as someone put a knee in the small of her back and started pulling her arms behind her. The exhaustion was coming on stronger now. The deck felt almost comfortable.

"There's a thing," Jordao said. "A thing they put behind an access panel. No savvy mé que, but I can show you where, yeah?"

"What was it?" the pistol asked Naomi.

Naomi shook her head ruefully. "Afraid you're going to have to go fuck yourself, coyo."

He hit her, stepped forward. Clarissa felt the zip tie going around her right wrist while the guy fumbled with her left. She rolled her head. Five of them, all told. All with guns drawn. The pistol came down, ready to end Naomi where she lay.

"You're sure you can find whatever it is?" the man said.

"'Course I am," Jordao said. "Where are your Marines? You said there'd be Marines."

"Change of plan. They're statues until we can get the lockdown codes undone." He looked down at Naomi. "Was that yours too, bitch?"

Naomi locked eyes with Clarissa. The calculation was gone. They were out of options. Which meant, really, that Naomi was out.

Clarissa always had one left.

It was a weird moment. Through the bone-weary tiredness, through the fear and the panic and the anger, something else opened up. Something like rage and joy, and more than all that, a profound relief. Naomi saw it in her expression, and her eyes widened. Clarissa pressed her tongue against the roof of her mouth, swirled it the way she hadn't in years. The fake glands in her body triggered, pouring their shit into her blood. It hurt. It didn't use to hurt, but this time, every one of them ached. Even the pain felt good.

Time slowed down around her. She bucked and the man on her back fell forward. He still had a hand on her right wrist, and he kept his grip as he fell. She felt her shoulder dislocate and heard the deep pop, but there wasn't any pain. Her legs were under her and she pushed off before he hit the floor. Her right arm was shredded and useless. Her muscles were thin and fragile. Just jumping, she felt the tendons in her knees and hips strain and rip, but she was already rolling, ready to hit the wall and launch again.

Pistol man didn't shift his aim from Naomi, but the other three were drawing down on her, moving slowly as someone underwater. One pistol barked, but the shot only tore into the anti-spalling fabric on the wall.

Clarissa spun through the air, her ruined arm trailing behind her. She led with her knee, and it felt like dancing. Like flying. Her aim was still good. She brought her bent knee into pistol man's nose, felt the cartilage give in her joint and his face, the two of them crumbling together.

She'd been sick for so long, she'd let it make her fragile. So much of her life had become nurturing what fading health she had. Rationing it like one canteen that had to get her across a desert. Now she gulped it, and it felt wonderful.

The two who hadn't fired did now at almost the same instant. One missed, but one bullet dug into the thin meat over her ribs. It hurt, but the pain was distant. She barreled into the closest of them. As they fell, she wrapped her good arm around his head, cradling it carefully so that when they landed, she could snap his neck. She hit the deck hard, pulled, and felt his spine give way.

I have killed. But I am not a killer.

She caught up the gun from his hand as the others turned. Clarissa felt the battle cry in her throat, felt the force of air and sound rattling her trachea. Felt the gun she'd stolen kick. The woman nearest her fired wild, and Clarissa placed a bullet in the woman's cheek, snapping her head back. That was two. The one who'd been on Clarissa's back jumped toward her. She put a bullet through his teeth. Three.

Naomi was scrambling for pistol man's fallen weapon. He was still down, holding his shattered nose like that was his biggest problem. Clarissa shot him twice in the center of mass.

There was only one guard left, and he was close to Clarissa. She could see down the barrel of his gun. She saw the fear in his eyes. He fired. He couldn't miss. Her leg gave way under her, but she fired a shot on the way down. It took the last guard in the throat. She landed hard, but her blood was still made from light and rapture. She rolled, knelt. Her abdomen ached and it was hard to pull in a full breath. Jordao looked at her like he was seeing the devil.

No! I'm sorry! he shouted in some universe close to hers.

Fuck your sorry. Sorry doesn't fix shit. She didn't know if she'd yelled or if it was just in her head. Either way, she shot him—once in the belly and when he doubled over, the crown of his head right where a little bald spot was just starting. Then the rush was over.

It wasn't as bad as she'd remembered. There was the retching and the feeling of illness. The helplessness. The pain. But at some point all of that had become familiar, so the experience of it wasn't as bad. Or else she was slipping into shock.

Shock, or something like it.

Naomi cradled her head and she noticed she was lying down. Her mouth tasted like bile. The guards and the traitor were spread throughout the hallway. The air stank of blood and gunpowder. It looked like a scene from hell. All of the years she'd spent living with her regret, doing quiet penance for the lives she'd ended, and now the only thing she could think was *That was fun.*

Words were happening somewhere nearby. *Stay with me, Claire.* She remembered Naomi was there and opened her eyes again. She didn't remember closing them. Naomi was spattered with blood, her face pale. Ren stood behind her. He was wearing some kind of black robe that made her think of Jesuits.

"I'm a monster," Clarissa said.

No you aren't, baby. You're not a monster. You're not. Which meant Naomi had misunderstood. Clarissa had meant, *I'm not afraid.* She tried to think what to say that would clarify that, but it was a lot of effort. And what did it matter really if anyone else understood? She knew.

Fuck it, she thought. *Some things you take to your grave.*

Clarissa Melpomene Mao closed her eyes.

Chapter Forty-Nine: Bobbie

When she was young, Bobbie had a recurring dream of finding a door in her room that led to some new, exotic part of her quarters that her family had forgotten or else never known about. Those dreams had been eerie but also beautiful. Full of promise and wonder and threat.

The *Gathering Storm* was exactly like being in one of those dreams.

The architecture of the ship had all the same aesthetics and design as the *Rocinante*. The central lift, the size and spacing of the hallways and doors, even the shapes of the hand- and foot-holds was familiar. Or if not exactly familiar, at least related. Part of the same family. Laconian and Martian had the same cultural DNA, and as much as anything else, the ship proved it.

But it was also *strange*. The decks didn't have seams or bolts. The foam and fabric on the bulkheads had the same uncanny fleshy texture as the hull. The lights were different somehow too. She didn't know if it was the spectrum or the brightness or the way that there seemed to be some kind of subtle motion in them, but everything felt a little bit like being underwater. Like the ship was a huge fish with the bioluminescent glow of the deepest seas.

It was home, but wider, larger, and *changed*.

They moved from hall to hall in strict formation, covering each other as they went. The rattle of PDCs was joined by something else she didn't recognize. Some Laconian version of torpedo fire was her best guess. The deck lurched and canted as the ship maneuvered around them, but the main drive never cut out, so down was always down.

She'd expected the ship's defenses to meet them at the central lift that led to ops. It was the obvious choke point, and holding that space meant controlling movement between all the decks it passed through. If she'd been in charge, all the hatches would have been open and a dozen rifles pointing down, ready to put holes through any head that popped out. Instead, there had been three Laconians with pistols retreating up it, and firing behind them, more to discourage Bobbie and her people from following them than to actually injure anyone. They were holing up on the command deck. She wasn't sure whether that was a good thing or a bad one.

"Amos?" she said, and when he didn't answer, turned up her broadcast power. "Amos, check in."

"Little hairy down here, Babs," Amos replied. "Made it to what I'm pretty sure is supposed to be a machine shop. Fucked if I know what half this stuff is, though."

"Any contact with the enemy?"

"Yeah, we lost a couple."

The sound that interrupted them was like something metal being torn by brute strength. It took a fraction of a second to recognize it as high-rate weapons fire. Amos was shouting over it— not to her. She waited, tension knotting her gut. She wanted to know what was happening, but not badly enough to divide Amos' attention. He grunted once, and she was sure he'd been hit. Something loud happened—a grenade, maybe—and the firing stopped.

"Still with me, big man?"

"Yeah," he said. "We just had a little thing there. Architecture's a little weird. And it looks like there's a bunch of stuff down here built out of...I don't know. Crystals? Or bug shells? You remember those buildings on Ilus? Like them."

The deck shifted hard to the right, and Bobbie's head went a little swimmy from the Coriolis. She grabbed onto a handhold.

"I wasn't on Ilus."

"Oh right," Amos said. "Well, like them anyway. But yeah, we're kinda stuck where we are unless we can make another hole. We're looking for something to cut through the bulkhead with. Would like to get that done before they decide to rush us."

Alex's voice cut in. He wouldn't be able to hear them unless she turned up her broadcast power a lot more, but the *Roci*'s transmitters had more than power enough. "Hey, y'all. The *Storm*'s breaking off our little dance out here. It looks like she's trying to get back to port. Might be a good time to launch anyone that wants to get launched. You're getting short on time."

Saba responded. "Still waiting for the prison stragglers. Any ship's ready, I'll get them gone, but keep that bastard off us as long as you can, yeah?"

"I'm on it," Alex said.

Bobbie ground her teeth. She wanted to break off, head down to back up Amos and his squad. Bad tactics. She needed to stick to the plan. Amos was going to be all right. She had to believe that. The lift tube went up the length of the ship, all the way to the ops deck. No one was waiting up there that she could see. That didn't mean no one was waiting.

"All right," she said to her team. "This is going to be just the same. Two move forward while three cover, and then the forward pair cover while the three catch up. Only instead of going from door to door, we're going up from deck to deck. If we start drawing fire, we'll try to get the lift going up before us, but it's probably locked down, and I don't want to announce where we are."

The Belters all gave their assent and took position. Bobbie and a tall man went first, climbing the handholds like they were free-climbing. She glanced over the top of the deck before she climbed up, but she would have been surprised to find an ambush there.

She leaned against the wall, gun pointed up. It looked like the hatch to ops was closed. Leaving the rest open gave the defenders a great line of fire, but they weren't using it. Not yet. She gestured to the others, and didn't take her eye off the enemy as they scrambled up beside her. The *Storm* was bigger than the *Roci*. There were eight more decks between her and ops. That last step was going to be tricky, but—

Gravity cut out, and she grabbed for a handhold by reflex as the ship spun around her, sweeping her legs perpendicular to the deck. As suddenly as it had cut out, it came back. A hard burn—four or five gs slamming her down. The impact knocked the breath out of her, and then gravity cut out again, a moment of spin on the float and another high-g microburn. She and her team were braced now. The float and burn happened three more times. It seemed ready to keep going forever.

"Amos?"

"Hey there, Babs."

"Is this you? Did you break something?"

"Nope. Whatever they're doing, this here is the product of conscious choice."

"I think—" A hard burn made her grit her teeth. Then the float. "I think they're trying to shake us around like bugs in a can."

Hard burn, and the float. "That's going make this inconvenient. They trying to slow us down?"

"Until they can get back to port." Hard burn, and float. Her mind shifted. Delaying and heading back to the docks made the most sense if the *Storm* was undercrewed. It also explained why she wasn't catching heavier fire from the command deck. If the

Laconians could get back to reinforcements, she wouldn't have a chance. And if she didn't, no one else would either.

Two more cycles of float, turn, and slam her into the deck failed to dislodge her from her place. When Amos spoke again, she could hear the effort in his voice. "That could be a problem."

"That's what I was thinking."

Another round of gunfire pressed its way through the radio. "Not sure I'm going to be able to stop that from happening."

"All right," Bobbie said. "New orders. Don't die until I say so."

"If I find a way to kill this bird?"

"Then act like I said so, but don't stick your head out just to look for it."

"You got a plan?" Amos asked.

"That'd be generous," she said, "but I've got something I'm going to do."

The ship kept doing its stuttering bounce like one of the first-generation exploration ships that exploded nuclear bombs as a propulsion system. Even for the crew that made it to crash couches, it was a miserable way to travel. She took a deep breath, felt the rhythm of it, and on the next float, pulled herself out to the lift shaft. Two good handholds, two good footholds, and suddenly she weighed five times her usual.

Her fingers and toes screamed in protest. Her back and shoulder flirted with cramping. The float came back, and the ship turned, but she was climbing up. Just one set of handholds before the weight came back. But she was closer.

If she fell, it was a long way to the bottom. But no one was going to be shooting down at her during this, and they didn't think she could climb while this was going on. That was it as much as anything. With every round of release and spin and high-g burn, she made her way higher, not looking back to see whether her team was with her. She needed all of her focus for this.

Sweat beaded on her forehead, and the suit's helmet fan kicked up to high so that her faceplate wouldn't fog up. She was burning through oxygen fast enough that a three-hour supply would last her maybe one. She thought about taking a break at one of the decks along the way and stripping off her helmet entirely, but if the Laconians decided to vent the ship after that…well, that would be unfortunate. Better to play it safe. Or as safe as free-climbing with a full destroyer's depth of decks below her in radically uncertain gravity could be.

Saba's voice came again when Bobbie still had three more decks to go before she hit ops. "Sensor arrays are down. We're launching everything. No more time to wait."

"I'll try to keep you covered, *Malaclypse*," Alex said. "The *Storm* is live and a threat. I can try knocking her torpedoes down, but treat her like she's got teeth."

"Bien," Saba said. "And I have a package on its way to you, *Rocinante*. Keep an open eye."

Alex swore under his breath. She didn't have time to guess why.

Another moment of float. Another collapse into terrible weight. The temptation to go faster, to try for two handholds up instead of just one, was a trap. It meant less time to get braced, and that was an invitation to fall. It hurt. It took forever. It was the right way. She couldn't get greedy. The pain in her hands was getting worse, but her feet almost seemed to be getting used to it. That or they were going numb.

She was over halfway up. Three and a half more decks, and she'd be at the ops deck. At the closed plate that kept the lift locked in place. Two and a half. One more. The float came again. She moved up. Her eyes were fixed on the seam where the lift plate would slide open. Where, if this was like the other Martian ships she'd been in, it would make the most sense to take cover and fire down at the boarders. At her. She waited for the next acceleration, but it didn't come. Only a gentle press as the ship maneuvered.

That was bad.

"The *Storm* is on approach to the dock," Alex said, and his voice sounded like ashes. "Anybody has a good idea, I'm listening."

Her arms and legs were trembling from the effort, and sweat

stung her eyes. She risked looking down. Her team was following, but they were only about halfway up. This one was hers.

Voices came from the ops deck. Sharp, barked orders. A clattering, probably from a weapon's locker. They knew there wouldn't be much time, but they were also thinking she had a lot more territory to cover than she did. The lift plate slid aside, and she reached in and took the blue-sleeved arm by the elbow and hauled the man attached to it through and down. He bounced against a couple walls before he caught himself, and by then her team had their guns on him and Bobbie was through the opening and onto the ops deck.

Three people, in the most oddly designed crash couches she'd ever seen. Bobbie raised her pistol. Definitely undercrewed.

A fair-haired man saw her first, and yelped, "Commander Davenport!"

An older man moved forward. Older than the others, anyway. He still looked like a puppy. "Get us into the dock! Whatever happens!"

"I am Gunnery Sergeant Roberta Draper of the MMC," Bobbie snapped. "I will kill every one of you if anyone touches the controls."

Davenport lifted a defiant chin. "You have your orders."

"Doesn't have to go like that," Bobbie said. "You know where that ends us. Your people dead. Mine too. Probably a lot of civilians if I have to ram this boat into the station to kill it. I said, *Don't touch those controls.*"

The pilot flinched back, shot a look at Davenport. He stared hard at her, like he was looking at his death. Like he was trying to talk himself into being brave and hadn't quite managed it yet. There was a chance there in the space between who he was and who he was trying to be. Killing these three wouldn't fix the situation in engineering. Wouldn't save Amos. Behind her, her team was floating up onto the command deck. She wished they wouldn't. More pressure on the Laconians was only going to cement their position. When she spoke, she tried to make her voice calm and soothing.

"Here's the situation. All your people die and all mine too, or all of us live. Now, you can decide whether this bunch of amateurs and assholes is worth a crew of Laconia's best."

"Hey!" one of her team said. She ignored him.

"You expect me to believe you won't steal the ship?" Davenport said. *Well, I wasn't planning to until just now*, Bobbie thought. *But since you mention it…*

"I'm not talking about the ship. I'm talking about you and yours either put out an airlock with suits and bottles or else killed here."

"I've seen the way you people work," he spat. "If we put down arms, you'll kill us anyway. You have no honor."

"Bite your fucking tongue," Bobbie said. "I'm Martian Marine Corps. If you live through this, you go ask your old-timers what that means. They'll tell you how lucky you are I didn't crack your ass the other way just for saying it. If I say you and yours are safe, then you're fucking safe."

Davenport said nothing, but there was something behind his defiance. She thought it might be hope. She opened a connection to Amos.

"Hey, big man."

"Hey, Babs," he said. He sounded winded. "I got us into engineering. Gimme another five minutes, I can light this bastard up. May take a bite out of the station when we blow, but I figure that's someone else's problem. How's it going up there?"

"Your team needs to stand down," she said. "No aggressive action toward the enemy. Confirm that."

There was silence on the line.

"That's not the plan the way I heard it," Amos said.

"Amos, listen to me. Stand down. Don't blow the ship. And if anyone down there kills another Laconian, I will shoot them myself. Including you. Understood?"

"Yup."

"Stand by. If I need you to go back to plan A, I'll know in about a minute."

Davenport looked from her to her team arrayed behind her. He scowled. Bobbie felt her breath go shallow. She waited.

"Thirty seconds, Mister Davenport," she said.

"You joined the wrong side, gunny," Davenport said. "You should have been one of ours."

Twenty-five minutes later, the surviving crew of the *Gathering Storm* were tethered together in the cargo airlock. Their arms were secured behind their backs, their ankles were tied together, and the maneuvering thrusters on their vac suits didn't have any canisters. Amos and one of his team went through checking their seals one last time and strapping emergency beacons to their knees. The Laconian commanding officer watched Bobbie now with the intensity of someone planning his revenge.

Amos knocked on Davenport's faceplate to get his attention. "Can you breathe in there? Getting good air? 'Cause if you're not, this is the time to say something."

He nodded once, a perfect physical representation of resentment.

Outside the *Storm*, ships were fleeing through the gates following the schedule Naomi had built. By and large, they were going to the smaller colonies where there was less traffic parked waiting for the gates to reopen. But some were going to the well-established places like Bara Gaon Complex and trusting to their ability to evade any traffic monitoring on the other side to get them to safety. There was still a little more than an hour before the last of them was slated to go, and then the *Storm*, following up at last. If things went right, Medina's sensors would be deep in their routing seizures for at least four hours. And the prisoners had enough air for ten. A six-hour window for pickup seemed like more than enough.

Amos gave her the thumbs-up, and Bobbie nodded him on. He undid the tether from the airlock deck, pushed off, and floated through to pull himself to a stop beside her. Bobbie cycled the lock, and when the outer door opened to the darker-than-space of the slow zone, she touched her radio.

"Okay," she said. "Let's see if the controls work the way they said."

"Copy that, bossmang," her new Belter pilot said.

The *Storm* shifted, pushing gently to the side. The prisoners seemed to float away, though really Bobbie was the one moving. Out beyond them in the darkness, a distant drive plume glowed like a star, and then, passing through a gate, went out.

"Okay," she said. "We're good. Make sure we get far enough away before we light up the drive. I don't want to save them just so you can burn them down in the drive plume."

"Sa sa," the pilot said.

"Alex?" she said, then remembered her suit was still on the low-power stealth settings. She changed it and tried again. "Alex? Where do we stand?"

A different voice answered. A man that it took Bobbie a few seconds to recognize. "We're hugged close to Medina for the extraction."

"Houston?" she said. "Is that you?"

"Now that you fuckers have come to your senses about the immorality of centralized power? Yeah, it's me. And I'm ready to accept your apology as soon as you untwist your diapers."

"He's gonna be a joy," Amos said placidly. "I kind of missed him."

Bobbie killed her mic. "I can't tell if you're being sarcastic. I need to know these things." She turned the mic back on. "We have a change of plan. We won't need pickup."

"Negative," Alex said. "I'm not leaving you behind."

"We're flying escort," Bobbie said. "The *Storm* is ours."

"No shit?" Alex said, then whooped. "Holy crap, you took a prize? Looks like you got yourself a ship after all, Captain Draper."

Naomi's voice cut in, clipping into Alex's last syllables. "I'm coming out."

"All right," Alex said. "Two to pick up, and then we can get in the flight queue out of this dump."

"One," Naomi said. "One to pick up. We ran into a problem. Clarissa went down fighting. I wouldn't have made it out without her. None of us would."

Bobbie's throat went tight. She looked over at Amos, and he smiled his usual amiable smile, shrugged. Just for a moment, she saw something underneath the expression. Pain and loss and sorrow and rage, and then he was just himself again.

"Damn," Alex said. "I'm sorry to hear that."

"Okay," Houston said. "I have you on the scope. We'll slide over and get you."

"Naomi," Bobbie said. "When you get on the *Roci*, I'll need you to find a safe place for the *Storm* in the escape queue."

"I'm on it," Naomi said. Now that Bobbie knew to listen, she heard the exhaustion in her voice. The weariness of grief. She turned off her mic, turned toward Amos, but he was pulling himself back toward the lift. She followed him, a little trickle of adrenaline coming in. Waiting to see what was coming next.

At the lift, Amos stopped and scratched his nose. "I was thinking I should probably get a few of the new kids. Go through the ship. Just make sure we don't have anyone on board we didn't mean to have on the ride."

For a moment, she thought about letting it go. Letting Amos fall back into his usual self. It would be easier. It would feel more respectful.

It was what Holden would have done.

"I need to know if you're okay," she said.

"I don't really—"

She pulled herself in close, almost nose to nose. She wasn't smiling and he wasn't either. "I didn't ask if you wanted to talk. I said, *I need to know*. Whatever ship I'm the captain of, if you're on it, that means you and I have clear, open, and honest conversations about your mental health. This isn't friendship. This isn't nurturing. This is me telling you how it goes. We both know what happens when you're off the rails, and I'm not going to pretend that you're anything more or less than what you are. So when I say I need to know if you're okay, it's an order. Are we clear?"

Amos' jaw clenched and his eyes went flat. She didn't back away. When he smiled, it wasn't the empty, amiable expression he usually reached for. It wasn't a version of him she'd seen before.

"I'm sad, Babs. I'm angry. But I'm okay. Going down fighting was a good way for her to go too. I can live with it."

Bobbie let herself drift back. Her heart was going a little faster than she liked, but she kept it off her face. "All right, then. Take your team and go through the ship. I'll warn you when we're going on the burn."

"I'm on it," Amos said. And a moment later, "You know, you're gonna be good at this captain thing."

Chapter Fifty: Singh

"This is exactly the kind of recklessness that has been underlying the Transport Union since its inception," Carrie Fisk said. Her face was flushed, her gestures sharp, and her voice had the buzz of rage behind every word. Her blouse was tan with black, and she wore the green armband that had come to symbolize antiterrorist solidarity among those loyal to Laconia and High Consul Duarte. "The union claimed that stability and safety were their primary mandate. That was the whole point of letting it administrate ring space! But the minute—the *minute*—someone arrives with the power to question that? Bombings. Theft. Murder. The hypocrisy is mind-boggling. It's *unreal.*"

The interviewer was a young man apparently well known in Sol system and on Medina. Singh watched the man nod and stroke his chin like an ancient sage considering a deep mystical truth. His seriousness made Fisk look even more formidable.

"And would you say the situation is stabilized now?" he asked.

"We can hope it is," Fisk said as she shook her head *no*. "When I look at the patience that the present administration has shown to us and the violence with which it was answered, it leaves me... not angry, even. Embarrassed. We called ourselves a civilization, and this thuggery is all we have to offer. I can only hope that the people who were fooled into thinking any of this could be justified are embarrassed too."

It was a sentence Singh had written himself and delivered to Fisk. She repeated it now as if it were an off-the-cuff thought, and she made it sound mostly convincing.

Of all the things he had done since he'd come to Medina, Fisk and the Laconian Congress of Worlds was by far the most successful. Everything else—moving up the timetable for the *Tempest*'s transit to Sol system, flushing out the underground, managing Medina Station—was tainted.

The catastrophe had lasted five and three-quarter hours from the launch of James Holden's ship to the restoration of full function to Medina Station. In that time, his best informant and the team sent to back him had been slaughtered, the station's external sensors had been compromised, the Laconian Marine forces neutralized, the detention centers broken open and fifty-two prisoners lost and not yet recovered, twenty union ships had transited through no one knew which gate or gates, and the *Gathering Storm* had been boarded and hijacked.

It was, without exception, the greatest failure of security Singh had ever heard of, and as governor of Medina Station, he had spent almost the whole time hiding in a public toilet. Humiliation sat in his belly like a stone, and he had the distinct sense that it would remain there forever.

Every decision he had made since he'd arrived at Medina returned to him in the light of his failure, and he considered each of them like a wound in his skin. If he had treated the local population with greater caution from the first, would Kasik have lived? If he had chosen to respond to the assassination attempt with a more focused response, would the underground have gained fewer followers and allies? If he had avoided the confusion of restructuring his security forces by retaining Tanaka, would they have exposed the underground in time to prevent this?

The list seemed to go on forever. And each choice he'd made—sending the *Storm* out despite Davenport warning him it was undercrewed, shipping James Holden to Laconia instead of questioning him more deeply about the underground, encouraging Trejo and the *Tempest* to move the timetable forward for the transit into Sol system—had led him here. So on some level each of them had been wrong. No matter how wise they had seemed at the time, how forgivable and subtle his failures of judgment had been, the final evidence was unmistakable. He had treated the people of Medina as though he were their leader instead of their warden. Instead of their zookeeper. And they had paid him back with violence, death, and dishonor. All of that was a given now.

There was no standing apart from the failure. It had happened on his watch, and so it was his problem to fix. And it didn't apply only to Medina. He saw that now. His mandate was to coordinate the empire from this, its hub. And that would mean crushing the underground wherever it had fled. Wherever it emerged from the fresh dung heap of the union's demise. He'd thought of Medina as a station to run, a logistical heart to sustain a glorious future for humanity.

He'd been mistaken.

His system chirped a connection request. He checked himself in the monitor, smoothed his hair, and straightened his tunic. He was done looking less than knife sharp. These were, after all, the first days of his career's rehabilitation.

He accepted the request. A woman's face appeared on the screen, a small identifier hovering above her to say who and what she was to him.

"Lieutenant Guillamet," he said crisply.

"Rear Admiral Song of the *Eye of the Typhoon* is requesting command-to-command, Governor."

"Of course," he said. The monitor flickered. He straightened his tunic again and felt immediately self-conscious that he'd done it. It was a sign of insecurity, even if he was the only one who knew about it.

Rear Admiral Song appeared. Her wide mouth was set in a polite smile. The light delay was almost trivial. Evidence that the *Typhoon* was on track to pass through the gate. "Governor Singh," she said. "It's good to see you."

"Likewise," he replied.

"We're on approach to the ring gate," Song said, then looked away. "I'm very sorry, but given everything that's happened recently, I have to ask you this. Can you assure me that this transit is safe?"

Singh settled more deeply into his couch. *Of course it is*, floated at the back of his mouth. *The* Typhoon *can come through the gate, and there won't be any rogue ship zipping through some other gate in the seconds before to change the safety curve. You and your crew will survive the trip and take its place as the protector of the ring space.*

He swallowed the words. It was like another fine cut on his soul to admit that he wasn't certain.

"I have had no new security alerts," he said. "We see no ships on approach through the other gates and have no reason to suspect any interference from fringe elements. But if you would like, I will consult with my chief of security to make certain we have done everything in our ability to minimize your risk."

"I would appreciate that," Song said, and her tone meant, *I'm sorry to ask it.*

"The safety of your ship and your crew are the most important thing," Singh said. "I understand your caution."

"I'll match orbit with the gate until we hear from you," Song said. "And thank you, Governor. I do appreciate this."

He nodded and dropped the connection. She didn't trust him. Of course she didn't. He didn't trust himself.

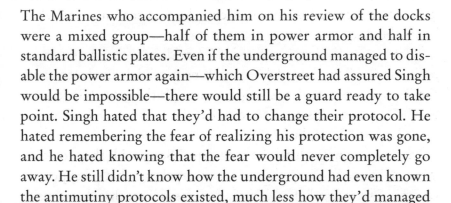

The Marines who accompanied him on his review of the docks were a mixed group—half of them in power armor and half in standard ballistic plates. Even if the underground managed to disable the power armor again—which Overstreet had assured Singh would be impossible—there would still be a guard ready to take point. Singh hated that they'd had to change their protocol. He hated remembering the fear of realizing his protection was gone, and he hated knowing that the fear would never completely go away. He still didn't know how the underground had even known the antimutiny protocols existed, much less how they'd managed to reverse engineer them. Was someone—a Laconian—a turncoat? Had they been careless? He had no way of finding where the information had leaked out. It was another little insult that burrowed into his skin.

He maneuvered through the docks on a small thruster of compressed air. The empty berths stared back at him like an accusation. The pocks in the decks and bulkheads where bullets had struck during the fighting hadn't been buffed out or painted over yet, though they would be. He felt the attention of the dockworkers. They were, after all, the audience for this excursion. Meant to see that the governor of the station wasn't cowering in his office, afraid to peek out from behind his desk. That he wasn't hiding in a public restroom. The heavy guard undercut the message, as did the fear in his gut. But he would pretend and pretend and pretend in the hopes that it would somehow become true.

So he lifted his chin, and made his way through the full round of the docks—even where the damage from the bombing of the primary oxygen tanks twisted and deformed the deck. He looked at the temporary plating with what he hoped was dignity and thoughtfulness. All he really wanted was to be done with this and back in his office.

The acting dockmaster followed along just behind him. The

anger in her expression was unmistakable, but he didn't know if it was rage at the terrorists who'd done the damage or at him for not preventing it.

"How long will it take us to make repairs?" he asked.

"That will depend on the supply chain, sir," she said. "Once we have the *Typhoon*, we should be able to get started in earnest, but they've been breaking more than we have the decking to replace."

"It's heartbreaking," he said because he didn't know what else to say. She didn't respond. "What is our capacity at this point?"

"It's not bad. The only berth that took serious damage was the first. Sheared off the docking clamps. Once that old gunship was out, the bastards took over my office. All the rest were released from the controls. That's one way it could have been worse, I suppose."

What if he'd brought Natalia and the monster had been here? Laconians had died in these uprisings. If his family had come to Medina, would they have been targets too? Would he have watched his daughter die the way he'd watched Kasik?

And yes, locals suffered too, but to have his people dead and hurt...And with what repercussions? The criminals had scattered like seeds on the wind, and taken his ship with them. What colony would see these images and not think that they could do the same?

He pushed over to the broken decking and put his hands on it. He'd been weak before. Lenient. He'd thought that by treating the people of Medina as if they were citizens of the empire, they would be transformed somehow. They would be civilized. The decking was half a meter thick, and twisted like a torn leaf. They'd been willing to do this, and he'd pretended he could treat them as if they were sane. Another of his mistakes.

He had hesitated to wield his power before. And the universe had taught him what rewards hesitation brought. Well, he'd learned his lesson.

"Thank you. I understand now," he said. Possibly to the acting dockmaster. Possibly to something deeper in his own soul. He turned to her. "This won't happen again."

"This was what they were building toward," Overstreet said. "The bad news is, they were by and large quite successful in their aim. I'm not going to make this pretty, sir, they trounced us."

"I agree," Singh said.

Overstreet leaned forward in his chair and threw the image from his wrist monitor to the screen over Singh's desk. A list of all the people presently unaccounted for on Medina. The people that they knew had escaped. Or died.

"On the other hand," Overstreet said, "their objective was defensive. This was a retreat. I've had the technicians make a complete audit, and I'm prepared to certify that it's safe for the *Typhoon* to make its transit."

"You're sure about that? Completely safe?"

"I think we've established that perfect knowledge isn't possible in this context. But in order to pull off this last series of attacks, the underground had to spend a tremendous amount of its resources and capital on Medina. If they'd stayed here, they could have used the same knowledge of the station and agents within the civilian population to protract the struggle here for months. Maybe years. Instead, they burned it all in one day."

"So this was a good thing?" Singh said.

"No," Overstreet said. "But it was all the bad things they could throw at us at once. I feel confident that they didn't hold anything back. So however bad this looks—and it looks very bad—we're going to end with Medina carrying a smaller insurgent population, with fewer resources at their disposal, and the main body of the underground scattered to the colonial systems."

"The colonies," Singh said. "Yes."

"The loss of the *Storm*... well, that's not inconsiderable. If we hadn't pulled most of the crew off to assist with other operations...

Or if your XO had scuttled the ship once it was clear they couldn't repel the boarders…"

"Talk to me about the colonies," Singh said.

Overstreet blinked his too-blue eyes in something like confusion. "Sir?"

"The colonies," Singh said. "That's where the terrorists have gone. That's where the next wave of this will take place, yes?"

"That matches my analysis, sir."

"So how we proceed here should be considered in light of the colonies. We should examine how likely they are to cooperate with the enemy. And how we can affect those decisions."

"Yes, sir."

"An example needs to be made. Something that not only restores confidence in the safety of Medina and the gate network, but displays what Laconian civilization stands for. What we believe. What we are willing to do to ensure our control over this situation."

Overstreet was silent for a moment. Singh paged through the lists of the missing. The faces of the enemy. There were pages of them, but not uncountably many. This was still a solvable problem.

"What exactly are we willing to do, sir?" Overstreet asked, and his tone told Singh that he knew what was coming.

"A white list," Singh said. "I would like you to identify the people who we are certain are not involved with the insurgency. The people we know absolutely that we can trust."

"And the others?"

Singh closed the image down. The enemy vanished. "An example has to be made."

Overstreet went very still. For a moment, the only sound was the hum of the air recyclers.

"I see," Overstreet said. "So a step up from counterinsurgency."

"It's been justified."

"The official position of the high consul is that these are all Laconian citizens. That the terrorists are Laconian citizens who are also criminals."

"I know," Singh said. "But I also know that I was placed in

command of Medina to learn from practice what theory can never teach. And this is the lesson that James Holden and his friends have taught me. Will you refuse to respect the chain of command?"

Overstreet chuckled at that. Singh didn't know why.

"No, sir, I will follow the chain of command, as is my duty."

"Good. Please prepare the cull, then. I will trust your judgment on who best belongs on the white list."

"Yes, sir," Overstreet said. "Only I have other orders. Sir."

A thrill of confusion moved up Singh's spine. "Other orders? From whom?"

"Standing orders I received from Colonel Tanaka when I accepted this position. So ultimately from Admiral Trejo. You see, sir, the high consul made it very clear to Admiral Trejo that the rule of the empire is permanent. And if history shows us anything, it's that people hold grudges for generations. Whole societies have lived and died because of their antipathy born out of events that happened generations before. Or maybe things that got so mythologized, they were just pissed off about stories of things that never happened in the first place. The admiral was adamant that we hold ourselves to a higher standard. As we always have." Overstreet spread his hands in a gesture that meant *What can you do?* His right hand held a gun.

Singh felt his heart catch and then stumble like it was running down a hill. "May I ask what your orders are?"

"I'm to set an example, sir. Restore confidence in the safety of Medina and the gate network, and display what Laconian civilization stands for. Including that we who have accepted the burden of government hold ourselves and each other to the highest possible standard."

Singh stood. His legs felt weak. This wasn't possible. This wasn't happening.

"But I was loyal," he said. "I've *obeyed*."

"You've given me an order to kill Laconian citizens who have not been found guilty of a crime."

"But—"

"For what it's worth, I don't disagree with you. These people are scum. They don't deserve or understand what we've brought them. For me, I think they never will. But their children might. Their grandchildren or their great-grandchildren. The story of Medina will be that Governor Singh mismanaged the station, lost his ship to a band of malcontents, lost his perspective. And when he let his wounded pride exceed the mandates of the high consul's directives, he was removed for the protection of the everyday citizens in his care. You see the difference? If you kill an insurgent, you're the enemy of all their friends. All their family. And then there's an expectation. Precedent. Enemies for generations. Forever. If you kill your own—even the highest among your own—to protect someone powerless, they remember that too. It sows gratitude. It sows trust. Generations from now your sacrifice will lead to the peace, prosperity, and fellow feeling among all humanity."

The air was gone. He couldn't catch his breath. His mind rejected everything he'd heard. He was going to see Natalia again. He was going to hold the monster in his arms and hear her gabble on about school and the dream she'd had and whether they could get a pet for their apartment. All of that was still true. It couldn't have changed. Not so quickly. Not so finally.

"Plus, it'll put Governor Song on notice," Overstreet said. He stood. "I'm very sorry about this, but it could be worse. You could be going to the Pen."

He lifted the gun.

"Wait!" Singh said. "Wait. Do you believe all that? About what killing me is supposed to achieve?"

"I am an officer of the Laconian Empire, Governor Singh. I believe what I'm told to believe."

Chapter Fifty-One: Drummer

It was three months before the *Heart of the Tempest* came to the transfer station at Lagrange-5. People's Home arrived behind it, like a servant waiting for the right moment to bow.

In those long, surreal weeks, the system had changed past all recognition. Or at least it had for Drummer. The surrender of the union ships had let the EMC fleet follow suit. There were some signs that the *Tempest* had suffered from the pounding it had taken—fluctuations of its heat signature, a reluctance to turn to port, the decision not to burn at more than about a fifth of a g. It didn't matter. If Laconia was bloodied, it was unbowed. Drummer couldn't say as much for herself.

A new armada of ships that had followed the *Typhoon* to Medina paused there for less than a day before they burned through the Sol gate. They were smaller ships, of a more familiar design, and fewer than a dozen of them dominated the solar system. The newsfeeds had nothing but the names of the new Laconian *Protector*-class destroyers—*Daskell*, *Ackermann*, *Ekandjo*, *Smith*—and their locations in the system. Where they were and where they might go.

Ganymede and Iapetus, inspired by God knew what quixotic impulse, declared that whatever the union and the EMC had said, they hadn't surrendered. Two of the new ships had gone to each station, and the defiant announcements had ended quickly after that. The independent feeds that called out against Laconia grew fewer and more tentative. Ceres Station had a welcoming committee when the *Ekanjo* docked there, and pictures of the governor of Ceres shaking the hand of the Laconian captain became the iconic image of the moment. Of the capitulation. Two smiling men. The end of one age, the beginning of something new.

The ship that came to escort People's Home was named the *Stover*, and by *escort*, they meant *occupy*.

By then, People's Home had gathered back most of the citizens who'd fled before the battle. Not all, of course. Some of the evacuation ships scattered themselves out among the smaller settlements and asteroids. Got quiet in hopes that with just a dozen ships, Laconia would overlook them. Maybe it even worked. For those who came back to the void city, Captain Rowman Perkins became their new leader. He was an older Martian man with close-cut white hair and skin the color of stained oak, with a folksy Mariner Valley drawl, kind eyes, and a fire team of Marines in power armor ready to make his wishes into law. When he'd come to her office, he'd had the courtesy to sit in the chair on the opposite side of the desk while they spoke. It was a small politeness that nailed in as much as anything had how utterly defeated she was. Laconia wasn't here to bully her or belittle her. It made no difference to Perkins whether he lost face before her. He'd come to take what he wanted—what he wanted was absolute authority—and he was going to get it. Gently was fine. Less gently was fine as well. The illusion of choice was hers.

She'd chosen.

House arrest was better than being in the brig. Her couch,

her clothes, her files and access, though without any broadcast privileges and a Laconian censor looking over her data streams. She dreaded the moment when Saba reached out to her and gave himself away, but that message never came. She assumed that the detention and cooperation of the Transport Union president was useful to Perkins and Trejo and Duarte. Her confinement rooms, her escort to the gym, her meals delivered by Laconian soldiers were all part of the narrative of victory, broadcast through thirteen hundred worlds as a warning to behave well. Before Laconia even the union fell. Even Mars. Even Earth. What hope could any colony world have against them?

That was speculation, of course. Newsfeeds weren't on her diet anymore. But she could watch old movies, listen to music, eat what she wanted, play games, sleep as much as she cared to sleep, exercise her way through all the routines she'd told herself she'd engage with if she ever had the time.

On the best days, house arrest was almost like an enforced vacation. For the first time in her adult life, she had no responsibilities. No long-term political aspirations to cultivate and attend to. No journalists or administrators or officials to spar with. The problems of who passed through which gate, of what artifacts were banned and which were taxed, of how to balance the needs of the colony worlds, all belonged to someone else now. Except for Saba's absence, it was the life she'd imagined retiring to when her term was complete.

On the worst days, her rooms were a box of crushing depression and failure, and death would be the only release.

Her handlers dealt with all of her moods with the same equanimity and insincere kindness. They were good to her because they chose to be. If they chose otherwise, that would be up to them as well. Her opinions didn't matter unless someone else decided that they did. And she had every reason to believe it was going to be like this—her rooms, the gym, her rooms again, under guard and cut off from humanity—for the rest of her life.

And then, three months after her surrender, the *Heart of the*

Tempest came to the transfer station at Lagrange-5, and Drummer went with it.

Vaughn came to her like a ghost from a past life. If she'd needed any measure of how her isolation had affected her, it was how glad she was to see him. His face seemed to have cracked a few new crags down the cheeks and across his forehead. He held himself with the same formality, but instead of radiating his usual low-level contempt, he seemed fragile. Like bread that had been hollowed out inside so that all that remained was the crust.

Or maybe that was her, and she wanted to see how she felt reflected in someone else. To not be so alone with it.

He stood in her doorway while she gathered herself.

"There's a meeting, ma'am," he said. "Admiral Trejo asked me to...help you prepare."

"Trejo?" she said, and it felt almost like a conversation they would have had before. "Is he here?"

"More that we're there, but yes. The secretary-general, yourself, and Admiral Trejo. A few others. They didn't give me the whole list, but they seem to want you presentable. And there's this."

He held out a hand terminal. She took it, spooled through the file trees it had access to. It was a thin list, but it had the advantage of being new. Things she hadn't already been looking at for weeks had a certain charm. A text file with her name. She opened it.

NOTE TO THE SPEAKER: It is important that the systems outside of Sol no longer be referred to as "colonies." In this and any off-the-cuff remarks, they are to be called "planets" or "systems." No primacy should be afforded to Earth, Mars, or the Sol system.

Questioner: Monica Stuart

Question: Is the Transport Union cooperating in the transfer of control?

Answer: The Transport Union has always been a temporary structure. Before our Laconian friends arrived, we were already in talks with the UN and the Earth-

Mars Coalition to draft a charter that would give over greater enforcement powers to a standing military. The Laconian fleet is the clear choice to fill that vacuum, and the union is pleased to work with High Consul Duarte and President Fisk to see that trade between the planets (see note) is efficient and free.

Questioner: Auden Tammet

Question: Is the union ready to pay reparations to Laconia for the damage done to its ships?

"Press conference, is it?" Drummer asked.

"That appears to be part of the agenda," Vaughn said. "You may, of course, choose to deviate from the script—"

"May I?"

"—but the Laconian censor will be reviewing everything before it goes out. And there are less pleasant accommodations than this."

Drummer spooled through the script. Three pages of questions, all of them staged, written, and approved. "So you're saying I should do this?"

"You gain nothing by refusing. And there is a certain dignity in living to fight another day."

"Or just living," Drummer said.

"Or that."

Drummer sighed. "I suppose I should make myself presentable. How much time do I have?"

The conference room was the same one she'd been in when TSL-5 had opened for business. The vaulted ceiling seemed grander now than it had. The wait staff circulated with flutes of champagne and hors d'oeuvres—tank-grown shrimp, real cheddar, dates wrapped in bacon that had once actually been a pig. The wall screens with their views of Earth and Luna, People's Home and the *Tempest*, were crisp and beautiful. High-level officials mingled and chatted as if the system of humanity hadn't been turned on its ear.

As if history were what it had always been. The absence of a few—Emily Santos-Baca, for instance—was something only she seemed to notice.

The secretary-general was in a pale suit with a collarless shirt and a golden pin in his lapel. He was smiling and shaking hands with the people around him. She'd expected him to be more somber, but in fairness, the transfer station had always been something of a humiliation for him. A place in the universe that defined the limits of his authority. Before, it had been her on the other side of that membrane. Now it was Laconia. So in a way, he'd already had more of a chance to get used to this.

The man he was laughing with, hand on his shoulder, was unmistakable. Admiral Trejo was smaller than she'd expected. Thicker about the chest and belly in a way that didn't speak as much to muscle or fat as genetics and age. His hair was thinning, and not styled to disguise the fact. His eyes were a bright green that would have seemed affected if they'd been fake.

Trejo noticed her, broke off his conversation with the secretary-general, and trundled over toward her. He was just the slightest bit bowlegged. Drummer felt an irrational twitch of betrayal. The man who'd destroyed and humiliated her should at least have been a bronzed Adonis, not a normal human being. It would have made it easier to swallow if she'd been beaten by a god.

"President Drummer," he said, putting out his hand. "I'm glad we could finally meet in more settled circumstances."

"Just Drummer," she said, and found herself shaking his hand. "I think we can dispense with the 'president' part."

"Oh, I hope not," Trejo said. "Transitions like this are delicate times. And the more profound the changes that are coming, the more important that it appear to have continuity. Don't you think?"

"If you say so," she said.

A waiter slid by, and she took a glass. She didn't need the alcohol as much as the idea of it. But, Lord, she needed something.

"I'm sorry your husband couldn't be here," Trejo said. There was nothing in his voice that couldn't just be a pleasantry, except that Saba's name had been linked to the embarrassment on Medina. She'd heard that much before her detainment. She felt a thrill of fear now. Did Trejo know something? Was he about to tell her Saba had been caught? Been killed?

"I'm sorry too," she said. "I miss him very much. But we have always had different careers."

"I hope to meet him one day," Trejo said, and she relaxed a notch. He wasn't dead. Trejo saw her response and smiled a soft, rueful smile. "It would be useful, I think, if you could help to resolve things with him. Chaos is bad for everyone."

"I don't have any way to reach him," Drummer said. She didn't go on with *And I don't know what I'd tell him if I did.*

"Fair enough," Trejo said. "We'll have that conversation another time, yes? Right now, there's something else I wanted to speak with you about. High Consul Duarte wants to convene the important people in humanity's new endeavors on Laconia. A kind of permanent convocation of the best minds and most influential people. He's asked me to extend an invitation to you."

The politeness of it was foul. The pretense that she was still autonomous, the master of her own fate. Oh, she could probably refuse. Duarte seemed smart enough not to welcome people into his projects who were willing to openly oppose him. But there would be consequences. That they weren't even spelled out made them more ominous.

"This is like the colonies, isn't it?" she said.

Trejo lifted his eyebrows, answering her question with a wordless one of his own.

"You're shifting everything to Laconia," she said. "Not just ships or money. The culture."

Trejo smiled. "Earth will always be the home from which humanity sprang, but yes. The high consul thinks that…fetishizing Earth is bad for the long-term future of the species. We will also put in place an accelerated repopulation scheme. Try to adjust the balance so that Sol system isn't such an overwhelming majority of the population either."

"You can't put billions of people through the ring gates," Drummer said. "It won't work."

"Not in our lifetimes," Trejo said. "We're talking about the work of generations. But...well, I was Martian before I was Laconian. Thinking for the long term doesn't intimidate me."

A woman in a white dress with gold at her throat and wrists sloped by, nodding to Trejo as she passed. He smiled back, glanced at her ass, and then back so quickly it might have passed for politeness.

"Your terraforming plan didn't work out too well," Drummer said more acidly than she should have. It just came out that way.

"It would have," Trejo said, "if something bigger hadn't come along. Anyway, please do consider the invitation. The high consul is looking forward to meeting you."

Trejo put a hand on her arm like they were old friends and made his way back out to some other conversation on his list. All around her, the eyes and attention of the crowd followed him and left her behind. She drank her champagne in a gulp and started looking for someplace to ditch the glass so she could get another one.

"Getting drunk, Camina? You think that's smart, or are you just past giving a fuck anymore?"

Avasarala was in her wheelchair. Her snow-white hair was pulled back in a bun, and her sari was a shimmer of green that almost hid the thinness of her body. She looked older than the last time Drummer had seen her. And she'd looked older than dirt then.

"I am taking the edge off the pain," Drummer said. "Because what else can I do?"

Avasarala turned her chair and started off toward the podium and the seats. They were empty now, but the journalists were starting to filter in. The show would be starting soon.

"I'd join you, but they tell me I'm on my last liver these days," Avasarala said. "No more liquor for me."

"You seem to be taking the conquest fairly well."

"The fuck option do I have?" Avasarala said. "I'm an old lady who spent her life trying to make peace between Earth and Mars. All this shit? It's like I missed a day at school, and everyone else learned to speak Mandarin while I was gone. I don't understand any of this."

"Yeah," Drummer said. "I can see that."

"It's the reward of old age," Avasarala said. "You live long enough, and you can watch everything you worked for become irrelevant."

"You're not selling it," Drummer said.

"Fuck you, then. Die young. See if I care."

Drummer laughed. Avasarala grinned, and for a moment, they understood each other perfectly. For a moment, Drummer didn't feel alone.

"Are you going to his orgy pit or whatever the fuck it is Duarte's setting up?" Avasarala asked.

Across the room, Vaughn caught Drummer's eyes and began walking toward the two women with purpose. Drummer didn't want to go with him. Didn't want to face the theater and falsehood of the next part. She turned back to Avasarala.

"I don't know. I suppose I have to."

"Always a bad idea to ditch the emperor," Avasarala agreed. Then, "Do you know why they're looking for Okoye?"

"Who?"

"Elvi Okoye," Avasarala said, and Vaughn reached them.

"It's time, ma'am," he said.

Drummer nodded and handed him her glass. Avasarala's claw of a hand grabbed hers, held her for a moment. "Chin up, Camina. These fuckers can smell blood. And this shit's not over, no matter what it looks like now."

"Thank you," Drummer said, and pulled away.

The seats for the journalists were full now. She recognized their faces. Sometimes even the way they sat, the way they moved. She'd done this for years. She'd never done this before.

Admiral Trejo made some brief opening remarks—thanked everyone for being there, expressed bright hopes for the future, extended the greeting of High Consul Duarte—and brought her up. The others would come later. The secretary-general. The speaker of the Martian parliament. Whoever else. But she was the last president of the Transport Union. Her dignity was first for the chopping block.

She looked out over the faces and remembered a time she'd enjoyed this.

"President Drummer?" Her podium identified the woman. Monica Stuart. "Is the Transport Union cooperating in the transfer of control?"

No, it is not. No, I am not. No, we have been conquered, but we will fight to the last breath because living with someone else's hand on our necks is intolerable, has always been intolerable, will always be intolerable. Not because of Laconia, not because of the union, not because of any of the authorities through all of history that have made rules and then dared people to break them. Because we're human, and humans are mean, independent monkeys that reached their greatness by killing every other species of hominid that looked at us funny. We will not be controlled for long. Not even by ourselves. Any other plan is a pipe dream.

In the front row, Avasarala coughed.

Drummer smiled thinly.

"The Transport Union has always been a temporary structure," she began.

Chapter Fifty-Two: Naomi

Freehold was pain. Some days that was a good thing. It gave her something to push against, something to fight. Other days it was just wearying.

The pencil-thin valley where they'd set the *Roci* down had steep, high mountains to the north, east, and southwest. A thin creek ran along the bottom with glacier meltwater. Pale-green treelike organisms clung to the stone with finger-thick roots and stretched out vines studded with pale-green bladders that floated into the open air as if Nature itself were putting up balloons for a party. A high breeze would shift the vines one way and then the other. Every now and then, one would break off and swirl away down the valley, maybe to die or maybe to find some new place to take root.

She understood it was all the product of evolutionary arms races. Photosynthesizing structures had spent centuries, maybe millennia, trying to choke each other in darkness until one of them had figured out how to both be rooted and fly, how to both command the high air and drop everything below it into permanent twilight. None of it had been created with the *Rocinante* in mind. It just worked out well.

The *Roci* itself huddled in a wide space where the creek curved around. The landing thrusters had scorched the landscape around it, but it didn't take more than a day or two before the local plants began growing back. The fight for survival made everything either resilient or forgotten. The floating vines made a moving canopy fifteen meters above them that would help hide them from observation, if anything ever came into the system to look. As hiding places went, it was decent.

The colony itself—the only other three hundred people on the planet—was in an arid biome a six-hour hike down the valley. At least it was for her. The locals could make the trip in half the time. Houston lived down there, among his people, and sometimes she and Alex would stay there too. But most days, she was at the *Roci*—her real home. There was maintenance to be done, restocking. Distilling the creek water until it was pure enough to put in the *Roci*'s tanks. The reactor could run for months without needing more fuel, but reaction mass was always a problem. If they wanted to go anywhere. If they just stayed put…well, less of an issue, then.

Today she'd spent half the daylight hours discouraging a cluster of very slow animals or possibly semimobile plants that were exploring whether the niches around the *Roci*'s PDCs would be a good place to live. When the light faded, she stopped for lunch. The planet's sixteen-hours-and-change diurnal cycle meant that most of her workdays had at least half a night in them.

The *Roci* had been built to rest on its belly in a gravity well. All of her systems functioned, even at ninety degrees from what she'd become used to. That seemed right too. Being at home, but also in a space her body didn't understand. Being in control of her day, but not of her life. Being achingly alone, but not wanting people around. It was all of a piece. If she'd dreamed it, it would have meant something.

As soon as she crawled back into the ship, she showered. There were compounds in the life cycle of Freehold that irritated her skin if she didn't wash them off. Then she pulled on a fresh jumpsuit, went to the galley, made herself a bowl of white kibble, and sat. A message was waiting for her from Bobbie, and she set her hand terminal on the table when she played it so she could use both hands to eat. The kibble was warm and peppery; the mushroom squeaked against her teeth just the way it was supposed to.

Bobbie looked exhausted and excited at the same time. Her hair was pulled back into a tight ponytail the way she wore it when she was working on machinery, not the bun she had for workouts. Her eyes were bright and the suggestion of a smile teased her mouth without ever quite appearing. She looked ten years younger. More than that, she looked happy.

"Hey, Naomi. Hope things are going well down there. I think we're making some real progress up here. I'm not positive, but I think I've found how the *Storm* manages its energy profiles. It's a little screwy, same as everything on this rig. I was wondering if I could get you to take a quick skim through the new dataset I pulled. Maybe you'll see something I didn't?"

The embedded data was structured as environmental-control buffers, and it was half again the size of the *Roci*'s. Naomi popped it open and glanced at the gross index. A lot of familiar parts, yes, but some strangeness in the large-scale structure. If it was anything like the other bits of the *Gathering Storm*'s operating code they'd harvested for analysis, it would get weirder the deeper in she went. She dropped it to a secure partition in the *Roci* and started unpacking it with her favorite tools, converting the language of the ships into something with handholds that her mind could brace on.

She set her hand terminal to Record. "Dataset received and in process. It may take me a day or two, but I'll let you know what I think. In the meantime, all is well down here. No need for rescue."

It was the rule. Somewhere in the message she sent up the well, there was always the word *rescue* and always would be until she needed one. Bobbie's word was *progress*. A message went back and forth every twenty-four hours at a minimum. Not that there was any real risk that Naomi could see, but protocol was protocol. The locals on Freehold had been at least willing to listen when they'd arrived with Payne Houston in tow, and there had been nothing but cautious goodwill since. Not that Naomi trusted that to last. The colony of Freehold would support her in her guise as a refugee and freedom fighter as long as it was convenient for them. She understood that having the only gunship in the system and a ring gate far enough away that she'd have a free hand how to use it for weeks before help could arrive figured into the local council's calculus of the situation.

Bobbie's improvised crew of Belters were with her on a little moon circling one of Freehold's three gas giants, tucked in an ancient lava tube and showing no signs of mutiny. Bobbie as captain and Amos as acting XO would, Naomi thought, be more than enough to ensure discipline. It also gave Freehold another reason to play nice, and a spare set of eyes on the ring gate in case anything nasty came through.

The *Storm* was slow to give up its secrets, not because of the internal security—though that was an issue—as much as the profound unfamiliarity of some of its technology. Its reliance on calcium, for instance, was an order of magnitude more than Naomi had ever seen, and the vacuum channels it used instead of wiring still made her head ache a little if she thought about them too much. With enough time, though, she was certain they'd come to understand the ship. On her good days, she thought they'd be ready, even if she wasn't sure yet what they were getting ready for.

While the *Roci* arranged the data for her and the kibble broke down pleasantly in her stomach, she lay back and let her eyes close for a few minutes. Her knees ached. Her spine ached. It wasn't even the gravity of Freehold. This world was smaller than Mars, and only a little bit denser. She'd been on long burns worse than this. Part of the problem was that she wasn't doing her exercises. She was doing work, and there turned out to be a suite of small, neglected muscles that had atrophied over the years and weren't happy to be put into service clearing vegetation and crawling around the bottom of a gravity well.

There was also, she suspected, something of a placebo effect. She'd spent so many years equating life in free atmosphere on a planetary surface with a constant, grinding full g, that now even though the gravity was actually fairly mild, she was primed to notice the discomfort. She expected it, and so it was there.

The *Rocinante* chimed to announce the completion of the data run, and then again almost immediately to announce Alex's return. It was less than a minute before she heard him walking up the hallway that was usually the lift tube. He was singing to himself. A light, lilting melody with words she didn't recognize.

"In here," she called as he came close.

Alex poked his head into the galley. He was more comfortable going into town, and the combination of long walks and sunlight had darkened his skin and given him his cheekbones back.

"Hola," he said. "Good news from Freehold. We're a business!"

He lifted his right arm. The satchel in it was heavy with batteries ready to be recharged. It was a minor convenience for the township to have Alex come by and collect batteries, recharge them from the *Roci*'s reactor, and deliver them again full up instead of waiting for their turn at the solar array. So Freehold's poor foresight on solar energy was now their cottage industry. At least for now.

Alex's grin widened. "And…"

"And?"

He lifted his left hand. A second satchel. "They paid in beer and curried goat. I've got a little cook fire started outside. It's going to be great."

Naomi started to say that she'd just eaten, but the joy in Alex's eyes was infectious. She swung herself up to sitting. "On my way," she said.

The moons weren't shining in the valley when she reached the airlock, but Alex's little cook fire was glowing happily next to the landing strut, and the stars glittered between the floating vines above them. They burned dried-out vines and the shed carapaces of huge, slow-moving animals that lived in shallow caves all up and down the valley. The smoke was pale and fragrant. The shards of carapace popped and cracked now and then, sending little sprays of spark up with the smoke to vanish as they cooled. The smoke kept away the night hoppers—tiny, nocturnal insect-like animals that usually found humans fascinating.

Alex had two skewers of meat dripping grease and curry onto the flames, and Naomi had to admit that they smelled better than kibble. She sat with her back against the landing strut. Alex took a bottle from his satchel, opened its neck, and passed it over. The beer was cold and rich and more biting than she'd expected.

"Robust," she said.

"Danielle likes a higher proof than some brewers," Alex said with a smile as he leaned back to look at the vines and the sky beyond them.

"Seems like you're getting along well with the locals."

"They're all right," Alex said. "Just don't get them talking about the nature of sovereignty and you're fine. Even then you're all right, it's just a conversation they've all had a lot. Tends to go along the ground they've already plowed."

He reached over and turned the skewers. High above them, something set off one of the vine bladders, and it glowed a pale yellow-green for a moment, then went dark again.

"Good to build rapport," Naomi said. "Freehold's going to have to look like a polite, compliant little colony for a while."

"No trouble. The council's on board for an 'enemy-of-my-enemy, hail Laconia, down with the union' stance. For the time being anyway. I think they kind of like having us here, actually. The founding impulse of Freehold is sticking it to the government."

"Loses some of its shine after you get elected."

"Right?" Alex tested the curried meat with his finger, pinching and releasing fast enough that he didn't get burned. He handed it over to Naomi. She waved it in the night air for a moment to let it cool, then took the first cube off the end and popped it in her mouth. The char on the meat was good. The spices that infused it were better. She chewed slowly, letting herself enjoy it.

"Do you think they'll sell us out?"

"Eventually, sure," Alex said cheerfully. "But not right away. And probably not for cheap, so long as they like us."

Her plan was the long one. The only one, really, that made sense. Laconia's strength seemed overwhelming. A force without weakness that nothing could ever overcome. That was an illusion. Earth had seemed like that once, when she'd been a girl scraping together a life in the Belt. It hadn't been true then either.

They'd wait. They'd watch. They'd be small and quiet and aware. Sooner or later, Laconia would show them where it was weak. And between then and now, life. Charging batteries in exchange for beer. Making friends with the township. Working to crack open the mysteries of the *Gathering Storm* with Bobbie and Amos. Keeping the *Rocinante* in good trim, and keeping herself from falling into despair. It was enough to fill her days. It would have to be enough.

"Which one of those is Bobbie?" Alex asked.

"Hmm?"

With the second skewer, he pointed up at the night sky peeping through from behind the vines. "One of those stars isn't a star, right? I mean, we can see her from here, can't we?"

Naomi looked up at the little slice of stars. The galactic disk looked the same as it had in Sol system, but the constellations not quite like her own. Parallax, she knew, was how they'd started mapping which systems were on the other sides of the gates. She'd seen a map once—the splash of systems that the gates connected. Thirteen hundred stars in a galaxy with three hundred billion of them. They'd been clumped together, the gate-network stars. The two farthest systems were hardly more than a thousand light-years apart. A little more than one percent of the galaxy, and still unthinkably vast.

"Look just above the ridge there," she said, pointing. "You see where the rock looks like a bent finger? The round knuckle?"

"Yeah, I see it."

"Track just up from that, and to the right. There are three stars almost in a row. The middle one is Bobbie."

"Hmm," Alex said, then went quiet. He wasn't singing anymore, but sometimes Naomi thought she heard a few hummed notes under his breath. It was maybe five minutes before he spoke again. "I wonder which one's Mars."

"Sol system?" she said. "I don't know."

"I think about Kit," Alex said and took another drink of his beer. "And Giselle, I guess, but more about Kit. I have a son out there. He's just starting his own life. His adulthood. I won't be there for it. I don't even know that I'd be any use if I were. I mean, when I was his age, I was getting into the navy, and Earth and Mars were the biggest things in the universe. Now...I don't know. Everything's different. He has to find his own way."

"That's always how it is," Naomi said.

"I know. Every kid has to find who they are without Mom and Dad, but—"

"History too. Mars before Solomon Epstein. Earth before the seas came up. Before there were airplanes and then after. When we figured out how to grow our own food. Everything's always changed."

"But up to now it wasn't my problem," Alex said, with an affected disconsolate buzz in his voice. They both laughed together. A half dozen of the vine bladders lit up and faded. She didn't know what made them do that, but it was pretty. She felt a pleasant warmth growing in her belly. The beer, probably. Or the meat, since she'd eaten almost all of it despite her expectations. Or the sense of being in midnight under stars in the middle of an ocean of air that wouldn't run out or leak away. It really was reassuring in a way that even the best station atmosphere could never quite equal.

"I think about Jim the same way," she said. "Not that he's beginning his adulthood, but he always wanted to take me back to Earth. To show me what living on a planet was like. Now I'm here, and I'm finding out, and he's not."

"He'll be all right," Alex said. "He always is."

"I know," she said aloud, but they both knew she meant *Maybe*.

Something crashed through the underbrush, made a high keening sound, and crashed away. They'd heard it before often enough that they both ignored it. Alex finished off the last of his beer and tucked the empty bottle back in his satchel. He levered himself up to standing and stretched his arms above him, looking like some ancient priest in the firelight.

"I should get these things hooked up," he said, hefting the dead batteries. "I said I'd have them back tomorrow. I'll probably take a sleep shift in town after that, if you're all right solo?"

"That's fine," she said. "Bobbie sent me a new dataset. I'll be working on that. I wouldn't be much company anyway."

"Should I douse the fire?"

Naomi shook her head. "I'll do it when I go in. I think I overate. I need to just sit for a little while."

"Right," Alex said, and trudged over to the airlock. He lifted himself in, and she heard him starting to sing again until the door closed behind him. She lay back.

Everything changed, and it went right on changing. A terrible thought when things were good, a comforting one now. Whatever happened, she could be certain that things wouldn't stay the way they were now. And if she stayed smart and clever and lucky, she'd be able to affect how the next change came. Or take advantage of it. She'd find Jim again, if she could just be patient enough.

One of the vines broke loose from the mountain wall and

drifted along with some high breeze that she didn't feel. She watched it blunder away to the southwest, catching on another vine for a moment, then losing its grip and floating on. Where it had been, there was a new spray of stars now, glittering from decades and centuries ago, their light only happening to fall on her here and now.

She wondered if one of them was Laconia.

Epilogue: Duarte

Winston Duarte watched his daughter playing at the fountain's edge. Teresa was ten now, and almost as tall as her mother had been. She was working with a clay boat, discovering the relationship between buoyancy and displacement for herself. Forming and re-forming the little craft of her own design. Finding not only what was the most efficient but also what was the most aesthetically pleasing. What would float and also steer and also be beautiful in its own right. Her tutor, Colonel Ilich, sat on the edge of the fountain as well, talking with her. Guiding her thoughts through the process, and helping her to connect the work of her hands to the lessons in mathematics and history and art.

He didn't know whether she was aware how lonesome a childhood she'd had. The State Building had facilities for the children of the government to live and work and attend lessons while their parents saw to the mechanisms of the empire, but most of the classrooms—like the offices—were empty. Prepared for a generation that was still just beginning. The timing was wrong for Teresa. Someday children would run and play together in the streets and parks of Laconia, but by then Teresa would be grown.

She leaned forward, lowered her latest design into the water. Ilich asked her something, and she replied. Duarte couldn't hear what they were saying from this distance, but he saw the change in the way she held the little boat. And more than that, he saw her mind change.

That had started more recently, and he wasn't certain what to make of it yet. A pattern of something around her head when she was thinking strongly. As she worked the clay, it infused her hands as well. Ilich had it too, though not as intensely. Of all the ways his changes affected his senses, this new one was the most interesting. He had the suspicion that he was, in some sense, seeing *thought*.

Teresa glanced over, and the whatever-it-was shifted just before she raised her hand. He waved back, returning her smile, then stepped away into the State Building to let her continue her studies undistracted. He loved his daughter profoundly, and the joy of watching her learn was better than anything else he had scheduled, but his presence wouldn't help her or the empire. Duty called.

He found Kelly waiting for him in his private office. The look on the man's face was enough to tell him that they had arrived. His heart sank. He had been dreading this moment since he'd heard that Natalia Singh had requested the personal meeting. It was her right, though. And his obligation.

"They're in the east drawing room, sir."

"They?"

"She brought her daughter."

Another little punch to the gut. But… "All right. Thank you, Kelly."

Natalia and Elsa Singh were dressed in matching clothes. Dark blue with white accents. Not the full black of mourning, but somber. He sat across from them as Kelly served tea and cakes. Duarte felt the temptation to focus on the whatever-it-was, to see if grief and anger looked different from Teresa's lesson with the clay boats, but it seemed impolite, so he didn't.

Kelly closed the door behind him as he left. Duarte sipped his tea. Natalia Singh didn't touch hers, but the little girl ate some cake. The sweetness of sugar overcame everything for children. Even loss. There was something profound in that. Beautiful and sad both.

"Doctor Singh," Duarte said. "I am so sorry for your loss."

Her chin lifted a few degrees, proud and defiant. He hoped she wasn't going to do anything stupid. Grief was a terrible thing.

"Thank you, sir," she said through a tight throat. The little one looked over, confused less by the words than by her mother's tone of voice. Elsa was a smart child, he could see that. Empathetic, which was more important really than other kinds of intelligence. She shifted on the couch, scooted toward her mother.

Duarte leaned forward, putting down his teacup. He laced his fingers together, and when he spoke, he tried to put as much warmth and care into his voice as the little girl had expressed in her movement.

"You asked to speak with me. How can I help you?"

"I would like to request a copy of the formal inquiry into my husband's death," she said, then swallowed.

Duarte slipped. His focus shifted, and the whatever-it-was— thought, consciousness, attention—became clear to him for a moment. It was tight in around Natalia Singh's head and chest, wrapping her like a shroud. The little one—Elsa—hers was diffused around her, thicker toward her mother, like something physical in her was reaching out. Longing to comfort and be comforted in a field effect that was something more, apparently, than just metaphor. He pulled his attention back to his more usual senses with a little echo of shame, as if he'd eavesdropped on something.

"Of course," he said. "I'll see that it's delivered to you."

Natalia Singh nodded once and wiped a tear away like it was an insect that had landed on her cheek.

"He was a good man," Duarte said. "I know that. You know that. In another time and another place, he would have been celebrated."

"He wasn't a killer," she said, and her voice had pressed down to a whisper.

"He was put into an extreme position, and he overreacted," Duarte said. "Our place in humanity is special. The rules that apply to us are harsh. You and me and him. But there's a reason for that, and I want you to know how much I honor his sacrifice. And yours. Both of yours."

Elsa looked at him now as if she knew he was talking about her. He smiled at the girl, and after a moment, she smiled back. He could see an echo of her mother's face in her small, soft features. Her father's too. He took Natalia's hand, and she didn't pull away.

"You will have the full support of the government," he said, "if you want it. Your daughter has a guaranteed place in the academy. Your work is important to us. To me. I know this is hard, and you have my word that you will not face this alone. We're all with you, whatever you need."

She nodded more slowly this time. She didn't wipe the tears away. Her daughter climbed into her lap, and Natalia put her free arm around her, rocked her slowly back and forth. It was heartbreaking, but he'd made the decision. He wouldn't look away from the consequences of it. This was his duty too.

"Is there anything else I can do for you?"

She shook her head. Speech was beyond her. While she wept, he poured her more tea, and sat, witnessing her sorrow and being present with her and her child. After a few minutes, she looked up at him, her eyes clearer, calmer. He took a deep breath, squeezed her hand gently, and released it.

"Thank you," Natalia said.

He made a little bow to her, a last gesture of respect, and withdrew. Anytime a Laconian died in the service of the empire, their family had the right to a private audience with the high consul. It was a tradition he'd begun when they first passed through the gate. It would have to be reconsidered as the empire expanded, but for now, it was still in his power to honor it, so he did.

Kelly was waiting for him in his office, a look of sympathy in his eyes. He didn't mention the widow or her daughter in the drawing room. Kelly was a man of perfect tact.

"A report from Doctor Cortazár, sir," he said.

Duarte pulled up the new file, opening it with a gesture. Cumulative update on the debriefing of Prisoner 17. Duarte spooled down the file, seeing Cortazár's questions, the prisoner's responses. They were only words. Designs of light drawn on air. After glimpsing the living thoughts of Dr. Singh and her daughter, mere language seemed sterile. He looked at Kelly, closed the file.

"I think," Duarte said, "it may be time I met this Captain Holden."

The man sat on the floor, his back to the wall of the cell. His splayed legs and bright eyes made him seem younger than his graying hair. As Duarte came in, Holden's gaze shifted between him and his guard—back and forth—until it settled on him. Duarte sat on the bunk, hands on his thighs, and looked down at the man who had caused so much trouble over so many years. He didn't look like anything more than an old ice bucker with a little too much curiosity and too little impulse control.

Duarte had known people like him from his time in the service. Hotheads and gadflies. The ones who were always sure they knew better than anyone else. The truth was, they had their place. Like anyone else, they could be apt tools if they were well suited to the task at hand.

Here he had no qualms about using his new senses. Holden was an enemy and an asset. He had no right to any privacy. And the pattern mind was...fascinating.

When he'd been a boy, Duarte had seen an optical illusion that changed one face into another as the viewer came near it. Holden was like that. There was something about the way the pattern of his thoughts moved that reminded him of dry riverbeds. The traces of something that had been there and was now gone, but not without leaving the trail of its passage behind it. Patterns inside patterns.

"You're Winston Duarte," Holden said, snapping Duarte's attention back to his more usual ways of seeing.

"Yes," Duarte said. "I am."

Holden pulled his knees up, rested his arms on them. His eyes were wide, and even a little bit frightened. "What the fuck happened to you?"

It took Duarte a moment to understand, then he chuckled. "Yes. I forget. I've been through some changes. Not everyone notices, but there have been some...I don't know. Shifts?"

"You're using that shit on *yourself*?"

"I think we're getting off on the wrong foot, Captain. Let me try this again. I'm High Consul Duarte. You and I have a shared interest, I understand, in the origins and function of the protomolecule. Did I get that right?"

"You have to listen to me. I saw what happened to them. To the things that made the protomolecule. There was a record on the ring station from before they got shut down."

"I read the report on that," Duarte said. "Even before I came here. It was part of what inspired me to take the steps I've taken. Not just"—he gestured at his own body—"but all of it. An empire is a tool, just like everything else."

That brought Holden to a stop. The pattern around his head was shifting and vibrating like a hive of angry wasps. Again, he had the sense of seeing the remnants of something in Holden's mind. Traces of another pattern. There was a term for this, but...

"*Palimpsest*," Duarte said aloud, then shook his head when Holden frowned. "I was trying to remember a word. I just got it. *Palimpsest*."

"You came here because of the thing that killed the protomolecule?"

Duarte leaned back, considered James Holden and, now that he'd met him, how best to build rapport. Radical honesty for radical honesty, maybe? Worth trying.

"I was connected to the MCRN intelligence services when the gate opened. The first one. Sol gate. And when the other gates opened, I saw the probe data sets as they came in. The early surveys of all the systems as fast as we could get them. And I saw an opportunity here. The most clearly intact ruins. A set of orbiting structures with what appeared to be a ship or something like it halfway through being constructed. And I recognized that the protomolecule had the potential to act as a handle of sorts. A way to interact with the artifacts that had been left behind. So I got the sample that we still had, and the best minds I could find on the subject. And through discipline and commitment, we developed new technologies faster and better than all the other worlds put together. Laconia is Mars. The Martian ideal taken to the next level."

"That's all great," Holden said. "Except for the part where something came and killed the shit out of all the things that made the artifacts. I saw whole systems going dark. They shut down the gates just to try to stop whatever was killing them, and it didn't work."

"I know."

"That thing that popped up on your ship? That's the same thing that killed the protomolecule. That wiped out the civilization that built all of this."

"I know that too," Duarte said. "Or I guessed, anyway. It seems the most promising hypothesis. And it's related, I believe, to the missing ships. Something deep, something *profound*, doesn't like anyone using these technologies and powers. Didn't like when the last ones did it, don't like it now that we've turned them back on. It's an interesting problem."

Holden stood up. The guard stepped forward, but Duarte gestured for him to stay back.

"Interesting problem? Something fired a shot at you. At your ship. It turned off people's minds all throughout the system, and that's an interesting problem? That was an *attack*."

"And it didn't work," Duarte said. "We aren't the same thing that got wiped out before. What killed them affected us, but it didn't destroy us."

"You seem pretty sure it's not going to find some slightly different approach that's going to wipe us all out. You're not picking a fight with the things that made the protomolecule. You're picking a fight with whatever killed *them*. Orders of magnitude above the things that were orders of magnitude above us. You've got to know this is going to escalate if we keep using these technologies."

"We were always going to keep using these technologies. That was inevitable the moment we opened the gates," Duarte said. "If you've studied any history at all, you know that. Never in human history have we discovered something useful and then chosen not to use it."

Holden looked around the cell like there might be something there to help him. Duarte didn't need any new fields of perception to see the agitation in Holden's mind. Duarte softened his voice the way he had with Natalia and Elsa, offering comfort and consolation in his tone if not his words.

"There was no path where we left the gates alone. No future where we didn't use the technologies and lessons we learned from them. And there wasn't likely to be one where we didn't face the same kind of pushback that killed the ones who came before us. There was only the way forward where we were scattershot and chaotic, or the one where we were organized, regimented, and disciplined. And the missing ships are a promise that the killers in the abyss will come back. That they've never really left. You, more than anyone else, should understand that."

"I did," Holden said. "I do. It's why I came here. To warn you."

Duarte leaned back. The bunk was thin and uncomfortable. He didn't envy Holden's having to sleep on it. But there was a breeze through the window and a bit of sunlight. The cell was still more luxurious than half of the ship cabins Duarte had been assigned early in his career.

Holden's hands were open as if he were offering something. And he was, but it wasn't what he thought.

"I don't need a warning," Duarte said. "I need an ally. You have seen things no one else has ever seen. You know things I need to know, and you might not even be aware of the significance of some of it. Doctor Cortazár has been trying to find that. Help him. Work with him. Work with *me*."

"To do what?"

"To take the shards of the protomolecule's broken sword and reforge it. To bring humanity into a single community that is functional and strong. And prepare us."

Holden laughed, but there was no mirth in it. Duarte knew he hadn't reached the man. That was disappointing.

"Prepare us for what?" Holden asked. "To poke gods with a sharp stick?"

"No, Captain Holden. No sticks," Duarte said. "When you fight gods, you storm heaven."

Acknowledgments

While the creation of any book is less a solitary act than it seems, the past few years have seen a huge increase in the people involved with The Expanse in all its incarnations, including this one. This book would not exist without the hard work and dedication of Danny and Heather Baror, Will Hinton, Tim Holman, Anne Clarke, Ellen Wright, Alex Lencicki, and the whole brilliant crew at Orbit. Special thanks are also due Carrie Vaughn for her services as a beta reader, and the gang from Sakeriver: Tom, Sake Mike, Non-Sake Mike, Jim-me, Porter, Scott, Raja, Jeff, Mark, Dan, Joe, and Erik Slaine, who got the ball rolling.

The support team for The Expanse has also grown to include the staff at Alcon Entertainment and Syfy, and the cast and crew of *The Expanse*. Out thanks and gratitude go especially to Matt Rasmussen, Glenton Richards, and Kenn Fisher.

And, as always, none of this would have happened without the support and company of Jayné, Kat, and Scarlet.

James S. A. Corey is the pen name of fantasy author Daniel Abraham, author of the critically acclaimed Long Price Quartet, and writer Ty Franck. They both live in Albuquerque, New Mexico.

Find out more about James S. A. Corey and other Orbit authors by registering for the free monthly newsletter at www.orbitbooks.net.